About the Author

Andrew is a retired Sales Business Consultant living in Cheshire. He is married with three grown up children. He has produced many tales but never had the confidence to write, despite considerable encouragement. He 'put pen to paper' during a particularly bad bout of insomnia, (worrying about the looming weddings of two of his children). He is a keen golfer, cyclist and walker.

For Grace

Andrew J Rexstraw

TORN

AUSTIN MACAULEY
PUBLISHERS LTD.

A CIP catalogue record for this title is available from the British Library.

ISBN 978 1 78554 405 7 (Paperback)
ISBN 978 1 78554 406 4 (Hardback)
ISBN 978 1 78554 407 1 (E-Book)

www.austinmacauley.com

First Published (2016)
Austin Macauley Publishers Ltd.
25 Canada Square
Canary Wharf
London
E14 5LQ

Acknowledgments

Dr Melanie Wynne-Jones. – For her invaluable help, brutal honesty and humour in proof reading and editing the manuscript, and also for her guidance and advice in tackling the complicated medical aspects of the novel.

Christopher Broster. – For his time and patience whilst proof reading and editing.

Jo Halliday, John and Joyce Glynn and Annetta Sinclair. – For their help and encouragement during the proof reading process.

Captain Tony Baker (Rtd). – For his invaluable military knowledge.

Captain "Anonymous" (Rtd) of the SAS. – For help with the 'black ops' description in Iraq and the medical discharge detail.

Paul Edgerton. – For helping me to understand and appreciate the devastating change that comes to a person's life as a result of a stroke.

Caroline Arden and Ruth Hunt from the Stroke Association. – For their advice on the Stroke recovery process.

Phillip (Jacko) Jackson. – For his invaluable nautical expertise.

Christian Mullan. – For his advice on criminology including, legal, police and coroner issues and procedures.

Tom Houghton – For his guidance with the Japanese translation and also in understanding the unique distinctions between formal and informal language.

To my mum and dad. – Dedicated bibliophiles who will never get to read this.

Finally, to my wife and family, there isn't enough room to write everything you have done for me. Thank you.

Apologies to David Bowie for changing the lyrics to 'Thursday's Child.'

'Love is not who you can see yourself with,

it is who you can't see yourself without'

PROLOGUE

My memory had been badly affected by the stroke, but when I found the box I remembered that due to its size, the book would be located near the very bottom. Beneath it would be the pistol, (wrapped in muslin), a box of shells, my passport and discharge papers, all put there hurriedly ten years ago.

Although somewhat faded and written in a child's hand, you could still make out the word, "KEEP" in red crayon on the lid. Apart from my sister, this little boy's old treasure chest, brown and dusty, was the only link to my past life.

I ripped the tape from the flaps and opened the box. Sitting on top was a stamp album with a red vinyl cover plus a few scattered cigarette cards. I removed the album and turned my attention to the cards.

My grandma had reluctantly given them to me, on her last visit to us in Germany. She had valiantly amassed them while smoking herself to death with lung cancer at the age of fifty nine. The collection depicting "Creatures of the Ocean" was scattered around and I could see why when I discovered a decomposed elastic band stuck to one of them. This one had a picture of a stonefish, which seemed very appropriate for my memory of her. Grey, ugly and liable to be venomous when disturbed. I don't recall her smiling in my company nor showing any warmth or affection but that was par for the course in my family.

I placed these items on the table beside me just as the door alarm of the shop below my apartment triggered. I knew from the tone it emitted that it was only Jordi opening the hardware store. I would have to remember to mention him when writing my final note later.

Along with the album and cards, I found my hard-backed school report, some first editions of my mother's books, a plastic bag containing some action comics, two envelopes, (one containing euros, the other Iraqi dinars), the deeds to the apartment, the registration documents for the car and my yacht, Sunbuoy.

As I placed my hand deeper in the box, a sound like rice sliding on a baking tray triggered the memory of a crumpled body at the bottom of the stairs and when I saw the child's rattle a scalding ache seared through my heart.

After regaining my composure, I put the heavy Montecristo cigar box on the table without opening it, along with Dad's old white leather bible, (which had some papers stuffed inside), and a sheaf of newspaper clippings. I slipped the gold lighter, leather cigar holder and silver hip flask, (which still had something in it), into the rucksack.

As expected, I found the book near the bottom of the box, wrapped in brown paper by my father, with the words, *"Rare Book"* written in his precise script diagonally across the packaging. He had found the volume in a junk shop in Germany on one of our infrequent family outings from the garrison when I was ten years old. This was the only thing he left me, when he died in 1994, apart from a bag of old clothes, the bible and an envelope, containing a letter and a cheque. His message simply said.

"Tez. This is for you. I realise no amount of money can make up for your suffering. I'm sorry I couldn't always be there for you when you needed me, I was weak. – Dad."

Then I found what I was looking for; the SIG Sauer P226 pistol. I pressed the magazine release and found the chamber had "one up the spout" which was all I would need later. I replaced the magazine and put the pistol into the rucksack.

3

I thought the box was empty but found a beige card under one of the folded flaps, it had the word, "MEMORIES" printed in the bottom right hand corner. It contained a black and white photograph, taken outside my school, when I was seventeen.

The past came flooding back to me as I realised the photograph featured,

a boy held responsible for the death of a two year old child,

a boy never loved by his mother,

a boy who lost his virginity at thirteen,

a boy abandoned by his father,

and a boy who had an affair with a forty two year old woman.

And now, twenty-four years after it was taken, as I sit in my apartment above the hardware store looking at the photograph, I know it also contains the image of a novelist, a linguist, a partially paralysed ex-alcoholic and a trained killer.

But, it also contains the picture of someone who has lost the only person he ever loved, his sole reason for living and who as a result, plans to take his own life in about two hours' time.

How do I know these things?

I know, because there is only one person in the photograph.

A boy with a kiss curl.

Me.

Tesla Coyne.

PART ONE

Chapter 1

I feel completely invincible today. After suffering the drastic change in my circumstances whilst in Iraq, I believe good times are just around the corner. I am truly happy for the first time in ages. My book has been published, there are rumours of an approach from Hollywood, and in a couple of hours I will be with Thursday's Child.

'Come on Jenny, you're going to be late,' I shout.

The front door is wide open and a stiff cold breeze is whipping in, making the chandelier's crystals shiver. A strong gust blows the letters from the telephone table onto the floor. The rain hitting the metal roof of my car sounds like a drum solo from one of those 70's rock bands no one remembers anymore. Then a voice booms from the floor above.

'We've plenty of time for God's sake! It's only just gone eleven, the plane departure isn't until two thirty.' I can picture her applying one last stroke of lipstick. I should be used to this sequence of events but I am still amazed at just how long it takes her to get ready.

'I know, but don't forget you need to be there at least two hours before take-off to check-in and I want to drop off the new manuscript at Poppy's on the way.' Jenny either has a memory like a sieve, or hasn't listened to me, or is too selfish to care about my plans. Yes, that would be it. She is just bloody selfish. I need to remain calm and be patient for just another hour or so.

'I know you do but why the hell can't you just drop it off on your way back from the Airport?'

"The reason my darling," I think to myself, "is I have some exciting plans after I have dropped you off." I start to explain, 'I told you she's going off for a week's holiday with Jacob and the girls, and I'd like to get it to her before she sets…'

She interrupts me. 'I thought you said she was going on Friday.'

'No she's going today. They'd rather go on a Thursday because the traffic is quieter.'

'You know, it can't be so bad for your sister if she can just get up and go whenever she wants.'

In the time that I have known Jenny, (it feels too long now), she has always had a bitter streak when it comes to my sister and her family. She resents Poppy, who makes a small income from her books on travel and the local recipes she discovers. She also dislikes Poppy's husband, Jacob, the proprietor of "Jacob Flood's Furniture Restoration" who can make ends meet with a smile on his face. I think what really annoys her though, is they have a successful partnership, two amazing children, and are happy together. Jenny strikes out on all three. She is a divorcee, has no children and I am not sure if she has ever been truly happy.

The shouting between us causes pressure to build in my head, making me screw my eyes tightly shut as a needle of pain sears between my temples. I become unstable and start to sway, so steady myself against the wall. I can't decide what I want most at this point, a painkiller, a cigarette or a stiff drink. I suppress the wish list as the moment passes. 'I'm going to give them a call to say we're on our way.' I fish my phone from my pocket, and hit speed-dial P.

Jacob answers, 'Hello.'

'Hi Flash, it's Tesla.'

'Yes, I know it's you Tez. I do recognise your voice.' He liked me using the nickname he acquired as a schoolboy. He didn't get it because he was fast over a hundred yards, but following a news report about a sudden downpour that burst the river's banks.

'Just to let you know we'll be on our way to you just as soon as Mrs Glacier gets her arse in gear.' I can hear Jenny upstairs muttering. 'Are you all packed and ready for your latest adventure?' I ask him.

'Yes mate, you won't be too long will you? We need to set off soon. Poppy's so excited about taking the girls to the Cotswolds.'

'No, I'll try to hurry her up. By the way, I forgot to ask, is this one of her potential writing assignments?'

'No, it's just a trip out for us to meet up with some friends and I'm going to look at some furniture I've been told about. I shouldn't tell you this but she's really excited about reading your latest draft.'

'Oh no! That could be the kiss of death! I just want her opinion before I take it further.' Suddenly, I hear movement upstairs. 'Look I'd better go. I think we might have lift-off.'

Jacob says, 'Right, see you in five minutes, bye.' I hang up and put the phone back into my jacket pocket.

'I'll go and start the car, will you lock up and put the alarm on?' I say as I move towards the door and the waiting deluge.

'Yes,' she says, in a harsh tone, 'I won't be a minute.'

I don't believe this. I snap. 'What the fuck are you doing now?' I knew the answer before I asked.

'There's no need for that language. I've just got to use the loo before we set off.'

My head is really pounding now; I feel hot and my face burns. I pull up my jacket collar as I move outside. The wind is bitterly cold but I welcome its cooling effect on my head and am glad I haven't got soaked running to the car. I open the door, get in and start the engine, then move it nearer the house to save her getting too wet.

When I turn on the stereo, I am pleased to hear the opening bars of Couperin's, La Sultane. The music makes me realise I have left my MP3 player and laptop in the kitchen where I was working this morning. I decide to call back and pick them up later. I let the sound of the violins waft over me, drowning the sound of the rain and kicking out the maggot of frustration as I wait. Within seconds I'm feeling better, calm is returning. I then hear a different melody as she enters the alarm code.

Jenny gets in. 'Right, I'm here let's get going, we've plenty of time. Oh and you can switch that medieval racket off before it gives me a headache.' Reluctantly, I turn the radio off. Our journey to Poppy's starts in uncomfortable silence.

Our relationship has been strained for a very long time now but I appreciate I should make allowances for her as she must be apprehensive about her big weekend. I turn to look at her and it is the first time today, no, actually it is the first time for a while, that I have really observed her. She is sitting bolt upright, staring straight ahead through the streaming windscreen. Putting aside her complex character for a second, I have to admit she really is beautiful.

'Gosh you look stunning.'

'What are you after?'

'Nothing, I just think you look lovely. Have you got all your music ready for tomorrow?'

This is the opportunity when Jenny may finally get what she describes as her "big break." She has been auditioning for many years to get a part in a major stage production ever since her career bombed after appearing drunk on a TV chat show. She had received a call from the show's producer, Ethel Cody, telling her she had been selected to play Cio-Cio San, the lead soprano in Puccini's Madame Butterfly. Although the provincial *première* wasn't scheduled to take place in Manchester for four months, Jenny was flying down to London today, to meet the cast and have a small party at the

Princess Theatre where the West End performances would begin early next year.

It was typical of Jenny's personality that this wonderful news was overshadowed by the pleasure she experienced in getting the part at the expense of her rival, Vanessa Tamerlane. "I'm so glad *the bitch* didn't get the part," she said, giving me a dirty look. I had met Vanessa at Poppy's when she came up to attend a charity event. They had been good friends since Vanessa had promoted one of my sister's travel books in an airline magazine. I had agreed to act as Vanessa's escort for the evening. It had seemed the "gentlemanly thing to do," seeing as she was alone and Jenny and I had split up for the umpteenth time. I did get immense enjoyment, seeing the rage boiling inside Jenny as she saw the two of us having such a great time together. Vanessa was a joy to be with, so warm, funny and engaging, you could see why she was popular and attracted many admirers. It's no wonder Jenny hated her.

'Yes, of course I've got my music ready; I know it all by heart. I've performed it enough times you know.'

'Ok, I just want everything to go well for you.'

'Everything will be fine. Nothing is going to ruin this chance for me.' We were silent for a while. As the rain began to ease, I switched off the wipers and she said, 'I meant to ask, why is your sister proof reading your latest book? I thought Kurt at Black Elk Books did a good job for you on your first one. What was it called, "The Amazon"?'

Sarcastically I said. 'Yes that's the title, well-remembered.' I thought. "How could she possibly have forgotten the name of my first book?" I continued, 'He did do a good job but that one was based upon historical intrigue; this one is taking a completely different direction. Kurt only knows about the outline of the plot as yet.'

'What? Your first book was so successful that someone wants to talk to you about filming it and you think it's a good idea to change direction?'

'Yes, I fancied a change. Besides, I'm still waiting for them to come up with a deal. This manuscript is one I've been working on for ages, so I thought I would ask Poppy for her thoughts as I value her opinion. *She is a writer.*'

'Yes, I know she is but her expertise is writing about tripping off to some obscure village in Somalia and discovering a recipe that looks and tastes like vomit.'

My voice rises. 'Why do you have such a downer on my sister, for God's sake?' My calmness is evaporating and I am beginning to feel light-headed as we arrive at my sister's house. I can see their car outside, packed to the roof with all their holiday paraphernalia, ready to set off on their trip. The twins, Pancake and Earache are at the front window looking out for me.

Just as I am about to get out of the car Jenny says, 'I know I'm not allowed to ask about the plot but at least give me a clue if it's such a big change in direction.'

'You know I hate to give details away, I believe it's bad luck. Are you coming in?'

'No, I'll wait here; it's starting to rain again. There's no point in me getting wet if you're just going to drop off the package.'

'Ok, I might divulge a little info about the plot on the way to the airport.' I pause. 'If you're in a better mood.'

'There is nothing wrong with me,' she spat angrily.

I reach back to pick up the white parcel off the back seat and open the door. 'I won't be long.' Jenny was right, it is raining heavily again but when the girls spot me, running towards the front door, the look of joy on their faces is like a ray of sunshine.

Jacob opens the door, 'Hi buddy come in. God this weather is foul. Pops will be with you in a minute.' He immediately turns away before I can answer and moves towards the oak panelled door leading to the cellar. 'Excuse me mate, just going to get the coats. Rush, rush, rush.'

I smile, 'No problem.' There is a wonderful aroma of burning honeysuckle coming from the incense holder on the bookshelf and the sound of "Blowin' in the Wind" by Bob Dylan, is drifting in from the kitchen.

The grandfather clock in the hallway chimes half past the hour as my two beautiful nieces come running towards me. 'Girls, calm down,' Jacob says in his most authoritative voice as he descends the stairs into the cellar. Happily, they ignore him and slam into me wrapping their arms around my waist.

'Hello Pancake,' I say as I scoop up Emily with my right arm. 'Gosh, you're getting heavy.' I can't believe she will be eleven next year.

'Mummy said you shouldn't call me that anymore, Runcletez,' she says in mock indignation. I smile at the realisation that the girls' nickname for me, and mine for them has stuck since I moved in with the family nearly eight years ago.

'I know, I promise I won't do it again, Pancake.'

Raising her head and looking towards the rear of the house she shouts, 'Mum! He called me Pancake again!'

The tugging on my left side reminds me that Melia, is feeling left out, so I bend down to pick her up with my other arm.

'Here we go Earache,' I say, as I begin to pick her up. She also starts to protest about being called by her nickname but I don't register her comments as I am alarmed that numbness in my left arm seems to be preventing me from raising her up as high as Emily. My sister comes into the hallway, tying her hair up into a ponytail with a bright yellow ribbon. I grin, thinking to myself "I need sunglasses to look at her." Her black polo neck jumper is tucked into an orange knee length floral skirt and her bright blue leggings are complemented by vivid red leather boots. She wouldn't be out of place, up to her knees in mud, at a music festival in Hertfordshire.

Her cheeks are ruddy as she smiles broadly at me. 'Come on girls. Go and get your coats on, we'll be leaving in a minute.'

'Mum, Uncle Tesla called us names and he wouldn't pick me up.'

'I'm sorry Melia; I had a funny ache in my arm. I promise I'll give you a huge hug when you get back from your trip.'

Emily folds her arms and says in a disgusted tone, 'Don't believe him Melia, he promised not to call me Pancake again, but he did.'

They run off to put on their coats. 'I was only joking girls, I love you so much.' I declare, perhaps a little too loudly. I take a moment to watch them follow their father into the basement. The thing is, I really do love them, I regard them as my "daughters." They have been a major part of my life since I moved in with the family after my medical discharge. Being close to them helped me to rebuild my life and that in turn, has spurred me to start writing again. I believe my dream of being a father will never be realised so I will never have the opportunity to provide love and care for my own children. The kind of love and care I craved when growing up.

I am conscious Poppy is watching me with a concerned look on her face, 'Are you ok?'

'Yes, I just got a funny ache in my arm. I must have pulled a muscle stretching to get the manuscript off the back seat.'

'Let's have it then. I'm looking forward to reading it.'

I hand her the package and start to move back towards the front door. 'I also want to ask you a couple of other things…,' I look through the window towards my car, Jenny will be getting impatient,'…but I'd better get going.'

'Well, ask away, it must be important.'

'OK. I would like to know what you think about the main character as I haven't included any physical characteristics. I want the reader to build their own picture of him. Plus I'm not sure about the title so I would like your help with that as well please.' I take another furtive look outside; I really do need to get going.

'OK. Didn't *she* want to come in?' There is an edge to her voice.

'No, you know what she's like. I don't think she wanted to get her hair wet.'

'I really don't know why you stay with her, hardly anyone likes her in the Dramatic Society you know.'

Before I can answer, Jacob appears from the basement, buttoning his coat and says, 'What time is Jenny Nasty Drawers flanning to ply to London?'

'Flanning to ply?' I repeat incredulously.

'Who said flanning to ply?' asks Jacob.

'You did Daddy!' the twins shout in unison, as they follow him back into the hall with their coats.

'Did I?' Jacob says, 'I'm sorry, I meant what time is she planning to fly to London.'

'Her plane is at two thirty, so I'd better get going.'

I bend down to give the girls a kiss and then I hold Poppy close. 'Have a lovely time all of you; I'll see you next week when you get back.'

Jacob opens the front door, 'See you next week Tez, take care.'

'See ya mate.' I have just stepped off the threshold and into the rain when I realise I have an envelope in my jacket pocket that I need to give to Poppy.

'Oh, I nearly forgot. Remember I mentioned I was having trouble with the title of the book? Well I've a list of ideas I'd like you to consider. Can you open the envelope when you've read the story and let me know what you think?'

'Of course I will, where is it?'

I put my hand into the inside pocket of my jacket but it isn't there. I say, 'Piggin Doggin,' in exasperation.

'Mum, he's swearing!' Emily announces.

'No, darling,' I say, 'you know it's just my special way of displaying frustration. The pocket is torn at the bottom, so it's dropped down into the lining.' I locate it with my fingers. 'Hang on, here it is, I've got it now.' I pull out the envelope and pass it to Poppy. 'Right, I'd better get off. Bye you lot, have a lovely time.' I turn up my collar and run back to the car.

I start up the engine but don't pull away immediately as I need to demist the windscreen. Jenny still sounds angry. 'So, why didn't you ask me to read your book first? I could give you some feedback. Aren't I good enough?'

'Please don't be like that, it's only because Poppy is connected to the literary field. If I wanted advice or guidance on opera or singing in general, I would ask you of course because of your expertise.' The thought also crosses my mind, "if I want instructions on how to be a miserable bitch, then I'll definitely ask you," but I keep this to myself.

'So go on, tell me what your book is about?' Jenny says above the sound of the blower which is on full blast. The screen is clear now so I pull away. We drive past the Floods as they pile into their car, waving frantically. I blow kisses to the girls; Jenny just turns the other way and feigns interest in a derelict Tapas restaurant across the road.

I have an epiphany as I realise I have had enough of her attitude. 'Well Jenny, the book is about a man called Aaron Jacks who lives with a miserable and venomous singer who can't be bothered to ask how his nieces are.' My anger is beginning to bubble to the surface. I seethe. 'She gets dropped off at the airport and later her plane crash lands on Rustic Island. It's terrible for her; she has to live there for the rest of her life without shampoos, hairdryers or moisturisers. Her only friend is an empty bottle of turquoise nail polish which she talks to and …'

She interrupts. '…very funny.' The rest of the journey to the airport is completed in silence.

I drop her off at the departure gate just before twelve thirty. 'Good luck tomorrow.' I shout as she slams the door. I don't expect, nor do I get, a reply. I think her hair is the colour of pus as she struts across the service road and enters the terminal.

Poppy is right, why the hell do I put up with Jenny? I have persevered for years with her mood swings and nastiness. It is at this point I make the decision to end it once and for all. I have chastised Grace for staying in an abusive relationship but I am no better. I love Grace. I don't want anyone else. I am content to live for our Thursday afternoons together and the dream she might leave Dick one day and be mine. I will tell Grace later I am exclusively hers, after she has told me her special news.

I then imagine Jenny as Madame Butterfly going behind the screen in act three and committing hara-kiri for real. Now that would get a standing ovation from me at least!

Chapter 2

Some very unusual thoughts went through my mind as I thought I was about to die. It had only taken me five minutes to get to the hotel from the airport. I drove around the area near the reception a couple of times but there didn't appear to be any suitable spaces available. Even after all my military training, I freely admit I am useless at reversing. So when I found two adjacent spaces on the perimeter, I decided this was the place for me. It still took me two attempts to get the car parallel. I switched the engine off and noticed I was next to the stop for the shuttle bus, about five hundred yards from the hotel. The rain was still torrential but I was happy in the knowledge that very soon, I would be with the only person I have ever loved. I still had a dull ache in my head as I lit a welcome cigarette and made a mental note to ask room service if they have any aspirin when I order our wine later.

I was about to get out of the car when I thought it would be a good idea to make sure I had the booking confirmation to hand. This was our regular Thursday arrangement but it would save precious time with the receptionist if I had the documentation, and save a sodden walk back here. (She had insisted on seeing it last week, when I left it in my glove compartment).I wiped the condensation off the side window with the sleeve of my jacket so I could see our usual room, next to the fire escape on the second floor. I used the fingers on my left hand to grope the inside pocket for the confirmation sheet, but there was nothing there. I gave out an exasperated sigh as my hand, wrist and part of my forearm followed my fingers into the hole. 'God Jenny, how many times have I asked you to stitch this fucking lining?' I asked the foggy, disinterested windscreen.

Bingo! I found it, it had worked its way into the dark recesses of my jacket, somewhere near my right hip.

I had tried, more than once, to repair my favourite jacket myself but had found I wasn't very good with a needle and thread and didn't fare much better when I used a stapler. Initially this seemed like a quick and easy solution to the problem, but after a while the staples came adrift, so every time I tried to access the pocket, I ripped the silk lining even more and once left my fingers a bloody mess from the protruding metal barbs.

I retrieved the confirmation sheet which I folded and put into my trouser pocket alongside my phone. I also found two old creased train tickets in the lining along with a pen and the hotel reservation from three weeks ago. 'I'm getting careless.' I said to myself, as I placed them on the passenger seat beside me, making a mental note to throw the incriminating evidence away later.

I was keen to get moving, so I undid the seat belt, opened the door and ventured outside. I do understand Grace is incredibly nervous whenever she comes to see me. Discovery and its aftermath is something too awful to consider but I had the feeling she was going to make today extra special. She told me she had something very important to tell me when I saw her briefly yesterday.

The rain had eased slightly but the breeze had picked up again. I locked the car and headed towards the reception. I was amused by the sight of business men running towards the hotel, some using brief cases as improvised rain bonnets. I laughed out loud when I saw suntanned groups, wandering around trying to locate their cars. Many of them wearing brightly coloured shirts, shorts and sandals and pulling cases through ever widening puddles, their comments indicating they were already missing the sun.

I had only gone a few paces when my left leg began to feel numb and I noticed my left arm ached again. The unwelcome tingle of pins and needles, down my left side, joined the party. I gave my limbs a vigorous shake, which I was sure, would give relief, then set off towards the dry sanctuary of room twenty two.

Suddenly, I felt as if I had a rucksack full of wet sand on my back. I fought with all my strength to stay upright but my legs began to buckle. I was conscious of my inane smile, trying to show the nosey and sodden observers I was in control – it was just a trip or a stumble, and I would be able to correct the mishap and stay on my feet. The collapse continued.

As I started my descent towards a grey pool of water, did I think about all the people I had killed? Whether my destination would be Heaven or Hell? No.

As my knees slammed into the coarse tarmac of the car park, did I think about missing the premier of "The Amazon" in Hollywood? No.

As my shoulder hit the ground with a loud 'thump' very swiftly followed by my head, was one of my last thoughts about Dr. Evans, wryly saying, 'I told you so?' No.

As I was lying on my left side, looking at the silver Mercedes above me, was my last thought about Poppy, Pancake or Earache? No.

All I could think was, "I'm in serious trouble." The blood started to flow from my gashed left cheek and I could taste the gritty texture of dirt on my lips. I tried to move my body to alleviate the pain in my face but my left leg and arm wouldn't move properly. I managed to turn my neck just enough to get most of my face out of the water, only to realise my vision was blurred. "Oh God what is happening to me?" I thought as I lay in the rain, unable to move.

'Are you alright mate?' said a voice. Despite the rain running down my forehead into my right eye, I could just make out a sun tanned foot in a fluorescent orange plastic sandal. I was disappointed to discover the very first person to reach me was stupid. I wanted to say, "Do I look alright, you prick?" But I thought that would be rude in my predicament, besides, I was abruptly filled with tiredness and didn't feel like talking. Then I heard someone running towards us.

'What's happened Billy?'

'Not sure Todd, this bloke just collapsed. He's smashed his face.'

'Come on let's lift him, get his head off the ground.'

Billy hesitated, 'Hang on a minute, should we move someone in these circumstances?'

I thought, "Yes, for fuck's sake get me off the ground. I'm cold, can't move, I'm bleeding, dirty, wet, very frightened, extremely uncomfortable and just to make matters worse, I have just pissed myself." On the plus side, I thought, "At least my groin is warm."

'I'm going to sit him up; I can't leave his head in a pool of water; look at all the blood. You phone for an ambulance while I try and make him comfortable.'

'Shall I tell them we're in the hotel car park Todd?'

'No Billy, give them some clues and ask them to guess where we are. We can play hide and seek with them when they get here. What do you think, you Tit?'

'Ok, there's no need for that, I was only asking.'

There is urgency in his voice. 'Tell them we're near the buttle shush helter.'

'Eh?'

'I meant the shuttle bus shelter.' His mispronunciation reminded me of Jacob.

'You call me a tit but you can't even talk properly.'

'Just help me get him up will ya?'

I hear a new voice to my left, deep, assertive and distinctly foreign. 'Hola, can I help?' He is definitely Spanish.

20

I want to say "por favor me ayude señor" but right now I'm incapable of showing off my linguistic prowess.

'Yes mate, could you put your umbrella over his head whilst I try and get him over to the shelter?'

'Si.'

'Come on buddy, let's get you out of this rain.' I was beginning to like Todd, a lot. As he put his hands under my armpits to raise me up, Billy the Tit confirmed the ambulance was on its way.

'Well done mate. You'll have to help me; this guy is a dead weight.'

'OK, will do.'

'Gosh Buddy, what's happened to you?' My new best mate said as they started to drag me carefully towards cover. I was glad I was in his hands.

I tried to say, 'I don't know,' but it only came out as a grunt.

Todd put his ear close to my mouth. 'What was that mate? I couldn't understand.'

I repeated the grunt. Why couldn't I make any sense? I am really alarmed now; I can't speak English, let alone Spanish.

Billy the Tit said, 'Do you think he's a deaf mute?'

Todd looked up at him and shook his head, 'How can he be deaf if he's tried to answer me? For God's sake have you left your brains in Ibiza?'

'Piss off Todd!'

That was the last I heard of the conversation between Todd, Billy the Tit and the Spanish Man. I was distracted by my phone's ringtone. My thoughts sandwiched between my version of the lyrics of David Bowie's song, Thursday's Child.

All of my life I tried so hard

I realised that Grace,

Doing my best with what I had

21

who would be waiting for me nearby,
            Nothing much happened all the same
was ringing to see where I was.
                Something about you stood apart
My penultimate thought was,
            A whisper of hope that couldn't fail
"I wish I could have held her one last time,
            Maybe I was born right at the right time
but please Lord don't let her see me like this,
                Building my life with you
I must look so pathetic."

                Love me tomorrow
            Now that we've really got a chance
                Love me tomorrow
            Everything's falling into place
                Love me tomorrow
            Hating my past, I'll let it go
                Love me tomorrow

I began to lose consciousness and at the point when I believed I was really about to die, as the music in my pocket reached the chorus, my very last thought was, "Why, oh why didn't I put a password on my phone or better still switch it off?" The call from my lover, Grace Perritano, would appear on my phone to be from someone called Russell, an alias, but that didn't matter, because the shit was really going to hit the fan and I wouldn't be around to protect her. I felt my heart being torn apart.

    Only for you I don't regret, you're my Thursday's child

Chapter 3

I am awake, and immediately have the sensation I'm gagging. My mouth feels as if a pair of rolled up socks have been substituted for my tongue and pushed down my throat. I am so dry; I don't think I have ever been so thirsty.

For a few moments, I believe I am pinned down. I consider whether I have been prepared for interrogation or to be tortured. That would be ironic after some of the actions I have performed in the service of my country. I remember the two Sunni Islamist terrorists we captured near the Cheekha Dar Mountain. It was their information, which led to the ill-fated operation near the border of Iran and Iraq, which in turn resulted in a political whitewash and my eventual medical discharge from the job I loved.

I try to suppress the panic rising in my chest. I think "Come on Tesla, use your training, and evaluate the situation."

I realise I am horizontal. Initially, I lie perfectly still and assess my position. Something is holding down my left arm, it is very tight and uncomfortable. I am alarmed to realise something is biting my left index finger. Fear is blossoming, I have to focus. My left arm will only move very slightly but my right arm seems to have good mobility even though there's something tight around it.

I become aware I am in a bed, naked from the waist down and lying in a very wet patch. I start to hyperventilate when I think I am blind but quickly calm down when I realise it is dark. I have no clear vision in my left eye but my right eye can just make out a blurred image of light below a door in front of me. I can vaguely see a monitor to my right; it has a green flashing trace with random numbers changing below it.

I decide it is time to explore my environment. Using my right arm, I reach for the source of the pain in my left finger and find a plastic clamp which I remove. And then, as I move my hand towards the edge of the bed, it hits metal. "I'm caged in!" This thought causes terror to flare and erupt in my chest. I am trying to shout for help but the sounds coming from my mouth sound bizarre. My right arm gets tangled in wires attached to my chest; I tear them from my body. My scream is dry and inaudible; I can hear an alarm sounding as my right leg joins my arm in slamming my cage for attention.

The darkness is shattered by a flickering harsh brightness as fluorescent tubes jerk into life. 'Mr Coyne, Mr Coyne it's OK. Don't panic. Let me help you.' I can just make out the outline of a female in a light blue uniform. She holds my hand as she says, 'So glad you're back with us. You are in hospital.' Her voice is soft, but confident and reassuring.

What am I doing here? She said, "Glad you're back with us." Where have I been? Who are the "us" she refers to? I want to get up but can't move on one side and I am consumed by fatigue. I try to say 'What has happened to me?' but the words are slurred and incomprehensible. I sound like the hunchback in that old black and white film, set in a cathedral in Paris. It's one of my favourite movies but I can't remember his name.

'Everything will be explained soon enough.' I can't believe she can understand me. 'Please just relax if you can.' She is standing right next to me at the side of the bed. I hear two loud metallic clicks and the cage disappears. I realise the metal is the side of the bed, no doubt there to stop me falling out. She smiles serenely as she takes hold of my hand. I feel more love and comfort in that moment with this stranger than I ever did with my mother.

'I know this must be awful for you. My name is Meredith Sanders. I am the staff nurse in charge of this ward. It's nearly midnight.' I can't believe it is less than twelve hours since I was supposed to be with someone but I can't remember who I was meeting. 'I'm just going to get some cloths to freshen you up a bit and get something to moisten your mouth.'

"Just get me a pint of iced water", I want to say but she continues, 'We need to do some tests before we give you a proper drink, just to make sure you can swallow safely. I'll change your bedding as well to make you more comfortable.' She moves towards the door, 'Your reaction is perfectly natural. It's scary to wake up like that and not be sure of where you are. I won't be long.'

As she leaves the room, I try to work out why I am here. I can remember a car park, I had fallen and smacked my head on the floor and there was someone there called Billy the Tit.

'Hi Mr Coyne I'm back now. It's me, Meredith, again. Let me freshen up your lips and tongue. This is called a mouth toilet, it's like a little pink lolly. It will help moisten your mouth, which will help you if you want to speak to me.' I remember I had damaged my water bottle once on an exercise in Brunei. I had gone sixteen hours without a drink but the relief that day was nothing compared to the joy of that little pink piece of moist cotton wool.

'We need to wipe away this stickiness from your eyes,' she said as she applied a cool, damp cloth to my eyelids. The feeling was exquisite.

'I made a couple of calls whilst I was out of the room. I've spoken to the doctor on call, who has suggested you try and get a good night's sleep. We don't need to do anything tonight. You've had a bit of a start waking up like that. Your own consultant Dr Invergordon will come and see you tomorrow after we've had all the test results. He will explain what has happened and the next steps.'

Meredith leans me to one side then the other as she changes what feels like a giant pad below my naked bottom.

She wipes me down and applies some cream. She pulls the covers back up to my waist, puts the oxygen monitor back onto my left index finger, checks the intravenous drip in my left arm and finally reconnects the wires to the sticky pads on my chest and the blood pressure pad to my biceps. She talks to me in a soothing way whilst she does this. Her voice reminds me of someone I love dearly. I fight hard with my memory, and then I remember. Of course, I was due to meet Grace but what the hell happened?

My thoughts are interrupted as she says, 'The police gave us the "ICE" number from your phone when you first came in, so we've called your partner again, to tell her the good news that you're awake.' I am confused, as I don't recall putting Grace's number in my phone to call in case of an emergency. 'She'll get here as soon as she can, as she is so keen to be the first to welcome you back.' Meredith adjusts my pillows and looks directly at me as she says, 'She came within an hour of you getting here you know. You also had another visitor but she left before we could find out who she was. Oh, I nearly forgot, your sister has called, she is back from her week away. She says she loves you loads and she will get here after Dr Invergordon has seen you.'

I feel myself sinking towards oblivion as the tiredness overwhelms me. I hear her raise the sides of the bed and turn to make some adjustments to the monitor. My eyelids flicker as I fight, in vain, to keep them open. She pauses at the door and says, 'Try and get some rest Mr Coyne. Goodnight.'

Oh Grace, I love you and I want to see you so much but I really don't want you to see me like this.

*

I am awakened by a sound and am aware of movement in the room. It is bright but the light seems natural, not as harsh as last night. I realise the curtains are open and it is morning, with sunlight filling the room. Although my movement is still restricted down my left side, there is no anxiety this time; I am calm.

'Good morning. I'm Connie Kirkendall.' I can't see her properly when she moves to the left hand side of the bed. My right eye feels crusty. 'Is it ok if I call you Tesla?'

I say, 'Yes,' but also nod, just in case she doesn't understand me.

She is walking around the room, placing things here and there but I can't make out what they are. It seems as if she is preparing to get me or the room ready for something. 'I took over from Meredith this morning. She told me what had happened last night. It isn't nice to wake up like that, is it?'

She comes over to the side of my bed and lowers the sides. 'I'm going to give your face a wipe and change your sheets ready for the consultant's visit. Is that ok?' I nod my head; I had forgotten that Meredith had mentioned last night, that a doctor would be visiting me today. What was it she said, "He'll explain what has happened and the next steps?" Connie continues, 'He'll be here at about ten.'

She follows the same procedure that Meredith had introduced me to last night. After she has smoothed the covers around me and checked all the equipment attached to my body she says, 'That's you all ready for your visitors. Can I get you anything else, Tesla?'

'Pink lolly,' I say but to me it sounds more like "stink rorry".

'Oh of course, you must be parched,' she says as she gets one of the pads from the table beside her, moistens it and wipes my tongue and lips. I groan with pleasure and gratitude.

'I must say that your speech is very good considering you've been out for so long,' she says as she begins to tidy up and moves towards the door.

I can't understand what she means by that statement. Out for so long? I have only been here for a night. 'What – you – mean – me – out – so – long?'

27

I still think I sound like the hunchback but she must have understood because she says, 'Don't worry about that now, your partner and the consultant will be here very soon to explain. I'm going to prepare another patient now for Dr Invergordon's visit so I'll see you in a little while. I'll tell my colleague Tamara that you're ready. She is keen to meet our sleeping author.'

I can't comprehend why she uses the reference, "the sleeping author," or, "out for so long." How on earth can Poppy have returned from her week away? I must have been unconscious yesterday when I fell and banged my head but I have just had about eight hours sleep.

My reasoning is disrupted when I hear someone enter the room. A new voice says, 'Mr Coyne, I'm Tamara Flint, I usually work on the same shift as Connie. She's gone to see another patient now so I thought I would come and say hello. Can I call you Tesla?' She pauses but before I get chance to reply or nod, she sets off again. 'I read your book, "The Amazon." I really enjoyed it, especially the love story between the steward and the Captain's wife. What was she called?' She held her chin as she pondered the question. Then her eyes lit up as she triumphantly said, 'Sarah Briggs, that's it, they disappeared along with all the crew. They should make it into a film.'

My ego and vanity want to tell her in my new slurring speech, that there actually has been talk of turning my story into a film but before I can interject she says, 'Oh, I'll just go and get a chair for your visitor.' With that, she quits the room leaving the door open. I can hear her walk away along the corridor. I turn my head to face the wall, nervous about what Grace will think when she sees me like this.

Within minutes I hear approaching footsteps. 'I'm back.' Tamara says as she quietly enters the room. I hear a scrape on the floor. It sounds as if she has put the chair near the monitor. I hear a slight creaking sound and realise she is leaning on the side of my bed. 'Tesla,' she says quietly. 'I have a surprise for you. Your partner is here. Is it ok for me to show her in?'

A lopsided smile forms as I recall how Grace had nearly jumped out of her skin in shock when I had held her hand for the first time in the supermarket car park. I think about when we made love for the first time in her kitchen, and of course our wonderful Thursdays together. At this moment I don't care how I look, I just need to see her again. 'Yes.' I grunt. I am excited, exhilarated and relieved she is OK. Love floods through me as the thought of her holding me again fills me with joy. 'Yes. Yes,' I repeat eagerly.

Tamara leaves the room and returns a few moments later. 'Here he is,' she says to the person she is escorting into the room. I slowly turn to face her, mentally cursing my poor vision, especially on my left side. I want to see her so much. My longed-for visitor walks towards the bed and stands in front of the bright sunlight coming from the window. I pray she will lean forward so I can see her lovely face again. She turns towards the door and very quietly asks, 'Can I be alone with him?' But something's not right. Grace sounds different. My head is in turmoil as I try to solve the discrepancy. I hear Tamara reply, 'Of course you can. I'll shut the door to give you some privacy. He doesn't *know* by the way, the consultant hasn't seen him yet.' The door is pulled shut with a click.

Hesitantly I say, 'Grace?' I am delighted because I know I have pronounced this special word correctly. I hear footsteps as she approaches the bed. There must be at least a second between each stride. The suspense is heightened as the last step is followed by total silence. I still can't see properly. It's too damned bright in here. It is at this moment, as the figure stoops over the side of the bed towards my face, that my life changes forever.

The panic is real and tangible this time as I realise the voice and contorted face now leering in front of me is not that of the person I love.

The voice is low but it has an edge to it that I swear could cut a diamond. 'No, it isn't Grace, you dribbling scumbag.' I can visualise poisonous spittle dripping from her mouth as she hisses. 'It's Jenny, your so called girlfriend, you fucking cheating bastard!' I try to back away from her as I remember I had dropped her off at the airport on my way to meet Grace.

'I can't believe I missed the plane because of you.' She keeps glancing at the closed door, I realise she isn't shouting because she doesn't want the nurses to hear. 'I came to be with you as soon as the police called me. I was concerned about you, then I found all the messages and the missed calls on your phone.'

Another flashback comes to me about yesterday. I thought I was dying as I was lying in the car park, and I could hear Grace's ringtone as she was trying to call me. I knew her husband would find out about us and hurt her badly and I wouldn't be there to protect her. Utter despair begins to grip me. 'I found the coded messages between you and your little actress friend. You must have thought you were very clever calling her Russell. It took me a while to work out it was that bitch Perritano. I thought her voice was familiar when I answered her call on your phone.'

I don't like where this is going. I want Connie or Tamara to come in and get Jenny away from me.

'Well, you pathetic bastard, I've some news for you.' She leans further forward, her face just a matter of inches from mine as she says, 'Your precious Grace or Russell or whatever other fucking name you call her, is dead.'

Dead? I try to back away from her vindictive lies but my body won't work properly and I am struggling for breath. I know Jenny has a nasty streak but this is beyond comprehension. She leans closer, so her nose is almost touching mine.

'You don't believe me do you? Well let me say it slowly so it sinks in. The slut died over a week ago, on the very same day, you became a fucking cripple.'

My brain goes into meltdown. How can Grace be dead? Why did Jenny say it happened so long ago when I have only been in the hospital for less than twenty four hours? I shake my head and try to say, 'How many days?'

She laughs as she straightens up and says, 'They haven't told you yet have they? I wanted to be the one to have the pleasure in telling you, you've been in a coma for over a week.'

I want this to stop. The sound from the monitor is no longer rhythmic, the tone is disjointed. I start hitting the metal side of the bed and try shouting 'Nurse, nurse.' It sounds as if I am saying 'durse, durse.'

'Durse, durse,' Jenny repeats mockingly, 'what's a fucking durse you pathetic piece of shit?' I begin beating the side of the bed with all my strength. 'Do you want to know how she died?' She is raising her voice now. I know instinctively I don't want to hear this.

She barks the words slowly into my face, 'Well I'll tell you. She died when she crashed the pile of crap she called a car. She got the door open but couldn't get out because she failed to undo the buckle. She was trapped and burnt to death.'

I am screaming now, ripping the wires from my chest, the drip from my arm and the clamp from my finger. I can hear alarms coming from the monitor and beyond the door but they don't drown out her voice as she shouts maniacally. 'They removed her body with a brush and dustpan you know; they managed to scrape together enough pieces for the funeral.'

The door suddenly bursts open as people rush into the room. Someone shouts, 'What on earth's happening here?'

Jenny grips the side of the bed as she screams, 'Yes Mr Cunty Coyne, your beloved girlfriend is dead. She was delivered to the Crematorium in a paper bag. The service was on Friday, hardly anyone turned up to say goodbye.' She is laughing as she delivers... 'They didn't even have to switch on the ovens.'

The noise coming from my throat doesn't sound human as I wail in anguish at this torrent of vitriol. There's a disgusting warm sensation underneath me as I realise I have opened my bowels. The smell is indescribable. I feel shame at what I have done but this vanishes when she hits me hard across the bridge of my nose. The nurses break the grip of her left hand on the side of the bed and start to steer her towards the door.

Jenny giggles as she delivers her penultimate retort. 'Just waste away in bed you cheating bastard. Waste being the operative word, by the smell of it. Who is going to want you now, Mr Ploppy, a pathetic cripple, who shits the bed?'

I hear one of the nurses say, 'Enough,' as they get Jenny away from the bed and through the door.

'I'll take you to court and sue you for assault you fat bitch,' is Jenny's final comment to Connie. This is followed by a loud bang as the door slams shut.

In that moment of silence, I believe what she has told me is true. I put my right arm over my face to try and block out the thought but it is no good.

I was an officer in the Special Boat Service, made love to countless women, published a successful novel and met someone who truly loved me. Now I am an invalid, deformed and lying in my own mess but worst of all, have lost my Grace in horrific circumstances.

I turn left to face the wall. I remember the scene where the hunchback rescues the maiden and shouts, "Sanctuary, sanctuary," to the hateful crowds who are attacking them. At least he had tried to protect her; I had failed Grace. Despair crushes me as a tear runs down my right cheek. I bury my face into the pillow as far and as deep as I can.

Is this an attempt to conceal my sorrow? I have shed tears before, especially when a chemical cloud enveloped me after the explosion in the cave. No.

Am I trying to muffle the sobs racking my chest? The weeping of a thirty nine year old trained assassin who defiantly refused to cry when ill-treated by his parents or when bullied at school? No.

I am trying to eradicate the image in my mind of the sheer terror on Grace's face, picturing her eyes wide open, as the flames engulfed her. What had Jenny said when she spat the words into my face? "She burnt to death?" Did she also say she was "trapped?" The image changes to my lover trying to escape. She is in agony, as the flames singe her hair and eyebrows. I imagine her skin, blistering, popping, peeling away with her blood boiling then bubbling through her broken flesh then erupting like lava. I squeeze my eyes together as tight as possible. The vision disappears to be replaced with a different scenario.

Why couldn't she get out? Was she so badly injured that she couldn't move? Just sitting there screaming as the heat melted her or was she dead already, her body smashed and shattered? It suddenly occurs to me she could have driven off in anger because I didn't turn up at the hotel. She had told me she had something special and important to tell me. Maybe she was pissed off because I didn't answer her calls? What if it was my fault she was dead? I feel even more despondent when I remember Jenny had said the funeral service was held on Friday, so I can't even pay my respects to Grace.

I tense as I hear the slight click of a door opening. A voice says, 'Tesla, its Connie, can I come in?' I don't reply. I don't need to; she enters anyway, approaches the side of the bed and puts her hand on my right shoulder. I stay where I am with my back towards her. 'We're so sorry about what happened earlier. She's gone now. The hospital security escorted her off the premises.' She gives my shoulder a reassuring squeeze as she turns to leave the room.

That is when I realise that I don't want to live in a world without Grace. An inner peace engulfs me as I decide what I will do. Only once before had I seriously wanted to die; that was after a beating from my parents, just after we had moved back from Germany when I was twelve.

Chapter 4

I realised, from a very early age, that my mother and father were not the most loving parents. I became aware they were different when comparing their behaviour to what I witnessed in school playgrounds and parties. Seeing the other mothers giving their children a hug and a kiss when saying hello or goodbye or for no reason in particular, made me envious. I would try to be a good boy, make my mum laugh or impress her with my school reports, but no affection was ever forthcoming. And to see the other fathers standing on the touchline shouting encouragement to their boys made me wish my dad would invest just ninety minutes to watch me play football. How I longed to see admiration in his eyes as I scored a goal or played a "killer" pass. Oh how I wanted him to ruffle my hair and say, "Well done, Son," as we walked off the pitch.

It was even harder for me to understand their behaviour when I saw how they showered my sister with love and affection. I honestly didn't begrudge Poppy in any way but I couldn't understand why my treatment was so different. I didn't think it was possible to get any worse but it did after the accident.

I couldn't remember a single time when my mother or father had hugged or kissed me or said. "I love you, Son." It was only later, after receiving my first beating, I realised this wasn't normal. I felt completely worthless.

*

Dad didn't normally use physical violence on me but he was goaded into it when my mother accused me of thieving. She'd also suggested he was weak and constantly refused to back her up in matters concerning my discipline.

It was a Saturday afternoon. Poppy had left with her friend at lunchtime to go to school; they were rehearsing a play for a performance the following week. I was in the back garden playing football when I heard a commotion in the house. Some papers had gone missing from my mother's studio, I could hear her, in one of her drunken frenzies, telling my father I was the culprit. My heart sank as I ran from the lawn towards the back door. I wouldn't be so stupid to take anything belonging to my mother but being one hundred percent innocent of the charge wouldn't save me.

On entering the kitchen, I pleaded with her to believe I hadn't touched her papers. 'Well who else could it be?' I considered whether Poppy might have taken them. It had been known for my sister, who was eight at the time, to take paper from Mum's studio to draw on or to make greetings cards. I certainly didn't want her to get into trouble, so I decided to remain silent. What was the worst that could happen? I was accustomed to the verbal abuse; hardened to it by now, so I wouldn't give them the pleasure of seeing me cowering before them.

My sudden change in demeanour and silence was taken as an admission of guilt. Talk about putting two and two together to get a Zebra. 'See, Harry,' she said pointing a finger at my defiance, 'you can tell by his face that he's taken them.'

My Dad looked uncertain. 'He said he hasn't taken them, Joyce. Perhaps you've misplaced them.' I cringed and took a step backwards. I knew his comment, suggesting she might be at fault, would be countered with the force of a nuclear strike.

I wasn't wrong. 'You're suggesting I've lost them are you? That's just bloody typical, you never support me when it comes to him.'

"Him?" I am twelve years old. I have a name and the creation of the two people in the room. I have to admit though, it is better than when she refers to me as *"it"* as in, "Is it back from school yet?" or "Is it up out of bed yet?"

I didn't realise Dad had moved towards me until I felt the slap across the back of my head. It wasn't a particularly hard blow, more a show of solidarity towards my accuser, I think. The surprise of it, however, caused me to fall backwards into a table. On it was a lamp and a porcelain figure left to Mum by Grandma when she died. I tried to grab them before they fell from the table onto the floor but my attempt was thwarted. My mother screamed. 'No,' as my father tried to deliver his next blow to my head, he missed but caught the fingers on my outstretched right hand instead. The sound of my fingers cracking was smothered by the noise of the smashed ornament, and my father shouting, "Shit."

My mother kicked me in the tummy as I fell. Shock, disgust and shame seared through me; as I hit the floor, I just as quickly sprang up and ran upstairs to my room. I could hear raised voices downstairs, the slamming of a door and a car driving away.

Later, when the house was silent, I ventured downstairs. Dad's car was no longer in the drive. I could see Mum's head moving through the glass door of her studio. I was beginning to feel sick with the pain now, especially my fingers. I noticed that the debris was still on the wooden floor next to the upturned table. I decided to clear it up, foolishly believing she would appreciate the gesture. I found a brush and carefully swept the pieces towards the wall. I had to be cautious because my right hand was useless, a slight knock from the broom handle made me wince in agony. I ripped a piece of card from a cornflake packet and by using my left hand, slid this under the fragments next to the skirting board. I dropped everything into the swing top bin then approached the studio door and knocked.

'Mum.' There was no reply. I knocked again a little louder and opened the door fractionally, 'Mum.' I repeated. She had her back to me as I walked into the room. 'Mum, I'm sorry about the ornament, I've swept the mess up.' She continued to ignore me. 'Mum, my fingers are hurting; I think I bent them back when I fell on the floor, can you take me to the doctor's please?' I thought that a better approach than saying, "My fingers were broken when Dad attacked me."

I was startled when she did turn around. The look of hatred in her face had reached a new peak. 'You should've thought about that when you caused all the trouble earlier, shouldn't you?' She paused. I could tell she was drunk, fighting to structure her next sentence. 'I'm busy; you'll have to get your dad to take you to the hospital.' With that caring comment she turned around, taking a deep gulp from a crystal glass. The liquid was dark brown. I had a bet with myself that it was brandy.

I went into the kitchen and ran some cold water over my hand. I have no idea why I did this but it just felt right. I wrapped a handkerchief around my sore fingers and left the house. I knew the Doctor's surgery was less than a mile away but wasn't sure if they would be open on a Saturday but decided to walk that way anyway to see if I could get help. I didn't know what I would do if it was shut. I knew the hospital was a half hour drive away at least. I blocked the thought from my mind; I couldn't contemplate walking so far.

Taking a short cut through a gap between some houses, I came out in a large field with a number of football pitches. The two closest to me featured matches with boys of about my age being encouraged by enthusiastic parents, other adults and a couple of blokes in jeans running up and down the touchline, raising a white rag above their heads at frequent intervals.

'That was never offside Ref,' I heard a man say as I walked towards the next pitch.

The match here had stopped and a number of players stood around chatting whilst a couple of men, (one in a blue tracksuit, the other all in black), crouched down next to someone sitting on the grass wearing a yellow shirt with a dirty number ten on the back. Moments later, the player stood up and ran, with a limp, towards the penalty area. The man in blue, carrying a large bag over one shoulder, jogged towards the touchline. Play resumed, and as I drew alongside him, he said to no one in particular. 'Alan will be OK; he got a knock to his ankle. He should run it off in a minute or so.' He dumped the bag right in front of me.

'Excuse me sir,' I said in my politest voice. 'I wonder if you could help me.'

He was a big man, with a large pink face; he smiled when he saw me. 'Well young man, you probably noticed I'm busy at the moment but what can I do for you?'

I said, 'Are you the trainer?' He nodded. 'I was messing around, watching my mate on the other pitch, when I fell and hurt my fingers. I think they're broken. There wasn't a trainer over there so could you have a quick look, please?'

'I shouldn't do really. Can't you get your dad to take you to the hospital?'

'No I can't. He went with my mum to see grandma.' I lied. 'He won't be back for a couple of hours. Besides he'll kill me if he finds out I wasn't at home doing my homework.'

'Ok, let's have a quick look,' I gingerly held up my hand to him. 'Did you wrap this hanky around your fingers?' he asked as he gently removed it.

'Yes, it made them feel a bit better.'

'Well, that was good thinking Son,' he said as he delicately moved my sore fingers. My dad had never called me Son. 'The good news is they don't look broken.'

He took some white tape and bound my aching fingers together. 'They should be fine now.' He said as he pressed something into the palm of my other hand. 'Here take this roll of tape with you; you can tell your dad your mate bound your fingers for you. Tell him it's a spare roll if he asks you where you got it from. OK?' I nodded and put the tape into my pocket as he said, 'Get your dad to take you to the Doctors on Monday if they still hurt.'

'I will. Thank you.' We had just finished speaking when there was the sound of a sickening collision, as if two large pieces of meat had slapped together, this was instantly followed by a shrill scream and the blowing of a whistle.

It appeared that Alan, the number ten in the yellow shirt, had taken revenge on someone for the earlier tackle. The referee was pulling players apart as I started to walk away. The kind man, who had bound my fingers, had had his back to the incident with "Alan the Number Ten," because he was concentrating on me. He must have been a magician though, because he shouted, 'Bollocks, ref, he never touched him,' even though he didn't see what had happened.

*

Dad's car still wasn't there when I got home. I entered the house gingerly. It was silent. I raised myself on my toes and looked into the studio. I could see my mother asleep at her desk. I went upstairs to my room, looked to see if Poppy was back as I passed her bedroom but it was empty.

I felt exhausted. I just wanted to sleep, even though my fingers were throbbing with the pain and my tummy was sore from my mother's kick. I decided to get ready for bed. It was difficult to get undressed and put my pyjamas on with a sore hand and I was shocked when I saw the angry purple bruise, running from my left hip to my navel.

I went back downstairs to get a drink and something to eat. I noticed the vodka bottle was still in the fridge when I went to get some milk. When I opened the base cabinet to get some biscuits, I found a pile of typewritten papers next to an upturned, leaking brandy bottle. These must be the ones that I had "stolen." The alcohol had gradually run out of the bottle, along the shelf, contaminating the manuscript on the way. It had dripped down onto the lower shelf and pooled on top of the airtight container, which held my supper, biscuits. The stale smell of booze caused me to lose my appetite, so I quietly closed the cabinet door and walked back upstairs with my glass of milk. I closed my eyes and imagined...

I see my dad stooping to get himself a chocolate digestive and discovering the papers. Realising his wife had left them there by mistake when she had prepared her breakfast of brandy and coke, he would have gone into her studio and awakened her from her drunken stupor. She would have cried in shame as he explained her mistake. She would run upstairs, (stopping only to have a wash, clean her teeth and comb her hair – she has to look nice and not smell of alcohol in my imagination, of course) before coming into my room and pulling me off the bed and into her bosom. She would hug me, kiss me and say the words I had never heard. "I love you, Tesla." I would close my eyes and savour the moment as she tells me she is sorry and promises that life will be good from now on.

... an impossible dream.

Later the next day, I tentatively opened the cabinet and saw the mess had been cleaned up and the papers removed. I recalled my mother's accusation that I was a thief and her violent kick to my tummy and my father's smack across my head and my 'broken' fingers.

There was no apology. I felt hollow, worthless and wished I was dead.

*

I feel the same way now, lying in my hospital bed. I hear the door open and recognise the voice. It is Tamara. 'Hi, Tesla, Dr Invergordon will be along soon, I'm just going to make you comfortable so you're ready for his visit. Ok?'

I grunt my assent and use the strength on my "good side" to turn and lie on my back. It is then that Tamara discovers the blood. 'Oh Tesla, what's happened here?' she says as she turns my head carefully. 'Your face and pillow are covered in blood.' Jenny must have caught me with her diamond ring when she hit me earlier. 'I'll be back in a moment to clean you up, love,' she says as she leaves the room.

I touch my face with my right hand. It is dry and crusty across the bridge of my nose and under my left eye and I can't feel my fingers on my cheek. I realise for the first time, that I have thick stubble where I was once clean shaven. I don't care about the blood but am concerned about the numbness in my face.

Tamara left the door ajar when she went out. I hear her say, 'Connie, can you give me a hand with Tesla please? Dr Invergordon will be here soon. You should see what the nasty bitch has done to his face.'

I don't hear Connie's reply. She just appears at my bedside moments later and helps me into a sitting position. She wipes my face clean with a damp cloth and I am relieved I can see a bit more clearly now. She moistens my mouth with a "stink rorry," removes the wires from my chest and changes my bloody gown. In the meantime, Tamara exchanges the marked pillowcases for fresh ones and applies a small plaster to the cut across my nose. Having settled me onto my back, they ease me gently onto my left side and rub my buttocks with cream. 'I'm just checking for bedsores Tesla.' I hear Connie say.

I discover that a part of me is working as usual when they massage my bum. I see a smile dart across Tamara's face, as she moves me onto my back and notices my erection. The wires are reconnected to the pads on my chest and the sides of the bed click back into place. Tamara says. 'We'll let the Doctor know that you're ready now.' I am sure she winks at me as she closes the door.

Chapter 5

The door opens and a tall, dark-haired man enters the room. His sleeves are rolled up to reveal bare elbows and hairy forearms, a blue and white tie is tucked inside his shirtfront. He is accompanied by Connie and two younger people. One is an incredibly handsome, dark skinned man, in a buttoned up white housecoat. The other, a woman with hair the colour of shimmering copper, is wearing a blue, green and red tartan skirt with a black polo neck sweater. She stands with her feet planted wide apart, hands pushed deep into the pockets of her jacket like a capital letter "A". The confident demeanour she displays is aimed solely at one person in the room. She can't take her eyes off the older man.

He is carrying a clipboard and a file of papers. He puts these on the table beside me and says, 'Good afternoon, my name is Doctor Invergordon. I'm the consultant looking after you. This is Dr Pancholi and Dr Sutherland who work with me.' I nod as they both quietly say; 'Hello.' The red head has a strong Scottish accent, 'and I believe you already know Nurse Kirkendall?'

He doesn't wait for a reply. 'I understand that it's ok to address you as Tez, is that correct?' I nod and say, 'Yes'. Connie smiles, which I take as an indicator my reply is clear and understandable. 'I would like to examine you now to see how things are working. Then we'll have a chat. Is that ok?'

I nod again as he moves to the left hand side of the room and he inexplicably vanishes from view. I hear running water and the washing of hands but I can't see him. The sound is followed by one of hands being dried on a paper towel, then the clang of a waste bin closing. He reappears, comes round to the right hand side of my bed and says, 'We're so sorry about what happened earlier, I understand you've lost someone very dear to you?'

The question is unexpected and unwanted; I am too stunned to reply. The image of Grace's flesh dripping off her face like wax, springs into my mind. I want to turn my head back into my pillow but his next comment stuns me. 'You've been with us for over a week now. Today is Monday. You were admitted on Thursday, that's ten days ago.'

This information devastates me as I realise it is true what Jenny has told me, I have now had it confirmed officially. Not only have I lost my one true love but also over a week of my life. I didn't believe things could get worse but they just have. The pain arrives like a red hot needle plunging into my chest. Nausea cascades through me like a waterfall. Connie moves over to the sink and begins washing her hands. I can't see her now either. Why do people keep disappearing from view? The consultant is taking a moment to check something in his notes.

'You probably won't remember this but we've already examined you a number of times and run some tests. We've also been moving your body to prevent sores and hopefully to help your rehabilitation in physiotherapy. I'd like to re-examine you now. Connie can you help Tez into a comfortable sitting position please?' She lowers the side of the bed and encourages me to shuffle upwards. I notice the redhead has moved forward to help but the consultant stops her, as he watches me use my right leg to push my body backwards. Connie gives me a gentle squeeze on my shoulder as she moves away and says, 'There you go Tez, I think you're ready. Are you comfortable?'

'Yes,' I say as she moves away from the bed. I don't want to mention that the hospital gown has somehow got creased and is caught painfully underneath my scrotum. I managed to straighten the garment and my appendages with my right hand, just as Dr Invergordon gives me his first instructions.

He stands to my right, gently supports my chin with his fingertips and says, 'I want to see how the nerves at the top are working.' I frown because I don't understand what he means. He must have seen my expression because he continues, 'When I say "top" I mean your head. So can you follow my finger with your eyes?' He draws an imaginary box in front of my face, emphasising the four corners, a point above my forehead and then another one at chest level. I track the movements without a problem. This is easy. 'Good,' he says.

He then covers my left eye with the palm of his hand, and says, 'I want you to nod when you see my fingers again.' He proceeds to wiggle his digits quickly, moving up and down, to the middle of my face and from right to…"where've they gone?" I think.

He then swaps hands, covers my right eye and says, 'Same again Tez, can you see my fingers?' I can see very well to my right but realise I am blind towards the left hand side.

He lets go of my chin and says, 'Relax Tez.' He makes a note on the papers beside me. He turns to his colleagues and says very quietly, what sounds like, 'a classic case of Anonymous He-man Phobia.' They both nod, I have no idea what that is but it doesn't sound very good.

He returns to my side and facing me directly says, 'Screw your eyes up tightly. Now grit your teeth. Open your eyes wide. Look surprised.' I do what he asks with each request. Then he says, 'Now let's have a big smile.' I think, "what the fuck have I got to smile about," but I comply.

'I'm just going to check your facial sensation now Tez. Let me know if you can feel me touch your face.' He touches me gently at various points, I dutifully grunt when I feel the contact. The brush of his finger on my left cheek is very faint. 'That's good.' He makes another note on his form and returns to the bed with what looks like a giant lollypop stick and says,

'This is called a tongue depressor.' He gently cups my chin as he says, 'Can you stick your tongue out please?' I do. 'Good, now wiggle it about.' I do as I am told. He then places the lolly stick on it and presses it down. 'Now say ahhh.' I do. 'That's really good Tesla. We'll do a swallowing test later which will give us a good idea of when you can have some proper food and drink but things are looking good.'

'I would like you to turn to face me if you can.' I do as I am instructed. 'Now grip hold of my fingers and squeeze.' I begin to apply pressure but am afraid of hurting him. 'Don't worry, just do your best.' I grip his fingers as tight as I can and realise my left hand wouldn't crush a paper cup but his fingers in my right hand are going darker. Then he says, 'Now, try to push me away and then pull me towards you.' It is becoming evident that there is a problem with my left side. He removes his hands from mine and returns to his notes. The next series of examinations confirmed what I had suspected.

I am asked to shrug my shoulders. Result, right one good, left one poor. Next comes holding my arms out like a sleep walker. Result, I can hardly move the left one off the bed but my right is excellent. Lifting each leg individually has a similar result, my left is virtually lifeless but my right is fine.

He moves to his notes again, scribbles quickly and then picks up a small metallic hammer with a rubber head from the table beside me. I don't miss his glance to Dr Pancholi as he returns to my side. The last time I saw a look like that, was followed by the delivery of very bad news. He sees the concern on my face as he says, 'Don't worry about not being able to move too much. Don't forget you're bound to be a bit stiff after being in bed for over a week.' Everyone in the room, including myself, realises that this is bullshit, but in a funny way I appreciate this attempt at kindness because it doesn't seem to sit naturally with him.

'Ok, we're nearly done now. I'm just going to tap lightly over your body. Let me know if you can feel it.' I grunted and nodded at the appropriate times, confirming that the right is good, the left pathetic. He returns the hammer to the table and takes hold of my right foot. He runs his fingers along my sole, my toes curl and my leg snaps away, nearly clipping his chin along the way. Tickling my left foot produces what feels like a stretch as my toes bend back.

Connie comes to the side of the bed as Dr Invergordon moves away. She rearranges my gown and makes the pillows comfortable behind me, as he has a few brief hushed words with his two colleagues. Turning to me he says, 'Normally, I would like to see you swing your legs over to the side of the bed and sit there ready to get up and stand but we'll leave that today. You can appreciate there is some weakness and you're probably feeling quite tired.' He moves to the foot of the bed and says, 'Tez'. I turn slightly to face him; he fixes his eyes on mine and continues, 'I can tell by your reactions that you can understand me. Is that correct?

'Yes.'

'Tez, is there anything I've said or done so far that you don't understand?'

'No.' But I think, "For God's sake, tell me what the fuck has happened to me."

'Excellent.' He returns to the table and scribbles some notes. Without looking up, he says to no one in particular. 'Did you know that Mr Coyne has had a book published, although I'm afraid I can't remember what it was called?' Dr Pancholi acknowledges the comment, seemingly with little interest. Dr Sutherland, on the other hand, seems to be having the same reaction that Jenny had had when she found out about my novel. I have never considered that having a book published could be an attraction to a woman. It isn't as if I am celebrity.

I feel like I am on a roll. My answers to the last two questions have been both clear and understandable. So I decide to try to provide the title of the book, even though my lips, tongue and mouth are dry again. 'Hamsun.' This is so fucking frustrating. Why do some words come out ok whilst others are unintelligible or totally different from the correct meaning?

'Samson?' Dr Pancholi said, his voice sounding thick and smooth like treacle. 'I love that story.'

I feel like screaming but Connie politely corrects him. 'Tez's book is called, "The Amazon."'

Dr Sutherland interjects. 'Oh, that's really interesting. Is it about the nation of female warriors from Greek mythology?' It was obvious that she's trying to impress the consultant and maybe me too, with her knowledge of classical literature. I really don't care though. My romantic novel about an abandoned ship has been morphed, first into one about a bloke who loses his strength when his hair is cut off and has ended up being about a nation of women, who kill off the men they have captured after copulating with them!

'No, it's a romantic maritime story,' Connie says before I have a chance to shake my head in disbelief. 'Nurse Tamara has read it. She said it's really good.'

This is the lowest point in my life but I would be a liar if I said that I didn't enjoy being the centre of attention as they discussed my book. I can tell the debate is about to continue but is cut short as Dr Invergordon picks up the open file, coughs discreetly (his way of demanding silence) and comes to my side. I raise my right hand and point to my mouth as I say, 'dwink peas.'

Dr Invergordon turns to Connie but she is already on her way with the sadly named "mouth toilet. "She starts to moisten my lips and tongue, as he says, 'I'm going to go through my findings with you now. Stop me if you want me to pause or to explain anything. Ok?' I nod my head.

'We have already done a brain scan which shows you've had a stroke. In other words your control centre has been damaged, which means that at the moment you can't control your body as well as you could before. The neurological examination shows the main problem is moving your left arm and leg and not being able to see what's on your left side.

Your speech is slightly affected at the moment but I'm hopeful that this will improve. We'll need to check your swallowing but I think this will be ok.'

'I realise that you will want to understand why the stroke happened and what the recommended treatments are, but I would like to give you a brief summary initially, as you might have some concerns following the exercises we have just been through. I'll begin by saying that you can clearly understand me, which is one of the biggest worries following a stroke. There is further positive news, as your verbal communication is very good when you are not agitated. This is also an excellent sign, because it means, in my experience, that very soon you will be able to eat and drink as normal. I will explain more about this later.'

His voice lowers as he delivers the next instalment. 'I'm afraid there's no easy way to say this, so I'll give you the next bit without frills because you obviously realise there are issues.' I tensed myself. 'The initial tests on your sight show that you have left homonymous hemianopia. This means you have lost vision on the left side which suggests you may have difficulty, particularly when reading and in seeing the left hand side of the page, I'm optimistic however, that you'll be able to write and use a word processor again. You don't have double vision, so you won't need a patch. We'll ask an occupational therapist to assess your problems and give you individual advice and treatment.'

So, just as I am thinking that things couldn't get worse, he now tells me I am effectively half blind and may not be able to write easily again. I could have laughed when he said that I wouldn't need an eye patch. Oh, what a shame! Why not give me a patch, stick a crutch under my left arm, put a parrot on my shoulder and watch my character miraculously transform from the hunchback into Long John Silver. I realise that I can remember some names and not others? Fuck!

He takes a deep breath, and says, 'Your right side is very strong and flexible which is good but your left needs help with mobilising. The physiotherapist will help you tackle the weakness and show you how to learn to balance and move around again although you may require a stick initially.' I think to myself, "Oh deep joy, and a cane now, how distinguished." He points to my head and says, 'Your right arm is working well; I noticed you've been curling your forelock whilst concentrating on what I've been saying.' That reassuring comment only serves to bring Grace back into my mind. She had loved my curl.

'Would you like a break Tez?' I shake my head; I just want to get this over with. 'We've tried to find out some more about your medical history to try and determine why this cerebral haemorrhage occurred. In your case we believe the biggest contributing factor was high blood pressure.'

I can recall Toby, saying, "I wonder why you don't look after yourself."

'We can find no records of you taking any of your recommended medication.' He definitely stresses the word "any" which seems to create extra interest in his colleagues. When he realises that he has their undivided attention, he continues with the air of a brilliant detective, who has discovered some astonishing revelation. I think I know where this is going. 'We have checked your records with your GP, Toby Evans. He says that you have not been collecting your repeat prescriptions and there is also a big gap in your medical history.' I am not surprised by this comment as there is no way the Marines would have released details of my misfortune. Connie has joined the group next to the bed. You can cut the atmosphere with a knife as they stand watching me intently.

The brilliant consultant takes a deep breath. There is a hint of exasperation in his voice as he says, 'Your medical records are only available up to 1991, and there is a gap before they pick up again in 2007 with Dr Evans. In summary, his notes say you have dangerously high blood pressure and an increased cholesterol reading. You are a heavy smoker and have an above average alcohol consumption. Your father died from suspected stroke at the age of forty two in Germany and your mother passed away with alcohol poisoning.'

He pauses at this point, to give me a moment to reflect on my parents' demise. I know that this gesture is out of respect for my feelings but I just want him to get on with it. I remained impassive, as he turns another page and meets my eyes again.

'You have some scarring to the lungs and some very slight damage to the left eye, apparently as a result of you being exposed to some Hydrochloric Acid vapour in an industrial accident.' No one in the room, including me, misses the emphasis made by Dr Invergordon on the word, "apparently." Toby hadn't believed my explanation either; I could hardly tell him the truth about what had happened in Iraq.

'You were prescribed drugs for your blood pressure and a statin for your cholesterol. I mentioned earlier that there are no records of you actually taking this treatment for the last four years. Not surprisingly, it was strongly recommended that you stop smoking and cut back on your alcohol intake.' It is only then that I realise I haven't had a cigarette or any alcohol for over a week. I am just considering that having a stroke is a drastic way to give up your vices when he says, 'The records show you did take regular exercise, which included, walking, swimming or going to the gym most mornings, with sailing being your favourite pastime.' The redhead smiles at me again, I wondered if she is attracted to an author who likes to sail? Perhaps she pictures me as Ernest Hemmingway cruising around the Caribbean while writing the Old Man and the Sea. I think, "Well darling, I can tell you I am not in that league. "She now appears to be totally focussed on me, just as the former object of her attention, Dr Invergordon adds, 'You're not too overweight and the records show that despite the high cholesterol, your diet seemed to be healthy.'

'We need to get you eating and drinking as soon as possible. I don't believe you will suffer from dysphagia, that's

50

a difficulty in swallowing, but we'll check this later today. A speech-language therapist will do a number of tests, including drinking a glass of water and if those go ok, we can remove the drip from your arm. We can arrange a dietician if necessary but I am not sure if this will be needed. We'll also get you out of bed and moving around, so that the physiotherapist can work out a plan for you. We'll also get the OT to help you with such things as washing, dressing and eating. And we'll need to discuss the best way to stop this happening again.

Dr Invergordon begins to collect his papers, indicating that our time together is coming to an end. He now seems to be in a rush to get away. He clutches my file to his chest and it is only then he asks me, 'Do you have any questions, Tez?'

I say, 'No,' clearly and do my best to smile.

'Excellent. Thank you for your time and I'll catch up with you again soon.' He turns and makes his way to the door. The other doctors follow him, Dr Sutherland pauses and mouths "goodbye" to me as she leaves the room. Connie shakes her head as we both hear Dr Invergordon say, 'Come on, we should be able to grab a cup of tea before seeing someone else.'

Although I feel like I am sinking in quicksand, I shrug my right shoulder, smile at Connie and start to formulate my plan.

*

I begin by evaluating my life.

My mother had hated me and my father had abandoned me. I had felt worthless after the way I was treated. I found a job in the forces that I adored, only losing it through a freak accident, which had left me with only the partial use of my lungs. I had fought back and found a purpose in life. I had had my book published and I had met Grace who had finally made my life complete.

This all collapsed when Jenny told me Grace had burnt to death, in horrific circumstances. I've also learnt I have been in a coma for over a week and as a result have missed saying goodbye to her. A couple of hours later, I have had it confirmed that I am partially paralysed, only have vision on my right hand side and have difficulty speaking. The fact I have also shit the bed is the icing on the cake.

I feel as if my life, my heart and my reason to exist have been torn from my chest. I am worthless. It will be good to die. I am surprised to find that there is weightlessness to this feeling of finally giving up.

Chapter 6

A familiar voice whispers softly into my ear. 'Tez. Tez. Come on, it's time to wake up.' There is a gentle pressure on my shoulder as someone moves me from side to side. It only takes a moment for the numbness of my deep sleep to disappear as I recognise it is Nurse Flint awakening me. When I open my eyes, the light from the window seems like a white explosion. The sunlight is causing patterns around the room, as it flashes through the trees outside and reflects off the stainless steel apparatus next to my bed. I think it should be dark by now. Tamara smiles down at me, as she says, 'Your sister is here to see you again. 'I frown as I don't remember seeing Poppy while I have been here in hospital. 'She came yesterday afternoon, about an hour after Dr Invergordon had examined you, but you had fallen asleep.'

I manage to say, 'Poppy – Yesterday?'

'Yes it was late when she got here, so we decided not to wake you. But don't worry; she is here now, you have had a good sleep and there's loads of time for you to talk.' I put my hand up over my eyes to shield them from the intensity of the light. 'Is it too bright for you Tez?' I nod as she moves to the window and closes the vertical blinds. The truth is, I love the vibrancy of the sunlight in the room but I want the room as dark as possible when my sister comes in and sees her pathetic and deformed brother for the first time since I dropped off the manuscript.

Part of me wants to see Poppy immediately but an equal part of me wants Tamara to take an age to freshen me up, give me a drink from the 'pink lolly' and comb my hair. To see her again will be such a welcome gift and I have so many questions that I need answering. But I certainly don't want her to see me like this and I am truly afraid of what I might learn from her. I am even about to tell Tamara that I want to be left alone as she walks to the door and says, 'Ok Tez, I'll show her in.'

I can hear movement just outside my door and a muted conversation as Tamara says, 'Can I ask you something before you go in?' I am pleased to realise that there is nothing wrong with at least one of my senses when I distinctly hear Poppy's whispered reply, 'Yes of course.' I feel something catch in my chest when I hear her voice.

'I wondered, did you come and see Tesla on the afternoon he was brought in?'

'No, I was on my way to the Cotswolds. Why?'

'Oh. It's just that one of the duty nurses mentioned there was a woman in the room just after his girlfriend got here from the airport. We thought she might have been family.'

'No, it wasn't me. What did she look like?'

'No-one saw her face but she had long black hair and horn-rimmed spectacles.'

'Gosh, that sounds like someone from a fifties film.'

'I know, she was probably in the wrong room. So you said you were on your way back from the Cotswolds?'

'Yes. I didn't know anything about Tesla's condition until I got back from Cirencester. Someone called Meredith rang me from the hospital on Sunday afternoon telling me he had woken up.'

'So you didn't know about him having a stroke and being in a coma?'

I can hear Poppy's voice waver as she emotionally whispers, 'No, we had a problem with our mobiles while we were away. It's a long story but sometimes they're more trouble than they're worth. It was only when we got home and got the messages off the house phone and the recharged mobiles that we understood the gravity of what had happened.'

'There is one thing more that I need to ask you before you go in. Have you seen or spoken to his girlfriend, Jenny?'

I really have to strain to hear Poppy's reply. I hear her voice harden as she says, 'Yes, she came round to see me yesterday. Why?'

'There was an ugly scene yesterday when she came in, it was horrible for Mr Coyne. I'm just letting you know because your brother was very upset. We had to escort her off the premises because she hit him.'

I can hear deep sobs as my sister takes in this information. They get louder as I hear her say, 'Poor Tez.' I then see Tamara's head briefly round the side of the door as she gently pulls it shut; to block out the sound of my sister weeping.

*

It seems like an age before Poppy walks into the room and shuts the door. Her beautiful, brave smile crumbles in the matter of seconds that it takes to walk to my side. I actually have to fight the urge to smile when I see the outrageous, purple, crushed velvet hat on her head. She bites her bottom lip, as the tears cascade down her cheeks. She is openly sobbing as she puts her arms around me and holds me tightly and says, 'Oh Tez.' The hat smells musty as the brim pushes into my left eye.

After a couple of minutes she gradually pulls away, releasing her warm embrace. She pulls a chair to the side of the bed, drying her tears with a tissue in one hand and holding my hand with the other. 'I had no idea that anything was wrong until I got back. I feel so stupid. I left my mobile in my office and we forgot the charger for Jacob's antiquated

55

"brick" of a phone so it wasn't until we got home and got the call from the hospital and the hundreds of messages that I could piece together what had happened. I didn't know about you and Grace. Oh Tez, what a total fuck up.'

The tears erupt from her again as she fights to continue. I squeeze her hand, as I prepare to speak to her for the first time. I don't want my affected speech to upset her any more than necessary, so I say, 'Toilet-mouf,' as deliberately and as clearly as I can. Although she smiles at my chastisement for her bad language, it doesn't take a genius to work out that the delivery and pitch of my speech is alien to her and has come as a shock. The tears are threatening to return, so I smile and say, 'Pops-tell-me-what-happened.'

She seems to be uncomfortable as she twists in the chair and says, 'It's too awful Tez; leave it until you're feeling a bit better. Ok?'

I hold her hand tightly; look pleadingly into her eyes, and say, 'Peas.'

She takes an age to answer. 'Ok,' she says as she releases my hand and stands up beside me. 'I'll just get some paper towels to dry my face.' She vanishes as she moves towards the sink. I don't dare mention I am blind on the left side, as this will surely set her off crying again. She probably hasn't been told about all my disabilities yet. She returns and sits down. 'I'm aware that Jenny has already told you some things yesterday, so I'll tell you what I know.'

'We got home quite late from the holiday, so I went straight upstairs to get the girls ready for bed, while Jacob made a brew. I was just coming downstairs to check for messages when the phone rang. It was someone called Meredith from the hospital, who telephoned to say that you had woken up after a week in a coma.' She squeezes my hand so tightly at this point that I grunt in pain. 'I nearly collapsed when I heard that you had had a stroke. It came as such a shock. The nurse was so apologetic though; she mistakenly thought I had already been told about it by Jenny.'

Poppy pauses to wipe her eyes again. 'I asked the nurse if I could come in to see you straight away but she said, "No." She explained that even though you had been in a coma for a week, the trauma of your waking up suddenly would leave you exhausted, so you would need to rest. I thought that was a load of bollocks, but she assured me it would be best to wait until you had completed some tests and been seen by the consultant. She said it should be ok to visit after he had seen you, which was yesterday afternoon. I told her not to worry about the mistake as it wasn't her fault that I couldn't be contacted. I asked her not to mention it to you but to make sure she told you that, "I loved you loads and would see you after the consultant." Did you get the message?'

I answer to the best of my ability. 'Yes-made-me-happy.'

'By the way, I did come to see you yesterday but you were fast asleep. I think the nurse told you?'

I nod as she continues. 'Ok, this is what I've pieced together. I checked the phones after the call from the hospital and found numerous messages from the police, the hospital, friends and reporters asking for us to call them urgently about what had happened to you. But there was also a load of other messages about Grace; I couldn't take it all in.'

'Most of the calls were from Jenny though, hysterically demanding I call her. One of them even said, "Stop avoiding me you bitch, I know you must be at home, you were only going away for a week." I felt bad enough about being away when this happened to you but we were having such a nice time, so we decided to stay until Sunday lunchtime. We thought it would be better to travel back in the afternoon when it was quieter on the roads.'

'Anyway, I had the pleasure of a visit from Jenny yesterday after she'd seen you. She came round to drop off your belongings, but oh my God she was so loud and venomous. She was standing in front of the house ranting about all sorts of things. She even demanded that I give her the manuscript you had given me last week. She said she was entitled to it because she was your "common law" wife. God, what a nutter! I stayed calm and lied to her. I told her I'd left it with a proof reader in Cirencester and would get it for her as soon as I could. This approach seemed to placate her, so I asked her in for a coffee. I've never liked her but I wanted to know what she knew. That was when she gave me her version of events. She talked for ages.'

I am so proud of my sister. Her tears have dried up and now she is in full flow, relating the chain of events to me. It is as if she is narrating an audio book of one of her recent travel adventures. She drains the last of her water then continues. 'Jenny had checked in at the airport and was just about to switch off her phone, when she got the call saying you had collapsed in a hotel car park and been taken to the hospital. She told the airline company what had happened and it appears that they were great with her. They explained that security procedures meant that they would normally have to remove her luggage from the aircraft before she could leave but they would make an exception in her case, if she wanted to go immediately to the hospital. One of the desk clerks was finishing her shift and dropped her off at Accident and Emergency on her way home.'

'They had just hooked you up to the life support system when she arrived. The hospital staff had told me that even they were impressed at how quickly she had arrived after receiving the call about your collapse in the car park. They said she must love you very, very much. They left Jenny with you whilst they went to get her a drink. She told me she was a bit suspicious as to why you were in a hotel car park and it was at that moment that she heard your phone ringing.'

A shiver runs down my spine as I remember the last thought that went through my head as I lay in the puddle in the car park, over a week ago. As the rain lashed down upon me, I had asked myself, "Why, oh why didn't I put a password on my phone or better still switch it off?"

I have a really bad feeling. Poppy looks at me seriously, as she leans forward and takes my hand in both of hers. 'Tez, the story gets really shabby from here, are you sure you want to hear this?' I nod.

'Your clothes and belongings were still in the room, because the hospital staff hadn't had time to put them away. Jenny heard music and realised it must be coming from the mobile phone in your pocket. It had stopped ringing before she got a chance to find it, so she checked to see who it was. She found that the missed call was from someone called Russell. She didn't recognise the name at the time. I think she was also trying to work out why you were in a hotel car park, when she also found the text messages. One said, "Is it the usual room? Lots of love from your Little Detective." It made her realise something was going on. She didn't know who this person was, so she phoned back, a woman answered and said something along the lines of, "Thank God you are OK, Tez, I was so worried." Jenny demanded she tell her who she was but she remained silent. So Jenny then shouted. "The cheating bastard is in hospital with a stroke, you bitch." That's when the line went dead. Jenny told me she couldn't identify the voice but she was certain it was familiar.'

Poppy gets up, walks over to the window and leans against the radiator. She sighs as she continues. 'I was shocked to hear about the "other" woman of course but I thought she might be mistaken. I was even feeling sorry for her at this point. Then she told me that she called the producer of the show, Ethel, in London and explained what had happened. Jenny said she would get the next available plane, so that she could still attend the launch party of Madame Butterfly. That was when she was told that Vanessa had been given the lead role, seeing as Jenny hadn't bothered to turn up. Oh Tez, she went ballistic.'

Poppy comes back to the bed, looks down at me and says, 'Are you sure you want to hear the next bit Tez because it concerns Grace?' I don't really want to hear anything about what happened to Grace but I do want the horror story that Jenny told me, to be proved a lie. I know this will be difficult for Poppy because Grace is one of her best friends, but I have

59

to know the truth, so I reach out, hold Poppy's hand and say, 'Yes-I-need-to-know.'

She sits down again. 'Jenny found a hotel confirmation in your jacket pocket. She found another one, from a few weeks ago, on the passenger seat when the police had located your car. She said you were probably up to no good every Thursday when you were supposed to be at the library, researching for your book. It was later that evening, when she was sifting through the data on your phone that she found a group of photographs in a hidden folder. Most of them were of Gracie, aka "Russell" but there were some of the two of you together. Jenny phoned Dick Perritano to tell him that you and his wife were having an affair, but before she could "spill the beans" he told her that Grace had died in a car accident and that he had just got back from identifying her remains. Jenny said he sounded as if he was pleased that she had died. *She certainly was.*'

Suddenly my body begins to cave in on itself, like a tent without poles. "Oh God. "I think. "Why didn't I put a password on my fucking phone?" Grace must have realised it would only be a matter of hours or even minutes before Jenny worked out who it was on the phone and called Dick to tell him. She must have panicked at the thought of what he would do to her and decided to make a run for it. I was too fucking stupid not to secure my phone. I have caused her death.

There is a knock on the door as Tamara comes in. 'Sorry to interrupt but I was just checking to see you were both OK or if you need anything?' I shake my head but Poppy says she wants a moment to get some air and to go to the bathroom. They leave together shutting the door behind them.

It had crossed my mind yesterday, that the shit might hit the fan if Dick found out about us and beat Grace up again. I then wondered if he had anything to do with the crash and her death as it all seemed too much of a coincidence. I really wished I had let him die in Portugal when I had the chance but I made a private pledge when I left the Special Boat Service that I wouldn't end anybody else's life. I really should have made an exception for him. The thoughts of murder and revenge are just about to replace my feeling of grief when Poppy re-enters the room.

She sits beside me, takes another deep breath and says, 'Look Tez, I hate to tell you all this bad news but I think it's best you hear it from me once and for all. I don't want you hearing gossip, rumours or lies, especially as it's been in the national press. People are bound to ask you about what happened.' I shake my head in disbelief as I consider how my stroke and Grace's accident have got into the papers. Poppy must be mistaken; she must mean the story was in the local rag.

Poppy says, 'I have pieced together this last bit from a lot of different reliable sources and from what I know to be fact. Dick was just about to leave work at five thirty when he got a call from the police to say there had been an accident involving Grace's car. It seems she'd definitely gone home and unloaded the shopping but that she left in a hurry, leaving the lights on and the house unlocked. There were reports that she had emptied the safe, taking money, passports and other important papers, along with a holdall of clothes.' I recall my deception, as I was the one who got her the key.

'We think the crash happened at about five o'clock. Grace seemed to have lost control on a bend in the road, the skid marks suggest she was conscious at impact but she couldn't get out of the car. Everything was destroyed in the…,' she hesitates for a moment before saying, '…inferno.'

So what Jenny told me yesterday was true. Grace had died in a burning car. A few moments ago I thought I could cope with all this pain but that feeling is disappearing fast. Poppy continues. 'I have something else to tell you Tez. The police did question Dick about Grace's death because of his alleged ill treatment in the past, but there was no proof of course, and because he was at work he had a ready-made alibi. Can you believe he was actually angrier about her clearing the safe than he was about her affair with you?'

She stands now, clearly agitated. 'Dick is so vindictive. He managed to get Grace's body released by the coroner and arranged a quick cremation. The funeral was on Friday so hardly anyone could attend at such short notice, not even Sebastian and Faith; I can't believe the bastard didn't contact her brother and sister. A couple from the Dramatic Society did manage to go because they noticed an announcement in the newspaper. They later told me he didn't arrange for a remembrance plaque for her or claim her ashes, he just had "her" scattered in the garden at plot six at the Crematorium. He then took his mother away on holiday.'

Another tear runs down Poppy's cheek. She has been so brave to tell me so much bad news about someone we both loved but I can tell she is worn out. She says, 'Tez, why don't you come back to live with us? We can arrange to have your rehabilitation there; the girls would love to have you back at home with us and they'll think you look like Father Christmas with your lovely white beard.'

I forgot that I hadn't had a shave for nearly a fortnight. I realise just how special my sister is, I pull her hand towards me raising my head off the pillow as far as I can to try and kiss her. She lowers her face towards me and as one of her tears falls onto my forehead, the door suddenly bursts open. The shock almost jerks the left side of my body back into action.

A bald, middle aged man approaches the bed. I can't make out too much detail about him because he moves so quickly. Poppy is about to say something but he is already speaking. 'Mr Coyne, I'm sorry about the interruption. My name is Norman Cody from Independent News. I was wondering if you could give me a statement about the death of Grace Perritano and whether there is any link to your recent collapse.'

Poppy screams, 'Get out.'

He just leans over the bed and says, 'You must have seen the headlines Mr Coyne, "Best Selling Author Collapses in Car Park." Is it true there were people from Hollywood discussing the rights to your book but this has been shelved because of your links to the death of the wife of a respected businessman?'

'Nurse, nurse!' Poppy is screaming now and I can hear people running down the corridor towards my room.

'Mr Coyne, did you leave the Marines because your last operation went horribly wrong and resulted in death and a political whitewash?'

Connie, Tamara and a heavy set man run into the room. Connie shouts. 'I don't believe it; this happened yesterday. Come on, sir, you have to leave.' He shouts abuse as they escort him from the room. Poppy's shoulders are shaking and I can hear deep sobs as she follows them out.

I begin to laugh hysterically. Anything that was holding me together has now evaporated. I am in turmoil as I pull the drip from my arm and wires from my chest, causing the alarms to sound again. I turn and push violently against the bedside monitor and watch it slam into the wall and topple onto the floor. I weep as I see that my green trace has disappeared from the black screen, just as Grace's life spark had been extinguished in her car.

Chapter 7

The lead from the blood pressure pad on my arm has ripped from the monitor and is swinging like an umbilical cord over the metal rail of my bed. A nurse I don't recognise, explodes into the room and shouts, 'Doctor, Doctor,' picks up the unit from the floor and starts to move the broken glass against the wall with her foot. She comes over, has a quick look at me and runs out. I distinctly hear her shout, "Smashed monitor" and then, "sedative" when she is in the corridor.

She came back into the room followed by Dr Pancholi and the red headed woman. They have a speedy conversation when they see the damage I have caused and immediately give some instructions to the nurse who quickly leaves the room. She returns moments later carrying a syringe. 'Would you like me to give you this, it'll help you get some rest?' I nod my head; I pray it is a lethal dose of morphine as she injects it slowly into the cannula.

I turn away as one of the doctors approaches the bed; I bury my face into the pillow, as far and as deep as I can, just like I did yesterday. I can feel myself sink towards oblivion as the medication takes effect. I start to weep again, with deep and exhausting sobs, but this time I really don't give a fuck if anyone sees them.

*

I awake, several hours later, to find that there is no evidence of my destructive tantrum; the room is immaculate. I am surprised that despite my grief and desire to die, a small part of me regrets my outburst; it must be my military training. Two nurses complete their routine tasks in my room and tell me a specialist will be with me shortly. There is no mention of the damage.

I am still feeling groggy when a woman enters moments later, wearing a cream uniform. 'Hello Mr Coyne, I'm the speech therapist, Miriam Du Bois. I'm here to get you started on the first stage of your rehabilitation – the swallowing test.'

She gives me liquids of differing consistencies, on a spoon. I have no idea when I take that first sip of water, that it will be over eleven months before I will leave the hospital. As I struggle with these first invasions of my mouth I fully appreciate the deadness in my cheek; it really does feel as if I have been to the dentist. There is an uncomfortable feeling, as I keep biting my tongue and the inside of my mouth. She has to wipe my chin when some of the liquid escapes and dribbles from my mouth. I feel like a child.

She is talking to me throughout the test and listening carefully to my replies. But I also notice she is watching the movement of my throat intensely. She smiles when she finishes and tells me the results are very good, and that I can now eat and drink again. I know this is good news, but I promise myself that no matter how ravenous and thirsty I get in the future, I will never forget the 'Pink Lolly.'

She makes a final entry in her notes, stands, packs away her samples, and comes to the top of my bed. She stretches over me with a cloth and I can lean my head back far enough to see her wipe the words "Nil by Mouth" from the white board above me. She pauses at the door. 'I guess that you're probably in a very dark place at the moment Mr Coyne but you're fortunate because there are some patients who never regain the ability to eat and drink properly you know.' I don't bother replying. 'Thank you for your time and good luck, I'll tell Hazel to see you now,' she says as she leaves.

I don't feel very "fortunate" when I remember how I had bitten my tongue and how she had to wipe my chin as the liquid escaped. I am fully awake now and wish I had the felt tip pen so I could write, "Just fuck off and leave me alone," on the board above me.

My wish isn't granted because a few moments later a stout, middle aged woman sweeps into the room. She is at my side in an instant. I can hardly make eye contact because her white blouse is looming above me and is struggling to contain her huge chest. She looks like a ship's figurehead albeit with a pair of spectacles swinging from a silver chain. Her voice booms, 'Hello Mr Coyne, I'm Hazel Peabody your psychologist.'

I nod and tense a little as I prepare for her to explore my mind. I am considering how inappropriate her surname is for her build, when she sits, produces a clipboard and requests that I repeat some sentences. I can see her properly now; her grey hair is tied in a bun on the crown of her head, she is wearing a dark brown skirt and white trainers. She makes notes as I reply and I begin to relax when she asks questions which include numbers in the answer. These, especially remembering my birth date, seem to be all too easy. The turning point comes shortly after she says, 'Dr Invergordon has made some positive notes about your speech when he examined you. Did he see you on his own?'

'No. Connie was with him and two doctors. Dr Pancholi and a red headed woman, with an accent but I can't remember her name.'

She smiles. 'Excellent, your speech is actually very good you know.' Her eye contact assures me she is sincere, I like her. She continues. 'Red hair and I'm guessing her accent was Scottish?' I nod. 'Yes, that sounds like Dr Sutherland.' She made another entry. 'OK, I just need to ask a couple more things.'

I realise she is not only testing my reasoning but also my speech.

'Do you put your shoes on before your socks?'

'Pardon?' I am not sure if my hearing has gone haywire as I think, "what an odd question."

She repeats. 'I said, "Do you put your shoes on before your socks?"'

My hearing is OK after all. 'Not normally, but I did once,' I reply.

There is look of alarm on her face, her pen poised above the clipboard. 'You've put your socks on over your shoes in the past?' Her eyes are wide open, eager for my reply.

'Yes, when I was a kid. It was incredibly icy, so I thought it would help me walk on the slippery pavement.'

'And did it?'

'No. I was frozen to the spot.' She bursts out laughing, her body shaking. Yes, I do like her. I can't help leaking a rare smile as I remember sitting in the snow, trying to break the elastic bands around my ankles, which were keeping the oversized socks in place over my shoes. In the end I had to leave them where they were, the woollen fibres welded to the ice crystals. God knows what passing pedestrians made of that scenario.

She wipes her eyes with a tissue and says, 'All things bright and beautiful…' I wait for her to finish the sentence but she pauses; she wants me to continue. The words are familiar, is it a poem? No, it's a hymn. I remember singing it as I took a loaf of bread to a church altar in Germany; there was so much food on display. I stall for time, I don't want to fail. Fuck, the words are just out of reach.

'Harvest festival?' I say hopefully.

'That's very good. Let's try another. Roses are red…'

I reply immediately. 'Violins are blue.' I am proud I could answer without a pause this time, but it doesn't sound quite right. There is a flicker of concern on her face.

'Ok. Your sister mentioned you love music. Do you have a favourite song?'

I nod and say, 'Yes,' as I remember hearing it as I was lying in a puddle in the hotel car park.

'What's it called?'

'Thursday's Child.' I am feeling pleased with myself, I am sure I have got this right.

She says, 'Oh, I'm not sure I've heard of that one, I'm into Cliff Richard.' I cringe as she makes more notes. 'Who wrote it?'

I can still hear the tune in my head but my mind goes blank as I try to remember his name. OK, I know it's a man, that's good, but who? Even the lyrics won't come to me, the special words that describe how much I love Grace. I feel as if I have abandoned her because I can't remember. Outwardly, I try to appear calm but I am frantic inside as my mind screams. "Fuckin' hell Tez, come on! "Panic sparks through my body, as I run through the alphabet, trying desperately, to reconstruct the letters of his name. Why don't I know the answer? I just need a couple of moments more to remember. I am running through the alphabet again as she moves in her chair; she is preparing to leave.

'Don't worry about the answer, you've done very well. That's all for now, you must be tired.' She stands and smiles down at me. 'The vision of your socks, frozen in the ice did make me laugh.'

I don't want her to go yet, I need to show her, and my beloved Grace, that I know the answer. I am so pissed off. Anger and frustration run through my veins like acid. How can I remember some things but not others?

She stops at the door. 'The OT will be here soon to go through the activities that we think are needed to get you moving again, especially those for "daily living." I frown because I don't understand what she means. She clarifies, 'Things like washing, getting dressed and making a cup of tea. See you soon. I'll be back to see you again. Bye.' With that she leaves and I am alone.

There is surprise in my voice as I say '*David Bowie.*' It has come to me, just as she has shut the door. Fuck!

*

I am still disappointed in myself, when a young woman also in a cream uniform, enters the room. She is small, very slim with an olive complexion but her defining feature is her shoulder length hair. It makes music as she walks. It is braided neatly, each strand encased in black and red beads. I guess she is in her late twenties and I can sense the energy radiating from her. 'Hello. I'm Mishap, the occupational therapist.' She actually claps her hands excitedly as she continues. 'I'm here to explain the plan to get you moving again.' I have known her for approximately six seconds and her enthusiasm is already exhausting me. I want her to get lost. 'What shall I call you Tesla or Tessie or …?'

I interrupt. 'Tez,' I say tersely.

'OK, Tez it is, nice to meet you.'

She explains in great detail the activities that she hopes will help me overcome my physical, mental and memory problems. I have to give her credit because she makes each dreaded task sound like an adventure, but I am not easily fooled. I nod in the right places, make positive statements about my intention to get well, and confirm my eagerness to be discharged. She also asks a list of questions it wouldn't take a genius to understand, are designed to evaluate my mood, and gauge the level of my depression and anxiety. I guess that this is because of my violent outburst, so I put on my most positive face and lie with nearly every response.

'You will be helped out of bed soon, and taken to the bathroom,' I don't fancy the sound of that; it seems like weeks since I've been to the toilet. 'Then for a shower and maybe a shave if you want one.' The idea of a refreshing wash, on the other hand, actually raises my spirits. 'I'll be working with you and the team to agree a programme to get you moving and back into society. Do you understand Tez?'

'Yes.'

My fake upbeat demeanour, (when I am actually feeling the opposite,) seems to hoodwink her, because the meeting finishes with a positive spin on my recovery. 'We'll get you moving in no time.' Part of me actually gets carried away with the optimism. I think Mishap must have that effect on most patients. 'I now have something very important to explain to you. No two strokes are ever the same. This is because the part of the brain affected and the severity of the damage differ from person to person. It's important you understand that there's potentially some good news. As the swelling of the affected area of the brain reduces, some of the issues like the deadness in your cheek and the limited vision could improve. Also the undamaged parts of your brain can eventually learn to take on some of the tasks of the affected ones.'

She moves towards the door. 'We'll be seeing a lot of each other, see you soon Tessie.' I am about to protest when she laughs and corrects herself. 'Only joking! I'll see you soon, Tez.' With that she leaves, sucking all my energy out of the room with her. I am asleep in seconds.

*

I know my mood is fragile and my memory is dodgy but I am hopeful that my body won't let me down. The optimism disappears when it comes to the simple task of getting out of bed. It takes two people to help me up and swing me to the edge of the mattress. I really want to tell them to "fuck off" when they proudly tell me they will teach me how to lie or sit, to give me a better chance to get up in the future, unaided. There is a chunk of sarcasm in my voice when I say, 'Great.'

There will be no walking for me on my first excursion, because I am lifted into what looks like a white garden chair with a hole in the middle of the seat. My robe catches on the bed as I am lowered, exposing my "meat and two veg." No one says anything but I do feel pathetic as strange hands rearrange the fabric to cover me. I can't do it myself because my left arm is useless and I am gripping the rail, with all my might with the other.

I discover that the garden chair has wheels when I glide out of my room. I am pushed down the corridor by Barry an auxiliary nurse. His deep voice seems better suited to advertising romantic getaways to the Maldives, than to small talk with me in a northern hospital. He reminds me of the American civil rights activist who proclaimed "I have a dream." I am running through the alphabet, again, trying to recall his name but I am interrupted before I can summon the identity of the brilliant religious orator.

'Hey Tesla, did you hear about the man who said to his wife? "I'm sick of you. You talk down to me, you push me around and you're always talking behind my back?"

'No Barry.'

'Well, she says.' He starts to giggle. *"You ARE in a wheelchair honey."'* His infectious laughter rattles through the ward; people nod and smile in our direction. This man is obviously popular. His joke seems a bit inappropriate but it did make me smile.

I say, 'Funny.' It stops me feeling sorry for myself for a moment.

'I've told that joke a thousand times and it still makes me chuckle. I can tell by your reaction Tesla that you'll be ok. Well sir, here we are, we've arrived at our destination.'

We enter a huge bathroom and he wheels me into a private cubicle and directly over a commode. A familiar pressure is building in my gut which I am keen to evacuate. There have been no other incidents since I had soiled the bed during Jenny's visit and I know that I have to face this challenge, but I am afraid.

Barry says, 'It will be fine Tez.' As he starts to pull the curtains around me, he must have seen my concern. 'Lots of people worry when they "go" for the first time.'

'But couldn't the strain…'

He interrupts as he laughs again, the tribal marks on his dark cheeks seemingly making his smile look even bigger. 'No, no, you'll be fine. You might find it a bit difficult after so long.' He said the next part of the sentence slowly, his voice incredibly deep and reassuring. 'But I can assure you Tez that it will not trigger another stroke! 'He puts the emergency nurse-call buzzer in my hand.

I say, 'Ok,' as he closes the curtains.

I can hear him open the main door and pause before leaving. 'Mind you, that's the least of your worries.' Fear grips me as his voice becomes that of a preacher from the Deep South. 'Your poo will look like sheep's droppings; smell like someone's died and your farts will sound like thunder.' He chuckles again and waits for a moment. Sure enough, I laugh at his sermon, not only was it funny but it triggers the name I was searching for, Martin Luther King.

'Take your time Tez. I'll pop in every ten minutes or so to see how you are getting on. Just press the buzzer if you have a problem, or if the smell is too much for you.' He sings the next bit in a brilliant bass baritone, 'And I'll a come a-runninggggg…' The actor who sang "Ol' Man River" would have impressed but I can't remember his fucking name either or why his comment about the "emergency alarm" stirs a faint memory of a story from Chicago's O' Hare airport from many years ago.

Half an hour later, after I have managed to clean myself, he opens the curtains and he wheels me towards the central shower. Another part of my dignity crumbles away when he helps me to strip and places me and the chair, under a cascade of delightful warm water. It isn't being naked that bothers me; it is being so pathetic, having to rely on him to undress.

I am given soap and a hospital monogrammed linen flannel but can only accept them with my right hand. I place the block of soap on my groin and begin to get suds as I rub it with the flannel; the sensation is delicious. I become aware of stiffening as the warm water and bubbles envelope my penis. I pray to all that is Holy he doesn't notice. The moment is gratefully broken when he holds up his left hand and tells me forcibly to, "use it or lose it". He demonstrates how to put the soapy flannel in my left hand and to use the support of my right to wash my face and chest. I try it and find that getting both hands to work together seems to have an instant impact on my arm's mobility.

He is laughing when he says, 'Well done Tez, the secret to your recovery is to keep the muscles moving, even if you don't really want too. Keep trying each day and you will have your left hand washing your bollocks and the cheeks of your arse in no time.' He then helps me to dry and dress myself in a fresh tee shirt when I have finished.

The final part of this first expedition is when I am re-introduced to a mirror. I can immediately see my left cheek is sagging slightly but it doesn't look as bad as I had expected and the nasty gash has healed. I look thinner and a bit pale but that's not surprising after eight days or so I have spent in here. My kiss curl is still evident but is almost lost in my untidy hair, and my cornflower blue eyes, once an asset for attracting women, look dull and lifeless. I also appear a bit rugged, thanks to the stubble. Tamara had said I looked handsome when she had seen my picture on the dust cover of my book but she thinks I would look even better with a full beard. I think I will let it grow, not because I am vain but because it might cover the slight slackness in my cheek.

By now I am exhausted but when Barry takes me back to my room I manage to get back into bed with only his assistance, instead of the two pairs of hands it took to get me out earlier. He settles me in bed; I am fighting to keep my eyes open when he says, 'You've done really well today Tez.'

I don't hear him finish the next sentence. 'I'll be back for you tomo…'

*

My food is blended for the first few meals, with bits of fruit, gradually increasing in size, being introduced into the hideous mush. I am euphoric though, a few days later, when I eat my first "proper" meal of steamed fish, potatoes and peas, entirely on my own. But this is short lived, when the meals start to arrive with items that are difficult to slice because I discover how weak my left arm is, as the nurses have to cut them up for me.

I am reminded to eat slowly and chew every mouthful to make sure I don't choke. I think I have done really well until I look and see the food down the front of my shirt and realise I can't even eat properly and the inside of my mouth is bleeding from where I keep biting myself. The blood thinning medication I am taking means there is a faint trickle down my throat, producing a nasty metallic taste. Fuck me I'm so pissed off with this.

*

I work hard to get back the use of my left side but the pins and needles in my arm, and the hot and cold sensations in my leg drive me crazy. My stay in the wheelchair is short lived though, as the hours I spend having massage, manipulation, and doing leg and arm lifts in my bed, start to pay off. My left side begins to wake up and respond.

There is always someone watching over me in these early days whenever I attempt the milestone movements. Getting out of bed and moving to the chair; rising from a sitting position to stand and walking around my bed. I discover my balance has been affected, it's as if my centre of gravity has shifted. I move like a marionette that's had the strings on the left side cut. I am encouraged to sit on a bloody enormous ball or stand on a cushion to improve my equilibrium.

I have to use a walking frame at first, but I quickly move on to a stick. I am pleased with these early wins in my mobility because I have set myself the target of walking to the Crematorium when I am discharged and at this rate it shouldn't take too long. I have difficulty in remembering some names but not the one I have to say goodbye to. Grace. I keep repeating it so it won't escape me. Grace, Grace, Grace.

It is really difficult to walk due to the paralysis down my left side. I have developed a technique that involves throwing my left hip to the side, in a movement to initialise the first step. I then have to repeat this, like a human "Newton's Cradle" to keep the momentum going. I catch a glimpse of myself one day, reflected in a glass door at the end of a corridor. Can that really be the same super fit soldier who completed the fourteen mile Brecon Beacons "Fan dance" with full equipment in under four hours? I am walking like Frankenstein's monster. This is so fucking infuriating. Not only do I look like some kind of freak but by mid-afternoon my left leg is dragging behind me. It looks like I have been shot.

The time comes to tackle a seemingly impossible task; the stairs. Initially, I manage a few steps at a time but I gradually build up until five months after my admission I complete all the flights and stand at the top of the second floor landing. I punch the air in triumph; I imagine I am the boxer from the film, who stands at the top of the steps of the Philadelphia Museum of Art. I have to shake the image from my head as it reminds me too much of the death of a little boy.

The improvement in my left side, especially my leg, means my partial paralysis is 'downgraded' and is now referred too only as 'my weakness.' There is definite progress but one thing that I can't seem to eradicate, is my left toe catching on the ground. I can lift my leg quite high but my ankle seems to have no strength, so my foot just hangs like a piece of meat and I stumble frequently. It is soul destroying. I am told that the technical term for this condition is 'drop foot' and the cure could be to wear a FES, which uses small electrical signals to replace the nerve impulses. But that's not for me. Apart from my stick, I want my last walk to Grace's resting place to be unaided. I can at least do that for her.

*

I get very little warning in the early days, when I need to go to the toilet but I manage to make it every time, admittedly with some help. The visits do get easier as I learn how to get out of bed so I can go on my own. My secret isn't speed but being able to hold "everything in". Some poor buggers on the ward will never have that luxury, no matter how much re-training they have; they can't control their movements, so never make it on time. You can picture their "dignity meter" running on zero. There is a big adjustment for me though. All my visits to the toilet are performed sitting down due to the unreliability of my left leg, I don't think that will ever change.

*

Another frustration is trying to cope in the kitchen. It isn't being unsteady on my feet that is the problem (I could always sit on the 'perching stool') it is doing the things I have always taken for granted. Opening the coffee and sugar containers with one hand takes a fucking eternity and by far the worst for me in the early days, is trying to butter a piece of bread. I can move my left hand high enough onto the counter to hold the slice but lack of control means the bread moves and ends up glued to the butter on the knife. There are marks all around the walls where I like others before me have thrown food in frustration. A slice of bread with peanut butter on it evades detection for weeks, as it is stuck to the side of the ceiling light.

I gradually learn techniques, which I use to aid my physical recovery, resulting in me being more patient and thus reaching self-sufficiency in the kitchen. I am invited to "the breakfast club," where I not only make a hot drink and butter toast but also cook some bacon. This is the equivalent of getting my green beret in the Marines. Word spreads through the ward that I have completed this major task. I am applauded as I make my way back to my bed, rocking from side to side, frantically balancing the plate with my dream sandwich in the crook of my once useless left arm. The aroma of the bacon is positively divine as I am thinking, "Please don't drop it, please don't drop it."

I sit in my room and hold it for a moment before biting. Savouring the moment, I slowly sink my teeth and the flavour plays a tune on my tongue. The taste, oh the taste, it's impossible to describe. It is almost worth staying alive for.

*

Looking back, I realise the move to the rehab ward has institutionalised me. I have become part of a structure that I don't really want to leave because I am safe here. I want to die because I don't want to live in a world without Grace but I don't want to be exposed to danger. That sounds like a contradiction, but I just want to be in a protective environment with the people I know.

There is "Irish Jimmy," whose stroke has left him almost unable to speak. He shocked us all a week before Christmas, however, when a local choir came in to spread some festive spirit. We just wanted them to fuck off and let us get some sleep as we didn't like them disrupting our routine. We were half-heartedly joining in with the carols when we heard a small voice from a part of the ward that is normally quiet. It was Jimmy. There was part of his brain working that allowed his Celtic lilt to add an unimaginable beauty to "Silent Night." There wasn't a dry eye in the house when we heard him singing, "Sleep in heavenly peace."

Then there is "Mixed Up Mickey" in the next bed. I do envy him because he can perform all the word association tests brilliantly and his memory is astonishing. What he can't do, is remember the simplest of instructions. I followed him once when he went to the kitchen to make a cup of coffee. He was wearing his vest over his jumper and I watched him make his drink with cold water and a spoonful of jam instead of sugar. I pitied him when I saw the confusion etched on his face, as he tried to work out the problem when he tasted it. He looked so lost.

There are, on the other hand, a couple of people who I am sure could drive me to killing again given the chance. One is "Peter Rewind" who will watch the same DVD time and time again. He can never remember what he is watching or more importantly the plot. He will continually ask the same question which will be answered with totally random replies. I know it sounds cruel but he will have forgotten what has been said to him within minutes, so it doesn't seem to matter.

The most annoying without doubt is "Harold the Swisher." He doesn't have the motivation to get well, which is his prerogative I suppose. He frequently exposes himself because his stroke has disinhibited him and he is never quiet when he's awake. He hits the metal side of his bed with the heel of his hand, a rhythmic reminder he is there. I know it's horrible but I have fallen asleep imagining myself kneeling on his face with a pillow between us.

And yet, I would rather stay here with them than leave the safety of the hospital. The thought is always at the back of my mind that if another stroke happens then I will at least be in the right place.

By the way, I am known as the "Scribbler".

*

I have been given puzzles and word association tests to keep my brain active but one of the specialists has suggested "why not try and write again." I don't really have the motivation because I'm afraid I won't be able to remember anything or be creative, but I give it a try and find that it isn't really a problem as long as I don't rush my thoughts. Poppy brings me my ancient laptop, phone and music to try to make the experience more enjoyable. That is when I discover the enormity of Jenny's hatred towards me. She has deleted all the contacts from my "cursed" mobile and my beloved catalogue of music from my MP3 player, that's over three thousand tracks. The coup de grace however is my computer, which has been wiped clean. All my photographs, correspondence and personal files have disappeared. In addition, all the ideas, drafts and completed chapters for the entire Aaron Jacks trilogy have gone. I do have a "backed-up" CD at Poppy's but it doesn't really matter because I won't be alive to finish it and see it published anyway.

I decide to try and make a journal of what has happened to me up until this point in my life. I try using the laptop but the battery keeps dying so I am provided with a writing pad and a pencil instead. This keeps me occupied for an hour or so every day instead of just sleeping.

I carry my notes around in the little rucksack that Poppy used to bring in my stuff. The euphoria of knowing I can fend for myself in the kitchen is balanced by the fact that I still struggle to fasten the buttons on my favourite jacket on those occasions when I venture outside to write in the small walled garden. The beautiful terrace within the hospital is scarred by discarded cigarette ends.

Observing the determination of the nicotine addicted patients reminds me of at least one miracle that has happened in me since having the stroke. I was the man who was described as having a balanced diet if I had a beer in one hand and a fag in the other. The only time I wouldn't smoke was when I was in the shower but I haven't had any cravings, for a drink or a smoke, since collapsing in the car park. It's a rather drastic way to give up – but it seems to work.

*

There are other observations that become apparent as the weeks on the ward tick by. It seems so strange to spend so much time in bed alone. Some people probably feel uncomfortable if they go to bed without cleaning their teeth but I still find it difficult to settle without a female body beside me. There were very few nights that I spent alone when I was away from the Marines.

Then there is the incredible tiredness which seems to affect all of us on the ward. I have gone from being an incredibly active person to one whose mantra is "just let me sleep." I resent being disturbed for my rehab even though I know I have to do it for Grace. And although, I long to see my sister and the girls, I feel so exhausted when visiting time arrives that sometimes I really don't want them to be there. I have no energy or inclination to talk or interact, I have even feigned sleep. Then it breaks my heart to see the concern on their faces. I hate myself even more for wishing they wouldn't come but then I miss them when they've gone. I am in turmoil.

*

The talk about my discharge gathers pace as I get stronger and there is subtle pressure on me to have a home visit even though I have no plans for a domestic future. The hospital arrange for one of the physiotherapists to visit Poppy's to check the access and floor coverings to make sure it is safe for me. They give their blessing and a date is agreed.

Jacob picks me up from the hospital. I have to breathe slowly and deeply to calm the panic rising within me, especially when we pull out into the road and enter the madness of the world outside "my" ward. Everything seems too fast and threatening. I am wearing my favourite jacket but the rest of my attire is new. The underwear, socks, tee shirt, jumper and jeans, all gifts from my sister, are appreciated as they fit better now having lost so much weight. It is the new-fangled trainers that set the alarm bells ringing. I have made all my progress so far, in the same pair of shoes and now I am wearing alien footwear with a higher sole and fancy Velcro straps instead of laces. I don't like them.

Jacob is so excited about bringing me "home." I know he won't understand the fear that is rising inside me as we approach the house. I concentrate using all the strength I can summon to show an interest when he speaks, and to smile as often as I can. I think I would rather be back in the ward with Barry than with the brother-in-law I love.

He has just pulled up outside the old Tapas restaurant to park and I immediately want the ground to open up and swallow me. There are neighbours waiting on the pavement, some are waving, and others have balloons. Poppy is bouncing up and down with joy that her big brother is back after so many months and I can see the girls with a "*Welcome Back*" placard. I know they mean well but I just don't want the fuss.

I want to ask Jacob to drive me back to the hospital, but I can't of course. I hold myself together as I unsteadily cross the road to the welcome reception. The girls don't run to me this time. There is a look in their eyes, a look that wasn't there before; is it concern, pity or even fear? I have no idea, but I don't like it. The poor darlings won't know how to act in the presence of someone so grotesque. All I can think is "please get me away from here" and I haven't even entered the house yet. I accept the well wishes and pats on the back as I shuffle as quickly as I can towards the front door. The neighbours suddenly disperse when I abruptly say 'I'm tired.'

The visit is a disaster of course. I catch my left foot in the deep pile of the carpet as I enter the living room and crash down into the bookcase, ending up on my back. There are so many hands fussing over me, and I know they are only thinking about my well-being, but I push them away. I just want them to fuck off and leave me alone. Blind rage is boiling inside me but I suppress it with all my might. I really can't be bothered to try and move myself but I have no choice, I feel like a turtle trying to right itself.

'Piggin Doggin,' I say through gritted teeth. I really want to shout "Fuck me!" at the top of my voice but I have to quell my frustration for the girls. 'That was clumsy of me wasn't it? Leave me to it; I need to learn to get up myself.' My voice appears to be calm and relatively controlled.

I manage to get up with them all watching. The tears in Melia's eyes, wound me deeply. Sweat is running down my back and my face is flushed from the embarrassment and anger. I have done so well on the tiled floor of the physiotherapy gym and the corridors at the ward but realise "home" will be like an assault course. I manage to make it into the kitchen, (thanking my lucky stars it has a stone floor), have a drink and then ask to be taken back. On my way back to the front door I fall again. This time it is serious.

I make the mistake of trying to talk and walk simultaneously. I have been taught to concentrate on one task at a time but forget this golden rule when replying to a question from Emily.

I stiffen my body as my head approaches the edge of the oak table. I am ashamed to say that all thoughts of saying goodbye to Grace leave me, as I pray for the finality of a broken neck. I think, "Please Lord let me die this time." Poppy's piercing scream is drowned by a sickening crack as my head smacks into the table.

*

I am blessed with nothing more than concussion. Although I am told I was only unconscious for fifteen minutes and that my recovery will be swift, my mood and motivation enter a world far darker than I could ever have imagined. What little there was left of my will seems to have left me and I just give up. I used to be brave enough to face anything but both my nerve and confidence have gone. It takes weeks before I remind myself that my road to rehabilitation was for the specific purpose of accomplishing a simple plan. I need to get well enough to walk to the cemetery to say goodbye to Grace, then go to the apartment to put everything in order for the benefit of Poppy and the girls. And then finally, to keep an appointment with a bullet. My decision is final and irrevocable.

*

So after six months I am moved into one of the modern rehab bungalows adjacent to the ward. (This is not the normal practice but it seems they proposed this out of embarrassment following my fall at Poppy's when they deemed it safe). The result is the hospital gets their bed, and I get a chance to try out the new accommodation. It is more private, and I have my own bathroom and kitchen, which are supposed to encourage my independence. Most of the people looking after me are special in their own way, with Connie, Barry and Mishap invaluable to my continued recovery. There is one however, Tamara, to whom I get very close.

She is pale, very slim, wears tortoise shell glasses and has a hint of ginger in her shoulder length hair. She isn't married, but lives with her boyfriend, Terry. She has no children although she wants them desperately, so she is attending a fertility clinic. She has a passion for literature, and plies me with numerous questions about "The Amazon" and how I managed to convey the feelings between the lovers.

She is very talkative, but her voice never tires me, I actually find myself looking forward to her shift. We talk constantly when she is attending me. Then she starts to visit me after she has finished work. There are frowns from some of her colleagues and even a disguised warning from her bosses about her spending time with me but she ignores them. I am pleased because I like her company; she is like an adopted sister. She brings me a polished briar cane with a silver handle one day. I refuse it, saying it is far too extravagant a gesture, but she insists I have it as, "it will only get thrown out if you don't." The alarm bells are ringing.

Tammy tells me Terry is a builder who occasionally ill-treats her when he has been for a drink. The memory of how Dick hurt Grace sticks in my throat, like a fist.

She comes to chat to me one day when I have been writing my journal. She goes into my kitchen to make a drink and I fall asleep, leaving my writing pad open. I see it is on her lap when I awake. She says, 'You were curling your hair in your sleep.'

'Was I?'

She holds my hand. 'Yes, you look lovely when you do that.' She holds up the pad with her other hand. 'You dropped your story.' I reach for it and I hope she hasn't tried to read it. I am so insecure about my grammar and punctuation but positively paranoid about my inability to remember names, and the correct words to use.

'Sorry Tammy,' I say as I take the pad from her. 'I didn't mean to be rude and fall asleep, I just feel so tired today.'

'Don't be silly.' She pauses, the pressure on my hand increasing. 'It's very good by the way.'

'What is?'

'Your life story, I couldn't help reading a few lines when I picked it up.' I can't work out if I am uneasy that she had read my story or whether I am uncomfortable about the way she is holding my hand.

What becomes apparent in time is her knowledge of the English Language is far superior to mine, which is how she becomes my proof reader. I pass each chapter to her and look forward to her feedback. We become incredibly close, which ultimately results in her being suspended from her job.

I write eighty eight chapters whilst I am in the hospital; (enough perhaps for a trilogy) almost two for each week I was there. These are the twenty three that are relevant to this story. I have tried to be accurate with the dates and chronology but I can't guarantee it with my memory.

PART TWO

Chapter 8

I still remember the day I lost my virginity. It was in the summer of 1986, she was called Verity Bane. I was thirteen.

My understanding of what the act involved was somewhat tainted by what I came to realise were stories and downright lies from the boys at my school, especially those who were three or four years older than me. Their vivid escapades, recalled in differing amounts of detail made me feel I was missing out on so much, but to be honest, some of their disgusting recollections made me wonder whether I was cut out for the exploration of the female form anyway.

Girls had been of interest to me from an early age. I had seen kissing on the television, of course, so I thought I would give it a try. My first attempt took place in the garrison school playground in Germany when I was ten. I plucked up the courage to approach the prettiest girl there; I think she was called Uta, the daughter of one of the senior Germans, working in the Quartermasters department. I ran across to her, put my hands on her shoulders, looked into her eyes and planted one on her lips. I regretted my action immediately. Her eyes were wide eyed with shock, her mouth gaping. I prepared myself for the scream and inevitable punishment from the headmaster. The screech didn't happen, in fact, she actually seemed to have enjoyed it. She looked at me fondly and her friends who had seen the whole episode appeared to be quite envious of her. I employed the same tactic on a number of girls at the school, almost always with the same result.

I suppose what I am saying is, although I believed I wasn't much to look at compared to some of the more handsome and athletic boys, I did have the confidence to at least try and approach the fairer sex. The vast majority of my targets appreciated the effort, the term "he who dares wins," was certainly true. There was only one real problem – where could I meet girls outside school?

*

We had been back in England for just over a year when my mother had taken Poppy and me to meet her best friend, Lucy Bane. Though I had never met her, I knew quite a bit about her from overhearing conversations between my parents. She was in her mid-thirties, about the same age as Mum, and lived with her daughter in a small cottage on the outskirts of town. Her husband had left her some years previously after he had caught her having an affair with a local tradesman. One discussion about Lucy had resulted in a heated argument when my mother had accused my father of having "the hots for her." I couldn't wait to meet Mrs Bane.

It was unbearably hot on the journey to their house in the country. The open windows did little to relieve the stickiness in the car. I sat in the back with Poppy. Many of my mates who had younger sisters, seemed to be embarrassed or ashamed to be seen with them. But it didn't bother me that my sister was four years younger and I had no qualms about holding her hand for the initial part of the journey because I loved her. We seemed to realise at the same instant that our hands were becoming uncomfortably clammy, so we released our grip simultaneously. She picked up her doll and started brushing its hair whilst looking out of the window. I turned my attention to my French vocabulary book.

I was very proficient in that language, as well as in German and Spanish, thanks to the excellent schooling I had received in Germany. Unfortunately, my French teacher, back in England, (Monsieur) Stanley Lyon, was a poisonous and vindictive bully who seemed to take an instant dislike to everyone. He loved to see his pupils struggle, as it made him feel superior. He seemed to hate me most of all for getting good grades, so I had set myself the task of annoying him even more on my return in the autumn.

It is worth noting that he was also responsible for teaching us gardening, which gave him another opportunity to ill treat us. He would change out of his brown brogues, stamp his feet into his black rubber boots and don his brown overcoat and beret, before coming to supervise the totally disinterested throng. We once had to dig a trench to accommodate some Hybrid Tea roses ready for the visit of some local dignitary. He took great joy in declaring that he would like us all to line up next to the hole, shoot us and cover us with soil. "You would make excellent fertilizer, that's all you lot are useful for," he said as he walked off to the greenhouse to light his pipe and sit and listen to Radio 3 on his transistor.

I initially hated the sound of the classical music that drifted towards us along with the smell of his aromatic shag, it was nothing like James Brown or Human League but gradually I began to enjoy it. There were many times whilst having a sneaky cigarette behind the equipment shed, that I would recognise a tune, probably from an advertisement, or a melody that had been stolen by a modern songwriter. I listened carefully at the end of the pieces I enjoyed, to find out who the composer was. So in a roundabout way, it was a sadistic, green fingered, Francophile bastard that I have to thank for introducing me to classical music and the start of an unusual collection of second hand records from market stalls and second hand shops.

I was humming "Greensleeves" as I took hold of a piece of my hair between the thumb and index finger of my right hand and slowly turned it over in a circular movement. I always did this when I was concentrating or under pressure. I didn't notice the rest of the journey nor the heat as I revelled in the concentration of the task that I had set myself.

My attention on the verb, *etudier*, was interrupted when we suddenly turned sharp left off the main road onto a lane that seemed to have more holes and craters than flat surfaces. We rocked from side to side as we drove towards a brown wheat field. You could smell the dust in the air. I sneezed, and my sister giggled with delight as she bounced around in her seat. I started to chant the declensions for *secouer*, as we approached a white cottage.

'Je secoue, tu secoues.'

'What does that mean Tez?' Poppy asked, her voice fluctuating in pitch as she was thrown violently from side to side by the uneven road.

'I shake, you shake,' I said, as the car drew up outside a white wooden fence. There was a small rectangle of stained wood nailed to a gate, proclaiming "Yellow Door Cottage."

'Very funny,' my mother said sarcastically, as she switched off the engine. At least Poppy thought it was humorous. She squeezed my hand and smiled.

The heat was stifling as we crossed the grass verge and opened the gate. The front wall of the building had a plaque above the centre window.

1748

That window and the one to the left were wide open. I could hear music playing faintly and recognised the closing bars of "Holding back the Years" by Simply Red. A row of tall rose bushes guarded the pathway to the front door (which was black, not yellow as advertised), with a bulbous brass knocker above the letterbox. Poppy said, 'Mummy, look at the butterflies on the flowers,' as the door opened.

'Hi Joyce, I thought I heard a car. It's great to see you.'

'Hi Lucy,' I heard my mother say as I looked towards the anonymous voice.

The brightness of the light bouncing off the cottage wall meant my eyes took a fraction of a second to focus. When they did, I could see why a local tradesman (and my dad) had found this woman irresistible. She was wearing blue and white striped shorts and a white blouse. A silver chain around her neck glistened as she stepped out onto the front step. Her dark brown hair was tied into a pony tail, she was suntanned, and I could just make out her gigantic dark eyes looking at us over the black plastic sunglasses perched on the end of her nose. She was truly stunning. I could feel a stirring in my jeans.

As she walked towards us I was convinced by the movement of her breasts that she wasn't wearing a bra. When she stooped to kiss Poppy, she confirmed my assumption. I got the briefest glimpse of a dark brown nipple before she stood up to welcome me. 'You must be Tesla?' She spoke slowly, her voice rich and warm, as if each word really mattered. I mumbled some kind of acknowledgement and prayed she wouldn't notice me blushing or how my hand had moved in front of my groin.

'Come on in and I'll sort out some drinks,' she said as she turned and walked into the house. I watched as she stepped away from me. Her legs were slender and although she wasn't wearing any shoes, her ankles seemed tiny in proportion to the rest of her body, I liked that. My gaze and my concentration had come to rest on her bottom when I realised my mother was watching me, so I made a fuss of Poppy.

I said, 'Come on Pops, let's get a drink.'

A clutter of big boxes stood in the hallway with some smaller ones stacked neatly on the stairs. It felt cooler here and I could see why as we entered the kitchen towards the back of the house. The back door and most of the windows were open; this must be creating a welcome draught through to the windows upstairs.

The music from upstairs had changed now to 'Addicted to Love' by Robert Palmer and I started to hum along with it. Lucy said. 'There you go Tesla. Here's some iced lemonade for you,' and she handed me two glasses, 'Could you take one up to Verity for me please?'

'Yes. Which room is she in?'

'Just follow the music.'

I left the two older women talking in the kitchen. Poppy was sitting outside on the lawn looking into an enormous rabbit hutch. The music had stopped momentarily but then the sound of a haunting synthesiser escorted me as I ascended the stairs. It was joined by a catchy beat as I crossed the landing towards a closed door and the Pet Shop Boys singing "West End Girls."

I was just about to kick the bottom of the door to gain attention when I heard, *"sometimes you're better off dead, there's a gun in your hand and it's pointing at your head."* I went to a dark place for just a moment. The lyrics reminded me of all the times I had thought I'd be better off dead, that's how my mum had made me feel so often. Cancelling this thought I set down one of the glasses on the carpet, knocked on the door and said. 'Hello. I'm Tesla; I have a drink for you.'

There was no answer so I knocked harder and repeated myself a bit louder. The music muffled as I heard. 'Come in.'

I opened the door and stuck my head into the room. 'Hello. I'm Tesla. Your mum asked me to bring you this drink.'

'Hi, she said you were coming over. I'm Verity.'

She was leaning against the windowsill, her face bright red. If I had been a betting man I would have said she had been dancing before I knocked on the door. She had dark brown hair like her mum and was wearing tortoise shell spectacles, and a dark red dress with a zip down the front. The thin straps over her shoulder showed off her suntan, as did her bare feet and legs. She smiled as I took the drink to her.

'Please turn the music back up. I like your taste,' I said as I handed her the glass.

'Ok,' Verity said as she restarted the CD player.

We spoke whilst listening to the music. I found out she was sixteen and revising for her exams but she didn't know what she wanted to do when she left school. It must have been a good hour later when her mum shouted up the stairs. 'Verity, we're going for a walk to the pub. Do you and Tesla want to come or stay here and listen to the music?' I don't really know why I did it but I looked pleadingly into her eyes and shook my head. I mouthed "no," pointed to the carpet, and whispered "stay here."

Verity shouted down the stairs. 'No Mum, we'll stay here. Tesla can help me with my revision.'

'Ok, see you in an hour or so. Listen out for the front door and the phone.'

I smiled broadly as I said, 'Thanks, I'd rather stay here with you and listen to the music.'

We talked some more. I told her some stories, and jokes to make her laugh. She described her recent holiday in Spain, and how her mum had been propositioned by loads of waiters. She also confessed that she put her room key on the bar one evening and a Swedish student standing next to her had said, "I will climb up to your balcony later and ravish you, now I know your room number." She said she had lain there all night, excitedly waiting but he hadn't shown up. She looked at me with mock sadness, then giggled and said. 'I was so disappointed.'

We were sitting on the bed as she chattered on. I confess I wasn't really listening as my mind wandered as I remembered the view down her mother's blouse. It was as I imagined my hand sliding down towards Mrs Bane's nipple that my attention was rudely awakened.

Verity had started to pull the zip down on her dress. She only lowered it by an inch or so but that simple action resulted in my undivided attention. I thought I was about to explode. 'Are you ok?' she asked cheekily.

'Oh yes, sorry,' I stammered. 'I just wondered what you were doing.'

'I'm just a bit warm. Why, are you getting all hot and bothered?'

Before I could answer, she pulled the zip right up under her chin and after a slight pause, whilst holding my stare, she started to slowly pull it down past the previous point, then back up again. She leaned towards me, offered me the zip. 'Would you like a go?'

My mouth was incredibly dry. This was the moment I had heard stories about and now it was happening to me for real. I was just about to say yes and take hold of the metal tag when she jumped off the bed. 'That was naughty of me; I'll put some more music on.'

'No,' I said a little bit loudly. 'It wasn't naughty Verity. It was like a dream come true. I haven't been with such a pretty girl before.' My voice wavered. 'I was nervous.'

'You think I'm pretty?'

'Yes, of course,' I said as the pulsating rhythm of "Word Up" by Cameo filled the bedroom.

'Oh, I love this,' I said as she turned to face me.

'Come on and dance with me then?'

This time I wasn't going to be unsure and delay my response to this opportunity. I stood, put my left hand onto her hip and pulled her towards me. She smiled as she said, 'You're very forward young man.'

I had the biggest smile as I moved her around the room in a totally random fashion, hardly in sync with the music but it didn't seem to matter to either of us. The track ended but we continued to dance to the following songs even though they weren't so familiar.

I was getting hotter and hotter from the physical exertion of the dancing but I just pulled her closer, my right hand finding the small of her back. She was slightly taller than me so my head came level with her naked collar bone. I remembered a comment made years earlier, whilst on holiday, when my dad had told my mother that she was sweating like a pig. She responded with a comment along the lines of "horses sweat, men perspire and ladies glow." Well I have to say that Verity was sweating like a horse and I loved it. We moved well together, we were laughing and happy, I never wanted this moment to end. We both collapsed onto the bed when the final track finished.

My left hand was under the base of her back as I raised myself onto my elbow and placed my right hand onto her tummy. She didn't pull away, move my hand or protest. She just looked at me, never taking her eyes from mine.

'Would you like me to cool you down a little?' I said as I moved my hand up towards her neck. I saw the faintest nod of her head as I fixed my eyes on hers and took hold of the zip. My heart was pounding as I slowly began to slide it open. I expected to be stopped at any moment but Verity just closed her eyes, sighed and turned slightly towards me. I took this as a hint she wanted me to kiss her. I leaned towards her and as our lips touched I slid my right hand into the opening of her dress and touched her damp chest. I moved my hand sideways and discovered she wasn't wearing a bra. Her dress created more space as she turned even further, allowing me to fondle her breast. My schoolboy dream was coming true but I had an overwhelming desire not to mess up. I pulled my lips away. 'Verity, please tell me what you want me to do.'

'You're doing fine. Just be gentle and I will give you clues as you go along.' I did as I was told. I listened carefully to her breathing. It seemed right to apply and reduce the pressure in time with our kisses. I was truly amazed that when I thought I might be hurting her she pulled me tighter towards her. 'That's so nice,' she said as she gave a deep sigh.

She suddenly pulled her lips away, put her hand on my chest and pushed me slightly. As she sat up, my world fell apart; I had thought I was doing so well. I felt so stupid, inadequate, inexperienced and embarrassed. I was about to apologise when she pulled the left strap over her shoulder followed by the right. Her dress fell down from her upper body and bunched around her waist. I gasped.

Her chest was an even golden brown apart from two small triangles of white with two bright pink tips in the middle. The left one was a darker shade and slightly larger due to my earlier attention. 'Come on,' she said as she put her arm around my neck and pulled me down onto the bed.

Verity guided my hands and mouth all over her body, showing me what pleased and aroused her. Then she started to stroke my groin, undid the top button of my jeans and unzipped them.

We touched and kissed, exploring each other's bodies and then she lay back and I knew it was time. I entered her and felt that I wasn't a boy any more. She held me tight, her legs gripping my waist and her cries getting louder as she neared orgasm. I couldn't hold on any longer and even now after all these years I cannot describe the excitement that passed through me when I collapsed into her arms. Her smile when she sat up next to me will live in my heart until the day I die. That was the best moment of my life so far.

Suddenly a thought came into my head, "What if I've got her pregnant. Oh shit, Mum will kill me." Verity must have seen the look of panic on my face and realised what I was thinking 'Don't worry, I'm on the pill.' She said smiling.

We were silent as Verity pulled the straps of her dress back over her shoulders and zipped it up. We smiled at each other as I pulled up my jeans and went to the bathroom. I heard the music resume as I washed my hands and looked into the mirror above the sink. Did I look different? I wasn't sure but I certainly felt different as I smiled to myself, looking forward to seeing her again. My brain was working overtime, as I went back into the bedroom, trying to work out how to get to see her without it being too obvious. She wasn't there.

I went downstairs and found her filling the glasses with lemonade. I put my arms around her and kissed her. She smiled again as she handed me the drink. I said, 'Thank you.'

She kissed me; she knew what I was really thanking her for. "I think I love you," I thought as Verity went back upstairs and I took my drink outside into the fierce heat. I realised I would be blushing as soon as our mother's returned. I would have to pretend I was crimson from a lack of suntan lotion. I lay on the grass, thinking about what I had seen and done since arriving at the cottage. I fell asleep realising that the memories would fuel my right handed activities for years.

*

Mrs Bane looked a bit tipsy when she walked us to the front door as we were about to leave. Verity waved from the top of the stairs and smiled at me as I turned and left. I was helping Poppy with her seat belt when I heard my mother say. 'I'm really glad I got to see you before you left.'

I think, "Oh, they must be going on holiday again," as I picture the Banes women sunbathing topless. I am jealous as I imagine boys flirting with "my" Verity. My thoughts are shattered when Lucy Banes says, 'Me too Joyce, I'll call you with our new number when we get connected. Make sure you come and see us next time you're in London.'

I caught a glimpse of Verity standing at the upstairs window as we drove off down the dusty and bumpy lane. I had just had the best moment in my life, only to be devastated seconds later by the news that she was moving away.

I heard a rumour some years later that there had been an incident between her and her mother's new partner, and that Verity had left the City and moved to America.

I didn't know if I would ever see or speak to her again.

Chapter 9

I lit another cigarette from the dying embers of my last and checked the itinerary again even though I had already travelled this route once before, when I had gone down to complete the three day, Potential Royal Marine Course. I wasn't nervous then, as I hadn't committed my future to the Marines, but now I had been selected I didn't want to be late. I wanted to confirm that it was just over four hours for the train journey to Exeter, St David's with a further hour (after a brief wait) to Lympstone Station and the commencement of my thirty two weeks training. No turning back now.

It was almost nine months since my initial call. The man on the main enquiry number had said, 'I can arrange for you to attend an ICP at your local recruitment office and if you are happy with that, we will give you an application form to complete. This will mark the start of the process for joining the Royal Marines.'

'What's an ICP?'

'It's an Initial Career Presentation. It will give you a taste of what the life is like and if you have any questions you can have a chat with the officers there. It only takes two hours. So, shall I book you in?'

I said, 'Yes please.' I gave him my name, age and address and he confirmed a date to attend a week later. I asked whether I needed parental consent but he said "no" as I had turned eighteen two days earlier.

The meeting at the recruitment office had gone well, or so it appeared. One of the officers asked some questions about my background. He commented that my fluency with foreign language, sailing ability and having an understanding of the need for discipline, (as a member of a "service family"), would stand me in good stead. He made a jovial comment about not wanting to mess with my dad, when I told him where he was stationed. It was all very friendly until I mentioned, stupidly, that I had hoped my dad's position might have an influence on my selection. This was not an attempt to get any preferential treatment you understand, it was just to find a way to speed up the process and get away from home as soon as possible. His voice became quite menacing as he said. 'Having a dad who's a fucking "brown job," counts for fuck all in the Marines sunshine.'

His tone and expression did soften somewhat when I explained I was just really keen to enlist. I didn't believe him when he gave me the recruitment application form and told me the process could take over six months from the date I submitted it, but it turned out he was telling the truth.

The psychometric test took place at the same recruitment office a week before I started my language course at college. I had spent most of the last year either revising for or sitting tests, so one more wasn't going to bother me. I actually enjoyed the numerical and verbal aptitude papers but my favourites were the mechanical reasoning and spatial ability tests

I had to juggle my lectures when I attended the medical, eye tests and selection interview, as I had already started my course at college. It was ironic that I had to feign illness to go to a fancy gym and take a fitness test that included completing a three mile run in twenty minutes with only a minute's rest half way through. Seven weeks after completing the security clearance and counter terrorism checks, I received confirmation that I had been accepted and was expected to report to the Commando Training Centre in Devon exactly one month later.

I waited until the weekend before I was due to leave before telling anyone. I called my father in Germany and was amazed he actually answered my call. He said it was good that I had joined up, but what about college? I explained they were disappointed that I had decided to leave, but they understood my decision was final. It didn't surprise me that he hadn't asked me what my mother had thought about me leaving the language course, but I guessed he would call her later. Poppy cried when I told her I was going away, she said I had promised I would never leave her. I put my arms around her and reminded her that I had never made such a promise, but pledged I would always remain in contact.

At that moment my mother came into the kitchen and saw Poppy quietly weeping in my arms. She shuffled across the room, still in her dressing gown, with her heels pressing down on the back of her stained slippers. She started to fill the kettle as she said 'What's the matter Poppy? What's he done to you?' Her speech was slurred.

'Oh Mum, Tez is leaving us tomorrow. He's joined the Marines.' Her words broken by sobs.

I clung to the hope that news of my leaving would spark a display of love from Mum. But the words seemed to have no more effect, than if she had been told it had started to rain. 'I know, your father rang, we both believe it'll do him good.'

Poppy said, 'But Mum, he might be called up to fight in the civil war in Sierra Leone.' There had been reports on the news that British Forces might be involved in the conflict. I was marvelling at Poppy's knowledge of current affairs when her next comment shook me to the core. 'What if there is another Gulf War? He might get killed.'

I have to be honest and say that the thought of dying "at work" hadn't occurred to me. At no point from the career presentation nearly nine months ago till now did I think I might never come back. My fourteen year old sister had made me realise the enormity of my decision to run away and made me realise just how much I wanted my mother to ask me not to go. I understood her priorities when she finished making her drink and said. 'Well he's made his decision Pops; it's up to him to stand by it.' With that, she turned and shuffled back towards her studio. Poppy pleaded with her to stop me going but Mum just shrugged her shoulders. My sister glared at her as she shut the door.

*

The taxi had arrived to take me to the station. I was standing in the hallway about to leave; Poppy was holding my hand, asking me yet again not to go. There was no sign of my mother as I heard the driver press his horn to encourage me to leave to catch my train. Poppy didn't release my hand as I walked to the studio and opened the door. My mum was sitting facing me but she didn't raise her eyes from the screen of her ancient word processor.

I said, 'I'm leaving now Mum.' There was no answer. Just one kind word would have stopped me. I could feel the tears welling up behind my eyes, like water filling a bath; I had to get out before they overflowed.

As I pulled the door shut, I thought, "It wasn't my fault Mum."

The sound of the car horn shook me as it summoned me again, so I pulled my hand away from Poppy's, picked up my bags and moved towards the front door. I left Poppy in the doorway to the studio, frantically screaming, 'Mum, please ask him not to go,' then turning to me and shouting, 'Please don't go Tez.'

I slammed the front door and hurried to the taxi and put my bags beside me on the back seat. I kept looking straight ahead as we pulled away from the house, pretending I didn't see Poppy running along the drive with tears streaming down her face. I shook my head as I remembered the small broken body at the bottom of the stairs and whispered, 'It wasn't my fault Mum.'

'Sorry mate, what was that?' the driver said as he looked at me in his rear view mirror.

'Nothing, I was just thinking out loud.' I had to turn away and look through the side window as the tears ran down my cheeks.

*

I watched the countryside pass by as I travelled towards my new adventure on the south coast. I put the thought of the accident in Germany and Poppy's tears out of my mind, and concentrated on the woman who had hurt me on my birthday, Maria.

I had been to the shop a couple of times with my mother and sister. Mum's conversation with Mrs Walters was usually about their school days or people they had known who had since got married, been separated or even died.

Mrs Walters had mentioned she would have to start shutting the shop at lunchtimes now that Ahab, who had worked there on a part time basis, had left. He was flying to Ireland for a fortnight's holiday at an uncle's in Cork, before going to a Kibbutz in Jerusalem for a month. She commented that although she didn't have children of her own, she thought she would find it hard to be separated from her son like that. I didn't miss the glance my mother gave me when Mrs Walters had said that – my mum would send me away forever if she got the chance.

Maria's husband Rick, who worked on oil rigs in the North Sea, often helped when he was on leave but he wasn't due back for a week or so. She explained that she hadn't had any response to her advert for a shop assistant, this was when my mother suggested I go to help out until her husband returned. The casual observer would see this offer from my mother as a generous and charitable gesture, but in reality it was just a ploy to get me out of her way.

102

Maria Walters was about my height, very slim, with a bulbous chest, a cute bottom and slim legs. She had thick auburn hair, wore horn-rimmed glasses and every time I had seen her, had been wearing either a dress or a blouse and skirt. She reminded me of Mrs Robinson from the film The Graduate, which I had watched on television a couple of nights earlier. The thought of Anne Bancroft seducing me, flashed through my mind before being quickly replaced with the vision of Verity Bane, lying naked beneath me.

I started work in the shop the next day.

My experience with Verity had cemented my confidence when in the company of girls and women. Following that encounter, I had found myself in female company more and more. Youth clubs, bus stops, the local park, shopping centres and the swimming pool gave me the opportunity to use my eyes and ears effectively. I began to understand what it was they valued the most. I realised a compliment about how well they looked when they had obviously made an effort was priceless. I taught myself to listen, really listen, when they were talking to me. I used eye contact to show them unsolicited and quality attention. I raised my eyebrows when they made a startling statement or a frown when I needed to express concern.

I used all these techniques on Mrs Walters. It was difficult at first, it was almost a chore but then I began to do it naturally and I enjoyed the results. She seemed happy in my company, we laughed a lot. I found most of her stories of interest but it was the day she was upset that I learned the most.

I had not seen or heard from her for a few weeks as her husband was home on leave and helping around the shop. I found a message on the fridge one morning.

"Mrs W rang. Can you go down and help this morning? Luv Pops xxx."

It was already after nine so I hurried to get washed and dressed and cycled down when ready.

I could see a couple of customers in the shop as I approached, so went round the corner and in through the back door. I stored the bike and saw the last customer leaving as I entered the living area. "Autumn" from Vivaldi's Four Seasons was playing quietly in the background as Mrs Walters walked quickly towards me from the shop. 'What time do you call this?' the tone of her voice was harsh. She sounded like my mother.

'I'm sorry Mrs Walters; I didn't get the message off Poppy till this morning. I came as soon as I could.'

'You watch the shop, I need to do something,' she said abruptly.

'Ok,' I said, as I went into the shop. She turned away and walked into the kitchen. She didn't close the door so I could hear her slamming things around. I didn't like this atmosphere, it reminded me too much of home. I heard her sobbing quietly. 'Mrs Walters are you ok?' There was no reply; I tried again, 'Mrs Walters.'

There was still no response, so I went round to the front of the counter and looked through both the large shop windows. Its position at the corner of a road junction meant the shop benefited from an abundance of light and a fantastic view in all four directions. It didn't appear there were any customers on their way, so I went back behind the counter and through into the living room. She was sitting on the arm of a chair, crying into a handkerchief.

'Mrs Walters, are you ok?'

'You should be in the shop,' she said in between blowing her nose and wiping her eyes.

'I can go in there as soon as I hear the bell,' I said as I sat next to her, 'what's the matter?'

'Oh, you wouldn't understand.'

'You're probably right but I'm happy to listen if you want to give it a go.' She didn't reply, so I continued. 'Listen I heard you in the kitchen before. It sounded like you were dabbling at porcelain tympani. Why don't I go and make you a drink in total silence?'

There was a hint of a smile as she said, 'Ok, that would be nice.'

I moved backwards and forwards, from shop to kitchen, as I served a few customers and prepared the drink. I looked at the clock on the cooker; it was midday, so I made a decision. I went through to the shop, taking the key from the dish on the table at the bottom of the stairs and went to the front door. On a hook on the door jamb there was a small sign with the words, "Sorry, Back at" written in red and a little clock below it. I moved the hands to show 12:30, applied moisture to the sucker and pushed it onto the glass door, which I locked.

'What have you done,' she said as I walked back to the kitchen.

'I've shut the shop for half an hour.'

'There's no need for that. I'm ok now.'

'I'm going to make you something to eat. Closing the shop for thirty minutes of peace and a bit of "you time" isn't going to break the bank.' As I started to prepare some soup I asked, 'Do you want to tell me about it, I hate to see you upset?'

'It's nothing really, just a few problems with Rick and his job. We never really talk things through when he is here and the next minute he's heading off again.'

I put the soup in a bowl, which I placed upon the kitchen table along with a spoon, a plate of cut bread and a cup of coffee. 'Mrs Walters,' I said as I looked at her sitting quietly, 'your lunch is ready.'

She came and sat down at the table. 'That looks lovely,' she said as she started to eat, 'tasty too. Where did you learn to cook?'

'Warming some soup is hardly cooking but I do make a lot of meals for me and Poppy.'

'Why's that?'

'Because Mum is usually too busy writing her latest book.' This was a lie of course, the real reason was she was almost always pissed out of her skull and couldn't be bothered to provide me with nourishment.

'Have you thought about training to be a chef when you leave school?'

'No, not really, I've been accepted to study language at college in the autumn. I'd like to be an interpreter.'

'That sounds interesting,' she said as she continued to eat the lunch I had prepared for her.

I said, 'I'll go and open the shop up now.' I put my hand gently on her shoulder as I walked past. I could feel her bra strap through her cotton blouse. 'Are you feeling a bit better now Mrs Walters?'

She turned, looked up at me and smiled as she said, 'You can call me Maria and yes, I do feel loads better now. Thank you for listening to me Tez.' I could see down the front of her blouse at this point and noticed the milky white flesh wobble when her chest caught the side of the chair when she moved. I was instantly aroused. I headed towards the connecting door to the shop, hoping she hadn't noticed the bulge in my jeans or my blushing face.

The rest of the day was spent serving customers, stacking the shelves and general chit chat. I was bent over behind the counter, at one point, when she walked past me. She patted my right buttock and said, 'Come on breathe in, you're blocking the way.' I was surprised that the chocolates on the tray above me didn't melt with the heat coming off my face. She smiled when she saw my youthful embarrassment.

As I prepared to leave, a couple of hours later, she said, 'Thank you for today Tez, you made me feel loads better.' She walked over to me, put her arms around me and gave me a hug. It was the most fantastic feeling to be held like that. I wanted to say something but before I could speak she held out some money in her palm and said, 'Here's a bonus for all the work you've done for me, I really appreciate it.'

I held her hand, and then folded her fingers into a fist, thus securing the cash. 'Just seeing you smile is good enough for me, buy yourself some flowers with the money. I wish I could buy you a bouquet.'

She said, 'Oh. You're so sweet.' I could smell lavender as she hugged me again, tighter this time, and gave me a soft kiss on the cheek. I felt light headed as her soft flesh pressed into me. I left the shop by the rear entrance and cycled home as quickly as possible.

I locked my bedroom door when I got home.

*

The following weeks in her shop are unbearable. The haze of her perfume makes my head spin and my body trembles when she brushes past me. I notice changes in her behaviour that make me giddy with excitement. The way she bends over the kitchen table making her pencil skirt stretch over her perfect buttocks and the extra button undone on her blouse, when she's not in the shop. And my favourite, when she's standing at the top of the ladders in the store room. How her dress rides up, showing off her legs and the glimpse of black elastic at the top of her stockings, as she reaches towards the upper shelf. Is she being provocative or is it my imagination? I don't know but I ache with desire.

I hear her walk down the stairs one morning, when I am in the kitchen counting the float for the till. She was cleaning when I arrived but had gone upstairs to change. When I look up, I see she is wearing a dark blue skirt, a crisp white buttoned shirt (with *three* buttons undone), black stockings and black court shoes. My voice can't disguise my lust when I say, 'Good God Mrs Walters, you look amazing.'

'Flattery will get you everywhere, you charmer,' she says, patting my cheek tenderly, 'and I've told you to call me Maria.'

*

She calls my mother one afternoon to ask if it is ok for me to go in early the next morning to help store away a big delivery that had just arrived. I hear my mother mention the words "heavy boxes" and "of course he can." It is settled without any discussion with me so I duly get up early the next day and cycle the three miles to the shop.

I let myself in at the back door with the key Maria had given me. The lights are on as I enter and I can hear the washing machine spinning. There's no sign of her. I wheel my bike into the kitchen, making a bit of a racket in the process, and head towards the door between the sink and the washing machine. This gives access to the garage and storage area. I take my bike down the two steps and lean it against one of the boxes near the window. I can see the delivery but the boxes are nowhere near as big or as heavy, as I imagined.

I can hear music playing softly somewhere as I re-enter the kitchen. 'Maria, it's Tesla, I'm here.' No response. The kitchen leads into the living room and further ahead I can see the frosted glass door, leading into the shop. There's no light in there so she must be upstairs. I call again a little louder as I begin to climb the stairs but again there is no reply. When I reach the landing I notice her bedroom door is slightly ajar. The bedroom is dark but by the light coming from the bathroom I see her sitting on the edge of her bed with her back to me. She's wearing a fluffy white robe and is drying her hair. I watch her for a couple of seconds, believing with every fibre of my being that she knows I am standing there gazing at her. I knock lightly on the door before pushing it further open. 'Maria,' I whisper.

She appears startled as she turns towards me and says, in a flat melancholic voice, 'I didn't hear you, come in Tez.' All I can think at this moment is, "Yes you did! You must have heard me crashing my bike through the kitchen and shouting up the stairs," but instead I say, 'Sorry, I didn't mean to scare you. What music are you playing, I really like it?'

'It's called the "Tallis Fantasia by Vaughan Williams."' Her voice sounds sad, just like the melody.

'Are you alright?' I say as cautiously I enter the room.

I'm standing at the end of the bed with my heart pounding, as she says, 'I feel a bit down today, I'm getting old and unattractive.' She looks small, gentle and vulnerable as she absentmindedly strokes her wet hair with a towel. I pluck up the courage to sit next to her on the bed, expecting a protest but none comes.

'Can I tell you something Maria?' She nods and turns to face me. 'I think you are really attractive, but that day when you wore the blue skirt…' I pause for a moment, turn towards the mirror and sigh softly. '…you looked absolutely amazing. I can't tell you what I wanted to do to you.'

'Tesla Coyne!' I think I detect a hint of mock indignation in her voice but I can't be sure. Have I made a massive mistake?

'Sorry, I shouldn't have said that.'

'Go on tell me,' she said, I catch just a hint of eagerness in her voice.

'No, you'll be angry or even worse, laugh at me.'

'Tell me,' she says with mild authority. She leans towards me, our shoulders are touching, my heart about to burst through my chest.

'I would come up behind you as you are standing at the sink and put my arms slowly around your waist. I would be incredibly nervous, expecting you to push me away but I can hear the heels of your shoes scraping across the tiled floor as you lean slightly back towards me and I would stand on my toes and kiss the nape of your neck.'

Our legs and hips are touching now. Maria is bending slightly forward, which causes her robe to fall slightly open. I start to turn towards her, putting my right hand on the small of her back and turning her face towards me with my left.

I kiss her.

'No,' she says and starts to move away from me. I release my grip enough to let her move away from me but she stops. She doesn't resist as I close the gap between us, pull her towards me and kiss her again. This time she responds. Her right hand pulls my face towards hers and our lips meet again. This time hers are parted, and her tongue licks mine causing them to tingle and open slightly. When our tongues are touching, exploring each other, and my head is buzzing with pleasure, I slide my hand inside her robe.

She pulls away from my kiss and puts her hand on my wrist to restrain me. 'No Tez, you're only 17.' At this moment I feel immature, disappointed, and totally confused. We've worked together for weeks, gradually getting more and more comfortable in each other's company. She has flirted with me and touched me as I walk past her in the shop. I am sitting with her now in her bedroom and she has responded to my kiss by exploring my mouth with her tongue. I know Maria is lonely, she told me so herself. Am I the first to be in this position or is she ashamed of her body? She told me earlier she felt old and unattractive. I take a silent breath, summon all the confidence I can muster and gently pull her towards me.

'I will be 18 soon and been with a married woman before. Plus I've always wanted you Maria, from the very first time I saw you.'

I can tell she is about to speak, so I stop her by kissing her again. She doesn't pull away this time, so I put my hand inside her robe and with the gentlest touch trace a route to the underside of her breast. I move from her lips and kiss her neck. She sighs as I begin to stroke her gently; this changes to a groan as I increase the pressure. Her hand, which has found my thigh, squeezes in time with my actions. Then she moves it slowly upwards.

The robe has started to fall away from her shoulders and the back of my left hand is no longer touching fabric. Her chest is exposed so I kiss her below her right ear, from where I can sneak a peek at her nakedness. The music downstairs doesn't sound sad anymore but uplifting, even joyous as she slowly undresses me and begins to caress my body. I pull her robe open and she slips her arms out of the sleeves, letting it drop onto the bed. Both naked now, we throw ourselves into an embrace, our arms and legs entwining and our mouths crushed together.

She squeals as her body shudders and she clamps her legs together, trapping me. I try to continue but she pulls away gently and says, 'No more, it tickles.' She is smiling up at me. 'Where did you learn to do that?' she says. I just smile put my arm around her and kiss her. We lie there for what seems like hours gently kissing and holding each other tightly until I break this idyllic silence, saying, 'I'd better get ready and go and sort out the boxes from the delivery, before we open the shop.'

She looks at me mischievously and says, 'Tez, I lied about the delivery.'

'That's ok, I lied about being with a married woman.' She looks surprised as I kiss her, fasten my jeans and go downstairs.

*

It didn't take a genius to work out that I'd been used. This had all been planned yesterday when she had called my mother asking me to go in early to help with the fictitious delivery. She must have heard me come in the shop. There was the racket I had made with my bike and my shouting her name repeatedly. Then there was the mood lighting in the

111

bedroom, as she sat there, semi naked, telling me she was unattractive.

I stood in the kitchen, smiling as I quietly said to myself, "Maria Walters you crafty, sexy beast, you seduced me. I succumbed to your trap and I will be eternally grateful. I think I love you."

We opened the shop, served some customers and glided past each other in silence, as if nothing had happened. When our eyes met, I was pleased to see her smile was as broad as mine. I was behind the counter when Mrs Eyres shut the door after buying a quarter pound of pear drops. The shop was empty. Maria came in with a drink and sat next to me. She took hold of my hand behind the counter (so no prying eyes would see) fixed her gaze upon me, and spoke to me in a whispered voice. I knew something important was about to follow.

'Tez, we need to have rules. You mustn't say anything to anyone about what happened today. Don't look too eager when you come here, as that could arouse suspicion. That goes for me too you know. We must be careful; you never know who might be watching.'

That was how our affair started. Over a week passed before there was an indication that "it" would happen again. I had arrived one morning to find her wearing the blue skirt and white blouse. She had a wicked smile as she saw me notice her attire and said, 'I think we will shut the shop for an hour at lunchtime.' The blue skirt was the confirmation that she wanted me. I would put the sign on the front door and go back into the living area to see what scenario would be played out that lunchtime.

I have so many wonderful memories from our time together. One of my favourites was the day I found her in the kitchen, standing at the sink washing some dishes. I went in, shut the door, moved behind her and put my arms around her. She pressed herself into me as I pulled the blouse out of her skirt and pushed my hands up and cupped her breasts. She reached back and unbuckled my belt which encouraged me to move my hands to the hem of her skirt and lift it up to her waist.

Her soapy hands on my nakedness, made me think I was about to pass out with pleasure. I had to think of something to stop myself climaxing too soon. The window over the sink looked out onto the backyard where I noticed the geraniums in the hanging baskets needed deadheading. She had pushed her backside against my groin as I realised the grout in the wall needed repairing. I also noted the windows needed cleaning, just as she pulled away from me and spun around. She pulled a chair from the kitchen table, pushed me back so I was sitting down and pulled up her skirt which had started to fall from where it was bunched at her waist. She straddled me. All thoughts of household maintenance evaporated as she took control and dictated the rhythm of her body riding against mine.

My body juddered and I held her tightly. 'Fuck me.' I said as I could see coloured lights explode behind my closed eyes. She gave me a tender kiss on the top of my head and slowly raised herself away from me.

I thought I had learned how to tap into a females' psyche, how to use my senses in order to seduce them, but it was Maria who taught me the lessons which otherwise would have taken an age to learn. She explained that what a woman says and what she wants is not necessarily the same thing. And what is more, all women are wired differently, so what works with one, may not tickle the neutrons of another. They can even change their mind as to what they like. It was so confusing, but I was to have so much fun over the years finding out which buttons to press.

*

The train had gradually emptied as we approached our destination. There was a definite buzz in the air as the remaining passengers arrived at Lympstone and stumbled out excitedly onto the platform and I started to recognise others from the recruitment process. A four tonne troop carrying vehicle was in the car park with a couple of blokes in uniform leaning against it but it was the man standing in front of me who quickly attracted my attention. I guessed he was about the same age as Dad, immaculately dressed with a green beret and a sash. He slammed himself to attention, gripped his swagger cane tightly and said, 'Fall in. I'm Sergeant Salad.'

I cringed when I heard a snigger behind me at the mention of his name. I definitely winced when the guy standing next to me said. 'I wonder who will be "tossing the salad" tonight.'

The sergeant suddenly shot forward from his position and marched purposefully until he was standing directly in front of me. His nose nearly touched mine as he spat the words, 'So you think my name is funny do you?' He stepped back, took his cane from under his arm and flicked the small curl on my forehead and said. 'Well, who do you think you are with a curl like that, Bill Haley? We'll soon have that shaved off! You and I are going to be seeing an awful lot of each other.'

There was a distinct clearing of a throat next to me as the true originator of the comment said, 'Excuse me Sergeant.' The officer brought himself back to attention and barked, 'Silence, come on you pieces of shit, make your way to the car park and get on the TCV.'

I was sitting on the hard iron seat when I got the first real sight of the joker. He leaned forward and offered his hand and said, 'I'm sorry about that mate. I was going to say something to him but he wouldn't let me.'

'Don't worry about it. It made me smile, besides I'm used to putting up with that kind of crap off my mother.' I shook his hand and said, 'Tesla Coyne.'

'Good to meet Tesla. I'm Eddie Tolmach.'

So it was on that day in 1991, the last time that I would have to think for myself for thirteen years, that I met my new best friend.

Chapter 10

It was a Saturday, the evening of my eighteenth birthday. I was sitting in the cinema waiting for "The Silence of the Lambs" to start, when I saw the advertisement that was to change my life. I should mention it had nothing to do with an invitation to visit the foyer to purchase a hot dog, popcorn or a fizzy drink but it had a lot to do with my forty two year old lover, Maria Walters.

The summer of 1991 was nearing its end. My sister Poppy was due to go back to school; I was still undecided about what to do next. I had shown my school report to my mother in the hope there would be some recognition of my achievements, but no praise was forthcoming. I guessed the reaction would have been the same from my dad, if he had been at home. It was not unusual to get this kind of response, but foolishly I thought that when my exam results came out, showing some of the highest marks ever attained in my school for English Literature, German, French and Spanish, that I would hear the words, "Well done Son."

I was above average at most subjects but had been classified as "gifted" when it came to English, (I love writing stories) and learning new languages. I taught myself some basic Japanese after watching an old black and white film called, Seven Samurai and dabbled at Cantonese. I found both surprisingly easy to grasp and somewhat empowering to be able to surprise people with my gift when the opportunity presented itself. Going into a Chinese take-away to order food was a particular joy. Usually resulting in amazing food (I think they made a special effort) and in one memorable case, an erotic encounter in the kitchen after closing time, with Lin-Lin, the shop owner's daughter.

This must have had an effect on me because I later applied and was accepted to attend a foreign language college, to study for a degree in Cantonese. I thought this would be a perfect stepping stone to my long term objective, which was to learn Mandarin. I had read that the Chinese economy was set to grow exponentially over the next ten to twenty years and I believed a career as an interpreter would be a good direction to take in order to help companies wanting to do business over there. One article had suggested there could be opportunities for language graduates following the upcoming transfer of sovereignty in Hong Kong in 1997.

Although the idea of being a business interpreter appealed to me, my misery at home and the thought of another three years of education, made me feel like getting away and trying something different but I didn't know what direction to take.

I was lying on my bed thinking about my future when I heard the sound of the letterbox snapping shut as the post landed on the floor in the hall. I decided to get up, to get a drink and some breakfast. I pulled on my jeans and a tee shirt, left my bedroom and walked towards the stairs. I stopped at Poppy's room. I knew it was hers because she had kindly stuck an A4 sheet of paper on the door saying "Poppy's Room." I smiled as I thought that if it wasn't for this piece of information I might not have known where to look for her. I knocked quietly and said, 'Pops, are you awake?' There was no reply. I knocked a little louder and opened the door slightly. She wasn't there. I noticed that her bed had been made.

I continued downstairs and checked to see if there were any birthday cards for me. There were three envelopes, two addressed to my mother the third for the attention of "The Occupier." Nothing for me. I went into the kitchen to make a drink, where I found Poppy's card on the table. Although she was fourteen, she still enjoyed making greetings cards for me by hand. I knew *she* would never forget my special day.

I could hear movement in the studio, which meant my mother was already in there working on her book. Surely she would burst through the door any second now, singing *"Happy Birthday dear Tesla."* She would be holding up a beautiful cake, there would be marzipan, (I love marzipan), covered in icing with eighteen sparkling candles lighting up her happy and smiling face. She would put it on the table in front of me and say, "Make a wish when you blow them out birthday boy." I would take an exaggeratedly deep breath and blow the flames out in a single gust. OH how we would laugh when I realised that the candles were the new joke ones, which came back to life when you thought you had extinguished them.

However, the door didn't open; there was no singing and no cake. The same as last year and every year for as long as I could remember. My dearest wish by the way would have been – "Hold me close Mum, give me a hug and a kiss and PLEASE tell me you love me."

Although Mum had ignored my special day again, I wondered if I would hear from Dad. He had a habit of forgetting to send me a birthday card but had been known to call me from Germany. He had joined the Royal Corps of Signals and moved to the Rhine Garrison, near the Dutch border, with my mum in 1973. I was born there six months later. No one in the family ever knew what Captain Harry Coyne did for Her Majesty. All I knew, was he could speak fluent German and Russian and he was often away from the garrison for weeks on end. One of the boys at my school said his mum reckoned my dad was a spy. The look Dad gave me, when I mentioned this to him one day, made me shiver with fear. I would never mention that word again.

When Poppy was eight years old, it was decided that we would move back to England. Mum said she was sick of living in the barracks and it was also mentioned the move would benefit my sister's education. The benefits of academic improvements for me were never mentioned of course. Mum had also had some interest from publishers about a children's book she had written, so she wanted to be closer to London. Dad moved back with us but couldn't settle, so returned to Monchengladbach after only seven months.

Dad would come home on leave quite often but the six weeks per year gradually became less and less, bottoming out at a couple of weeks around Easter or Christmas. We thought that when the Berlin wall came down in November 1989 that he would move back in with us, but this made no difference. Mum said she didn't care, "he probably has a fancy piece out there and she's welcome to him."

I stopped thinking about my parents, picked up the pale yellow envelope, containing Poppy's card and opened it. I instantly recognised the folded piece of cream card was the same my mum used to separate the publishers rejection letters in her filing cabinet.

The front of the card had a picture of a small sailing boat on it with a boy at the tiller. I knew it was supposed to be me because the boy was wearing a blue and white striped jumper (one of my favourites) and the distinguishing feature was the big kiss curl in my fringe at the right of my forehead. She had named the boat; "Prendre la Fuite" which I had told her was French for "take flight." She knew I was desperately unhappy at home and dreamt about getting away. She often begged me not to leave her but I could never give her that assurance.

The sky above the boat and boy was a beautiful blue, interspersed with white clouds and swooping seagulls. The word BROTHER with two blood red hearts on either side was the banner across the bottom. I opened the card to find the boy with the kiss curl was now blowing out the candles on a cake. She had written 'Happy Birthday Tez' and below it 'From Pops. Love you loads.' At the bottom of the card were eighteen crosses representing a kiss from her, for each year of my sorry life.

I had put the card back into the envelope and was about to leave the kitchen when I heard the door to the studio open and my mother came out wearing her pyjamas, carrying a glass and a small plate. She didn't acknowledge me as she lit a cigarette, shook the kettle to make sure there was enough liquid inside then pressed the switch to boil the water for a drink.

'Mum. Where's Poppy? She isn't in her room.'

She turned to face me; she hadn't even noticed me sitting at the table, directly in front of her. Her hair was stuck up somewhat and her mascara was smudged. I wondered if she had fallen asleep in her studio and had slept there all night.

'She's gone to the Skyler's,' she said abruptly. She was slurring her words; she must have had at least one glass of vodka already that morning and it wasn't even midday yet. 'Sebastian picked her up earlier. Are you going out?'

I said, 'Yes, I'm going to pop into the shop this afternoon to see if Mrs Walters wants any help and then I'll probably go into town tonight to see a film.'

Just the mention of Maria's name made my mind race off into a sexual wonderland trying to imagine what adventure would be awaiting. I blushed as I remembered the day, two weeks ago, when Maria was standing on the ladders, in the stockroom. She looked over her left shoulder as I approached her and widened her stance on the top step. She sighed as my hands moved slowly up her stockings, stopping briefly when I felt her cold pudgy flesh next to the elasticated band. Her breathing faltered as she squatted ever so slightly onto my fingers and pulled my head against her. She was groaning as she said. "God, that's so dreamy." I was just about to replay the part, where she came down the steps and lay back on the chest freezer, when my thoughts were interrupted by my mother.

'Good…' Regaining my concentration, I recalled that Maria had told me she would shut the shop early, as she had a special gift to give me for my birthday. I knew she would be driving to the airport later to pick up her husband, so I could go and see the film I had been dying to see, since reading

Thomas Harris's book. I was wondering what surprise was waiting for me, when Mum continued in her usual harsh tone. '…I don't want you hanging around here all day.' That was the end of our dialogue. I watched as she opened a cabinet and selected a beaker. It was the same cabinet in which she had misplaced the manuscript, six years ago, which had resulted in my father nearly "breaking" my fingers.

She put three spoonfuls of coffee and four of sugar into the cup and added the water when the kettle had boiled. She turned away and walked unsteadily back to her literary shrine. When I say literary shrine, that's exactly what it used to be. She had always made a steady living from her stories which were popular, especially with girls up to Poppy's age. Recent years had seen the trend for popular stories to be darker and more menacing. Fourteen year old girls were now being entertained by stories about a telekinetic schoolgirl or a teacher who turns out to be a wizard.

The last book she had published was "Pauline Pepper and the Secret Secretary," nearly three years ago. I knew she had submitted two other books since then that had been rejected. This had resulted in her drinking even more excessively and getting depressed. I wouldn't have believed she could have neglected me more than she already did but now she was openly hostile to me most of the time.

"Why do you stay in this abusive relationship Master Coyne?" I had asked myself this question so many times in the past. I was too young to escape before, but not now… now I am officially an adult.

I remembered her talking on the phone one day saying she had tried to change the theme of her books; only to erupt in rage after the person on the other end of the call had obviously told her that her writing was juvenile. "Juvenile! What do you fucking mean my book is juvenile?" she had shouted at the receiver, "I've written it in the same style as the crap that's being sold now." I have no idea what was said to her then but when I heard the phone thrown against the wall I decided to get out of her way. I made a mental note to buy copies of Mr

Majeika and Dahl's, Matilda and to leave them lying around, just to piss her off.

The house was totally silent now. I folded Poppy's card and put it in my back pocket, made myself a coffee and put some bread in the toaster. I decided to wash the pots that had accumulated over the past couple of days. I raised the glass that my mother had used to my nose; it stank of stale gin, which means she must have run out of vodka. Things must have been bad because she hated the taste of juniper berries. The plate had a piece of crust on it, evidence she had had a sandwich. I am amazed my mother had introduced solids into her body.

I was just about to go back to my room when I heard Poppy come in through the back door. 'Hello birthday boy,' she said as I walked towards her.

'Hi Pops, thanks for my card. I'm glad someone remembered me,' I said as I gave her a hug, 'did you have a nice time?'

'Yes, I went round to the Skyler's to play with Faith and Gracie, they've got a Gameboy you know and it's really good.' I had had a go of one of the new electronic consoles; I was hopeless, so I couldn't see what all the fuss was about, I much preferred a good book. She continued, 'Sebastian showed me one of his new paintings, it's really brilliant.'

Sebastian was the twin girls' older brother and guardian. He had become their "protector" after the death of their widowed mother. I remember being dragged from a sailing holiday in Germany to attend the funeral. I suspected that my sister was infatuated with him. I'd seen him many times when he had called round in his sky blue VW campervan, to pick Poppy up. He was in his mid-twenties, very tall and gangly, with long hair, normally tied back in a ponytail. He looked as if he had been transported through time, maybe from the Woodstock festival of 1969. He was softly spoken, gentle, very calm and laidback. I really liked him; it would have been good to have him as a brother. He spent most of the summer months with his sisters on the south coast, where he indulged his passion for wind surfing. The rest of the time he spent painting. One of his pieces had been bought by a dealer, when he displayed some of his work at an exhibition in his final year at college. The painting was subsequently sold by a gallery in London with commissions following from as far afield as Milan and Chicago. One of his paintings had been used by a band as a CD cover which had resulted in fame and fortune for him when their music had "gone platinum."

'He's going to paint on a Greek island for two months,' Poppy said as she took off her coat.

'Who is?' I said, setting the trap.

'Sebastian. He's going away for part of the winter to stay at his dealer's house while Gracie and Faith are at their aunties.'

'Sebastian, Sebastian. Sebastian. That's all you talk about. You really fancy him don't you?' I teased.

'No I do not,' she shouted, 'besides he's too old for me.'

'See, you do fancy him but you're disappointed you're too young for him.' I began to dance around her. 'Poppy loves Sebastian, Poppy loves Sebastian,' I said as I giggled and continued to torment her in a childlike voice.

'No I don't.'

'Yes you do.'

'No I don't,' she said beginning to look upset. 'Tez stop it, I hate you.' Her voice was rising higher now.

'Yes you do.'

'Well Gracie Skyler fancies you,' she said triumphantly.

That stopped me in my tracks. I had seen Grace when she had been round to play with Poppy. She was pretty but very quiet and shy, unlike her sister, Faith, who was a bit wild and seemed full of nervous energy. Grace was cute but she was… 'Don't be silly,' I said, shaking my head in disbelief. 'She's far too young for me.'

'Oh, so you would fancy her if she was older?'

'Touché,' I said as I realised my little sister had outflanked me. Time to change the subject. 'I was only teasing you Pops. Thanks again for the card.'

'Ok,' she said quietly. She took a book from a pile on the windowsill and sat at the kitchen table. I finished tidying up, made a fresh drink, buttered the toast and decided to go back to my bedroom. The silence between us was uncomfortable.

I stopped as I was about to leave the room, turned to face her and said, 'Love you Poppy.'

'Love you too Tez.'

I was pleased to see she was smiling. I don't ever want to hurt her as she's all I've got. I walked up the stairs thinking about what Poppy had said about Grace. There is definitely something about Gracie Skyler that intrigues me but I can't put my finger on it.

*

I closed the door to my bedroom and listened to Violator by Depeche Mode on my CD player as I ate my toast and drank my coffee. I decided to have a nap, so I set my alarm for two which would give me time to get ready and get to the shop before four o' clock. I lay back and thought of the time Maria seduced me. There was only one thing for it before I had a sleep. I loosened my jeans and pictured my forty two year old lover kneeling in front of me.

I was excited when the alarm woke me. I went to the bathroom, had a quick shower and returned to my room. I put the CD of Baroque Classics in the player and got dressed to Handel's Water Music. When I was ready, I had one final look in the mirror and turned off the music as Bach's Brandenburg Concerto finished.

Poppy had the television on when I got to the front door. I could just hear the announcer as I opened the front door *"...news headlines followed later by Five O'clock Shadow with Jenny Monr…*" I left just in time to catch the bus to town.

*

I could see the lights were off in the shop when I turned the corner, so I went around to the rear and let myself in. She was standing in the entrance to the living room, barefooted and wearing a green floral dress. She approached me, put her hands on my shoulders, pushed me towards the wall where we couldn't be seen from the street and kissed me. I couldn't help noticing a look of sadness in her eyes as she moved away and said, 'Happy Birthday Tez, I have a special surprise for you.'

'Why thank you,' I said as she walked into the kitchen. 'Are you ok?'

'Yes I'm fine,' she said unconvincingly, 'you go upstairs and have a soak for twenty minutes. I've run the bath for you already.'

I went up and through her bedroom, noticing the white towels on the bed. I entered the bathroom, undressed and put my clothes on the wicker chair next to the sink. My arm encountered over six inches of bubbles, before it reached the water to check the temperature. Finding it at just the right heat, I lowered myself into the bath.

I could hear the faint sound of someone outside the front of the shop, trying to open the door, no doubt wondering why it had shut early. A little later I heard Maria behind me, 'does that feel nice?' she said as she took her bathrobe from the hook on the back of the door.

'Yes, it's great but I'm getting hot now.'

'Ok, get out when you're ready and lie face down on the bed. I'm just going to change,' she said as she closed the door.

I stood up and dried myself rigorously as I didn't want to delay the arrival of my surprise. I stepped out, dried my legs and feet and wrapped the towel around my waist. The bedroom was dark when I entered, apart from the light from two scented candles on the dressing table.

I had just lain face down on the bed when I heard her enter the room. She sat on the left hand side of the bed and as I turned to her I could see she had placed a glass jug on the bedside table. I could tell by the wisps of steam rising from it, that it contained warm water. There was a bottle of oil bobbing around in it. She was wearing her robe; I closed my eyes when she placed her hand softly on my neck.

I sneaked a peek as the pressure on the bed shifted slightly. She had taken the oil from the water and flicked the cap up. Her right hand left me briefly as she pooled some oil in her palm then brought it to my back and shoulders. The warm sensation was wonderful. I sighed gratefully as I remembered what Verity had told me about giving clues with sounds and gestures, to indicate what you like. Maria continued down my arms and onto my lower back and sides. I counted five deep strokes for each section of my body, gradually working her way lower. She stopped abruptly when her hands encountered the towel; I was disappointed she hadn't continued going further.

She slowly raised herself from the bed. "Please don't go." I said to myself. She poured more oil on her hands and knelt between my legs. I made a sound that would have been universally acknowledged as "thank God you're back." Part of me had got caught in the towel as it had swollen. I was very uncomfortable but refused to delve down to release it, as it might have destroyed the "moment." She placed her hands on my calves and slowly applied pressure upwards towards the top of my thighs, stopping once again when she reached the towel. I was disappointed again, that she had stopped and removed her hands from my body.

She must have applied even more oil because her hands were wet through when they returned and moved upwards again, towards my bottom. This time she didn't stop at the towel. I hummed with anticipation as she allowed her fingers to slide under the material. She lowered them again, teasingly, but pushed up immediately, slightly further this time, repeating until her fingers and thumbs were kneading my bum like bread dough. I groaned with pleasure as she raised my hips off the bed and her wet hands continued to stroke me.

Then she lifted my shoulder in such a way that I knew she wanted me to roll onto my back. I obliged as she lowered her head towards my groin. I held her chest fleetingly and stretched out my arm to try and satisfy her. She stopped me by pulling my wrist away from her, and then continued to focus her attention on me. I tried reaching for her again but was halted again.

'Let me touch you,' I whispered. These were the first words I had spoken since leaving the bathroom.

She disengaged me from her mouth and said, 'No, this is your treat today.'

'It's not fair Maria, let me,' I said as I reached for her yet again.

She held my wrist as she said, 'Look Tez, not now. I can't.'

'Why? I don't understand why you won't let me?'

She sighed, and then said, 'I can't because Tom is visiting.'

'Tom! Who the fuck is Tom?' I said loudly, as I started to rise from the bed. 'Why have you arranged for someone to call round when we are doing this?'

She laughed out loud as she said, 'Calm down, it's not a good time for me. Just let me treat you.' I felt stupid and immature at that moment and I could sense my face beginning to flush with embarrassment. Maria spared me the feeling of ridicule as she returned her attention to me, only to sit bolt upright moments later, when she heard my breathing catch.

I don't know if it was the effect of being smothered with warm oil or the feeling of panic as I thought we were about to have a male visitor, or maybe the sensation of her tongue exploring my body or perhaps a combination of all three, but something had had a profound effect upon me. The jet of liquid shot onto my chest, across my chin, nose and into my eye. I saw her smile as I tried to clear my vision. I prepared myself for her wit but she said, 'Wow that was amazing. I have never seen anything like that before. Don't rub it! I'll get a cloth and clean you up.'

She got up from the bed and went to the bathroom. I lay there feeling that life couldn't get much better than this. That is, apart from looking like a giant snail had crawled up my body and left its trail petering out in my eyeball.

Maria reappeared with some damp tissues and cleaned me up. We lay together in silence for ten minutes. I was turning the hair round on my fringe with my finger and thumb, when she sat on the bed and said, 'We'd better get ready now; I need to get to the airport.' She gave me a kiss, touched my forehead and said, 'I love your little kiss curl,' as she went back into the bathroom.

*

I had just finished getting ready when Maria came back, sat next to me and said, 'Tez, I have something to tell you.' I'd sensed something was wrong earlier and could tell by the look on her face that I was about to get bad news. 'You know I have to go to airport now to pick up Rick, don't you?' I nodded. She continued, 'Well he rang me this morning to tell me he has got the promotion he was after as a Subsea Specialist,' she paused before adding, 'in Houston, Texas.'

I was pleased the news didn't appear to be as bad as I had anticipated. I smiled as I asked, 'Will that mean we can spend more time together?' I admit the tone of my voice had a hint of desperation in it as I continued. 'I'll have more free time when I start college next month and he won't be coming home as often as he does from the Scottish rigs.'

'No Tez, this will be the last time we can be together.' I couldn't believe what I was hearing. I think I was just staring at her; my mouth hanging open. 'He's coming back tonight on a month's leave, to put the shop on the market and get everything ready for the move. I'm going with him, first to Florida for a holiday then onto Houston.'

This can't be happening. She can't leave me now. 'What if you can't sell it before he has to go, surely you will have to stay on?' I said pleadingly.

'It is highly likely that could happen, darling, so he has arranged for his sister to run the shop until we sell it. I'm sorry Tez. I wanted to make today special for your birthday but the news came as a shock, he didn't expect to get the job.'

I couldn't think of anything to say. I knew it would come to an end one day but wasn't prepared for it now. I caught a glimpse of my face in the bedside mirror. I looked like a miffed and petulant little boy, which was exactly what I was at that moment.

I got up and walked to the bedroom door, I had reached the landing when she said, 'Please don't be angry with me. I will miss you. You are very special you know.' She got up to follow me as I started to walk downstairs. 'You are a good person and you were there for me when I needed someone.' I had reached the bottom of the stairs and started to walk towards the kitchen. 'You're a good listener, very funny, confident and really caring.' She was standing right behind me when she said softly, 'And you're an amazing lover with a wonderful body.' I wanted to turn around and kiss her, plead with her not to go but I didn't want her to see the pain in my eyes. I thought. "Why do women always have to hurt me so much?"

'Do you want a lift to the cinema?' she said as I put her key on the kitchen table and opened the door.

'No, I'll walk,' I said as I lit a cigarette. Those were the last words that I ever spoke to her.

*

There was no belated card from my mother when I got home. There was no message that there had been a call from Dad wishing me Happy Birthday. I felt as if a part of my soul had been torn from me as I realised I wouldn't see Maria again. I could just about bear living here if I could see her from time to time, but now even that had been taken away from me.

I spent the whole of Sunday in my room waiting for nine o'clock on Monday morning to arrive. That's when I called the Royal Marines recruitment office.

Chapter 11

The Intel briefing before the mission, was just like all the others I had attended in the thirteen years since joining the armed forces. Even now in the SBS there was the usual banter before the CO and his team were due to come in and bring the briefing to order.

Tommy Culver was sitting directly in front of me but had spun round excitedly in his seat so he was facing me, Eddie and Smithy. He was telling a story about how he had developed severe stomach pains at O'Hare Airport on a trip back from Chicago. He had dived into the toilet opposite to the American Airlines transfer desk to ease his discomfort, as he didn't believe he would make it to the toilets nearer to the departure gate. It was kind of him to describe his "evacuation" in detail. The emphasis on the quantity and aroma of the event helped to paint the picture; it was almost as if we were there. He got quite animated when he raised his voice for the climax of the story.

'I had just finished wiping my arse when I thought I'd better get a move on, otherwise I would be late boarding the plane. I was keen to get rid of the debris so I yanked the toilet flush cord as I was pulling up my trousers.'

I groaned as I called him a 'dirty bastard.'

'Unfortunately, it wasn't the flush for the bog after all but the emergency alarm. It was only then I realised I was in a disabled facility.' He was standing up now, laughing hysterically, holding his belt in one hand whilst waving his other arm around his head. 'I was trying to buckle my belt and waft the smell from the room as the high pitched siren was joined by people hammering on the door.' I was smiling broadly as I imagined the scene. He continued, 'I pushed the correct flush button on top of the reservoir, fastened my pants and opened the door. There was an airport utilities bloke standing there along with some cabin staff and numerous business commuters, all looking to see what the emergency was. I stepped out unsteadily. I said, "Sorry I thought I had a problem opening the door. I'm ok now." I then swayed from side to side, impersonating Douglas Bader's gait.' Tommy started to walk around, rocking from side to side, with his legs locked stiffly. 'I carried on like this until I got around the corner, which was when I sprinted to the gate. God, I was so embarrassed.'

I turned as I heard Eddie's booming laugh beside me. Our paths had crossed a number of times since meeting on the station platform on my first day in the Marines. We had both ended up being selected for M Squadron specialising in anti-terrorism and helicopter assault. If you heard his voice on the phone you would picture him as tall and built like a brick shithouse. My best friend was less than six feet tall, very slight, extremely strong and ruthless.

He was also a devout Christian. I had seen him chastised and ridiculed for his beliefs on a number of occasions by recruits and officers alike. He had handled these situations serenely until the morning a huge, new recruit to the squad had slapped him across the back of the head, as he was kneeling next to his bed praying. Eddie sprang up from his position, spun around in mid-air and crashed his fist into the offender's throat, this was followed by a blow to the nose which erupted in a spray of blood.

'Fuck me; there was no need for that,' the guy said as he sat in shock on the floor. 'I was only having a laugh; I thought you lot were supposed to turn the other cheek?'

Eddie took a towel from his cupboard, bent down and passed it to the bleeding giant. 'Turning the other cheek is my

131

way of avoiding responding to verbal insults; it isn't a lesson in being a pacifist. Your smack across the back of my head crossed a boundary. The teaching of Jesus is not against killing but against murder. My understanding of his love means I will defend myself and others from evil and I believe there is no greater love than to lay down my life for a friend, even you.' He might have been my best mate but fuck me he could be a bit heavy at times. I made a mental note, years ago, "not to cross him."

I had been "on jobs" with Tommy on a couple of occasions, I really liked his extrovert personality. Eric Smith by contrast was a very quiet ball of nervous energy. I didn't know him that well, but we gravitated together by chance, when he heard me humming "Habanera from Bizet." We spent hours talking about our love of music and became good mates.

Although I didn't know the detail behind the operation, I couldn't have picked a better group to work with; I had no idea it would be the last one for Eddie and me.

*

We were in a tent in a remote compound some eleven miles west of Yuksekova in Turkey. Smithy and I had been there since dawn and had been involved in the interrogation of two Islamist terrorists who had been captured just south of Cheekha Dar Mountain. They had been brought across from Iraq by Kurdish activists who were supporting our search for enemy threats along the border. It was their information, that there was an Al Qaeda stronghold some eighteen miles from where they were captured, that led to today's operation.

Commander Kelsey gave us the briefing. He explained that the four of us would be taken across the border at 01:15 hours tonight by Lynx helicopter and dropped five miles from the coordinates he had provided. We were to work in pairs and he confirmed this would be a "black op" to neutralise the terrorist threat. He finally detailed the communication procedures and the recovery plan, then we were dismissed to get a meal and prepare our equipment.

*

We moved quickly from the drop off site and arrived at the observation point about two hours before dawn. We were wearing dark clothes to have a better chance of melting into the background should things go wrong. Our position, on the banks of a dry riverbed, gave us an excellent view of the eastern side of the suspected site of the Al-Qaeda camp and the makeshift road leading to it. But this location just didn't "feel" right. The plain running from the Zagros Mountains in the east, stopped at a hill shaped like the back of a camel. It seemed out of place in this type of terrain; it was too elevated and exposed and could be seen from miles around. Although it was still the dead of night, the clear starlit skies and moonlight illuminated the landscape sufficiently to show us it was unlikely there was any terrorist threat there.

It was overcast, cold and starting to snow as we set off. The snowfall reminded me it would be the twin's third Christmas soon. I shook my head to remove the thought of my nieces from my mind; I hadn't seen them since I visited them just after their birth. I reminded myself about the task in hand, we were here, on a secret mission, to "neutralise a terrorist cell."

We decided to split into two groups. Eddie and I, Alpha team, worked our way along the edge of the road until it petered out and became a dirt track, just south of the highest point. Bravo team, Smithy and Tommy, continued further west and took a position in a rocky outcrop at the base of the hill amongst some bushes and small trees.

I crawled up towards the side of the road while Eddie covered me from a position below a fork in a riverbed some twenty yards away. I didn't set foot onto the surface in case it was mined but I could see no evidence of any recent activity. It was obvious heavy traffic had used this road in the past but it seemed odd that it ended in what appeared to be a goat track. It was then I noticed a small gap between a boulder and some small trees growing behind a pile of rocks. I probably wouldn't have paid any attention in broad daylight but the glow from the moonlight seemed to highlight the fact that the road continued towards Tommy and Smithy's position. The rocks had been put there as a roadblock.

I waved Eddie over and showed him what I had discovered. We skirted the end of the track, and then doubled back on the other side until we came to where the road was blocked. It was getting lighter now as we climbed over shale and some larger stones to where we found the road again heading downhill towards the north and a dense wooded area. Eddie signalled to the Bravo team who joined us minutes later.

We agreed to travel north along the edge of the road as the alleged Al Qaeda camp was more likely to be in the woodland at the base of the hill than where the captured Islamists terrorists had originally suggested. We took the western side, threading our way through the bushes while the others took the east, making their way through the debris at the base of the slope.

We were able to keep each other in view as we followed the road, but there came a point about two miles along when the Bravo team suddenly disappeared from view. I had just followed Eddie through a dense thicket of scrub when we realised we were alone. The road was still in front of us running along a sheer rock face topped with trees that clung to its edge, but there was no sign of the other two.

We had just started to track back to look for them, when I heard the sound of a finger clicker, come from some trees, across the road. Three times in quick succession was the signal to stop. We saw them at the side of a giant boulder, they were waving to us, they had found something. It was too far to double back this time to avoid any mines, so we'd have to cross near here if we were to join up with them. We tracked back about fifty yards to a point in the road where it narrowed, close to some overhanging rocks. Smithy followed us on the other side, and climbed up into an overhanging tree and attached a rope so we could swing across. Eddie crossed first, missing the surface of the road by inches. I followed, raising my arse as high as possible to avoid triggering the mines that could be waiting for me below.

We followed Bravo team after retrieving the rope and quickly realised why they had disappeared from view. The road split at the base of the cliff and forked slightly eastwards into some denser tree covering, behind which we found a cave.

The entrance was shaped like giant avocado pear; it was wide enough at the base to admit two trucks but narrowed at the top, about twenty feet above the road. We proceeded cautiously towards the cave noticing signs of human refuse along the way. There was a broken wooden pallet, a partially buried Iraqi Army glove, a dirty Coke bottle and numerous cigarette butts. Because of its sheltered location, the weather's effect had been minimal. We found more broken pallets, a concrete loading bay and rusting metal drums just inside the entrance. Electrical wiring and broken lamps ran along both walls eventually disappearing into the darkness. It seemed fairly obvious the area had been abandoned decades ago. There was no way a terrorist cell was located here.

We paused at the concrete wall of the loading bay. The large metal plates and the rotting timber behind us didn't look safe. We noticed heavy chains hanging from a girder above us as we took on some water and weighed up our options. The mission was to find a terrorist camp but this location was too important to leave without investigation. We decided that we would recce the cave for thirty minutes then call in at the pre-arranged time to inform base about the changes to the operation. We would return to the road after our deviation and continue north towards the woodland we had spotted earlier and report our findings when we returned.

Eddie decided to lead, I followed with Tommy with Smithy as our rear-guard. We attached laser lights to our rifles and set off cautiously at thirty yard intervals. We were on the lookout for mines but realised the sandy ground in the cave was covered in animal tracks indicating that we were safe from this threat. We saw skeletons and carcasses of animals and birds of various sizes as we progressed. It seemed odd that they had died here; I had a very uneasy feeling about the remains in the tunnel. My senses were on prime alert as I continued deeper into the cave.

All I could hear was the very faint sound of my footsteps in the soft sand.

All I could see was the sweep of the light on my rifle, illuminating the way ahead and the occasional beam from my mates.

All I could feel was the rifle in my hands and the annoying crease in the lining of my helmet, behind my right temple.

All I could smell was someone cooking. *Cooking*. My nose was playing tricks. I swear I could smell garlic.

The passageway narrowed significantly within two hundred yards of the entrance but there was still enough room for a small vehicle, maybe a fork lift truck but nothing much bigger. Eddie stopped and pointed his light at what looked like a small alcove set back in the wall. He continued and disappeared round a right hand bend.

I reached the alcove and found what I thought was a wooden wall. I turned to my right, just as I could see Eddie's light fading as he moved further inside. I wanted him to pause while I checked out what was behind the wall. I looked back, it was pitch black, Tommy's torch must have either failed or he was way behind me. I focused my attention back on the wooden wall and realised it was actually a number of crates tightly stacked on top of each other. I then saw a faint light approaching from my left and heard Tommy moving towards me.

There have been occasions in my life when an hour has appeared to pass in a heartbeat. The following seconds however, seemed to tick in slow motion.

Tick… The crates are dusty but I can see faint writing and symbols. I place my weapon on the ground with the light facing the alcove I carefully brush the sandy film from the labels and make out the words, "Schwefel-Lost, K.Kobe." I think, "Oh Shit, no," as…

Tick… I hear a high pitched squeal (like leather and wood rubbing together) along the passage to my right, just as I see Eddie's light illuminating a door…

Tick… I think. "Don't open it," but I realise it's too late, as the noise from the hinges continues. I shout. 'Eddie, No!' just as I hear the sound of a metallic spring triggered, followed by Eddie's voice distinctly say, "Sweet Jesus."…

Tick… I shout, 'Fuck,' as a brilliant flash of light is followed by an ear shattering explosion. The curve in the tunnel protects me from the majority of the blast but it is still forceful enough to slam my head into the wall.

I don't know how long I was down, but as soon as I was conscious, I was fighting to get to my feet to go to Eddie's aid. My eyes were on fire and tears were streaming down my cheeks as I was pulled up from the floor and dragged away from the alcove. My ears were still ringing from the blast but I could hear Smithy's voice screaming as he put something wet into my hand. I could see it was his lucky green beret that he carried with him everywhere. He had soaked it in water and shouted, 'Put this over your face, breathe through it, protect your eyes.'

'Eddie, get Eddie,' I said as I tried to break free.

I was still protesting when Tommy joined Smithy in pushing me towards the entrance to the cave. I was screaming about going back for Eddie as Smithy told me to calm down and let him attend to the wound on my head. Tommy squatted down with the radio as clouds of dust billowed behind us. There was a brief crackle on the airwaves, then his voice.

'Golden Sword to Lionheart. Two down. Dijon.' I realised the name for the city in Burgundy was the code word for chemical weapons. 'Immediate Casevac.'

Smithy crouched down by my side. 'Tez, listen. This has been a total fuck up. You've lost a hell of a lot of blood in the blast. We have requested urgent casualty evacuation. We have to get out of here.'

I tried to sit up but the pain in my head was overwhelming. 'I have to go back for Eddie,' I said as I was pressed back onto the ground. 'He was caught in the blast.'

'No one is going back in there until the Lynx arrives with the proper equipment. Eddie must have triggered a booby trap that has fractured some of the canisters stored down there. There are hundreds of old crates of mustard gas.'

My head seemed to be filled with a wave of splashing treacle as I tried to get up and go back into the cave for Eddie. There was a sickeningly strong smell of garlic as I collapsed backwards. Tommy caught me and said, 'He's gone Tez. Come on, we have to get moving.'

The last thing I heard before I passed out was Tommy saying, 'Blister agent Smithy, the fucking bastards did have blister agent after all.'

*

I drifted in and out of consciousness and could only piece together snippets of information. I remember Kelsey was there for the recovery and he had a look of total catastrophe on his face. I was initially taken to a Turkish military hospital and then to a secret British Medical Facility.

I experienced itching in my eyes within twenty four hours of my arrival; this developed into severe conjunctivitis, and then blisters on my face began to weep a yellow fluid. Thankfully, these symptoms settled down within five weeks but my eyes continued to give cause for concern, so I was given lubricating drops to give me some relief. I was informed by the Medical Officer that further tests had confirmed it was unlikely that I would suffer from persistent corneal scarring. He said I was very lucky that my injuries weren't worse. Tommy's quick thinking and my clothes had protected most of my body. I didn't feel lucky when I was also told I had suffered some bleeding of the lungs which would result in some difficulty in breathing and possibly a persistent cough in the future. I thought his interpersonal skills were sadly lacking when he told me that my sperm count might be affected but I was shocked when he demonstrated how to use an inhaler, handed it to me and said. "Take this, as you might suffer from respiratory cancer in later life."

I had numerous visits from the psychiatric staff. I seemed to spend hours answering their questions about the explosion and the death of my friend. One of the doctors said it was unlikely I was suffering from Post-Traumatic Stress Disorder but he would recommend a course of Citalopram to help with the anxiety and depression he had identified. I agreed to take them but didn't really think they would be necessary, I was sure I was strong enough to cope.

I was moved to Hamworthy Barracks after my convalescence, and was met by Kelsey and the MO, who debriefed me about what had happened. I was told I was to say nothing about the blister agent, and to keep to the story that a training exercise had gone wrong. I had no idea whom I could have told because I was kept in virtual isolation the entire time, and had a guard on my door to stop me talking to anyone apart from the doctors.

They were not sure if we had walked into a trap, or if the two we had captured had really believed there was an Al Qaeda cell located near there. The recovery team had gone in wearing protective clothing to recover Eddie's body and had found a store of mustard gas canisters, in old packing crates which had probably been destined for use during the Iraq and Iran war of the eighties. It was their belief that the entrance had been hidden and the contents booby trapped, probably around the time of the search for weapons of mass destruction by Hans Blix as there had been no evidence of any activity there for decades.

There was a glance between them which I knew could only be followed by bad news. They explained that the guard on my door was to ensure that the real outcome of the "black op" didn't get exposed. Although we had discovered WMDs, the government couldn't release this information because we shouldn't have been there in the first place. They confirmed they had blown up and blocked the entrance and that the official story was that we were caught in an explosion in a chemical factory. In closing, they informed me that my medical assessment indicated that I was no longer "fit for role" which would result in a medical discharge, effective immediately.

It was less than four hours later that I left barracks for the final time. I was loaded into a military vehicle along with a bag of medication and all my possessions, and taken to my apartment in the town. My discharge papers were in my jacket along with a letter explaining that detail of my compensation and pension would follow later.

I think I was still in a state of shock as we drove along the coast road towards Minecliff Road. Was it really only weeks ago that my best friend had been killed, and I had been caught in a blast and cloud of gas, that left my lungs permanently damaged? Had I really just been told that I was no longer FFR and had lost the job I loved?

As we were passing a restaurant where a group of office workers were stumbling out wearing party hats, I remembered Kelsey's final comment as I left the briefing room.

'Hope you have a terrific Christmas. Got anything special planned?'

Chapter 12

I am in my penthouse apartment, listening to the murmur of traffic and pedestrians on the busy street at the front of the building. This sound is drowned out, at regular intervals, by the crashing of waves on the rocks beneath my rear window. It was the view of the sea and the dramatic sheer drop to the beach and rocks below that convinced me to buy the property with the "apology" money my father gave me.

I recall what Kelsey had said to me. I really don't think he meant to be sarcastic when he gave me his best wishes for the festive season. How could I be jolly in the circumstances? I believe that he had been in the forces for so long, he had lost the ability to understand other people's feelings and he had learned to cope by putting up defence mechanisms, to avoid being overwhelmed when people were faced with personal loss.

So what am I going to do for Christmas? Remembering my thoughts about Emily and Melia as we approached the hill in Iraq, I have an overwhelming desire to see my nieces again. The brutal events in Iraq make me want to cry out for sight of their innocent faces. And Poppy of course, yes to see Poppy and spend Christmas with her and her family would be perfect, especially as I don't have a clue what to do with myself.

I light a cigarette and go downstairs to the shop. Jordi is reading at the counter when the buzzer on the door announces my arrival. His face beams when he sees me. Jordi has been there for me from the early days when I bought the apartment above his shop. I introduced myself and left contact details if he needed to get in touch. There was a bad leak one February when some pipes burst. He arranged for all the repairs and redecoration with the insurance company, so I trusted him from then on. He has keys to my apartment and I have given him access to all my non-personal mail. I also leave a cheque for him for essential expenses for my home, car and boat. We have become very good friends and frequently go sailing together when I am on leave.

'Tez. Oh my God, long time no see.' His outrageous accent can swing from Wurzels to Wałęs within a single sentence. He springs up from his seat and makes his way around the light bulb display.

I am genuinely glad to see him. 'Hi Jordi.'

'I thought you were back, I saw the curtains were open. I was going to pop up later to check. What's the matter with your eye?

'I'm ok. Had an accident on a job, slight case of conjunctivitis, nothing serious but I've left the Marines now.'

'Fuck off! You've left them? Why?'

'I can explain everything later mate. Can I use your phone to call Poppy?'

'Yes of course. I'll go and make a drink. It's been quiet this morning but I'll come back if I hear the door.'

I am standing behind the counter, surveying the winter wonderland before me. Jordi's attempt at festive decoration even manages to raise a smile on the lips of this miserable observer. The aisle leading from the front door has a piece of green tinsel on either side of the shelves. The strand nearest the door is somewhat shorter than the other, no doubt due to being caught on winter coats when customers push past. The small tree next to the till is illuminated by a set of lights that would be better suited on the one in Trafalgar Square. I swear I can feel heat coming from the gazillion lamps as I pick up the telephone.

'Hi Pops,' I say brightly when she answers.

'Oh, what a lovely surprise, I was expecting your call nearer to Christmas. Are you ok?' The joy and enthusiasm in her voice never ceases to amaze me.

There is no point in worrying her by telling her I have lost my job and my health. 'Yes, fine thanks. How are you and the babies?'

'Everything is wonderful here Tez. The girls are no longer babies though. They're walking now and fascinated by all the decorations and the presents under the tree. They potter around like a couple of old ladies, they're so funny. I wish you could see them.'

'Well that was the purpose of the call Pops, I was wondering if it would be ok for you to set another place at the Flood's Christmas dinner table this Saturday?'

There is a brief silence on the line as my request sinks in, followed by an ear piercing squeal. 'Tez! Do you really mean it; you can be with us for Christmas?'

'Yes, I've got some time off so I thought it would be nice to come up and stay with you over Christmas. Maybe spend a bit of time writing if you can find some spare room?' I say sarcastically.

I visualise their house with its labyrinth of rooms and my favourite, the studio in the loft. I can hear her shouting excitedly in the background as I wait for an answer. She'll be at the back door shouting across the garden to Jacob's workshop, telling him that her absent brother wants to come and stay. She is out of breath and sounds excited when she returns. 'Of course you can come for as long as you want. We've refurbished the studio since you came last time; it's a lovely little self-contained guest flat now. We had the Perritano's staying with us last weekend; they said they really liked it. I'll get it ready for you.

'That's brilliant I'm looking forward to seeing you all.'

'Are you coming up today?'

'No Pops. I have a few things to sort out here at the apartment and with Jordi. I thought I might come up on Thursday evening so I can be with you on Christmas Eve morning.'

'Tesla Coyne that will be one of the best Christmas presents I've ever received.' I smile at her words, they radiate such joy. She continues, 'Jake's delighted you're coming up and says he has some fine malt for you to try.'

'Sounds good,' I say, as the buzzer sounds on the shop door. An elderly lady enters pulling a shopping bag on wheels, narrowly missing the tinsel as she approaches me.

'Do you sell bags for a vacuum cleaner?'

'Just a moment madam I'm just on a call.'

Poppy says, 'I know you're talking to me.'

'I know Poppy, I'm talking to someone who's just come into the shop.'

'Pardon, I don't want a poppy, I want bags for my vacuum cleaner.

'Listen Pops, I'm in Jordi's shop. I'll have to go. I'll see you, the girls, Jake and the scotch at the end of the week. Ok?'

'Ok Tez, drive safely. Love you loads.'

'Love you too,' I say as I hang up the receiver.

'Love me? I only want bags for a vacuum cleaner, do you sell them?'

'Piggin Doggin.'

'What?'

Jordi appears at my side and passes me a drink. 'Here you go Tez why don't you go into the back while I serve Mrs Fallowfax? Relieved to have been rescued, I quickly make my escape.

'Morning Mrs Fallowfax, what can I do for you?'

I can hear the resulting conversation faintly as I walk into the living area and can see the kitchen beyond. The layout reminds me of another shop and triggers the memory of my eighteenth birthday and my affair with Maria. I wonder whether she is still in America.

My thoughts are interrupted as I hear the buzzer followed by the shop door closing. Jordi comes to join me, he is laughing. 'She is brilliant. Comes in here virtually every week to get something, I'm sure it's just for the company. She used to be very close to my dad after my mum died. She is hard of hearing and was a bit confused when she found you behind the counter. She told me you were trying to sell her some flowers, then said you loved her and that you had some pigs and dogs in stock. Anyway, she has gone now. So, tell me what has happened to you.'

Let the lying commence. There will be no official records of what really happened in Iraq and my medical history will never see the light of day. So I relate the story I had agreed with Lieutenant Kelsey and the medical officer.

'There isn't much to say really. We were on a routine operation when there was an accidental explosion in a disused factory. I got caught in a cloud of sulphuric acid vapour given off by some old lead batteries. I got mild damage to my left eye, I still get a bout of conjunctivitis occasionally but it will clear in time. My lungs however took a bit of a hammering. I have some scarring to my respiratory system, so they medically discharged me.'

'Bloody hell Tez, that's a bit drastic, couldn't they offer you a desk job or something?'

'No. The government cutbacks mean they're trying to encourage people to leave, plus I really don't think that would suit me, even if that option was available.'

'So what are you going to do for money and a job and things?'

'I'm not bothered about the money side. I'll get compensation for my discharge and I have some savings. I have just spoken to Poppy about going to stay with her for a while, so I'll go up there on Thursday. I'll chill out there and think about what to do. I have a play I want to finish and the draft of a book I'm working on.'

'Ok mate, is there anything I can do for you?'

'I was hoping to take the DS to drive north to Poppy's. Is it in running order and more to the point is there anything I owe you?' I had found the 1966 Citroen DS Convertible in La Baule-Escoublac, when we sailed to Bordeaux in 1999. I got into a conversation with the owner of the black series two after I had noticed the sign "à vendre" on the filthy windscreen. He was a surfer preparing to head back to Paris and his job in the City. The car was dusty and appeared battered and open to the elements with surf boards abandoned on the back seats but I wanted it because I knew it was rare. We shook hands on the deal and I arranged for Jordi to pick it up at the end of the month; he took it straight to a restorer. The renovation cost me double what I paid for it, but now it was in pristine condition.

'You don't owe me anything Tez. The car is running as sweet as a nut. I took it out in August and that Vernon Verdonck bloke from the golf club offered to buy it again. I told him it wasn't for sale at any price. It was serviced at the end of October and also passed its MOT last month so it could do with a good run out. I have left all the paperwork and the keys in the file in your apartment. I will move my bike from the garage so you can get the car out without a problem when you leave.'

'Thanks mate, do I owe you anything?'

'No, some of the bills have gone up and we needed to have some sails replaced on the boat but this was all within budget.'

I finish my drink and stand to leave. 'Ok, mate thanks again for looking after things for me I really appreciate it. I'll drop another cheque in to you to cover things whilst I'm away. I don't know when I'll be back.' The thought of spending some time in the studio at my sister's and writing again seemed like the most wonderful idea.

Jordi gives me a big man hug as I walk back into the shop and prepare to leave. 'Sorry you lost your job mate, but I'm sure you'll be fine. Enjoy the time with your sister and her family.'

'Cheers buddy,' I say as I leave the shop and turn left to the entrance to my apartment. The three sets of stairs have never been a challenge to me before but now the damage to my lungs is evident as I find myself out of breath by the turn of each flight.

*

I spend most of the next day sleeping. The events in Iraq and their aftermath have taken their toll on me. The explosion, my injuries and the shock of Eddie's death were devastating, but the political 'cover up' and my sudden discharge were the ultimate kick in the bollocks. In addition, the drugs from the military hospital haven't quite worn off so my body is telling me it's time to shut down and rest.

On Wednesday I awake feeling refreshed. The weather is bright and clear with the sun's rays bouncing off the sea making me feel brighter. I decide to follow Jordi's advice and take the car for a run before the long journey north tomorrow.

The car looks immaculate when I remove the covers and reveal the deep black shine of the body work. I lower the hood, clip the protective cover in place and turn the key. It starts first time. The cold air bites into my face as I emerge from the garage and pull away, but the ancient heater and my favourite tweed jacket keep the chill from my body. I have time to think about the plot of my book during my journey along the coast, before stopping at a bar on the sea front. I sit with a drink and a cigar overlooking the beach, hearing the occasional strike of a golf ball on the links behind me. The tranquillity is punctured by my coughing as my lungs struggle to cope with the smoke but there is no way I am going to give up on a Monte Cristo. I decide to set off back as grey rain clouds start to gather.

Arriving at the apartment at dusk, I make a quick meal and read through my discharge papers as I eat. I later place the documents, my passport, pistol and foreign currency carefully into the old box that has been with me since I was a boy. I seal it and put it on the shelf in the storage cupboard, and start packing for my journey. I fill a holdall with clothes, some important papers and my ancient laptop.

I check the folder containing my story ideas. There is the original version of The Philately Phairy, a children's tale, which I wrote in crayon when I was eleven. A plan for a play based on a detective story by Laurie R King. A draft of a trilogy of stories based on Aaron Jacks, a man whose Christian name innocently causes disaster. Then finally, a maritime love story about a famous ghost ship whose working title is "The Amazon."

*

I leave the apartment on the afternoon of the 23rd December after crossing out the date on the calendar above the sink in the kitchen. Jordi is serving some customers when, as promised, I go in to give him an envelope with a brief note and a cheque. He waves and shouts. 'Have a great Christmas buddy.'

'You too mate, I'm not sure when I'll be back but I'll definitely return to take the boat out with you soon.'

I get in my car and set off towards the north, with Stephen Pendleton's suicide at the front of my mind.

Chapter 13

I begin to feel a strange sense of detachment and unsteadiness as I drive to Gramplington to spend Christmas with Poppy. I reflect on losing my job and recall the headlines about the hardest and most gifted soldier that I ever met.

'Special forces veteran Stephen Pendleton found hanged after suffering from post-traumatic stress.'

Steve joined at eighteen and spent over twenty one years in the force until a helicopter accident in Belize left him with a damaged skull. An operation to relieve some swelling was deemed a success, but his fitness was severely compromised resulting in him, like me, being discharged on medical grounds. Everyone who knew him realised he had gone to pieces at this point. He began to have major panic attacks and told his sister he was terrified about re-entering civilian life.

Although he had a loving family and a girlfriend who adored him, they couldn't fill the hole in his life created by his departure from the Marines. He just couldn't adapt to the life outside. He started drinking heavily and living rough. In the end he hanged himself less than a year after his discharge.

So what does the life and tragic death of Stephen Pendleton have to do with me? Well, if a medical discharge can so tragically affect one of the most confident men I have ever known, then what does life have in store for me? I am alarmed that my mood has plummeted to such a point that the thought of driving off the road and ending it all seems an attractive option. Yet to be honest, I feel more concerned about damaging my classic car in the quarry I just passed, than I do about destroying my life.

Although at eighteen I hadn't fully understood the implications of running away to join the Marines, I'd already been exposed to life in the forces through my father's postings in Germany. I found the life suited me perfectly. Every day was structured from the time you got up until you went to bed, and I was fortunate enough to have other interests, especially sailing, to keep me occupied on leave. Joining the SBS exposed me to extreme discipline and training but also brought me into contact with an extraordinary breed of men.

They were fit, hard and seemingly unbreakable colleagues. The camaraderie and banter allowed no evidence of weakness. Any story about someone in the forces suffering from stress or a similar problem was met with derision. "Weak bastard," the usual comment. There could be no chink in our armour. We all knew of Marines who had successfully gone back into society after a medical discharge and allegedly got on well. Those that didn't were forgotten and rarely discussed.

I don't think the enormity of my discharge had sunk in when they gave me the news. It had all happened in a blur but now I have left the safety of the hospital, I feel lost, depressed and abandoned. I am detached from reality as I try to clear my head and decide what I am going to do with my life.

I entered the military world effectively as a child, and now thirteen years later, will have to fend for myself. I've been told I qualify for compensation due to the difference between my fitness levels now, i.e. after the explosion, and when I joined. And my pension will be considerably increased due to my injury being long term, but money doesn't seem to be important to me now.

I am too proud to accept the offers of help that were made available to me. I'm not interested in an appointment with the psychiatric staff to check out my mental health, nor do I want rehabilitation treatment to prepare me for civilian life. I know these offers of support are there for a reason; who would know better than they, the devastating effect that leaving can have on someone? But I, like many before me, am too macho to accept it.

Their parting gift was a letter referring me to the county hospital should I require help in the future, and a bag containing lubricant drops for my eye, an inhaler for my chest and some boxes of pills.

*

I arrive at Poppy's in the early evening, light a cigarette and pause for a moment outside the front of the house marvelling at the flashing lights around the front door and the heart shaped holly wreath hanging on the brass centre knob. Inside is a brightly decorated Christmas tree, which takes up half of the front window; the room beyond looks warm and homely but most of all inviting. The dark cloud of gloom, so dense within me on the journey here, begins to dissipate.

Jacob has done an amazing job renovating this three storey Victorian property. He bought it in an auction and found very little had been changed in over a hundred years. Although he has totally renovated it, he has managed to retain most of the period features and created a magnificent home in the process. It became known as the "Skiphouse" because of the length of time a metal container was situated outside. The neighbours joked it would qualify for its own postcode one day.

I was going to drive around to the rear of the house and leave the car near the garage beside Jacobs's workshop, but decide instead to get out now, so as not to delay being with my sister and her family any longer. I grab my bag from the backseat, lock the car and try to jog up the steps to the front door but I am out of breath before I reach the top. While taking a second to recover I realise I haven't brought any gifts. My thoughts are rudely interrupted when the door shoots inwards and Poppy bursts out in the opposite direction. She shouts, 'Tez!' as she throws her arms around me. What on earth was I thinking earlier when I thought I had nothing to live for? Wouldn't I rather be here in my sister's arms than in a crumpled heap at the bottom of a quarry? She starts to pull away from me but I hold on for just a couple of moments longer. I give her an extra special squeeze and sigh as reluctantly I release her.

'It's wonderful to be here Pops. You look so well.'

She looks so happy and content. I know she is delighted to see me but can tell there is also an inner peacefulness I wish I possessed. She is wearing pyjama bottoms and a lime green woollen cardigan, (the victim of countless washes at the wrong temperature), hangs from her shoulders like a deflated windsock; she would need arms about three feet long to reach the pockets which are nearly at ankle level.

'Come in for a moment, put your bag down then I'll help you bring the rest of your stuff in.' I don't get a chance to tell her I have nothing else to bring in as she continues. 'What's wrong with your eye?'

'Nothing really, it's just a bit of conjunctivitis. I haven't got anything else to bring in Pops, I'm travelling light. Has Flash got the key to the garage?'

'He's out delivering a desk he's restored for someone as a Christmas present. He's got the key with him, so you'll have to sort the car out later when he gets back.'

We go into the kitchen and sit at the table to talk while we have a drink. There are toys, papers and piles of clothes scattered all over the surface. I can't believe that someone like me, who has been steeped in precision, order and discipline for so long, can find joy in this chaos. I am wallowing in the comfort of "home" when a droplet of water splashes on my forehead; I look up to see garments drying on a laundry maid. The warmth from the wood burning iron stove makes me feel sleepy but incredibly comfortable. I'm so happy to be here. We talk about the family and what they've all been up to. I say I am keen to see the girls and she explains that they are asleep but I can spend time with them tomorrow. Then the inevitable question comes winging my way.

'So, how come we have this big surprise of you being here for Christmas?'

'Well, basically, I left the Marines on Monday.' Poppy lets out a gasp and her eyes widen as I continue, 'so I thought how I'd love to be with you all.'

'You've left? I don't believe it Tez. I thought you loved it.'

'I do. Sorry, I did love it but there was an accident, which meant I had to leave.'

'Oh my God, were you hurt?'

I tell her the lies about the blast in the factory and the battery acid vapours and that I am not really bothered about leaving. I play down the damage to my lungs and my weeping left eye, my subsequent medical discharge and the fact that a couple of hours ago I wanted to "do a Pendleton." She starts to make a fuss but I just reiterate that I'm happy, and that government cuts are really to blame, and quickly change the subject.

'Did you mean it when you said that I could stay as long as I want?'

'Yes of course, why?'

'Well while I'm here I want to take the opportunity to finish a play that I'm working on, and have a go at a book I've drafted. I promise I'll stay out of the way.'

'Tez, it'll be wonderful to have you here. What are the play and book about?'

'The play is called, "Pirate." It's about a female detective called Mary Russell who investigates a dodgy company making a film of Gilbert and Sullivan's "Pirates of Penzance." I've based it on an original story by Laurie King.'

'Sounds interesting. I know our amateur dramatic society is looking for new plays to perform in the next couple of years or so.'

This takes me by surprise. 'Whoa! Hang on a minute sis, that's jumping the gun a bit.'

'Is it? You know you've always been gifted with your stories, so why not a play?'

'My stories were nothing special.'

'Tesla Coyne, don't you dare say that! We both know Mum stole some of your ideas for her most successful publications and in any case, like a lot of other societies we're always on the lookout for new stuff to try, so let me have a read when you've done it. What have you got to lose?'

'Ok.'

She continues, 'You mentioned a book as well?'

'Yes, it's called, "The Amazon," it's a romantic mystery. Don't want to say much more about it though.'

'Ok, listen you can stay as long as you want. I can't wait to read what you've written. Go and make yourself comfortable. Jake will be home in an hour or so, we can eat then.'

'Ok, I'll go and freshen up while you're getting the meal ready.'

I take my time walking up the stairs. I am stunned at how such a short climb can leave me so breathless. It's ironic though that it doesn't stop me going into the studio, opening the window and lighting a cigarette. The smoke bites into my chest as I inhale; I decide to blame the pain on the freezing night air. Perhaps I should give up as the medical officer had suggested. Poppy doesn't like me smoking so I flick the stub into the garden and watch the arc of the red ember as it lands in a children's sandpit below. "Piggin Doggin." I think to myself as I close the window. I'll have to make sure I remove it tomorrow.

I put my clothes away, take my wash bag into the en suite bathroom and have a quick shower. There's a sharp pain in my foot as I step behind the door to grab a towel. A small, circular piece of metal sticking into my heel turns out to be a tiny gold earring with a green stone in the band. I get dressed and put it in my trouser pocket before making my way downstairs.

The amazing aroma of Poppy's cooking is enticing me, but I stop on the first floor landing next to an open door. I can hear the breathing of the two infants within. One is rhythmic and peaceful whilst the other is erratic and fitful. I put my face into the gap, taking care not to push the door any wider in case the hinges cry out and wake them.

There is no smell of food cooking here. The fuzz of warm blankets, boiled milk and vomit hangs in the air. I can just make out their shape in the beds so obviously made by their dad, with their initials carefully chiselled into the middle of each end panel. There is very little movement from the one with an 'A' on it, but the other with an 'E' actually rocks at one point, as the covers are kicked from one side to the other. I pull away and continue down and into the kitchen.

As I enter, Poppy smiles at me and takes the lid off an enormous saucepan. The all-too familiar stench slams into my face like a wall. Garlic!! Panic wells up in my throat as I remember the blast and the gas burning my lungs. I make a choking sound as I try to back away to escape the pungent smell.

She says, 'You OK? You've gone pale?'

I take a second or so to recover my composure. 'Yea fine, it's just the smell of the cooking; it reminds me of the explosion and the battery acid.' I know it sounds ridiculous as I say it, but this is the best excuse I can think of. She is frowning so I say, 'Seriously Sis, I'm fine. It was weird but the fumes smelt just like garlic.'

She relaxes and smiles. 'Blimey, I didn't realise my cooking was that bad.'

I laugh. 'It's OK, I'm going to have to get used to it. I can't wait to taste it.' I pull back a chair and sit down.

'Pour some wine for us both will you?' she says and turns back to the stove.

The table has three place settings, candles and an open bottle of wine. The space has been achieved by pushing the papers, toys and clothes into an untidy pile at the end nearest the wall. 'Yes of course. By the way, I found an earring in the bathroom,' I say as I fill a couple of the glasses with the wine. The label says "Elderberry Wine – Chez Flood – 2003." I prepare myself for the first sip. Their homemade wine has won awards and almost killed people; it depends on luck and which batch you are offered!

'Oh that must be Gracie's. She stayed over with Dick at the weekend. She didn't mention she had lost one though.' She comes over and picks up the glass and takes a deep quaff. 'Mmmm delicious,' she says as she takes it over to the cooker.

'Well someone did,' I say as I hold it up to show her. I sip the wine cautiously; it is surprisingly good. 'Who's Gracie?'

'You know her. Grace Skyler, Faith's twin sister. I used to play with them all the time when I was little. She had a crush on you.'

I laugh as I recall the disagreement between us from years ago. 'Well what about you and her brother Sebastian?'

'Don't start that again, he never showed any interest in me, besides he moved to Greece years ago and I'm more than content with my Jake thank you.'

'I remember them now, they were very pretty girls. Grace was very quiet and a bit timid but Faith seemed a bit wild even a bit unhinged at times.'

'That's right. Grace married Richard Perritano and Faith basically went off the rails.'

'Perritano! Isn't that the bloke who made a fortune from buying disused farm equipment? He renovated the good stuff and sold the rest for scrap?'

'Yes.'

'That's right, I remember him when he used to go riding at weekends; always jovial and friendly. Didn't he pass the business to his sons years ago?'

'Yes. Two of the lads went to university before joining the company but the eldest, Richard, joined straight from school.' There is a definite edge to her voice when she mentions him.

'I met him a few times; a big, athletic looking guy. He strutted around like he owned the planet but he seemed ok, maybe a bit arrogant but I guess that's understandable if you get things handed to you on a plate.'

'No, not necessarily, Don and Marcus didn't let their dad's help affect them at all, they're really level headed. Dick on the other hand, does appear to be dynamic, attractive and very charming but there is a side to him I just don't like. It's hard to explain but I can just about put up with him in small doses.'

I am confused. 'So why do you socialise with him and let him stay here if he irritates you so much?'

'Because it's the only way I can really get to see Gracie.'

'What do you mean?'

'She hardly ever goes out without him or his mother, Isabella, being with her. Isabella is the true head of the family by the way, a real battle-axe. It's as if they're watching Grace all the time.'

'That's a bit odd.'

'I know. She used to be able to meet up for a coffee or go shopping with me but this has gradually changed to the point that I don't even embarrass her by asking anymore.'

'Is she afraid of them?'

'I don't know. She never complains and appears happy but it just doesn't feel right. She never says anything negative to me; it's just a feeling I get.' I think Poppy must be exaggerating. 'I'll introduce you to them soon, especially if you get involved with the GADS. They're both members.'

'GADS?'

'Gramplington Amateur Dramatics...'

'Oh yes, of course,' I interrupt as I realise the abbreviation. It would be nice to see Grace Skyler again; I wonder how she has changed. 'How did you and Jacob get involved with them?'

'By accident really, we both pitched in ages ago to help Gracie but now Jacob has ended up doing most of the scenery and carpentry and I help with the costumes.'

'OK, I would like to get involved. By the way, whatever happened to Faith Skyler?'

'She's back in prison.'

'Prison, again! Gosh, it just shows how out of touch I've been whilst I've been in the Marines. I remember the time she really rattled me.'

'How did she do that?'

'The Skyler's were over at our house one day; they were playing with you downstairs. I bumped into Faith when I came down for drink. I don't think I'll ever forget the chilling words she whispered to me.'

Poppy turns towards me and says, 'Go on you've got my attention, what did she say?'

'She stopped me in my tracks, looked furtively over her shoulder, and fixed me with a penetrating stare and whispered. "The trees are coming to get me." I felt very uncomfortable. I started to walk past her but she held on to my arm and I could see the deep fear in her eyes. I think you called to her because she ran off. That look of hers will never leave me.'

'Well she definitely had a lot of health problems. She got in with a bad crowd, then into drugs and married at sixteen. She was arrested for possession and got sent down for dealing. She seemed to calm down for a while when released and tried for a baby but had no luck there. She found she was infertile and subsequently went off the rails again. She was apprehended for possession again, then prostitution and sent back to prison.'

'Blimey, so she's still in there?'

'Well yes, she's still in prison.' Poppy pauses and sighs. 'Although she did get out for a while but got sent back for GBH!'

'I'm getting confused.'

'She got released for good behaviour last year and went for a holiday to Sebastian's in Greece for a couple of weeks. She came back to stay with Grace and ended up being detained within hours of her arrival. She's been inside ever since.'

'What happened?'

'There are two versions. The first is – Faith arrived at "Perritano Towers"' and found Grace was absent because she was in hospital after accidentally falling downstairs and breaking her ankle.' I have a horrible flashback to what had happened in Germany. Poppy sees the sudden blaze of pain in my eyes and quickly continues. 'Faith attacked Dick with a kettle of boiling water. He said it was because she'd demanded money for drugs and erupted when he refused to give her any. This resulted in her getting arrested, she accused Dick of attempted rape but Isabella was a witness and testified against her. Everyone who knows Faith thought she should be sectioned but she was sent back to prison. God help her, the poor girl is ill.'

'So what's version two?'

'She went to stay with Grace only to find she was in hospital with a broken ankle. There was speculation by the way, that this had happened because Grace had been pushed downstairs by her "loving" husband. He tried to rape Faith when he'd got her drunk but she fought back and scalded him. He had ripped her clothes when he tried to rape her but his mother testified that they were torn when he fended her off.'

'What do you believe?' I say as I walk past her, open the back door and light a cigarette.

'I don't know for certain. I told you earlier that Grace refuses to discuss her relationship with Dick but I get a feeling there is definitely something wrong between them. A lot of people think they're the ideal couple but I've known her since she was little and I can see sadness in her eyes.' There is a loud bang down the hallway as the front door slams shut. 'That will be Jacob! I hope he doesn't wake the girls.'

I flick my cigarette into the hedge as Jacob comes into the kitchen muttering. He is clearly agitated but his demeanour changes when he sees me. 'Hi Tez, saw your car outside, it's really great to see you.' He embraces me and pats my back affectionately. 'Have you been here long?'

'No not really. I've had a shower and a chance to settle in a bit. You OK, you seem a bit stressed?'

'I'm OK, but I do need a drink.' He grabs a glass from the table, pours himself a large measure and takes a mouthful.

Poppy holds out her glass. 'You can fill ours up as well and tell us why you're in such a mood.'

He empties the rest of the bottle into our glasses and gets another from the rack. As he opens it I try to get a glimpse of the label to see if it's the good stuff. 'I'm sorry about that; I don't think I woke the girls. It's just Dick, he can be such a bastard at times.'

Poppy looks at me and raises her eyebrows. 'That's funny we've just been discussing him, what's he done this time?'

'You know the antique desk I refurbished for him?'

'Yes.'

'Well, he refused to let Grace pay for it.'

'You're joking. I thought that it was her present to him for Christmas. Surely it's up to her to settle up?'

'Well it is, but he said he wants to check it over first before he authorises the payment from her. He can be so bloody awkward at times!'

'Didn't he look it over when he stayed here?'

'Yes but I think he was still pissed when he did.' He takes another mouthful of wine. 'I think he was just showing off to Grace and his mother, mind you I won't give him the keys until he pays up.'

It was my turn to speak. 'What keys?'

'Well, whenever I fit new locks to any furniture, especially desks and cabinets I always keep a spare key. You wouldn't believe how many people contact me asking for help when they've misplaced or lost theirs. Anyway, in Dick's case, I also fitted a miniature safe in one of the drawers, so I've kept all the keys until he pays up. Call it my insurance policy.'

'You said they stayed over the other weekend, do they live a long way away?' I asked.

'No. They live in the big house on the top road on the way up to the stables and the "Gallops." 'It amuses me as he looks towards the back of the house, in the direction of the steeplechase course north of the town. He continues, 'We had a great night out with them, followed by too many drinks here afterwards, so they stayed over. Anyway, let's change the subject; we've a lot to catch up on.'

Poppy serves the food. Fortunately the pungent aroma that panicked me earlier is no longer so overpowering. We replenish our glasses and take our places at the table. The wine really is excellent but I can't resist the temptation to switch allegiance, when Jake produces a bottle of my favourite tipple; malt whisky. The hours pass as the conversation swings from the girls to amateur dramatics and then to Poppy's latest travel book.

I am so proud of her. She has always travelled extensively and written copious notes about all the locations she has visited with a special emphasis on the interesting recipes she encountered and the best local restaurants to sample them in. She had the idea one day to send some of her "guides" to the major airline companies so they could include them with their booking info. This was very successful but created a demand that she found difficult to manage after the girls were born. She now concentrates on guides to the British Isles, receiving commissions from tourist information groups across the country.

Jacob and I are left alone for a while when my sister goes upstairs to check on the girls. We discuss my car and some of the repairs I had to have done to my yacht "Sunbuoy." It sprang a leak when a board worked loose sailing back from Le Touquet in the summer.

I am on my second glass of whisky when Poppy returns. She reaches across, takes my hand in hers and raises her glass with her other. She says, 'To my big bother Tez, you being here is my best Christmas present ever! I will look after you now. Love you loads.'

Something is blocking my throat as immense joy erupts within me. The tears are back and my voice is a whisper. 'The conjunctivitis is really bad now Pops – it's in both eyes.' She stands and kisses me softly on the cheek, then playfully tugs the kiss curl on my forehead before returning to the table.

Chapter **14**

I wake early, just as I always did in the forces. It's no surprise that this continues in my civilian life regardless of how drunk I get the night before. The difference on this Christmas Eve morning however, is the crushing pain in my skull. I flap my arms in a futile attempt to push the concrete blocks off my forehead. There is nothing there of course but the simple act of moving exaggerates the intense pain. I try to cry out but my mouth is so dry it appears to be welded shut. So this is a real hangover. I realise now what they meant at my discharge when they told me that my "health had been compromised." I've never felt this bad, even after drinking twice the amount we did last night. I recall the elderberry wine and the bottle of malt Jacob and I finished before we crept upstairs, giggling as we tried not to wake the girls. I had a final cigarette at the open window, smiling broadly, as I drank a nightcap of industrial strength Russian Coffee.

I hate the idea of wasting a day so I raise my head gingerly and check my watch. I realise I have slept fully clothed, diagonally across the bed. My pillow is untouched with a wrapped chocolate upon it still awaiting my attention. A nice touch from Poppy but her drunken brother was too pissed to appreciate it. The thought of eating chocolate makes me gag.

I get up and as I make my way to my bathroom, I hear muffled voices from the landing below, so I stop and open the bedroom door quietly.

'...but why can't he come today?' It's a child's voice, sounding as if she is out of breath.

Poppy says, 'Because it's one more sleep before Santa can come.' She sounds tired.

'Not fair!'

'Calm down Emily.'

'Mum.' This voice is different, the pitch slightly lower than the first. 'What's wrong with Daddy?'

'He's not feeling very well today...'

I close the door missing the rest of the conversation. I smile as I enter the bathroom, pleased because it seems that Jacob is in as much pain as me. I clean my teeth and start to come alive after my third glass of water. My hot shower followed by a couple of minutes under an ice cold blast sets me up for the day. I dress and go downstairs and am just about to enter the kitchen when I hear the excitable voice again. I make a mental note that it's Emily. 'Whose is this yucky thing?'

'Don't be so rude, it's your Uncle Tez's.' She must have noticed my favourite jacket on the back of the chair. I love the directness of her appraisal of it.

'Mum. Who's Runcletessers?'

Poppy laughs. 'Sorry Melia. It belongs to,' she emphasises the name, 'Uncle Tesla, my brother. He has come to stay with us. You'll meet him soon, I heard him moving about upstairs.'

I realise that they won't know me. I've only seen them twice, once just after they were born and again after their first birthday. I cough as I walk into the kitchen; the two girls are sitting at the table. At first glance it appears that they are truly identical but then I notice slight differences. The one further away, has tiny freckles across the bridge of her nose. She sits quietly with a colourful picture book open in front of her. I recognise it instantly, even from this distance, because I have seen it a thousand times before. The other, nearer to me, is perched on the edge of the chair where I sat last night. She kicks her legs excitedly and pulls the sleeves of my jacket around her neck as if she is being strangled. She is making a "gagging" sound but stops when she sees me.

They stare at the stranger before them. Poppy puts down the pan she is drying and walks to me. 'Good morning,' she says as she hugs me close and plants a kiss on my cheek. 'How's the head this morning?'

'Clear as a bell.' I grin and grimace to indicate the "white lie." 'But a strong black coffee would be appreciated.'

Both the girls are silent as I walk over to my jacket, put my hand on the collar, bend forward with an exaggerated bow and say. 'Good morning Terence, I see you're giving this beautiful young lady a hug.' I close my eyes and say very slowly, in my best theatrical "séance" voice, 'Can you tell me something about these delightful girls please?' I open my eyes dramatically and say, 'Thank you, Terence.' The sleeves are instantly released when I say, 'Good morning Emmeline.' Her jaw drops and her eyes are wide as saucers at this announcement. Before she comments I turn and say, 'And good morning to you Amelia, I see you're reading a book.'

Poppy is smiling as Amelia breathlessly asks, 'How'd you know our names?'

'I know because this old, yucky thing told me.' Emmeline's eyes grow even wider and she looks a little sheepish when she hears these words. 'Ladies let me introduce you to the "Amazing Terence Tweed."'

Amelia asks, 'Is it magic?'

'Oh yes it is,' I say as I walk away from them towards the hallway. I spread my arms and announce. 'There are special times when I touch or wear him that "Amazing Terence Tweed" performs miracles and sometimes make wishes come true. He not only told me your names but other things as well.'

'Like what?' Emmeline says suspiciously.

'Well, he told me that the book that Amelia is reading is "The Philately Phairy."' She looks at the book in wonder, holds it high above her head to show her sister and mummy that I am right. 'And, Terence told me you're both very excited about his friend Santa Claus coming tomorrow but he knows that you, Emmeline, would like him to come today.'

She turns in her chair, closes her eyes and addresses my ancient tweed garment. '"Mr Tweed" make Santa come today?' She opens her eyes; they are shining with expectation.

I walk over, put it on and I give a little shimmy as if a spell cascades through me. 'I'm sorry girls but he says it's impossible for Santa to come today.'

'Why?' they both say in unison.

'Because there are gazillions of little girls around the world expecting surprises on Christmas morning. The "Amazing Terence Tweed" can't use his magic against that kind of power even if he wanted too.'

Poppy hands me my drink and says, 'Right girls, that's settled. Santa will still come tomorrow if you're good. Leave Uncle Tez alone now and have your cereal.' I'm grateful for the interruption before I get out of my depth. Already I can see they will be a challenge, especially Emmeline, and they aren't even three years old yet.

Just as I am about to go outside, I hear a deep sigh from the hallway. 'Daddy!' The girls shout as they jump down from the table and run to Jacob who is standing in the doorway. He looks terrible and stumbles when they slam into him, wrapping their arms around his legs.

'Gorning mirls.' He manages a smile as he attempts a bit of humour.

He visibly winces as they scream. 'Talk properly Daddy!'

'Sorry girls, come on let's sit down, I need a drink.' Amelia goes back to her book but Emmeline sits on his knee and strokes his forehead. She looks like she's petting a puppy.

'Head hurt?'

'Yes darling.' He gives her a big squeeze and smiles as Poppy places a steaming cup of coffee in front of him. He looks at me. 'Have you met the girls Tez?' He hugs her again and continues before I can answer. 'This little devil is Melia and the bookworm over there is Emily.'

I think for a nanosecond that I got their names wrong earlier but the "bookworm" shakes her head, gives a long sigh and says in an exasperated voice. 'Daddy's got us mixed up again Mummy.'

'I know Melia, he's a silly Daddy.' Poppy smiles as I walk past her to open the back door.

I go into the garden for a smoke and start to retrieve the butts, (discarded from my third floor window,) and throw them under the hedge. I think about the tremendous warmth that has enveloped me since arriving here yesterday and marvel at the affection that the twins enjoy. I can't help wishing that I had been loved like Emily and Melia. My parents made me feel like a discarded cigarette.

*

It's Christmas Eve and the energy of the girls seems to increase proportionately as bedtime approaches. They positively sparkle with excitement when they are tucked under their duvets. We can hear them whispering and giggling for hours as the three of us sit quietly drinking wine. I deliberately limit my intake to two glasses; I want to be clear headed for the next day. We take it in turns to wrap and hide presents whilst listening for the approach of tiny feet on the creaky stairs.

It's well past midnight when the silence becomes deafening and we take this as our cue to bring in the girls' main present. Jacob and I cross the rear garden to his workshop and silently open the doors. I can make out a white sheet hiding something; I imagine it's a huge rabbit hutch until he removes the cover. It is the stable that Poppy had mentioned he made out of an old wardrobe. I can tell he has done a remarkable job, even in this poor light. 'Welcome to the Bethlehem Hotel,' he says as we take a corner each and walk back towards the house.

'It's wonderful...' I want to say more but the breathlessness returns. My chest burns as I try to cram more air into my lungs.

Jacob says, 'I've treated it, so that it can be an outdoor playhouse, in the summer.'

Poppy is waiting at the open French doors as we enter and place it in the centre of the playroom. We adorn it with tinsel and a giant pink bow. Poppy puts her arms around Jacobs's neck and kisses him deeply. 'You're so clever Mr Flood, the girls are very lucky.' She holds his hand as she makes her way out of the room. I make my way upstairs as they turn off the lights before following me up. As I begin to climb the stairs to my floor I hear two clicks. I shiver and feel a trickle of sweat run down my back as the sound instantly reminds me of the Bravo team call sign before we discovered the cave in Iraq. I turn to see Jake snapping his fingers to attract my attention. Poppy is next to him, waving me back. When I re-join them they take me into the girls' bedroom and I understand why they want me to see them. Both girls are on Melia's bed, lying on top of the covers. It looks as if they have been dropped from a great height. There is no movement, just deep breathing. They are obviously exhausted from keeping each other awake so late. Poppy puts a spare duvet over them and whispers as she ushers us out of the room. 'Leave them as they are, we don't want to wake them.' I start to creep back upstairs. 'Night Tez, I'm so happy you're here.'

I turn, and as I look down at her face I know I will never forget this moment. My whole being is full of a wonderful but alien feeling. My voice breaks with emotion when I whisper. 'Night Pops that was the best day...' I pause for a moment as I hold her attention, '...ever.' She blows me a kiss as I turn and make my way to bed.

*

Excited voices greet me as I awake on Christmas morning. At first I think I've overslept but my watch confirms that it is my usual time. The voices are accompanied by the hammering of two pairs of tiny feet running along the landing below. I hear Jake shout, 'It's too early; he won't have been yet,'

'We go and look?' I am sure this voice is Melia's.

'No! Go back to your room; we'll all go down in a bit.'

'Aw.' I am certain that's Emily. 'Please?'

'Come on, back into your bedrooms.' Poppy is up. 'Let's get your dressing gowns on; we'll go down in a minute when Daddy is ready.' I hear a distinct groan from Jacob as the girls cheer. It sounds like Poppy is at the bottom of my stairs. 'I hope Uncle Tez is up.' The emphasis in her voice makes this sound more like an order than a statement. I jump out of bed and hurry into the bathroom. I wash and dress quickly, realising it has been spelt out to me that I am family and I have to be there.

*

There is pandemonium on that special morning when the girls discover that Santa Claus did indeed call and leave presents for them. Poppy sits carefully next to the tree and hands out the presents one by one. She winces as one of the needles from the tree penetrates her pyjamas. The unwrapping is furious but I love the way both of them pause when they discover each of them has the same present as the other. It hadn't crossed my mind until now that buying the twins identical gifts avoids conflict and jealousy.

Christmas carols are playing in the background as Jacob and Poppy trade kisses for their respective "surprises" and I genuinely feel awkward when the girls hand me mine. I regret

169

not having bought anything for them when I discover the fifteen year old malt and a box of my favourite Monte Cristo cigars.

Things begin to settle when all the presents have been handed out and the girls focus on their favourites. Melia unsurprisingly, sits on the floor and leans back against a chair reading a story to her new doll from a pristine picture book. Emily on the other hand, is a bundle of energy as she ignores Jacobs's protests and begins to eat some chocolate from a selection box. She has put some of the wrapping paper on her head to act as a crown as she walks around the room humming an indistinguishable tune. She stops at the sliding doors to the playroom, reaches for the handle and says, 'Why shut?'

'We've another surprise for you,' Poppy says as she stands and moves quickly to the door. There is a blur as Melia flashes across the room to join her sister. They are both giggling and bouncing on the spot, full of excitement. Jacob joins Poppy and they hold a handle each. 'Now try and calm down and close your eyes.' I can see that one has her eyes screwed shut but the other is peeping. 'Emmeline Flood! Close your eyes.' She eventually complies as Poppy says, 'Dah dah!' They slide the doors apart.

They open their eyes and scream with joy when they see the stable. 'Is that where baby Jesus was born?'

'Yes Melia,' Jacob says as he smiles at me. 'It's Uncle Tez's special present for you.'

I am about to protest at his selfless gesture but Poppy shakes her head. "No" is her silent message to me as the girls squeal with delight. Their faces beam when they look at me, Melia says, 'Thank you Runcletez,' as they run to explore the stable and its contents.

I try to express my gratitude but Poppy just waves me away and says, 'There'll always be room at the inn for my special brother.' I manage to hold myself together but when "Away in a Manger" comes on the stereo; I have to go outside for a cigarette because it's just too much to bear. The serenity on Melia's face as she rocks to sleep one of her new dolls (that is now christened "Baby Jesus"), reminds me of my dead brother. I miss him so much.

The stable is a stroke of genius as it keeps the girls occupied for hours. I am drafted in as one of "the cattle are lowing," but am soon dumped because I am too big to get inside and don't for the life of me know how to "low."

The turkey dinner is followed by chocolate, cashew nuts and champagne. I get a proper chance to explore their house as the Christmas songs continue, occasionally interspersed with the odd contribution from Led Zeppelin and Leonard Cohen; Jacob and Poppy's respective choices. I marvel at the racks of books including the section dedicated to her travel journals. I love the sound of the ticking clocks, the smell of the joss sticks and the family clutter. I feel as if I belong.

In the afternoon, I sit quietly in a huge wingback chair with a large measure of malt. I feel a special bond already with the girls when I see the happiness in their faces as they come and sit on my knee after the lavish dinner. Melia shows me Baby Jesus and Emily tugs at the curl on my forehead. The highlight comes later when they both lie quietly on either side of me as I read them a story. Poppy catches my eye and silently applauds; I know instinctively this is because they are both quiet and settled. Soon after, I notice they are both asleep, so I put my arms around them, settle back and close my eyes.

*

I am dreaming about the Virgin Mary giving birth to twin girls and the three wise men bringing gifts of whisky, travel books and joss sticks when I feel a gentle, rhythmic pressure on my shoulder. I am a little groggy when I open one eye, (the other is glued shut with pus again) and see Jacob cupping a hand to his ear and mouthing "phone." Carefully, he helps me to move the sleeping girls. I leave the room wondering who could be calling me. I pick up the phone in the hallway and whisper, 'Hello.'

'Happy Christmas!'

'Oh.' It's Jordi, how did he get this number? 'Same to you mate.'

'You don't sound like you're with it. Are you ok?'

'Yes. Sorry, I've just woken up. This is a nice surprise.'

'I was concerned when you left mate, I've never seen you looking so down.' I remember the image of my death wish; my car leaving the road and smashing into the quarry. 'I tried calling your mobile a couple of times to see if you'd got to your sister's ok, but didn't have any luck. I really began to worry when there was no answer and then I remembered the call you made from the shop and luckily her number was still in the call list.'

'Oh bollocks, sorry about that, I had to hand the old mobile phone back to the Marines. I kept the memory card for when I replace it; I'll give you a call with the new number.'

'OK. So how are you?'

'What?'

'I asked, are you Ok?'

Poppy comes into the hall and picks up some muddy boots. 'Yes buddy, I'm more than ok, I'm very happy here.' She stands and turns to look directly at me, aware that the words were really intended for her. 'You were right about how I looked when I left you. I don't mind admitting I was a bit depressed about my health and felt pretty shitty after losing my job, but being here has put things into perspective. 'Poppy walks to me, she has tears in her eyes as she stretches up to kiss my cheek. 'I'm actually thinking about staying here indefinitely, to work on the writing I mentioned to you, if they'll have me.' It's my turn to smile as my twenty seven year old sister bounces on the spot like a child, waving her arms in the air as she silently shouts, "yes, yes, yes, yes, yes, yes, yes, yes, yes, yes, yes."

'Good for you. Let me have your address when you call me with your new number and I'll forward any important mail to you in the New Year.'

'Ok, will do. I'll try to get down in the summer; perhaps we can take "Sunbuoy" out?'

'Abso-fuckin-lutely.'

I go into the kitchen after we have said our goodbyes to find Jacob waiting for me. 'Poppy and I both feel the same way; you're welcome to stay here as long as you want. This is your home now.'

Poppy comes into the kitchen beaming with happiness. Jacob walks towards the French doors with some tools. He gives Poppy a tender kiss and pats her backside as he leaves to go to his workshop. She smiles deliciously at her loving husband as I "anchor" the memory of the time since I arrived here, as one of the happiest in my life.

*

I go for a long walk on Boxing Day with a happy chatter of thoughts about the twins and my new life at Poppy's. Ideas for my book and the play also bounce freely around my head, along with plans for my future. I make my way up towards the "Gallops" with all the subjects jostling for attention. I absentmindedly step out into an avenue heading towards the public footpath, just as a large SUV sweeps out of a gravelled drive, alarming me. I turn just in time to see the passenger; she is beautiful. Our eyes meet for an instant, I feel a jolt as I realise she looks familiar.

I light a cigarette and watch as the gates swing noisily towards me. There is a loud metallic judder as they slam shut; I notice the ostentatious brass plaque on the pillar.

"PERRITANO"

Chapter 15

I am standing in the hallway after returning from my early morning walk, delighted that my fitness level seems to be improving. Poppy and Jacob are in the lounge discussing the GADS New Year's Eve party. Jacob sounds exasperated. 'Well we both can't go Pops! Why don't you take Tez? I bet he'd love to go with you to meet the crowd.' I cough discreetly to announce I am there, I don't want them to think I'm ear wigging.

Jacob says, 'Oh you're back. How do you fancy putting your glad rags on for a party on Friday night?' Poppy appears to be excited as I enter and sit in my favourite chair. The twins are on my lap in an instant.

'Why can't you both go?' I say as I tickle the girls, making them giggle.

'There are two very good reasons on your knee. Our babysitter Suzanne has just returned with a dose of dysentery after spending Christmas in Goa. It's too late to get anyone else, so I thought you might like to go with Poppy. I'll look after the girls and a very large glass of malt while you're out.'

I give the twins a hug as I say, 'I have a better idea, why don't I look after them? You can go together, have a nice time and I will have the girls and…' I pause for dramatic effect, 'that large glass of malt.'

The girls sit up straight, twitching excitedly. Emily says, 'Please say yes Mum,' Melia pleads, 'Let Runcletez look after us Dad. Please!'

174

Poppy shakes her head. 'No girls. Uncle Tez has only just got here, it isn't fair to…'

'…I would be honoured Sis.'

The girls continue their urgent request. I feel a rare emotion of being wanted. Jacob and Poppy look at each other and nod.

Poppy says 'Ok.' The girls cheer and snuggle back down beside me.

*

I have no idea what time Poppy and Jacob got in last night but they are still in bed after lunchtime when the girls and I decide to go for a walk. I am pleased they are having some time to themselves and delighted to be alone with my nieces. It is brilliantly bright with no wind reducing the temperature on this crisp cold day. I find a pub about a mile away with a play area and watch the girls on the swings while I chain smoke and drink Guinness with brandy chasers. They complain of being cold so I buy them both a hot chocolate with a marshmallow on top and a bag of crisps. The light is beginning to fail when we head back. Melia skips ahead of us as Emily grips my finger and chatters about how much she loves chocolate.

We have just come out of the park as a car is pulling away from the house. It is only when I see the passenger that I realise it is the same car that had startled me on Boxing Day. This time there seems to be a smile in her eyes as she sails past. I am still thinking about her when we open the front door and are met by enveloping warmth and the aroma of spices from the incense burners.

'Here they are,' Poppy shouts towards the back of the house, presumably to Jacob. She says to the girls, 'Have you had an adventure?' They nod enthusiastically. I think "Phew" as I am grateful they didn't say I just sat and drank whilst they played. She addresses me. 'You're a godsend, thank you for looking after them. I'm afraid we had a very late night.'

'No problem, I've had a great time with them. Have you just had a visitor?'

'Yes it was the Perritano's. I told them you were out with the girls; they said they're keen to meet you, it's a shame you missed them. Dick went into the workshop with Jacob to get the keys for the desk as Grace gave me the cash. She was actually alone with me for a couple of minutes. I was laughing when I told her to look out for a handsome, limping man with two little girls when she was driving home.'

'Why?'

'I gave her the earring you found and told her you're permanently scarred after standing on it in the bathroom.'

'And what did she say?'

'Just that, "she's really sorry about crippling you." I definitely saw a twinkle in her eye when I mentioned you; I think she still has a soft spot for my big brother.'

'Don't be silly,' I say, throwing my coat on the banister and hurriedly going upstairs. I lie on the bed feeling tired after my day with the girls. The brandy begins to kick in as I drift towards sleep. I playback Poppy's comment and quietly say, 'Soft spot? Ridiculous.' Yet I have to admit, that the sparkle in Grace Perritano's eyes is haunting my final conscious thought.

*

I soon settle into a routine at Poppy's. I enjoy my first cigarette of the day as I lean out of the bedroom window reviewing the weather. Heavy rain means a walk to the fitness centre about a mile away for an early swim or a session in the gym. Dry conditions signal a quick breakfast followed by my favourite, a walk.

I usually go through the park opposite the house and down to the river. Turning right takes me down to a bridge which I cross and follow the path to the weir before joining an old farm track and continuing back to Poppy's. A left turn at the riverbank takes me through the village towards the stables at the bottom of the hill continuing on a circular route which leads back to the park. Thursday is when I pass through the stables and head up towards the "Gallops," an old steeplechase course. I always stop at the last house on the top road and look out for a speeding car before I cross in front of the "Perritano" driveway. I then climb up the footpath to watch the horses early morning training sessions and take in the view across the plain.

I try to get back before seven thirty as I love being there when the girls wake up. I help with the breakfast and enjoy trying to keep them amused whilst their parents prepare for their respective day's activities. I relish being a part of their lives and know my help is appreciated during the early morning chaos. Poppy normally takes care of the girls for the rest of the day while Jacob is in his workshop and I sit at the writing desk in my room. But when the deadline for Poppy's next book looms, my role as babysitter becomes more involved.

I care for the girls until early afternoon when Poppy takes over from me. This enables her to get on with her writing and allows me to spend the rest of the day working on the "Pirate". This arrangement is particularly advantageous to Jacob who can concentrate on his renovations in the workshop and his deliveries without having to be drafted in to perform child minding at a moment's notice. I offer to keep the same morning schedule when the girls start "Tiny Tots Nursery".

People joke that you can probably see the small village hall from outer space, on account of the garish artwork along the side of the building. The cats, dogs and farmyard animals are all depicted in primary colours along the walls, but the "pièce de résistance" is the giant snail at the door, its open mouth forming the entrance. How children avoid having nightmares is beyond me. I take the girls across the park and deliver them to the psychedelic gastropod before returning to the house.

I spend the mornings writing next to my open window, often hearing Jacobs's music as it blasts from his workshop and sears across the garden, only to be met by the acoustic melancholy from Poppy's study. My own taste in music has been resurrected by an act of kindness from Jordi. I had mentioned to him months ago, that I missed the collection of CDs I had left in the apartment; he proceeded to download the majority of my favourites onto a MP3 player as a surprise and send it to me.

Midday is the time the "Floods" meet in the kitchen to prepare lunch and it's my cue to return to the nursery to pick up the girls. Whilst walking across the park one day I speak to Mana for the first time.

*

My compulsion to be with women is as strong as ever. I chalk up numerous relationships as the months turn into a year at Poppy's. There are many female visitors to the house and I'm introduced to lots of people when out and about with either Poppy or Jacob. I find the most success in meeting eligible women in some of the more vibrant bars around town, with the gym and swimming pool also providing some nice encounters. There is, however, never any permanency in these relationships; they all just seem to fizzle out because they just don't excite me enough.

Poppy tells me that female "tongues are wagging" about her mysterious brother who suddenly appeared from nowhere. She is asked so many questions about me that the innocent snippets of information she supplies result in me becoming the most eligible bachelor in town. The rumour is that the man with the "kiss curl," is a rich war hero who drives a classic car and spends his spare time writing. Playing down this perception when I am in company has the opposite effect; it just increases the favourable glances from interested women.

I try to avoid flirting with the mothers at the nursery even though some of them are extremely attractive and make it very obvious that they are "available." I do however make one exception, for Manami Tanimoto.

I notice she always walks to school, unlike the majority of the mothers who drive. I am seriously attracted to her; she is small and slim and her body has a tautness that makes her look incredibly athletic. Her olive complexion and sharp oriental features are dominated by her eyes. They are virtually the same colour as her jet black hair, which is held back with double pins at her forehead. I particularly like her femininity; she wears either a skirt or a dress every day. I never see her in jeans or those awful grey tracksuit bottoms favoured by many of the mothers who can't be bothered to make an effort when they dress in the morning. Keen to learn more about her I mention to Poppy, that I have noticed a beautiful "oriental child" in the nursery.

Poppy guesses that the little girl is called Sora and tells me that her mum has a complicated name, so is known simply as "Mana." She moved here from Tokyo over a decade ago to open a Sushi bar with her husband but it all went horribly wrong and resulted in bankruptcy and an impending divorce. She decided to stay here for the sake of Sora when her husband went back to Japan. Poppy says she speaks fractured English and thinks that she may have a partner, as she has seen her walking with a man in the village from time to time.

I'd learned some basic Japanese just before I decided to study Mandarin all those years ago. Even though a career as an interpreter bit the dust, I am amazed that substantial amounts of foreign languages still remain so clear in my memory.

I plan the walk to the nursery with the girls, to coincide with her leaving her house. I am successful one bright spring morning when she appears before me as she shuts her gate. Our eyes meet, I smile as I say, 'Ohayou.' She looks shocked.

A flash of panic courses through me as I think "Maybe Poppy has got her nationality wrong." Is she offended? She might be Thai or Vietnamese or, or, or…

I am so relieved when she breaks into a dazzling smile and says, 'Ohayou.' I realise she'd looked shocked because she was startled to hear a westerner speaking her language.

I spread my arms as I look up to the heavens, an exaggerated look of wonder on my face. I can feel the sun's warmth on my face as it peeks from behind the clouds in the pale blue sky. A plane leaves a trail as it crosses high above us, and swallows dart and swoop around our heads. I turn to her, smile and utter the word I hope will describe this amazing morning. 'Kirei ne?'

Her face lights up with joy as she looks around and nods. 'Sou ne,' she says as she clasps her hands together at her chest and bows forward repeatedly. 'Sou ne,' she says again and repeats the actions. I have only said two words to her and believe I am in total control but I am wrong.

I am silently congratulating myself on being an "Ace Seducer" and formulating the sentence to introduce myself when the moment is broken by Emily. 'Why you talking rubbish? Sound like Daddy!' Mana must understand some English because she bursts out laughing, but not in a way to cause offence to my cheeky niece.

I kneel down to give Emily a hug; Melia rushes to my side as she doesn't want to be left out. I'm holding them both closely as I say, 'I was speaking Japanese to this beautiful lady…' I flash a quick smile at her. "Nice touch" I think as our eyes meet. '…saying what a gorgeous day it is.' I am feeling pretty pleased with myself, especially with the girls showing what a wonderful father figure I am. I stand and begin to usher them towards the village hall. I look over my shoulder and nod as I say, 'Sayōnara.'

'Sayōnara,' she echoes as she bows again, points at me and says, 'Namae wa?'

I say, 'Tesla Coyne.' As I turn to leave, I can see her mouth trying to form the words of my name. 'Have a good day, Manami Tanimoto,' I say in English just to throw her a little. It looks as if the trouble I had taken to get her full name has paid off when I take one final look back. She is standing stock still, with her mouth open, her daughter pulling at her skirt, as she realises she has an admirer.

*

I deliberately stagger the time slightly when we leave for the nursery over the next week or so. I need to know if she is interested in me. Sure enough, I notice on a couple of occasions that she is performing some minor gardening tasks as we draw level with her house. I know it sounds arrogant but I'm sure she is waiting for me. I am glad.

We have a brief conversation when we do bump into each other over the following weeks and nod and smile across the playground when we don't. One day we find ourselves walking back towards the park together after dropping the children off. She is wearing a pleated skirt with a white blouse and a navy blue cardigan which she pulls tightly around herself even though it is a very warm morning. She looks beautiful but nervous as we stop at her house; the passageway leading to the park is next to us. I drag the back of my right hand across my forehead as I puff out my checks, the escaping air sounding a pronounced "Phew." I say, 'Atsui desu.'

There is a moment's indecision, as she turns around to see if anyone is watching. We are alone as she makes a drinking motion and says hesitantly, 'N-n-nomimono?'

I say, 'Hai.' And try not to seem too eager as she leads me to her house, but my heart is racing. There is one final glance as we enter to see if anyone witnessed us before she gently closes the door.

The hallway appears wide until I realise there is no furniture, hanging coats or discarded toys, creating clutter and

181

an obstacle course like the one at Poppy's. I follow Mana towards the back of the house but stop at the room on my left. 'God,' I say as I marvel at the immaculate interior. The floor is wooden with a huge white rug placed precisely in the middle of the room. There is a long, outrageously low table at its centre the same colour as the floor, with four black patterned cushions at each corner. I notice the bonsai, a framed kimono on the wall and bamboo screen with a flowering cherry tree design, before I make my way to the kitchen.

She is standing facing me, leaning against a wooden worktop "island" as I approach her. I sense a static charge in the air even though it is cool inside. Perspiration glistens on her upper lip as she hands me a glass of water. I take it from her and see goose bumps on her forearm as our fingers briefly touch. She looks so beautiful and vulnerable; I have a raging desire for her.

We both jolt as our knees touch when we sit on two of the high chairs next to the wooden unit. We manage to communicate by using a mixture of words from our native languages. I tell her briefly about being in the army, living with Poppy and trying to write in my spare time. She seems to be comfortable in my company; we laugh as I struggle with some of the words. It is when I ask about her life that the floodgates open. I fall silent and concentrate as she tells me about the Sushi bar, the marriage split and Sora. She gradually introduces more English into her narrative as her confidence grows but her voice gains an edge as she tells me about Benjiro, a distant relative, who drives down from Northumberland most weekends.

'Benny is kind man. Ask me to be his girl one day.' She is really agitated now. 'No I say. He like a brother.' Her voice is rising. I must be the first person she has spoken to for an age. She is opening her heart, to me, a virtual stranger. 'I try hard, make life here, on my own. No good.' She doesn't protest when I instinctively take hold of her hand. She tells me she is going back to Japan in the summer to introduce Sora to the grandparents she has never seen. I can hear the hurt in her voice when she mentions her parents. I envy those feelings. She has tears gathering as she continues. 'May not come back. I am so lonely here Tesra.'

I love the way she mispronounces my name and appreciate how she shares her feelings with me. I am genuinely sorry for her as she confides in me. My silence and attentiveness seems to have prompted years of repressed emotion to bubble to the surface. My heart is racing as my instincts tell me the situation is moving at breakneck speed towards a familiar conclusion. She leans closer to me, her eyes moist from the tears. 'Arigatō,' she says as she touches my face.

'Why are you thanking me?' I say, as her hand strokes my face, her fingers finding the curl on my forehead.

'For listen to me.' She pulls me towards her and kisses me passionately. I don't break from the kiss as I stand and pick her up from the chair. She wraps her legs around my waist; I can't help gasping at her strength. She is pulling me into her chest, the scent of spices on her blouse, making my head tingle.

We don't make it out of the kitchen. I want to carry her down the hallway for a rendezvous with a white rug and a couple of black cushions, but she has other ideas. She releases the grip of her legs, slides down my body and starts to undo my belt. I am devastated to feel her perfect bum leave my hands but compensate by cupping her breasts as she crouches in front of me. I am hard and exposed, my jeans bunched up around my feet as she stands to kiss me again. I open her blouse and pull the white silken bra up towards her neck. I see her erect nipples as she suddenly backs away from me and perches on the edge of one of the chairs. She hitches her skirt up to her waist, spreads her legs and pulls her panties to one side, exposing herself. She rips her blouse wider as she cups her breast in her other hand and says, 'Fakku me Tesra.'

I make my way to her, shuffling like a penguin to gladly obey her order.

*

There are many more mornings like the first but each time subterfuge has to be employed. She is insistent that "we" have to be discreet; she doesn't want anyone to know our secret. I don't know if this is a case of Japanese honour or simply because she is still married. I had asked about maybe taking her out one day, 'My sister can babysit Sora.' This was met with a flat refusal.

We meet outside the nursery, hardly acknowledging each other's existence; we can't be seen to be too friendly. A simple nod in my direction and the code word, "Atsui desu" means we'll be fucking in a matter of minutes. If the code isn't forthcoming then I leave the playground, cross the park to Poppy's and sit at my writing desk until it's time to return for the girls.

The signal is my cue to enter the house unseen and search her out to perform whatever she has in mind for me. When the coast is clear I leave via her rear garden gate which gives access to the park, cross the playing fields, marvelling at the amazing sex and the fact that my damaged lungs and headaches never stop me ravishing her.

I am running one particularly brutal session through my mind when I get back to the house and the inevitable question from Poppy. 'You're late getting back again. What're you up to?'

'Nothing, I just went on an errand.' I go upstairs to try and stop the bleeding from the deep nails marks on my back and try not to lean back in my chair as I resume writing.

One day, about a week before the summer break, I see a man looking over the hedge at the end of the garden as I come out of Mana's kitchen door. He definitely has oriental features but has gone when I look out of the back gate before stepping into the deserted park. I dismiss the incident as I make my way home.

It is three days before the start of the summer holidays when the code changes. I say, 'Ohayou.'

She doesn't nod but replies, 'Ashita odoroki oaru.' I know the last word instantly but the other is outside my comprehension. It's only later that night I realise what she is implying. I have difficulty sleeping as the excitement builds up in me as I try to work out what unthinkable "gift" she has in store for me the next morning. I fall asleep wondering if I need to check if there are any bandages in Jacobs's first aid kit in the workshop.

I get the girls to the nursery earlier than usual, only to find Sora sitting, reading to one of the teachers. I say, 'Morning Margaret.' And then smiling at Sora, continue. 'Someone is up early this morning.' Melia and Emily run off to the toy box next to the stage.

'Yes Tez,' Margaret says. 'Mrs Tanimoto was already here when I arrived, she said she had something important to sort out this morning.' I am excited as I wave goodbye to the girls and make my way to Mana's, pondering what she has in store for me.

I check that no one is looking and slip through the gate and up to the kitchen door. It is unlocked. I can hear faint music drifting down the stairs when I enter; a flute, a drum and a string instrument that I don't recognise. Emily would call it a "plunking guitar". I make my way upstairs and enter the dimly lit bedroom.

Mana is standing, facing me. Her face has a thick white base with a slash of bright red lipstick and black pencil around her eyes. Her hair appears to be a foot tall with combs and brightly coloured hairpins holding pieces of cotton in place. Her kimono is turquoise with elaborate embroidery, I approach her quickly as I want to hold her. She stops me, makes me sit on the bed and removes my shoes. She bows as

185

she serves me green tea and waits patiently for me to finish then replaces the tea bowl on a white linen cloth.

She commands the situation, as usual, slowly removing my clothes before taking them from the room. She comes back, smothers me with kisses and then straddles me. Her kimono gapes open, exposing her body, heightening my desire. It is only when I throw her onto her back that I discover that her elaborate hair is a wig. It becomes detached from her head and topples onto the floor. I make a mental note not to stand on it later: those combs and pins could injure me. Our union is frantic, urgent and greedy. We are trying to outdo each other for stamina, not wanting to be the one to give up first.

Later, when we eventually collapse into each other's arms, sticky from our excesses, instinct tells me this treat is her way of saying goodbye to me.

*

Mana is still fast asleep when I awake; her kimono is undone, exposing her tiny delicious body. As I get out of bed I cover her with a sheet, she murmurs softly as I kiss her. I set the small alarm on the dressing table, so that she won't be late for Sora, and pause at the door to look at her before going downstairs. She is like a beautiful, lonely whirlwind. I think that with time I could fall for her and perhaps she could learn to love me.

I discover a note in my pocket when I get home. The paper feels like vellum, the script is neat, a work of art. It says:

"I hope my writing of English is better than my speaking. Benjira is impossible, he won't leave me alone. I am going back to see my parents tomorrow and plan to stay there all summer. My husband has requested a meeting to discuss reconciliation. Good for Sora to have a Daddy again. Thank you. I will always remember my sexy Tesla! XXXX"

My thought, seconds earlier about a possible future with Mana, is dashed as I consider she is yet another woman who is deserting me. I wonder if I will ever see her again as I lie on my bed, drifting, exhausted, towards sleep.

Chapter 16

Going sailing in my spare time is my passion. I was taught just off the coast of The Hague during the summer holidays away from the barracks. But if it's not possible to sail, then I try and write. I always get a kick out of creating stories and though I haven't had any published, I've been told that some of them are pretty good. Even my mother "used" some of my tales as a basis for some of her bestselling children's stories.

I also want to try and write a play, so I've started one I've entitled "Pirate" based on a book by Laurie King. The original story is about a female detective, Mary Judith Russell who is the prodigy and later wife of an ageing Sherlock Holmes. The story has her infiltrating an English silent-film company suspected of engaging in criminal activities. She works undercover, assisted by Holmes, joining a film crew making a film, about a fictional film crew, making a film version of "The Pirates of Penzance." I realise it sounds complicated and outrageous but it just happens to be the plot, so I think it will be fun to try and adapt it for the theatre. The project went so well in the early days; I'd shown excerpts of it to Smithy in the barracks and he told me he was being honest when he said he thought it was really good and made him laugh out loud. He said it was a miracle he felt that way because "quite frankly Coyne, I fuckin' hate Gilbert and Sullivan."

I've been working sporadically on the "Pirate" since arriving at Poppy's but my enthusiasm is starting to wane. I am ashamed to admit that the euphoria of being with the Floods has begun to wear off. I can feel myself spiral down into a dark place as my mind begins to fill with negative thoughts. Any creativity disappears for days as melancholy begins to eat into me. The summer break means that the girls are predominately cared for by Poppy and Jacob and are away a lot on trips and holidays, plus, the departure of Mana means I have no real highlights in my day. My fun times with the girls and frequent mornings of exhausting, aggressive sex have been replaced by days of blankness, staring at a flickering lap top screen, wondering, what made me think I could write a play in the first place.

Even music can't seem to lift me. I spend hours lying on the bed, wearing my headphones, flicking through the thousands of tracks on my player trying to find something that will raise my spirits. Nothing seems to work; favourites that have inspired me in the past now seem dull and irrelevant.

I find myself going for an early afternoon walk with a rucksack casually slung over my shoulder. 'Where are you off to?' Poppy asks as I fail in my task of leaving without being seen.

'I'm just going out for a walk.'

'You must be going for a while. Are you taking provisions?'

I attempt a casual laugh. 'No, I'm just taking my "story folder" with me. I might pop into the library while I'm out.' The real reason for the rucksack is to conceal the bottle of whisky that I will be sneaking back into my room. Even though I am in my early thirties, I still feel embarrassed to have my younger sister know I am drinking so heavily in the afternoon. I lock my door and find that chain smoking and an early afternoon tipple takes my mind off my loss of creative juices and briefly obliterates the feeling of inadequacy.

It's when I am drunk and stumbling around in front of the girls early one evening that Poppy intervenes. She follows me into the garden when I go outside to have a smoke. 'Tez, what's the matter with you?'

My speech is slurred. 'Nothing, why?'

'Tez, you're my brother, I know there's something wrong. I know you're drinking in your room during the day, I can smell it when you go out.' I am about to protest she's invading my privacy but manage to keep my mouth shut. 'I can also hear you coughing your guts up all the time, from the cigarettes that you chain smoke up there; it can't be good for your lungs. And finally, you seem to be really fed up, even the girls are wondering what's wrong with their "Runcletez." The alcohol in me wants to fight back but being told that the girls have noticed my decline, stops me in my tracks. 'Now, please tell me what's going on?'

I could tell her I am finding it difficult to get up in the mornings and my headaches are getting worse. And that it's hard to accept my lungs will never be the same as they were before the explosion. I could mention I still visualise Eddie opening the door that ended up killing him and how maybe, just maybe, I could have stopped him, if I hadn't paused to look in that fucking alcove! How about telling her that after all the structure of the forces, my days seem aimless now and I just seem to drift along with no purpose? Shall I open the old wounds relating to Mum and the death of my brother? How about informing my sister about the overwhelming need I have, to find someone who will love and not desert me?

I don't say any of this. I know I have a box of monsters screaming to escape but I will just sit on the lid rather than let them out, no matter how much din they make.

There is something that I can tell her. 'It's this bloody play I'm trying to finish. It's doing my head in. I wish I had never started the fucking thing.'

'Why, what's the problem?'

'I can't seem to get the structure right.'

'Ok, I might be able to help you. By the way are you taking the medication that the military doctor prescribed? You look awful.'

That is a brilliant question because I haven't touched the package of potions, apart from the one for my eye (I like that one) that were given to me when I was discharged. 'No.'

'I bet that's the problem, you silly sausage. You've been through such a lot and they wouldn't have suggested the pills if they thought you didn't need them, would they? Come on, let's get you taking your medication, that'll help you and I've an idea how to get your play back on track.' I have to admit she has a point. I did feel low when I left the apartment to drive to Poppy's but gradually over the months it's got worse. It seemed to creep up on me. I could cope with the odd day feeling down but now it seems constant and I can't seem to pull myself out of it.

We go back into the house and she watches over me as I use the spray and take my tablets. She says I must promise to keep taking them and sort out an appointment with a Doctor. I nod my agreement. She also listens attentively, as I explain what is bothering me about the play. She goes into her study, returning minutes later with some old scripts to help me. One of them will be particularly useful when it comes to getting the stage directions correct for the songs.

I do my best to keep my promise to Poppy and make sure I keep taking the medication, but I'll admit that sometimes when I'm feeling a bit brighter, I simply can't be bothered. I apply myself to the writing and sure enough begin to feel better as the weeks and months pass by. My mood and creativity improves to such an extent that I finish the "Pirate" and hand it, with trepidation, to Poppy to read.

*

I found a programme, inside the pages of the script that Poppy gave me. It's for their production of "My Fair Lady" from a few years ago. It contains some names I recognise.

Eliza Doolittle was played by Grace D Perritano and the production was directed by her husband, Richard. I mentioned to Jacob a few weeks ago that it seemed strange that I'd not seen them back at the house since New Year's Day. (I can still visualise Grace and her eyes). Jacob said Dick had probably "seen his arse" because he had stood up to him about not handing over the keys without being paid. He also said that Dick can be all over you like a rash when he wants something, but can drop you like a stone once he's got what he wants.

The programme shows that Professor Henry Higgins had been played by Toby Evans, the Flood's family doctor. I'd heard his name mentioned a few times around the house and met him once when he'd dropped some papers off at Poppy's. Dr Evans was tall, slightly overweight and had a deep Welsh accent. I liked him immediately. He suggested that it might be an idea to register with the practice when I admitted I hadn't arranged any medical cover since moving in with Poppy. I'd said I would.

I don't recognise the names of any of the production personnel apart from Poppy and Jacob who were credited with costume and scenic design respectively. Then I notice a name that surprises me. The Music Direction and Choreography are credited to "Jenny Moriarty, (née Jenny Monroe star of the hit TV show, Five O'clock Shadow)."

I know that she had been in a show in the early 90's that was popular with teenagers but I remember her principally from when she appeared on light entertainment programmes later in her career. She was beautiful, had a stunning body and if that wasn't enough, was a great dancer and had the voice of an angel. She had the reputation of being pretentious and difficult but I didn't care because I had a huge crush on her.

She had continued to appear in the theatre and on TV after an acrimonious divorce from Guy Moriarty, a professional footballer, but had disappeared off the scene after her appearance on a chat show had gone horribly wrong.

Guy had left her for a young shop assistant and there were pictures of the happy couple at their wedding in the tabloids and magazines on the very same day that Jenny appeared drunk, on the show. She became agitated when the interviewer casually asked her how she felt about, "the nation taking the young girl to their hearts." The show's host (sensing an opportunity to get an even bigger reaction) showed her the headline from one of the morning's newspapers. "*Moriarty transfers pompous banshee for shop assistant angel.*" The response was cataclysmic. They managed to edit out the torrent of abuse she hurled, but the smashed jug of water and her staggering exit, effectively heralded the end of her career on TV.

I can't understand why Poppy has never mentioned that a famous ex TV star is connected to the society. I don't recall her name ever being raised around the house.

*

I put the play out of my mind and concentrate on my maritime love story, "The Amazon." Poppy has been going to her weekly meetings with the group and came back one evening to tell me that their next production, "Shirley Valentine," was nearing the final rehearsals and I have been invited to discuss the possibility of staging "The Pirate," the following year. She tells me she loves my play and those in the GADS who have read it are keen to consider staging it. So, it is on a warm evening that I accompany Poppy to an upstairs function room at the rear of the Green Man to attend a meeting of the GADS to discuss forthcoming productions.

I thought I was going to the meeting with no ulterior motives but after being informed that someone is not attending, that I realise that I've been subconsciously looking forward to seeing a certain person again. I feel immense disappointment when I am introduced to everyone, to find that Grace is on holiday with Dick and her mother-in-law, at their villa in Portugal. I am wondering when I will see her again when I hear a slight commotion; someone is arriving just as the meeting is about to start. I turn towards the doorway as someone behind me whispers, "She always has to make a fuckin' grand entrance."

I recognise the woman standing in the doorway. She has paused to allow every eye in the room to drink in her image. I remember her hair being short and blond like a bundle of white candy floss. Now it's shoulder length, immaculately straight and the colour of pale honey. Her knee length black leather boots, drainpipe jeans and sky blue polo neck sweater give her a casual look which would not be out of place in Beverley Hills. I get a clearer look at her as she moves into the room; the babble of conversation resumes. She still has a feline look about her, with the high cheek bones but now she looks a bit drawn, perhaps because she is so much thinner than when I last saw her on television. "She is still beautiful though," I think as Jacob nudges me and says, 'I'll be back in a minute Tez, I'll go and get Jenny and introduce you.' I notice that Poppy has turned her back on the new arrival.

*

My introduction to the beautiful ex television star is a disaster. Jacob is steering her towards me. Her eyes light up as he says something to her. I just catch the end of his sentence as they arrive in front of me. '…my brother in law who wrote the play. Tez, this is Jenny.'

I am conscious that people are watching us as I extend my hand. I think I will impress her by remembering her surname. 'It's nice to meet you Mrs Moriarty.' I realise I have made a terrible mistake when I hear the gasps around me; see her jaw drop and her face flush bright red.

She is seething when she says, 'My name is Monroe. Ms Jenny Monroe. I don't want to hear that bastard's name around me again thank you.' I can see Poppy smirking in the background. It's now that I realise the programme I found was from a production well before Jenny's divorce. I need to rescue the situation.

194

She starts to turn away from me. 'I'm sorry Ms Jenny Monroe, I humbly apologise for making that mistake. I was a bit nervous about meeting you, so I hope you will forgive me.' She doesn't look as if she is going to relent as she begins to move away. I lower my voice. 'Jenny, I'm truly sorry about offending you. It was an innocent mistake; I was just trying to be clever. I wish I'd said that I have had a crush on you for years and that I came to watch you when you played Carmen in London.' This is a lie, (I remember Eric telling me he had seen her there when we discussed Bizet's opera) but she stops, turns to me and I see her eyes widen; she is definitely softening. 'I was smitten when you sang Habanera. I really wish I could take the comment back and start all over again but I can't. I'd love to work with you on my play, that's if the GADS decide to put it on, but I would understand if it was vetoed.' I begin to turn away from her and step towards the exit. 'I think I'd better go…'

Jenny puts her hand on my shoulder. 'Ok.' Her voice is softer. 'I accept your apology.' We smile at each other as she turns to address the others. 'Shall we start?'

Jenny chairs the meeting with hardly a murmur from the attendees; I can't make out whether this is down to respect or fear. A small group gathers round me when she calls a break after an hour of listening to previous minutes and financials. They appear to be delighted to speak again and there is light hearted banter and some barely disguised attempts to quiz me about my past. I try to be vague without being offensive, but I really felt quite uncomfortable which doesn't stop Poppy and Jacob waxing lyrical about me. At one point it becomes cringingly embarrassing and sounds as if they are advertising for a partner for me. I want to scream, "Stop it."

Someone mentions they've seen me driving around the village in a beautiful car. They say how unusual it is, so Jacob just has to confirm that it's a valuable classic. I attempt to play it down but then the apartment on the south coast and my yacht enter the equation. I can see where this is going; it's the "eligible bachelor pitch."

"Roll up, roll up Ladies, this is Tesla. He has a yacht, a vintage car, an apartment near Sandbanks; he is a war hero, a linguist and a writer. Don't let this opportunity slip through your fingers."

Jenny keeps in the background for most of my inquisition but I can see her back stiffen when a very striking woman sits next to me. I hope the interloper doesn't see me jolt slightly when I see her appearance. Her hair is crimson and piled on top of her head with brightly coloured pieces of cloth tied in bows. The numerous metal studs in her ear lobes are overshadowed by the silver spike in her nose. She is wearing a black tee shirt with gold writing across, but I can't look long enough to see what it says as it would give the impression that I am looking at the movement of her unrestrained breasts beneath it.

'Hello, I'm Candy Evans.' She shuffles a bit closer and grasps my forearm. I feel rather uncomfortable at her close proximity but that turns to embarrassment when she says 'Why hasn't someone snapped you up? Nice car, yacht, luxury apartment and you can write as well. Is there something wrong with you?'

I laugh heartily. 'No, I don't think so. I just haven't been in a place long enough to settle down. I am looking though.' There are a few chuckles at this but I feel a huge wave of relief when Jenny calls the meeting back to order.

I am asked to leave whilst they discuss the upcoming production of Shirley Valentine and their future plans, so I go for a welcome drink in the bar downstairs

There's applause and pats on my back when I am brought back and told it's been agreed that "Pirate" will be staged but much earlier than originally planned. Candy and a couple of other members sit with me in the bar after the meeting. We chat for a while; I tell a few stories which makes them laugh. I am really enjoying the company and the alcohol. After a while Poppy and Dr. Evans join us.

'Tez, you remember Toby Evans, our doctor.'

196

'Yes of course, it's nice to meet you again. I keep meaning to call your surgery.'

'Hello, nice to see you. I see you've met my sister.'

'Oh, yes. I didn't realise you're related.'

He smiles broadly. 'I try to keep it a secret, don't I Sis?' He bends over to kiss the top of Candy's head; it looks like he's plunging his face into a psychedelic nest. She playfully pushes him away. 'Don't let her appearance put you off Tez, she's a brilliant cook and would make a wonderful wife.' Laughter bursts out all around us, Poppy's is the loudest.

This is beginning to sound like a "setup." I make a grab for my sister saying, 'Are you trying to get me married off?' Her giggles are all I need to confirm that she has indeed persuaded them all to tease me on my first appearance at the society.

Dr Evans says, 'Yes Tez, your sister has been a bit mischievous. She's told us a lot about you. Do you still want to register with me?' Poppy smiles at me, I can't be angry with her; I need a doctor and her ploy with all the questions is just a clever way to get me "accepted" into the group. I also have a small glow inside because it made me sound quite interesting.

'Yes but I keep forgetting to call the surgery.' This isn't entirely true. I've picked up the phone a few times but replaced it in its cradle without dialling. I avoid making the call even though I have days when things are not right with me, especially when the oppressive headaches kick in.

'Why don't you come round to the surgery at 8am on Monday morning, I can see you before the rush starts.' He then looks at my sister. 'Poppy he needs to register before I see him; can you get him to the surgery to fill in the forms?'

Poppy glances at me; she looks like she's imploring me to accept. I say, 'That would be great, thank you for making that available.'

'No problem, I look forward to seeing you.'

He is just about to move off when I ask, 'I was wondering if I could be cheeky and ask you a couple of questions about Laudanum when I see you?'

He frowns and hesitates before replying. 'Why, are you planning to bump someone off?'

I laugh. 'No, it's a couple of questions relating to a book I've been working on for ages.' This comment creates a bit of interest to those around us at the bar. Jenny is standing behind the doctor, smiling.

'Ok but I'll have to kick you out before 8:30; it starts to get busy then.'

'That's great, thank you.'

I really enjoy the evening. I am made so welcome and end up talking to nearly everyone there. Later, when I am sitting alone in the bar on a battered Chesterfield, I'm joined by Jenny who waves away my attempt to apologise again. Our conversation is cordial at first but gets more intimate as the night progresses. We sit undisturbed for the rest of the evening as if there is a force field around her that the rest of the group are afraid to breach.

We talk mainly about her career and how I had a picture of her in my locker at the barracks. This wasn't true of course but it makes her melt a little bit more. I avoid talking about football and her ex-husband and make sure that my background doesn't enter the discussion. I have heard enough about Tesla Coyne to last a lifetime.

I offer her a lift home when she mentions that she'd got a taxi to the Green Man because her car was at the garage. She accepts. There are some strange glances when we leave together and I see that Candy appears to be disappointed, but I don't care, I have an ex TV star on my arm.

It is warm when we get outside, so I put the hood down to take advantage of the fresh air. We talk constantly on the journey. I glance at Jenny as she leans back to laugh at one of my stories, her hair bounces in the breeze; I think she wouldn't look out of place being driven in a classic convertible Mercedes Benz, by a movie star through the streets of Monte Carlo.

I refuse her offer to go in for a coffee when we arrive at her home. It is a hard decision to make because I really want to see how the evening will end but I have developed a pounding headache, causing spots in my vision so I just want to get home. I also think that turning down the invitation displays that I am not desperate and it might "keep her keen." This seems to have worked because she jumps at my suggestion to go for a drive and perhaps a meal at the weekend. I smile to myself as I calculate that it has taken me less than four hours to convert her antipathy towards me for getting her surname wrong into a possible romantic union.

Chapter 17

Trepidation nibbles away at me, as I wait in a cafe around the corner from the doctors surgery. It isn't the recurring headaches, the gunk that keeps weeping from my left eye or my scarred lungs that's bothering me. It's the mornings when I awake with a cavern of sorrow and blackness inside me, that I find it hard to cope.

I had always considered myself to be super fit and mentally strong when in the SBS but slight misgivings have started to fester, leading to an ever-widening chink in my armour. I can feel fine for weeks but suddenly plummet into a world of sadness and hopelessness. I ought to see a doctor but I try to avoid it because part of me is afraid to open myself up, in case I find there is something seriously wrong with me.

The reception is deserted when I enter the surgery at exactly 8.00, but there is already some activity in the office area behind the louvered glass. I can see two women in matching teal and white dresses working at their computers. I stand dutifully at the window waiting to be acknowledged but when this isn't successful, I find myself checking my reflection in the glass to make sure I haven't suddenly become invisible. My impatience is about to bubble over because I really don't want to be here and I am considering walking out, when another teal-attired woman enters the room with a tray of drinks. I recognise her as the one I gave my registration paperwork to earlier in the week, when Poppy had dragged me here to fulfil my promise. She waves and loudly says, 'I'll be with you in a moment.' I nod just as Dr Evans blusters into the room.

'Good morning ladies,' he says as he removes his coat and notices me, alone, in the reception area. He continues. 'It's OK Louise; I'll take Mr Coyne through. I asked him to come in last week.' She frowns as he leaves the room. He reappears at the reception door. 'Come through Mr Coyne.' Her eyes trace me as I enter the corridor and follow him.

I say, 'It's good of you to see me so early doctor.'

'Oh, don't mention it. I'm doing this as a favour for Poppy really. She said it's difficult for you to find the time to call and register, so I thought I would speed the process up for you. Come on in,' he says as we enter his consulting room. His tone is an indication that he knows the opposite is true. This is not normal practice for him; I'm getting special attention. Poppy must be really worried about me.

He questions me about my background and mentions it is odd that my medical records seem to stop in 1991. I explain that the data since then is held by the military and I lie when I tell him I expect they will forward it to me at some stage in the future. I continue the deception when I tell him the lies about the explosion and my exposure to the acid fumes and omit to tell him about my medication for PTSD. I am not ashamed to confirm that I have an inhaler spray for my lungs and lubricating drops for my eye.

I remove my jacket and shirt when he asks and he listens to my chest. He takes my blood pressure and makes a couple of notes before checking it again. He has taken the reading for a third time and is frowning when he says, 'You can put your shirt back on now Mr Coyne.'

'Please call me Tez,' I say as I start to button my shirt.

'Ok, as long as you call me Toby. Do you smoke?'

'I have the odd one now and again.'

'Yes, I thought I could smell tobacco smoke on your shirt.'

'I did have just the one before I came here.' This is another lie. It is only just past eight in the morning and I've already had six; even I can smell the stale smoke.

'Do you drink alcohol?'

'Yes.'

He smiles. 'I like your honesty, especially as I've seen you in action. You need to moderate the drinking and try to give up the cigarettes you know.'

I don't sound at all convincing when I say, 'OK, will do.'

He looks at the clock. 'I have arranged for Jacquelyn to take a blood sample before you leave and I'm going to ask her to fit you with a 24hr blood pressure monitor as well; your reading is a little bit too high. OK?' I nod. 'Smashing, there are instructions with it, just bring it back to the reception next week so I can check the readings. Now, you mentioned that you wanted to ask me a question about laudanum when we were at the Green Man.'

'Yes,' I say as I delve into my jacket pocket to get my notebook and a pen but they have fallen through a hole into the lining again. I fish inside for them and decide I really need to make an effort and get it mended. I make a mental note to sew up the torn pocket when I get home; I don't want to bother Poppy with it.

I explain that I have always loved sailing and was so fascinated about a famous maritime enigma that I had started to write a mystery novel about it some years ago and would appreciate his help with a key part of the plot.

'We've another ten minutes if you'd like to elaborate.'

'My story is about the Mary Celeste.'

'Oh. The ghost ship found abandoned in perfect working order?'

'Yes.'

'I thought she was called Marie Celeste?'

'No but the confusion is understandable because Arthur Conan Doyle wrote a fictional theory about what had happened…'

He interrupts me. 'The same Conan Doyle who wrote the Sherlock Holmes stories?'

'Correct. As I was saying, he wrote his theory about what had happened which was extensively published but he called the ship the "Marie Celeste" which seems to have stuck in most people's consciousness ever since.' It suddenly occurs to me that my play, "Pirate" not only has a nautical theme but also has a link to the famous writer. 'My story is about a love affair between the captain's wife, Sarah Briggs and one of the crew members. I can't tell you which one because that would spoil the plot but it involves incapacitating the crew. Would laudanum do the trick if enough was administered?'

'Yes, it was used a lot at that time as a painkiller and as a cure for diarrhoea but it's an extremely potent formulation of opium, so could be lethal if an overdose was given.'

'That's great thank you,' I say as I make a couple of notes, stand and put my jacket on, I don't want to eat into his time any further.

'No problem.' We shake hands, and he says, 'Just go back into reception and Jacquelyn will call you to take the bloods and fit the monitor. We can then arrange a follow up appointment to discuss the results and any medication you might require. See you at the rehearsals and please take heed about what I've said about the smoking and the alcohol.'

'I will.' I know it sounds a hollow commitment as I say it, so I change the subject. 'By the way, how's Candy'?

'Oh she's fine. She said she enjoyed meeting you.' I had just opened his door and was about to leave when he asks, 'By the way, can I ask what your book is called?'

I say, '"The Amazon."' I smile when I see the frown on his face.

*

Jenny and I start to spend more and more time together as we go for walks, to the theatre and to a number of restaurants. She seems to relax in my company but she makes it clear, as I get to know her that she doesn't trust men, especially after her husband cheated on her. She thinks men are only attracted to her because she has been on TV or because they assume she is rich. I play the waiting game by pretending I have no real interest in her, apart from being her companion. Nothing can be further from the truth of course. I get a kick from seeing her on my arm. I am single and have the chance to be with someone I have always desired.

I try not to have any real feelings for her because every time I find a woman who I think is right for me, they either leave me or destroy my expectations. I have learnt not to fall too deep because I don't want to be disappointed or get hurt again. This doesn't stop my drive to be with them however, I ache for their company. Every woman is fair game to me. It doesn't matter if she is rich, beautiful or supposedly unobtainable; attempting to seduce them has become second nature to me. Not because I am particularly tall or handsome but because I have the cheek to try.

I achieved exposure to copious numbers of "exclusive" women when I went sailing with Jordi; hopping from one exclusive port to another. I was able to apply for extended leave from the Marines for most of the longer journeys, sometimes managing to get special dispensation for adventure training, or pre-ops or even a charity race. It seemed outrageous that I could get time off and sponsorship from my employers to enjoy my two main loves, women and my boat.

"Sunbuoy" is a fifty foot classic counter stern yacht, with a long keel and cutter rig. I bought it for a pittance when the craze for plastic hulls caught on. It's moored to an anchored float in Upton Lake near Cobbs Quay in Poole. Jordi and I would row out to it in our dingy and marvel at its beauty as we approached. The curves of the hull are a joy to behold; we would both smile involuntarily as we never tired of its uniqueness. Our advance would be mirrored in the varnish of the pristine wooden hull and the highly polished brass dorade vents would sparkle in the sun. I always love the way the breeze makes the halyards and the topping lift rattle against the mast. It's as if the boat is welcoming us aboard with Morse code, saying "she is eager to leave." It's one of her ways of communicating with us.

An immense sense of pride fills me, when an old man with a weather-beaten face stops me one day and calls her, "a proper gentleman's yacht." I don't classify myself as a refined man (especially when I consider some of the outrageous antics I have got up to on board) but I understand what he means about her class.

Although "Sunbuoy" has a perfectly operational engine we only use it sparingly, preferring the peace of sail as we leave the lake on the ebb and float with the tide out to sea. Her beauty stands out as she passes the other boats; their hulls all synthetic and angular, with "artificial" posing women adorning the sun decks. We don't stand out as competent sailors with our cut off faded jeans, threadbare polo shirts, Breton jumpers and ancient deck shoes, but we are. I am a very good sailor but Jordi is a genius, he would grace any around the world yacht race if he was so inclined, but he is happy to concentrate on his recreational activities. His love for my yacht is so profound that I refer to it as "ours" and have given him full use of it whenever he pleases. I have also promised him a ten percent share of any profit if I should ever sell it. We both hope that that day will never come.

One memorable time we took "Sunbuoy" along the west coast of France to the Port of Haliguen in Quiberon Bay. We couldn't believe our luck when we radioed ahead and were told there was one spot available at the end of the visitors berth. We knew it would be busy because not only was it Bastille Day but they would also be celebrating the repulsion of the émigrés landing, that happened there in 1795. We smiled at each other as we heard the pompous French accent on the crackling VHF radio tell us "it'll be a tight fit for a "fifty footer"" and then advise us not to come in too fast because the breeze is "tres fort."

The sun was setting on the hot summer's evening, as we passed the island of Belle Ile to port and entered the bay. The air was scented with flowers, even this far from land; it reminded me of a sirocco I had experienced once off the coast of Libya. We were in excess of five knots and on a broad reach as we approached the harbour entrance. Jordi decided to sail past to refresh his memory of the layout. He quickly tacked the boat and hurtled towards the narrow passage.

"Sunbuoy" appeared to be airborne for a moment, when we hit the last wave before entering the marina. Jordi squealed with delight as the boat hit the flat surface of the sheltered waters and picked up speed. Through the sea spray, slapping into my face, I saw several cocktail parties in full swing. I could see the glistening blazer buttons of the men and I swear some of the women were wearing tiaras. Our approach attracted the attention of many on the boats and those on the promenade. There were crowds on the harbour wall behind us pointing, expecting a disaster. The people on the boats had moved closer to the guardrails and pulpits, curious to see if something bad was about to happen. I took a sideways glance at my mate; even I wondered if he had over-cooked it this time.

There were isolated shouts of "imbécile" and "stupide anglais" as our dazzling wooden boat, flying the Red Ensign, arrowed towards disaster. The adrenalin was searing through me as I started to silently recite the "Lord's Prayer; "then switched to 'Fuck me.' as Jordi abruptly tacked the boat again, almost throwing me violently overboard. I heard a flapping sound above me, like bed sheets drying in a strong wind, as the Genoa and Main began to luff. I let go of the halyard and the sail dropped in an instant. The boat began to stall, so Jordi pointed "Sunbuoy" towards the vacant visitors berth. He had timed the turn to perfection, allowing the gleaming varnished hull to slide serenely into the berth between two colossal plastic-looking boats. I let out a sigh of relief, slapped Jordi on the back and shook my head in amazement. I lied when I said, 'I never doubted you for a moment mate.'

The shouts had turned to "bravo, merveilleux and come to our party," as we both casually stepped ashore to secure the boat to the jetty. There were a couple of cheers when I produced a bottle of champagne and a sabre and performed a sabrage ceremony for the spectators. The first wave of fireworks, celebrating the public holiday, erupted as the cork was beheaded and flew into the air. The effervescent wine symbolically ejaculated onto the landing stage. We had announced our arrival.

I awoke at midday with a naked woman lying on each side of me, and no memory of how I got there. My mouth felt as if it was welded shut and I had a stabbing pain in my forehead. I thought I was experiencing one of my worst hangovers ever, and then realised I had fallen asleep, wearing just a tiara.

*

My experience in affluent European marinas influences my approach with Jenny. I demonstrate I am not overawed by her. She normally asks me in for coffee when I take her home but I always politely refuse. On one occasion, when she looks particularly flushed and agitated, she says, 'You can stay over tonight if you want,' there is a look of eagerness as she hurriedly adds, 'in the spare bedroom of course!' Her nervous laugh at the end of this comment suggests she is ripe for picking but I politely shake my head, kiss her gently on the cheek and go home.

It is a chance conversation with Jacob, a couple of weeks later that prompts me to think that maybe it's time to try to become something more than just Jenny's companion. He mentions he has heard she has been subtly asking questions about me; trying to find out why I don't try to seduce her. "Doesn't he find me attractive? Is he gay?" We both laugh at the suggestion as I decide to finally "charm" her, if the opportunity presents itself.

We had been to an outdoor musical festival at a local stately pile. When we arrived at her house, as usual, she offered me a coffee. Her voice had no trace of hope of me accepting but this time I turned to her, smiled and said 'Yes, I'd love to.' She couldn't disguise her glow of anticipation as she heard those words. I guessed she was excited. So was I. All those months of fighting my natural desire for her, along with that night's music, picnic, champagne and pyrotechnics had got my sap rising. We did talk for the last few miles to her house but I can't recall the detail because my mind kept wandering, imagining her naked beneath me.

Her modest detached house is in a quiet and affluent part of the village. She encourages me to wander around while she goes upstairs to "change her shoes." I hang my jacket on the rack next to the telephone table and I cringe when I notice that some of the junk mail is still being addressed to Mrs J Moriarty.

The hallway is quite unnerving, nothing short of a shrine to her past glories. The walls are covered with gold leaf photograph frames and award statuettes stand on a small table near the living room door. One wall has pictures of her with guests from the "Five o'clock Shadow Show," others from chat shows and some TV specials. The facing wall has theatre posters (with her name headlining), framed newspaper articles, reviews and magazine covers, all dedicated to her, along with copies of articles she has written as a singing coach for the BBC.

I wander around the rooms on the ground floor and see that the rest of the interior looks like a show house for a design magazine, every room is ordered and neat, an antiseptic tribute to white, beige and calico. Within minutes, I am longing to see a primary colour, a pile of books or even a discarded sock to make this feel like a home and not an advertisement.

I return to the hall and notice there are more photographs at the end, near the staircase. There are three of her at the Taj Mahal, the Grand Canyon and a "red carpet" film premiere in London. They are unusual because her stance makes it appear she is being embraced by a ghost. I realise that she has had the photographs digitally edited to erase someone from the memory. I guess it's her ex-husband, Guy missing from the picture. I find it odd that she would go to so much trouble just for the sake of proving she had been to those swanky places.

These are my thoughts as I hear a noise and she appears at the top of the stairs. She is bare footed as she walks slowly down toward me. It gives me a moment to drink in her beauty. She has removed the clothes she wore at the festival and replaced them with a knee length white dress; I can tell by the way that her body moves that she is wearing very little beneath it. Her smile is breath-taking as she links my arm and steers me into the living room.

We sit, side by side on an enormous grey linen sofa. One of her CD's plays quietly in the background, as we drink wine and talk into the night. I watch her with a deep longing each time she leaves me to bring me something to look at or to get another bottle; I limit my intake to a single glass when she offers a top up. My cheeks flush when she hitches up her dress, spins her legs beneath her on the sofa and leans into me. She hands me a scrapbook of newspaper articles about what appears to be her favourite subject – "*Jenny Monroe*." I feign interest in the gushing reports (about her), as I imagine her long, smooth legs wrapped around my neck.

We have a wonderful evening. She is charming and funny. I really enjoy her company. I wonder why some people are obviously not keen on her. It is getting late, so when she finishes the second bottle of wine, I start to make my move to leave. I can't make the mistake of assuming that tonight is the night. I put my arms around her shoulders and kiss her goodnight and head into the hallway.

I am about to put on my jacket and open the front door but she grasps my arm and turns me forcibly towards her. She kisses me gently at first but then her tongue enters my mouth with such velocity that it nearly dislodges the crown on my front tooth. My excitement is at bursting point as she leads me towards the staircase; I try to imagine what we will get up to in her bedroom but that isn't our destination. I am surprised, when she pulls me down onto the floor and begins to undress me.

I am lying at an uncomfortable angle with my upper body on the stairs, when she takes me in her mouth. She is greedy as she stuns me with this display of lust. The pain in my neck and back becomes irrelevant as I lift her shoulders and pull the dress over her head. I gasp at her nakedness. Her symmetry and perfection makes me wonder why on earth a man would cheat such a beautiful and desirable woman as this, let alone leave her. She takes control as she shows me what she wants; she takes my hand and encourages me to explore her. I feel her body start to twitch as she rises and stands with her legs either side of me on the stair. Her eyes never leave mine, as she puts her hands on my shoulders and squats slowly; lowering herself towards my desperate groin. I swear my penis stretches a little, eager to intercept her.

*

I feel uncomfortable after our first fuck on the hallway floor. It isn't the oak boards threatening to send splinters into my naked buttocks or my spinal cord practically snapping on the lower step of the stairs that unsettles me; it's the audience of "Jenny's," the row upon row of her eyes watching me from the walls above. They are as lifeless as the ones staring down at me now. Her hair, the colour of French mustard, is damp from the physical exertion. She raises herself from me and without speaking, goes into the downstairs toilet. I lie there naked and wilted for what seems like an eternity, as I think she might be kind enough to bring me something to clean myself.

She eventually re-enters the hallway, as I am gingerly pulling my clothing over my stickiness and trying to stretch and straighten my tortured back. There is no eye contact as she walks towards me. I think she must be embarrassed that she has given herself to me so openly, so I smile and go to kiss her. I say, 'You OK?' as she avoids me with a deft side step and finally looks at me as she unlocks the front door.

The passionate, delightful woman from earlier looks like she has been replaced by someone who's been sucking lemons. Her voice is lifeless and staccato as she says, 'Yes fine. It's late, you'd better go.' I am dumbstruck as she gives me the lightest kiss on the cheek. It feels like a butterfly has landed for a moment and immediately flown away in embarrassment.

I say, 'I had a great evening.' There is no response. I can't believe what's happening as I am ushered out of the house. 'When shall we do it ag...?' I don't get to finish the sentence as the door clicks shut. I stand for a moment, looking at the closed oak panelled door and shake my head in disbelief. I walk back to the car and drive to Poppy's. I have time during the journey, to consider what has just happened between us; perhaps I have just had an indication of why Guy left her.

*

I am confused when I see Jenny at GADS a week later. She acts as if nothing untoward has happened between us. She even suggests we go away together that weekend, which only reinforces my thought that being with Jenny is like dealing with two completely different people.

She can be funny and attentive for days on end. We will have great times together and she is a joy to be with but this part of her character is only the tip of the iceberg. Just as I am beginning to think she is relaxed and comfortable with me her mood will swing and a dark side will emerge from beneath the waterline. She will become cold and distant, her face blank with indifference or contort from beauty into a sneering ugliness. She will act like a stranger, shutting me out for days, even weeks, without contacting me.

I resist the temptation to call her however. I don't think she is used to this tactic because she eventually contacts the "Floods" and leaves a message, virtually pleading me to get in touch. I leave it at least a week, (on a point of principle) before I do. Even then, I can detect a hint of annoyance in her voice at being ignored for so long.

I wonder why I put up with her behaviour as I arrange to meet her again. Perhaps I am prioritising design over substance. Being with Jenny is like owning a beautiful sports car. The experience is exciting and exhilarating; people turn their heads, envious, wishing they were in my shoes. But they don't realise she's not someone that can be recommended for everyday use, she is temperamental, unforgiving and uncompromising. You start longing to find someone who can be a part of your everyday life and therefore priceless, someone that you can love and respect, who in turn reciprocates those feelings. My life so far, has taught me that the chances of that happening are remote, so I might as well try and make it work with Jenny and attempt to put up with her notorious antics.

It is less than a second after making that decision that I think about Grace's smiling eyes.

*

I start to spend more time seeing Jenny and often stay with her at weekends and if the chance arises, I work on "The Amazon." But I always find myself looking forward to returning to my sister's. I am wanted and loved there, and I can relax without having to concentrate all the time on what I say or what I do.

I still have the habit of rising early when I'm at Poppy's but I go for a walk every morning now, regardless of the

212

weather. The swimming pool and gym are no longer a haven even if the rain is lashing down because I am on the lookout for someone.

I don't turn right anymore when I reach the riverbank. I am drawn to the left with the lure of maybe seeing Grace as I walk past her house on my way up to the steeplechase course. I used to go this way once a week to see the horses train but now I pass every day to see if I can catch a glimpse of her. I walk slowly up the public footpath, looking over the hedge into the garden as I make my way up the incline, just in case I can see her. I am thirty four years old and I am acting like a lovesick schoolboy. Every day is the same; there's no sight of her. Disappointed yet again, I continue upwards, sit on a bench at the top of the hill and try to sort out the turmoil in my head.

*

Jenny's birthday starts promisingly. I have stayed over after working late on my laptop, with the intention of treating her in the morning but it's me that is awakened with a pleasant surprise. I see the bedcovers moving down my chest as a hump beneath them creeps slowly towards me. I feel hands sliding up my body and kisses alternating from one thigh to the other. Jenny emerges, naked, from her linen hiding place and without a word, slides herself onto me. She doesn't look at me as she moves rhythmically; it occurs to me that our union is totally one sided. Apart from her initial kisses, designed for my arousal, I realise there is no regard for my needs. In fact, I might as well have been a toy, running on batteries only to be returned to a bedroom drawer when I have completed my task. There is no warmth from her.

Later, after she has graciously relieved me, I make her a birthday breakfast. She seems genuinely excited when I tell her I am going to drive her to the coast for a treat at her favourite seafood restaurant. It is situated in a quiet street near the "Pier Theatre" and is frequented by celebrities. She likes it particularly, because they always make a fuss of her and ensure that we sit at the table with her photograph above our heads. She likes to feign surprise when other diners ask for her autograph.

I have just put on my jacket and am standing in the hallway as we are about to leave. I can hear her humming a tune from "Carousel" as she is getting ready. She comes down the stairs and the tune stops abruptly when she sees me. My heart sinks; her harsh tone is back. 'Do you have to wear that?' I am perplexed for a nanosecond as I try to work out which part of my attire she is referring to. I didn't have to wait long. 'You've loads of nice clothes; I can't understand why you keep wearing that shitty looking jacket. You know I hate it.'

She is right, I do have other things to wear but it's like my second skin. It had been my dad's, it fits me like a glove and I feel comfortable in it. Besides it isn't "shitty," it has been cleaned regularly and in my opinion it looks as good as new. Dad had it made by a bespoke tailor in Savile Row when he had been at a meeting in London for three weeks. (I overheard him mention something about "Box500" to my mother before he left. It sounded like a collection of Lego or a jigsaw. I was so excited; I crossed my fingers, praying for a gift from Hamleys, only to be disappointed on his return. It was only when I joined the SBS that I realised that "Box500" referred to something far more sinister than some plastic building bricks or a child's cardboard puzzle.)

I attempt to change the subject. 'Well my darling, at least my favourite jacket contains a little gift for you.' She seems to soften as I rummage in my pockets for the small velvet jewellery case containing some pearl earrings. They seem to be evading discovery, which in turn, lights the fuse of her impatience. I find the box just as I see she is about to erupt, it had slipped through the torn inside pocket. 'Happy Birthday!' I say cheerily as I hand the present to her. I should have left it there; I am not thinking when I follow it up with. 'Could you sew the pocket for me when you have a minute please?'

She stares at me for a second, and then throws the box at me; it bounces off my cheek. Her words are spat at me. 'You can just fuck off! I'm not a seamstress you know. Why not ask your precious sister to do it for you?' She opens the door and ushers me out. I wonder why my life has come to this as I stand on the doorstep like a scolded child.

No one asks for my autograph when I sit alone at the table later that evening. I decided to keep the reservation for two reasons. Firstly, I had to leave my credit card details when I booked, so I would be charged anyway for a "no show," but the main reason is to be near the ocean and away from my vitriolic birthday girl. My initial sips of the ice cold Chardonnay are replaced by deep gulps as I plough my way through three bottles during the meal, ending with a large brandy.

I leave my car at the restaurant and walk unsteadily up the incline from the esplanade, to the hotel overlooking the bay. I drink the complimentary champagne provided for booking their "luxury suite," then fall into a drunken sleep in the four poster bed.

I feel so miserable and alone.

Chapter **18**

I am back at Poppy's making good headway with "Amazon." She is away with Jacob and the girls on a two week holiday, so being alone helps to focus my mind on the story. There are times however, when the silence of the house eats into me. I am pleased to have the peace lacerated by a ringing telephone downstairs. I nearly do myself an injury as I hurtle down to answer it; to hear a voice, any voice.

I pause for a moment before picking it up. Firstly to catch my breath, (I still forget my lungs are damaged) and second because I realise it might be Jenny. I haven't heard from her for nearly a month, which is the longest she has left me without contact. I have had plenty of time to think about our last fall-out and realise I could have been a bit more tactful on her birthday. It has occurred to me that it may have been partly my fault she behaved the way she did, so I tentatively lift the receiver. 'Flood's residence.'

'Hi Flash.'

'No, it's Tesla. Who's speaking please?'

'Oh, hi Tez, it's Toby Evans. I was wondering if Jacob or Poppy were in?'

'Hi Toby, no they're all away. Can I help?'

'Well it's just an invite to an impromptu barbeque this Saturday evening at my cricket club. I wondered if you'd all like to come.

'They won't be back for another week, so…'

'…why don't you come anyway? The weather forecast says it's going to be scorching; it'll be great to see you.'

'Ok, thanks for the invite. I'll try to get over if I can.'

'Oh by the way, did you drop your prescription off at the chemist?'

I bite my lip as I lie to him again. 'Yes.'

I had dropped the monitor off at the surgery as promised; I had no choice because Poppy virtually dragged me there. Toby informed me at my follow up appointment that my cholesterol reading was too high and my blood pressure was a real cause for concern. He prescribed a statin and two different tablets to stabilise my hypertension. I hadn't had chance to drop it off at the chemist yet but I wasn't too concerned because I was feeling fine again.

'Ok, good. Hope to see you on Saturday. Take care.'

We say our goodbyes and I return to my room. I smoke a cigarette at the window, wondering if Jenny has been invited. I decide I will definitely make an effort to make it work with her if she is there. I take my seat in front of my laptop and in the time it takes to awaken from its slumber, I find myself hoping that someone else will be at the cricket club.

*

It is blistering hot on the day of the barbeque, so I decide to walk along the riverbank to the club. I do this for the exercise, to take advantage of the searing heat but also because I fancy a few drinks and don't want to risk driving home later.

I run the outline of my story through my head as I walk along the dusty path above the slow moving river. My tale about the ill-fated merchant brigantine has flowed onto the page, giving me a foundation on which to build.

I have always been intrigued by the story of the Mary Celeste and my love of sailing prompted me to try and write a story about what might have happened to cause the mystery. It was only when I started my research into the incident that I uncovered some remarkable facts about her background that made the story even more bizarre.

The ship was originally called the Amazon when she was launched in May 1861. Her first captain died of pneumonia on her maiden voyage, which might appear to be unfortunate but when you learn what happened next it is hardly surprising that the ship seemed doomed from the start.

It's not generally known that two more captains were to pass away on board, there were collisions at sea and a fire broke out in the middle of the deck before she finally ran aground in 1867. She was re-named Mary Celeste a year later (was this because the name "Amazon" was deemed to be unlucky?) only to become the greatest maritime mystery on 4th December, 1872 when she was found abandoned near the Azores in perfect working order. There have been numerous books written with versions of what might have happened but my research came up with an alternative theory, so I thought I would give it a go.

I have already worked out what I believe to be the skulduggery in the plot which explains the numerous, so called "unlucky incidents," but as I concentrate on the romantic twist that causes the crew's disappearance, my thirst suddenly becomes unbearable. The dryness of my throat is accompanied by the buzzing of flies, trying to quench their own thirst on the sweat weeping from every part of me. I am flailing my arms about like an uncoordinated windmill, trying to fend off the aerial attack, when I notice a possible oasis. I am about a mile from the promise of a charcoal-flavoured feast when I see a pub overlooking a silted bend in the river. It is shimmering, like a mirage in the heat so I head towards it.

I shiver as I enter the dark interior. The air conditioning is welcome but it brings on a violent headache probably due to the dramatic swing in temperature. I order two double whiskies and a pint of cider as I pass the bar on my way to the washroom. I rinse my face, neck and arms then let the water run over my wrists for a few moments, cooling me even further.

There is only one large glass in my hand once I have paid for the drinks and taken my place outside on the veranda. I light up a Monte Cristo and watch in satisfaction as the billowing smoke drives away most of the irritating winged marauders. Knocking back the doubles at the bar had made me wince and my eyes water slightly but this soon passes as I sit back to watch some children paddling below in the pools left by the unusually low water. There are adults lying on the grassy banks taking drinks and food from cool boxes and hampers.

My face starts to prickle as the sun begins to catch me. I smile as the children laugh as they play and then squeal when they splash water over each other. I think about Emily and Melia and how much I miss them when they are away. There is no breeze in this sheltered spot. I can smell the wood of the veranda and the plastic furniture toasting around me. The plants in the hanging baskets above me are wilting in the searing onslaught. I wish I had put some sun block on as I close my eyes and let my mind wander. How many people will I know at the barbeque? Do I really feel like moving? Fuck me, it's hot!

I sigh with pleasure as I roll the cool glass against my forehead, and my thoughts turn to Jenny again. Is she really all that bad? Being apart from her has made me realise we have had a few good times together. Maybe she behaves the way she does because she is fearful of rejection. Perhaps she is afraid of getting too close to me because I might hurt her; maybe she is worried I will leave her as her husband had done.

The heat is unbearable as I stand up; I peel my sticky frame from the seat and make my way back inside, to enjoy the refrigerated atmosphere. I enjoy two more drinks in the coolness of the bar watching a re-run of the 2003 America's Cup on the widescreen television. I wish that I was on the ocean with a cooling breeze hitting me, as I marvel at the grace of the yacht of the Société Nautique de Genève as it completes a whitewash over the boat from New Zealand.

The wooden terrace is still warm, even though it is in shade when I venture back outside. I am light headed as I return to my seat with yet another pint of cider. I have taken only two quaffs when an overwhelming bout of tiredness hits me. It's bliss to close my eyes for an instant.

It is still bright when I awake. The children and families have gone from the riverbank and the veranda is busy now with groups of young couples, many sneaking a look in my direction. I am shivering from falling asleep in the open air and my face is burning but this is nothing compared to the pounding in my head and the dryness of my mouth. I gag when I take a couple of gulps of flat warm cider; (avoiding the wasp that is trying to escape from the glass) it feels as if I have pieces of carpet welded into the roof of my mouth.

I am unsteady on my feet as I stand to stretch the cramp in my legs. I want to go back to Poppy's rather than run the risk of making a fool of myself at the cricket club. I hear a distinct comment of "Tomatoman" from a girl facing me which rubberstamps my decision to go home. There is a chuckle from the next table as I stumble into the wall as I leave.

*

It is dark when I wake up in my favourite chair at Poppy's; I have no recollection of how I got here. A couple of glasses of water followed by a few whiskies makes me feel better (and a bit tipsy again) as the pain in my face and head subsides. I reach into my jacket for my cigar case as I fancy one more luxury smoke before bed. "Piggin Doggin" I think, as I find that it's slipped into the lining through the torn pocket.

I remember Jenny's reaction was venomous when I asked her to fix it for me but I realise it was tactless of me to do that, especially on her birthday. I make the decision that now is a good time to mend it myself. I get a needle and thread from Poppy's sewing kit to repair the tear once and for all. I have to admit that it is not a neat job and I do catch my finger a couple of times on the needle but at least the problem is resolved.

I am sucking the spot of blood bubbling from my finger as I notice the flashing light on the telephone handset. There is a missed call. It's from Jenny. She has left me a message.

*

I am having a coffee and a smoke in the garden, (a welcome break from my writing), when I hear the commotion of the "Floods" return from holiday. I just manage to steady my swaying seat and am about to greet them when my nieces erupt into the garden. Melia shouts as she outruns Emily, "Runcletez. We're back, we're back!" She is breathless when she jumps up next to me; her sister joins us seconds later.

I say, 'I'm so glad you're home, I've missed you so much.' Emily and Melia sit beside me on the hanging garden chair, in the shade of the back patio. We swing lazily in the breeze but they still feel hot and sticky when they cuddle up close to me. They are wearing sleeveless summer dresses with a leopard print design. There's a sheen of perspiration covering their exposed skin. They are both tanned but Melia's freckles make her look darker. It's wonderful to have them in my arms again.

Emily rests on my chest, playing with the curl on my forehead as she chatters about their adventures at the seaside. Melia sits quietly watching me. It reminds me of the day she lay in the crook of my arm when she was a baby. She smiles as her sister tells me about the crabs they caught in the rock pools and the sandcastles they built with Mummy. We all laugh out loud when Emily tells us that Jacob had gone into an old fashion sweet shop and asked for "a bag of liquorice and a quarter of sharley bugar." Apparently "Mummy wasn't happy."

Jacob waves from the French doors and gestures for me to stay with the girls so he can go and unpack. My sister emerges moments later with a pitcher of lemonade and glasses on a tray. I shake my head in disbelief when I see her latest fashion statement. She is wearing a white cotton kaftan, over a grey tee shirt and a pair of bright red shorts. The largest, roundest sunglasses I have ever seen finish off the look. I can't work out if she looks like a bluebottle or Jackie Onassis. I am smiling when she reaches us and says, 'What've you been up to?'

I update her on what has happened over the couple of weeks that they have been away. I mention the invite to the BBQ and tell her I had phoned Toby to apologise for not going. I confirm I have been working hard on my book whilst it was quiet in the house but I am glad they are all home safely. She gives me a sideways look as she asks. 'Have you heard from Jenny after the way she treated you?' I had made the mistake of mentioning Jenny's outburst to Poppy just before she went on holiday. She was smug when she said, 'I told you to be careful with her. She's an odd one. 'I have to admit I agreed with her at the time.

'Yes,' I say and proceed to tell her it was virtually a month before I heard from her.

I relented when I heard Jenny's message virtually pleading with me to contact her. Her voice was soft and grateful when she heard it was me and she apologised for her outburst. This is a side of her I liked. I told her to forget it and said I was sorry to have been so insensitive on her birthday. I said yes when she asked if I would meet her to discuss the upcoming rehearsals of the "Pirate." We arranged to meet at her home.

When I enter, she welcomes me with a warm embrace, whispers "sorry" into my ear and kisses me tenderly. She is wearing the pearl earrings I bought her and I see her dress is backless as she turns and leads me through the hall, past the watching photographs into the living room. I imagine sliding my hands inside the dress, cupping her breasts and pinching

222

her nipples. The pressure of my erection means I have to re-adjust the fabric around my groin as I sit on the grey sofa. There is a bottle of champagne in a bucket of ice and two fluted glasses on the coffee table in front of me. Jenny kisses me as she kneels at my side and strokes my upper thigh. I groan as she moves her hand to clutch me; her lips don't leave mine as she loosens my belt and exposes me. She is stroking me gently as she leans back and cheekily says, 'I've missed this.' I am about to reply but she kisses me again, mounts me and guides me into her. The realisation that she isn't wearing any underwear and squeezing her cool buttocks heightens the intensity of my penetration.

She is in total control again as her hips snap against me with the rhythm of an urgent metronome. I hear soft moans as her arms wrap around my head, her face buries in my hair. She leans away from me as she arches her back and loosens the bow behind her neck. The dress cascades from her, exposing her chest which she slowly brings towards me. She presents her nipples to my mouth and says, 'Bite them Tez, bite them.' She moans and says, 'That's so dirty,' as I spit on them and start to lick. I then take each in turn between my teeth and nip them rhythmically. She gasps, 'Oh God!' as her hips smack into me, like the recoil of a shotgun; she's twitching and wailing like a wounded animal. Her muscles clamp me so tightly that my body convulses and I erupt.

We spend the rest of the evening, exhausted, side by side, flicking through the television channels, drinking champagne and eating cherry brandy liqueurs. She leaves me for a moment and returns with a small package wrapped in shiny gold paper. I open it to find a new mobile phone.

'I thought I'd treat you. You need one so that I can keep in contact with you.' I am about to get carried away with the gesture when she adds, 'I've already downloaded some of my songs onto it and put my number in for you, so that people can contact me in case of an emergency.' I shiver as she kisses me again and says, 'I would hate anything to happen to you.'

There is a faint alarm ringing as I think. "What the fuck am I letting myself in for?"

*

It is warm and clammy in the school hall when Jenny and I enter. There are groups of people dotted around the room, some are talking loudly. I hear, "Why's the bloody heating on?" and "Who's playing Sherlock?" I see a man pointing at me; it's not hard to read his lips, as he asks a man next to him "Is that Tesla Coyne?"

I can see Poppy and Jacob across the room talking to a woman who has her back to me. She drops a pile of papers on the floor and I am just admiring her backside when Jenny, (who has already told me she has been asked to help with musical direction and choreography,) claps her hands for attention. I am stunned by her forcefulness as the room immediately falls silent. She sweeps her open palm towards me like a quiz show hostess, presenting a family hatchback and announces, 'Evening everyone, this is Tesla Coyne, the playwright.' There are a few muted hellos and nods as Jenny resumes. 'Please can you all take a seat whilst production and pre-production get organised?' She turns away without another word. I watch her hair swish from side to side as she skips exaggeratedly over to a small group stood next to an upright piano in front of the stage. Her hair looks the colour of maize today.

I see everyone making their way to a group of seats set out in the shape of a horseshoe. I follow to sit with my sister, I am not shy but I just want to be with her at this first meeting. I time my walk to intercept her but then I see that the woman she had been talking to earlier is already sitting at the end of the row nearest to me. She looks familiar. She looks beautiful. I take the seat about two metres from her on the other end of the shoe.

I realise its Grace Perritano. I replay the image of her smile when she flashed by me in the car. She is talking to someone next to her, as I lean forward slightly, (not too obviously I hope) to get a better look at the girl that I haven't seen properly for nearly twenty years. Her hair is shoulder length, light brown with long deep waves. It shines as if it is damp from the shower. There is a wayward strand that sticks out at the back; I instinctively want to reach across and gently smooth it down.

She turns and looks directly at me, tilting her head to one side with a slight nod in my direction. The parting of the hair at the left appears at first to be too far over, but I like the way that locks fall free and she pushes them, temporarily back into place.

Her eyes fix on mine. Even from this distance I can see they are pure and clear but her irises are remarkable. They seem iridescent, changing from light brown to amber as she moves. I think I see love, kindness and happiness radiating from her at that instant. I feel my gut do a somersault; I am compelled not to break the gaze.

Her skin seems tight and it shines with health. Her arms are slender, her collar bones pronounced and her shoulders seem angular. She looks fragile almost birdlike. There is no flesh protruding from beneath the narrow straps of her yellow, halter neck dress; its colour accentuates her tan.

Her smile blooms slowly; dimples appear in her cheeks as her lips part. There is a small chip in the corner of her front tooth; this missing triangle makes her look sweet and cheeky. I love this imperfection; it is so refreshing after Jenny's flawlessness.

Her voice summons an image of warm liquid chocolate when she says, 'Hello Tesla.' I feel an odd tingling in the back of my head and the base of my neck, I am transfixed as I curl my forelock, she continues. 'Lovely to see you agai...' She stops and leans back abruptly. The wonderful, sparkling look of kindness and happiness crumbles and disappears, to be replaced by a look of fear and sadness. She quickly looks away as I hear a booming voice behind me.

'Is this our playwright Grace?' I turn to see a large man, and I recognise him from the car that nearly hit me. It is the same bloke I met years ago but he has changed drastically. When I had seen him then, he was a handsome and fit rugby player. I remember he called himself a "babe magnet." Now he looks as wide as he is tall. His face is flushed. I can't tell if he is angry or just has the kind of complexion that makes him look like he has had a bottle of red wine for breakfast. He extends his hand.

'Yes, I'm Tez,' I say as I stand and accept his handshake. His hand is clammy but his grip is firm and strong. 'But I don't consider myself a playwright just yet. "Pirate" is my first attempt at…'

He interrupts and talks over me. 'Richard Perritano, I think we met some years ago?'

'…a play. Yes, that was a long time ago but I think I've seen you driving around the village recently.'

'I'll be directing the play.' There is an edge to his voice as he adds, 'I see you've met my wife Grace, aka Mary Russell?'

I can't believe that she has been chosen to play my heroine. I reply, 'Yes.' I catch a glimpse of Grace from the corner of my eye. Her body is bent over as if she is expecting a blow or as if her life force has been sucked from her. She glances at me as I hear him move away. Her eyes seem to be soft with sorrow. I am considering whether she is sad because she is playing the lead part or because she's afraid of Dick, when my thought is interrupted.

'Right everyone, shall we start?' he says as he walks and takes his chair next to Jenny at the front of the room.

So begins the first read through of "Pirate."

I sit quietly as I witness this small village dramatics society bring my play to life. I realise that the change in Grace's demeanour and apparent sadness is linked to the proximity of her husband. When she starts to act, I have to fight not to stare at her, as she transforms from a nervous, thirty year old housewife, into a confident, twenty-eight year old detective. She comes to life as she grows into the part and the rest of the cast interact with her. Her speech is clear as she experiments with different accents. Her husband chooses a soft Cornish inflection as the one for the role; she sounds like one of the girls employed in Jordi's shop. He looks over to me when he has made the decision. It's not a look seeking my acceptance, more a challenge to see if I disagree. I get my first hint of dislike for him as I graciously nod my approval.

My heart misses a beat, when Grace later emerges from "wardrobe" wearing a black glossy wig with a red Alice band, brown horn-rimmed glasses and a heavy tweed suit. She starts to read from act one, about taking a new case, with the famous detective.

She becomes Mary Russell. It's as if a bubble surrounds her. The rest of the room and its inhabitants seem to disappear when she speaks; I can see that this opportunity to be another character, gives her strength and confidence.

Then our eyes meet for an instant. Even at this distance I can say, I have never seen a look in a girl's eyes like it before. I feel something inside again, that is alien to me, but this time it feels like a tiny electric shock is buzzing in my stomach. I felt it when she tilted her head to one side and smiled at me earlier, and I feel it now, as she battles with Holmes and Inspector Lestrade over an intriguing case concerning a British film company. I don't know what the feeling is, but it is very pleasurable.

There is a lot of fun and laughter as the company make their first foray into the performance of my creation. I breathe a sigh of relief as it looks like they are enjoying themselves. Jenny takes pleasure in telling me on the way home, that Grace once had a very small part in a TV show but she never looked like "making it." I don't like the way she belittles her. Then she is at pains to tell me that she could have played the lead role in "Pirate" if she wanted but she hadn't; something to do with "giving others a chance" and the terms of being a member of the actors' union forbids her. She sounds jealous and shallow.

*

They don't mind that I attend most of the rehearsals. I have to admit that I revel in seeing my interpretation of Laurie King's story come to life. I can see over the weeks that Jenny works well with Dick. I try really hard to keep two simple rules. Don't interfere with the Dick's interpretation of my play as I don't want to come across as being "precious," and try not to make it obvious that I am intrigued with Grace.

I gradually get to know Grace again by stealth. I have very few moments to talk to her properly at the rehearsals because it feels like Dick is continually watching. I can tell she is pathologically nervous when he is around but even he can't be there all the time, so I pick my moments carefully to speak to her.

I tell her it's wonderful to see her again after such a long time. She says she didn't think I had noticed her.

I tell her she brings Mary Russell's character to life. 'It's down to your writing,' she says.

I smile when I tell her she looks beautiful. She looks at me in disbelief.

I am nervous when I tell her that I walk past her house most mornings. She says, 'OK.' Then blushes and turns away.

I like it very much when I make her laugh; it makes her eyes sparkle which results in the fluttering inside me starting again. Can I really be the same person who was trained to kill? I feel young and giddy in her company.

*

I see movement when I pass her drive one morning but there is no one there when I step back to check. I continue up the footpath and pause when I reach where it turns, near the top of her garden. I think I hear a faint sound. I can see the rear of her house and am about to continue to make my way uphill, past the old mines, when I hear a faint voice. 'Tez?' I can't see anyone at first, as the hedge is too high but it is spindly and bare in parts where the weather has battered it. Then I see someone moving behind it towards a wooden door with a yellowing pile of grass cuttings dumped next to it.

I say, 'Grace?' as the door opens slightly, the squeal of the hinges assaults my ears. It is just wide enough to see a pair of amber eyes.

'Yes. Hello. I thought it was you.' She speaks quietly. 'I've seen you a few times.' My heart leaps, does this mean she has been looking out for me? A metal bucket rings against the jamb as she opens the door another few inches.

Her hair sticks up and out at erratic angles. There is what looks like a small piece of twig hanging down from a lock near her temple. There is the slightest smudge of soil on her cheek. She looks so natural, the imperfections attracting me.

I am suddenly tongue tied. 'I come this way a lot – I sit at the top – Think about my book – Except for today – Watch the horses.' This is the first time I have had a chance to speak to her properly and I can't think of anything clever to say. Her eyes leave me frequently as she looks furtively over her shoulder. 'What're you doing today?'

Her eyes meet mine again. 'The same as every Thursday, I'm going shopping this afternoon. I thought I would tidy this part of the garden before I set off.' She pauses as she looks behind her again. 'It is nice to see you Tez.' The sentence is said slowly, it feels as if it has been rehearsed but she still sounds nervous.

'It's great to see you again Grace. Why do you have to go every Thursday?'

'Only time I get to be alone...' Is she giving me a message? '...my mother-in-law, Isabella, goes to play golf in the afternoon; otherwise she is with me all the time, like a chaperone.' She tries to make light of the comment but it doesn't work. She looks really downcast.

'She sounds more like a prison guard.' I pause for her to disagree, and continue when she doesn't. 'Where do you go to shop?'

'Usually the department store and supermarket complex near the airport.'

'Oh, I know where you mean. Where there's a hotel next to the roundabout.'

She suddenly drops the bucket and jolts with alarm, as a harsh voice, from the rear of the house, splinters the moment. There seems to be the hint of a foreign accent. 'Grace, who're you talking to?'

Grace shouts, a little too loud. 'It's just a hiker Isabella, asking for directions.' She starts to shut the gate, she whispers urgently. 'You'd better go.'

'Why not just tell her who I am?'

I can hear panic in her voice as she urges me. 'Just go! It's too hard and complicated to explain, I should never have come out to see you in the first place.' She turns to leave as I hear the heavy breathing as someone labours up the lawn towards her. I catch sight of an older woman approaching.

I quickly whisper, 'I'll see you at the rehearsals on Saturday. Please meet me upstairs at the fire escape when the rest of the cast perform the "Major-General song.' I don't know if she hears me as there is no reply. I hear the hinges protest again as the door slams shut. I can hear the older woman's voice questioning Grace as I slip out of sight round the corner.

I run the encounter through my head as I walk to the top of the hill. Grace is petrified to be seen with me but she just happens to be there, at the exact moment I walk past. I smile as I remember what she had said. "I've seen you a few times."

There is a spring in my step as I convince myself our meeting today hasn't been a coincidence.

*

I had nipped upstairs earlier in the evening, on the pretext of having a smoke at the fire escape. A couple from the Society acknowledged me when they approached to use the toilets, on the same floor, at the end of the corridor. It was Dave Bentley and his wife Mandy. She smiled at me as she entered the ladies room, he said. 'Having a crafty fag Tez?'

'Yes, I'm just getting a bit of practice in before the smoking ban becomes official in July.' I laughed as I continued. 'I like to be prepared.' He smiled as he entered the men's room.

I wait for them both to re-appear and make their way along the corridor. I quickly pull the fire door to, placing a piece of card between the latch and the strike plate to prevent it locking. I jog to catch up with them and we chat as we go downstairs into the theatre. I return to my seat at the back to watch the rehearsals.

The dialogue stops and starts as Dick guides the company through the script. I have to admit he makes a good director; firm and encouraging with all of them – except Grace. His voice is harsh when he addresses her. Some would no doubt say that he can't be seen to be giving special treatment to his wife but I can see it is unfair and verging on bullying. I watch in wonder as she pauses, nods at his recommendations then says, 'Yes darling,' before repeating her lines. She doesn't appear to be fazed by his attitude; I can't tell if it's Grace or Mary Russell that is responding.

I am nervous as the scene approaches where Mary exits the stage, leaving the rest of the company to perform, "I Am the Very Model of a Modern Major-General. "This is the moment that I have asked her to meet me. I am sure no one notices as I slip out through the main entrance and go outside.

I have a sickness in the pit of my stomach, as I speculate if she will show. The sun is setting as I climb the metal stairs at the back of the building. I think "what the hell is wrong with me," as I remove the card from the lock, open the fire door and peek into the corridor. It is dimly lit and deserted.

There is still no sign of her as I hear the music and female chorus strike up below. I shake my head, as I realise that I am a fool to think she would run the risk of meeting me. I am about to return to the theatre when I hear the demented xylophone in the orchestra and then the tongue twisting lyrics, but I stop, as I detect another sound, footsteps, hurriedly approaching.

I think I have made a cataclysmic mistake, when I see a frumpily dressed woman approaching with long dark hair and spectacles. I am just about to duck out, back onto the metal staircase when I realise who it is. I had forgotten in my nervousness that she is wearing her costume. I cough discretely and whisper, 'Grace' as I emerge before her. She freezes when she sees me. I say, 'Grace, please don't go,' as she suddenly makes a move to walk away.

She stops, her voice shaking. 'I shouldn't be here, it's so dangerous.'

'We can be alone for a minute, we'll be able to hear anyone if they come up the stairs. You can say you've been to the toilet and I can leave via the fire escape.'

Her voice trembles. 'Tez, I've got to go. He'll kill me if he catches me talking to you.'

I say, 'Grace we are ok for a few minutes,' as I move towards her, 'I just want to know if I can meet you on Thursday. I'd love to have some time alone with you for a chat.'

'Tez, I won't have time. I have so much to do whilst Isabella is out.'

'Would you if you could Grace?'

She looks at me blankly, as if my question is a trap. I didn't intend it that way but I know her answer could be a turning point in my life. She lowers her head so I can't see her eyes; her voice is hushed as she says, 'Of course I would but I can't.'

'I'm sure we can have fifteen minutes together. I'll be at the store next Thursday. I'll park Jacob's van near the trees at the far end, it's fairly secluded and quiet there. We can say we met by accident if we're seen. 'My voice takes on the tone of a conspirator, 'We can say we were discussing the play. Just tell me what time to be there.'

We both look towards the end of the corridor as the music reaches a manic crescendo, signalling it's time for us to part. I lean forward to kiss her goodbye but she pulls away slightly. I move back in embarrassment, just as she moves forward. We are out of synch as our heads thump together but miraculously, our lips meet. The kiss is clumsy, her glasses dig into my cheek and our teeth collide. I wonder if that is how she chipped her tooth. We are both flustered as we pull apart; I smile as I reposition her glasses. She is alarmed when we hear a slight noise from the bottom of the stairs. She looks petrified as she scurries away from me and heads down the corridor. She suddenly stops before the corner; her demeanour seems to change. She looks confident and stands erect as she says something in a distinct Cornish accent before she disappears from view.

I duck through the door, shut it quietly behind me, and head down the stairs, two at a time, back to the rehearsals. Grace is on stage when I get back to my seat at the rear of the theatre. She is no longer petrified, she looks relaxed and carefree, as if nothing has happened; she really is a great actress. I see a newspaper on the seat beside me; I memorise the date of the day I kissed Grace Perritano for the first time. I run the words that she said to me as she left, over and over again.

'I'll be there at one o'clock.'

Chapter 19

Time moves at glacial speed in the days leading up to Thursday lunchtime. I can't concentrate on my book, even Poppy and Jenny comment at different times that I appear to be preoccupied. When I go for my walk, I linger like a stalker when I get to her house. I look out for her, expecting her to come and tell me it is all a terrible mistake and she can't meet me but there is no sign of her.

I have long discussions with myself. That kiss upstairs at the theatre was just two people saying goodbye. It was a platonic gesture, it had no real meaning. It was just a chance discussion...But what happened at the end of that dim corridor in the theatre didn't happen by chance.

I start to weigh up what I believe are the facts. I had told her I walk past her house most mornings and she was there less than a week later, waiting for me. She must have been looking out for me because she told me she had seen me many times. I told her where I would be at a certain time at the rehearsal and she came, even though her husband was downstairs. Then I remember her eyes when I saw her drive past at Christmas. There was something about the way she looked at me – or can she disguise how she feels? Finally, she has agreed to meet me. I smile as the pleasurable feeling washes inside me again.

*

Jacob hands me the keys and tells me he won't need his van until later in the afternoon. I use it quite often. He doesn't mind because he understands that I don't like to get my car out for just running around. I tell Poppy I am doing some errands, and plan to spend the afternoon in the library when she asks me where I am going.

My phone comes to life; its Jenny's ring tone, I don't answer it. I really don't want a conversation with her; she has been acting weird again. I don't want today of all days spoiling.

I am delighted when I drive into the supermarket car park to find the bays at the far end, partly shielded by shrubbery, are vacant. Its midday, I am excited and I have time to kill, so I walk to the far end of the complex to the department store where I buy some reams of paper and print cartridges. I don't really need them but they will be useful evidence to show my sister and Jenny if they check up on me.

When I return to the van, I sit twitching from side to side, furtively looking this way and that for Grace. I hear a car approaching from one side and look to see if it's her but it's just a customer picking up a pre-order. Then I see something out of the corner of my eye, I think, it must be her this time but it turns out to be a lorry with a delivery.

It's now well after one thirty, I feel despondent and foolish, and consider leaving. I have already started the engine when I see her car pull up beside me.

I wonder if it is up to me to get in her car as I hear my passenger door handle being pulled. I am amazed by her confidence but this is quickly replaced by a feeling of incompetence when she doesn't appear beside me. I can't believe I haven't released the central locking. It's a matter of a fraction of a second but I can see that she is about to get back in her car and drive away. I press the door release and wind the window partly down and urgently say, 'Sorry Grace, please don't go.'

She pauses with her back to me. I imagine her hand holding her key, ready to unlock her own car. She is considering her next move. She can drive away now, no harm done or... It seems like an eternity before she slowly turns, opens the van door and climbs up next to me. I don't really know Grace Perritano, but I instinctively know that getting in beside me is one of the most challenging and dangerous things she has ever done. Her voice is soft and fearful as she says, 'This is so wrong Tez. What if someone sees us?' She is scared stiff and shaking with nerves as I reach over to hold her hand, to calm and comfort her. Her voice is high pitched as she snatches her arm away. 'Don't, I've got to go. I shouldn't be here.' She is holding the handle of the door about to open it again.

'Grace,' I say as quickly and casually as I can. 'Grace, please just stay for a moment.' She is still holding the handle but I see her shoulders relax slightly. 'No one can see us. Let's just talk for a minute?' She turns to me. It is the first time she has looked directly at me since getting in the van. There are so many emotions etched into her face; she looks so unhappy, I want to hold her in my arms. 'I'm so happy you're here. I'd love the chance to talk to you properly; it's so difficult at the rehearsals.'

'I'd like that as well Tez but I can't. What would people think if they saw us?'

'They would say, "There's Tez with his sister's best friend. I bet they're discussing the "Pirate."'

'Look I have to go; I've so much to do.'

'Why the rush?'

'Because between Isabella leaving for golf and returning later, I have to complete all the shopping from the supermarket and department store and get home to make the evening meal and do all the chores. They'll ask questions if I haven't completed everything.'

I am about to say, "You're joking," but I can see by her expression that she is frighteningly serious. I have an idea. 'Can you give me your number so I can call y…'

I didn't get to finish the sentence. 'No,' she says as she reaches for the door handle again. 'You can't call me. And before you ask, I can't call you because he checks my phone and my bill.' She is really agitated now; I've made a real mess of this.

'I'm sorry Grace, I really am. I just wanted a chance to get to know you a bit better. Forgive me?' I am really sorry for what I am doing. I realise this isn't a game and my actions can have serious implications. I am genuinely astonished that this conversation means so much to me. I really care about this person; she isn't some conquest in a French marina but someone that I don't want to hurt. I can't explain why.

'Look Tez. Don't be sorry, I wouldn't be here if I didn't want to be but I don't know how to handle it, OK?'

I am about to concede defeat and say goodbye but I remember her voice as she left me in the corridor on the night of the rehearsals. An idea comes to me and the sentence is out before she can open the door and leave.

'How would Mary Russell handle it?' Her look is one of disbelief as she processes what I have said. She is silent. A spike of anxiety sears through me as I utter what I feel at that moment is the most important sentence of my life. 'Could Mary meet me here at the same time next Thursday?'

She looks at me in astonishment for a heartbeat, and I see her manner change as she unlocks the door and begins to slide out. She appears to be strong and confident as she looks over her shoulder and fixes her eyes on mine. The West Country dialect is back as she says, 'No.'

I have heard that word hundreds of times from women when it has only been a minor glitch but this time I feel unparalleled disappointment. I turn away and look through the windscreen. I notice it's filthy as the sun tries to break through. There is dust all over the dashboard, I will clean it for

Jacob when I get back, after all it's good of him to let me use it and let me live in his house. These irrational thoughts are interrupted as the van rocks slightly as she gets out; I realise I am alone but I haven't heard the door close. I am gutted as I fight the urge to look at her leave but then she speaks in the distinctive accent again.

'Meet me here at four instead; I'll be more relaxed if I do the shopping first.' I am stunned as she shuts the door and walks off. I see her get a trolley from the shelter in the next car park and cross to the store entrance. She turns and smiles at me just before the hedge in front of me cuts off the view.

Chapter 20

My relationship with Jenny has calmed somewhat.

I savour the moments when she is warm and considerate to me. They may be rare but at least they happen. Like the time she surprised me with a romantic weekend in a secluded coastal hotel in Wales. I really loved our time together; our walks down the deserted beach and making love in the dunes will always be a special memory.

I, in turn, have been as true to my vow to be patient and make allowances, even when her behaviour hasn't warranted it. It's like walking on rice paper sometimes. I make a special effort to get on with her because I have got into the routine of staying at her house most weekends and also on rehearsal nights. I have to admit that maintaining this charade is exhausting and I only keep my sanity because I always look forward to being back with the "Floods."

I am back at Poppy's one evening; we have finished dinner, celebrating the girls seventh birthday. They are sitting on my knee, as their bedtime approaches. Emily is fidgeting as usual; Amelia toys with the curl on my forehead and asks. 'Can you tell us a story Runcletez?'

I look at Poppy as she nods her consent. 'Of course, you've had some nice story books for presents. Why not go and get one of those?'

Emily says, 'Tell us one of your stories instead?' She is still for a moment as she fixes me with her "angelic and pleading" look. 'Please.'

'One of mine?'

'Yes, Mummy says you're good at stories.'

'That was a long time ago. I can't think of one right now.'

Amelia joins her sister in looking imploringly into my eyes. Their heads are a matter of inches away. God! I love these two so much. How can I resist? 'OK,' I say, as I hug them close.

'*Once upon a time there was a Prince...*'

Emily interrupts. 'Is he handsome?'

'You will have to wait and see. It might not be important to be handsome in this story.'

'I think all Princes should be handsome.'

'Do you want me to tell you this story or are you going to interrupt me all the time?'

Amelia says, 'Shush Emily; I want to hear the story.' Emily looks shocked; her normally placid sister has told her to be quiet. 'What's the story called Runcletez?'

'Mmmmmmmmmmmmm.' I only had a rough outline of a story, but no title. Then it comes to me. 'It's called, "*Spencer Spackman's Spectacular Spectacles*."'

The girls look at each other, their mouths frozen in the shape of perfect circles. Poppy's voice behind me says, 'Try saying that quickly girls, it's quite a tongue twister.' They try to outdo each other, to show their mum that they can master it, but they quickly tire of the challenge and settle down. Poppy is out of sight but I know she is sitting at the table in the next room.

'*Once upon a time there was a Prince who lived far-away in a land made ugly by war and hatred. He had fought many many battles without defeat but he longed for someone to love him.*'

'Didn't his mummy and daddy love him?' Emily interrupts again.

'He can't remember because he ran away from the King and Queen when he was a little boy to join the army. Shall I continue?' Both girls nod.

'One day, he decided that the time had come to find his love and settle down. He travelled the globe by land and sea to find a beautiful Princess to marry.'

'His journey was long but also very dangerous because he was a stranger in a strange land. He was attacked many times along the way by bandits and scoundrels. Each time he vanquished one, he would ask. "I will spare your life if you tell me where can I find the most beautiful Princess in this land?" And because the Prince was a great warrior they would point to the horizon and say, "Go that way, you will find the most beautiful Princess in the world."'

'So he would set off on his stallion, Stan...' They giggled at this. *'...to ride to the very edge of the world to find his Princess.'*

'In Pleasingtown he met the most pleasing Princess he had ever seen'.

'In Stunningtown he met the most stunning Princess he had ever seen.'

'In Charmingtown he met the most charming Princess he had ever seen.'

'In Gorgeintown he met the most gorgeous Princess he had ever seen.'

'So in each land he found what he thought was the perfect fit to his dreams but he wasn't happy.'

'Why not Runcletez?' Amelia asks.

'Because as he got to know them, he found that none was really suitable. In each case, it was whilst the arrangements for the wedding were finalised, that he realised they were only concerned about marrying a Prince and not him, as a person. He thought that was wrong. He wanted someone to love him for what he was, not for his title.

So when he left Gorgeintown, he decided to throw away his fine robes and his suit of armour and travel not as a Prince but as a common man to the land where he had been told there lived another beautiful Princess.'

'It was as he was travelling that he realised something very very important. Can you guess what that was?'

Amelia: 'She won't look at him because he doesn't look rich anymore?'

Emily: 'That he'll get killed by bandits, 'cos he hasn't got his armour.'

I think "bloody hell, clever girl," I hadn't thought of that issue in the story. I have to think quickly.

'No, he still had his sword and his shield to protect him. What he realised, was he was going from land to land looking for a beautiful Princess when he should really be looking for a beautiful person.'

'He was hot and tired and pondering how he could see whether someone was truly beautiful when he came to a sign that said, "You are entering the kingdom of Grimingtown."

'He thought to himself, "Well, I guess I wouldn't have found a beautiful Princess here anyway. I bet she'll be really grim." He stopped at a nasty bend in the road and tethered Stan to a tree. He sat down in the shade and was about to drink the last of the water from his bottle when he heard a clack CLACK – clack CLACK – clack CLACK – clack CLACK – clack CLACK...coming from a ditch across the road.'

'He got to his feet, cautiously crept to the edge of the track and looked over the edge...'

I pause for dramatic effect. The girls haven't budged for ages and I am aware that Poppy is sitting behind me listening to every word. I can see the story building in front of me but I have a pounding headache and really need to stretch my legs. Remembering P. T. Barnum I make the decision to stop, "always leave them wanting more."

'Right, that's enough for now girls, it's time for bed.'

Uproar! It feels like I have broken a spell as both girls protest. "Can't leave it there."

Poppy says, 'They can stay up a bit longer. What happens next Tez?'

'What's in the ditch?' Jacob asks. I didn't realise he was listening.

I decide to milk their eagerness for a little longer. 'No! It's a boring story. Come on; let's get you two rascals to bed,' I say as I move to stand up. Four voices plead loudly in unison.

'Please Runcletez – Aaaww not fair – You can't leave it there Tez'

I sigh as I relent and settle back. I decide to give them just a little bit more. 'Ok, here's a tiny bit more.' The girls both cheer and snuggle back down beside me. Poppy says, "Bloody good job." I don't think the girls hear her swear.

There at the bottom of the ditch, lying on its side was the smallest carriage you have ever seen. The words, "Spencer Spackmans Spiffing Spells" was written in red above a teeny tiny window. One of the wheels was turning slowly; a twig sticking into the spoke producing a rhythmical clack – CLACKING sound.'

'And there kneeling on its haunches, was the smallest pony you have ever seen, trapped by its harness.'

Emily interjects. 'Does the pony die, Runcletez?' I ignore the enquiry.

'It thrashed its head from side to side as it tried to escape and became ever more frantic and alarmed as the Prince started to slide down the dusty slope to help.'

'He jumped onto the side of the carriage and was about to release the pony when he heard a soft moan. He looked over the top and saw the smallest head he had ever seen sticking out from some black treacly mud. Two of the smallest hands he had ever seen emerged from the sticky mess and carefully

removed the smallest pair of glasses he had ever seen. A pair of the palest blue eyes he had ever seen regarded him as a tiny mouth opened and spoke to him. It was the voice of a Titan.'

It was time for me to impersonate the Giant's voice from "Jack and the Beanstalk."

"That was clumsy of me; I didn't see the bend in the road. My name is Spencer Spackman, Superior Specialist in Spiffing Spells. Could you pull me out kind sir and help me rescue Pony the Pony?" The Prince smiled at the little man with the big voice. He climbed down into the mud and pulled the man clear. "Thank you," said Spencer as he stood dripping in mud, "I would normally have used my wand to get me out of this sticky mess but I forgot to charge it last night!"

'Runcletez.'

'Yes Amelia.'

'Why does his wand need charging?'

'It's because his wand is the "Strontium Sepulchre Series Six; it can only be charged by the turning of the wheels of the carriage and he had forgotten to connect it up. He should have upgraded it to the "Strontium Sepulchre Series Seven" when he was in Gorgeintown.'

'Why?'

'Because the Series Seven can be charged by snores.'

'Snores?'

'Yes. Snoring will replace its energy if you put it next to your bed at night. And I forgot to tell you that Spencer Spackman, Superior Specialist in Spiffing Spells is a Splendid Snorer. Now, shall I continue?'

'Yes,' Amelia says as she snuggles beside me again.

The Prince was happy to be of help. They both pushed the carriage onto its wheels, (the tiny man was Surprisingly Strong) and got "Pony" hitched again then pulled everything back up to the road.

Spencer's voice boomed again. "Could I have a drink of water please? I'm very very thirsty." The Prince's heart sank as he handed the last of his water to the tiny man. He could have cried when he saw that most of it went to washing the black gunge from his tiny face. The tiny man went over to the pony and said, "Are you hurt Pony?" And the tiniest pony he had ever seen shook its head and whinnied in a horsey tone. "NNNNnnnnnooooooooooooo."

The Prince was astonished. He was thinking, "Can the pony really understand him?" when Spencer climbed onto a board at the back of the carriage and opened the doors. "Oh no," he said. "It's going to take some serious magic to sort this mess out."

'The Prince hopped up next to the tiny man and looked inside. It appeared that all the contents had been thrown onto the floor. It was complete chaos, just like your bedroom!' I said. I gave the girls a playful hug when they protested.

"That's odd," said Spencer. "The only item that hasn't fallen off the shelves is…'

I stop there.

'I'll tell you why the Prince gets the "Spectacular Spectacles from Spencer Spackman" early next week.' Everyone moans as I refuse to continue with the story. The girls reluctantly give me a goodnight kiss before Jacob ushers them upstairs.

Poppy starts to tidy up around me, she kisses the top of my head as she walks past me into the kitchen. 'That was a nice story Tez.' There is a moment of silence before she continues. 'Tell me, what's Spectacular about the Spectacles?'

'No can do Sis. You'll have to wait! I'll finish the story early next week and I'll tell you and the girls then.'

The placing of tea cups in the sink takes on a noise level somewhat higher than necessary. My exasperated sister utters a single word. 'Sod!'

Chapter 21

There is more traffic at this time of day but it is virtually deserted where I am parked. There is no sign of Grace's car but that doesn't worry me at first because I guess she will park at a more convenient location so as not to have as far to walk to load her shopping.

My stomach is churning as I wait to meet her. I check the time, 4:23pm. I realise she isn't coming. I try to shrug off the disappointment, as I grip the ignition key and start the engine. I raise myself from the seat for one last look over the hedge to see if I can spot her. I don't see her car, but a familiar figure is hurrying towards me. I smile as I turn off the engine and watch the woman push through a gap in the shrubs in front of me. She opens the door and climbs up beside me; she has long jet black hair a red Alice band and is wearing horn rimmed glasses. She says, 'This is so naughty.'

I hold her hand lightly, (so as not to alarm her) and lean over to kiss her cheek. I am pleased that she doesn't pull away. I tell her I am happy she is here; she tells me she is glad to see me but she can't stay long. I say that I am impressed by her ingenuity in wearing the props from the play; she says there is less chance of her being recognised. She laughs when I say that I like the summer dress and blouse she's wearing and I think the frumpy tweed suit would have attracted more attention than necessary. I laugh in return, as she seems to be relaxing, so I ask, 'So tell me, am I talking to Grace or Mary Russell?'

She frowns and considers my question carefully before replying. 'Part of Mary Russell will always be here whenever I come to see you. I think that's the only way I can cope.'

'I don't care as long as you're here. Are you looking forward to next week's premiere?' The first matinee performance is scheduled for next Thursday afternoon. She won't be doing the weekly shopping trip because she will be on stage.

'Yes, of course I am, I love being on stage and it's great to be performing your play for the first time. It's a shame we haven't sold all the tickets though.'

I am impressed with her diplomacy because having not "sold out" the performances is an understatement. The feeling that all is not well leading up to the production of "Pirate" is justified when we discover, less than a week from the premier, that the ticket sales are nothing short of a disaster. A cock up with the staff rota in the box office means that it hasn't been staffed for days on end and to make matters worse the sales by society members is woeful. Jacob told me that the plays marketing is suffering because it's brand new and a lot of people back off when they realise that it isn't a *bona fide* performance of Gilbert and Sullivan's, "Pirates of Penzance".

'I heard a rumour that they were going to cancel it?' I am feeling sorry for myself. 'It wouldn't surprise me if they did; I was probably too ambitious in the first place.'

She spins to look at me. 'No! GADS wouldn't do that. Low ticket sales often happen with new plays especially by unknown playwrights and every production, even the "Mousetrap" had to start somewhere. You should be proud that at least you've had a go and it was chosen by the Society on its merit, not because you are related to Poppy and Jacob. Imagine how thrilled we will be if it's a success and we were the very first society to perform it.' She holds my hand and says, 'And I am honoured to be your leading lady.'

Her comment reminds me why I had to miss some of the rehearsals. It wasn't because I was uncomfortable watching

247

my creation take shape nor that I was rebelling against Dick's direction or Jenny's autocratic treatment of the singers and dancers, (I have to admit they were both surprisingly good). It was Dick's tone when dealing with Grace that irritated me.

'I love you playing Mary Russell but I hate the way Dick speaks to you.'

'Don't be silly, it's just his manner. Besides, he has to push me to make me work harder and he can't be seen to be soft with me. I don't want to be accused of benefiting from nepotism.'

'Ok, it's just that he seems to be openly hostile to you at times and you have said yourself that you can never be on your own…?'

'…I don't want to talk about this now, I have to get going.' She kisses me and moves to open the door. I gently stop her.

'I'm sorry to interfere in your marriage Grace,' I say as I kiss her. 'Good luck next week.'

'You're supposed to say, "Break a leg."'

'I could never say that to you.'

She smiles as she leaves the car. It looks as if she is skipping across the road when I see her through a gap in the hedge.

*

I have to admit that my ego is massaged when I go down to the theatre and see my name in lights above the entrance.

"Gramplington Theatre presents PIRATE by Tesla Coyne."

I go in through the stage door, say a few brief hellos and then get out of the way. I have a feeling its bad luck for me to be there.

I take a seat in the stalls about twelve rows back from the stage and listen to the chatter as the sparse numbers enter the theatre. A group of elderly ladies take their seats directly behind me, they are complaining about their journey. The subject moves onto the weather, and seamlessly onto bunions. Then I realise that they have moved onto the programme as they start to discuss the cast. I can only hear clips of what they say because the orchestra has started to tune up.

"…seen her before. Lovely girl."

"…a very good Doctor."

"…nasty piece of work. His father was a gentleman though."

"…she told me there are bodies under the mine workings behind his house."

"…his brothers are the talented ones, you know."

"…trophy wife. Treats her badly, you know, never lets her out."

"…shady business dealings. Bankrupt…"

"…rumour he was in the SAS…"

I am keen to hear what they would say about me next when the conversation in the theatre is suddenly silent as the thunder from the kettle drums announces, Act One of "The Pirate." The curtains open. Sherlock Holmes is sitting in a leather wingback chair, reading a police file. A door, (stage left), swings open and a confident female enters, struts over and stands in front of the great detective. She puts her hands on her hips, leans forward and speaks in an exasperated tone.

"Honestly, Holmes? Pirates?"

There are fewer than a hundred people there to witness Grace's Cornish accent. I don't care because at that precise moment, something blossoms in my heart.

*

Everyone associated with the production is very kind, but the simple truth of the matter is that my play "stinks." My curiosity provides me with the truth. I lurk near the entrance as the patrons leave, most are silent but I hear a man say "terrible" as he passes me. I am having a smoke outside as one of the elderly groups congregates alongside a pair of minibuses. Two ladies shuffle past me, I can't see their faces because they are bent over double but I can hear their voices.

'I would've left earlier if they hadn't put my Zimmer frame in the cloakroom.'

'He should have stayed in the army!'

The after-show party takes place on the Friday after the "Pirate" has closed. There is one true highlight from the staging of my first (and probably last) venture into writing for amateur dramatics and that is sitting next to Grace. Poppy has arranged the seating plan to mix everyone up a bit, so I am delighted that my luck is in and I am sitting next to the leading lady. Jenny and Dick are sat directly opposite us; three other couples make up the numbers on the large circular table.

To my relief very little is discussed about the play. The subject matter mainly ranges from opera, to films, sport, (Dick gets animated for a while when the men discuss football and cricket) and then books. I am asked how the "Amazon" is going but quickly change the subject by saying. 'Well, if it is as good as my effort with the play, then I can't ever see it being published.' There is polite laughter around us as other people hear my self-deprecating comment.

The failure of "Pirate" has seriously dented my confidence and I really don't want to carry on with my novel. I nearly jump out of my skin when Grace's leg presses against mine. I immediately look around to see if anyone has noticed my reaction to her touch but everyone is in deep conversation. Grace looks carefully at Dick; when she is satisfied that Jenny has his attention, she whispers, 'Don't you dare give up Tesla Coyne.' Her voice dissolves my melancholy.

The conversation around the table continues to swing from subject to subject throughout the evening until it settles back upon books again and our favourite authors. Dick is quick to admit he doesn't bother reading apart from sports biographies. Jenny laughs, elbows him and calls him a "heathen." It crosses my mind that not many people could get away with calling him that; it's nice to see her in a good mood.

Most of us eventually start to debate whether we prefer modern literature over the classics. I admit that I had discovered a love of reading with Edgar Allen Poe and John Steinbeck but it was when I read Jane Eyre by Charlotte Bronte that I realised I had been missing out on the great British writers. I explain that I then "devoured" Dickens, Austen, Conan Doyle and Wilde.

Conversation about literature goes on for over an hour. I am really enjoying myself, and the alcohol is increasing my devilment. So I introduce one of my favourites into the discussion. 'I really like Rebecca by Daphne du Maurier.'

One of the singers from the production, (I think his name is George), says, 'I wouldn't categorise it as a classic but it's a good read.'

George's wife says, 'I liked the film. Laurence Olivier was such a dish.'

My words slur a little as I attempt to explain why I introduced the book into the discussion. 'I love the way it's written, especially the beginning when the narrator describes how she went back to Manderley, you can just visualise it. But what I love the most is the contrast between Rebecca and the "second Mrs. de Winter."

George says, 'What do you mean?'

'Well, you have Rebecca, who is a selfish and manipulative woman.' I glance at Jenny as I say this; I think Grace is the only one who notices, 'who makes everyone around believe her to be the perfect wife and a paragon of virtue. On the other hand you have the narrator, who is only referred to as the "second Mrs. De Winter," who is shy and vulnerable,' I press my knee against Grace's leg. 'It's no wonder that Maxim proposes so soon after meeting her, he couldn't let someone that lovely get away.' Grace applies pressure back to me. We smile at each other but the moment is shattered by Dick's voice.

'Bloody hell Coyne, you sound like a right ponce.' He puts on a girly voice. '"She was so lovely, he couldn't let her get away."' He takes a sip of his wine then leans back in his chair and closes his eyes. He continues. 'Wake me up when you want to discuss rugby.'

There are a couple of nervous laughs but I hear a quiet voice beside me. Grace says, 'I have always wanted to read Rebecca.' It is so rare for her to speak up in company, especially when Dick is around, so hearing her now seems to quieten the table.

My voice is nonchalant as I coolly say, 'Well I've got a copy; I can pop it round if you'd like to borrow it?' I have made the offer casually; Dick has heard me. Grace looks at him. I am not sure if she looks fearful or whether she is worried about gaining his approval. I try to appear indifferent as I look at Dick and ask, 'Is that ok?'

He waves his arms; his voice bombastic as he says, 'She can read what the bloody hell she wants; books bore me.'

I smile as I look into his eyes and quickly change the subject. 'So Dick, who'd you think will win the Rugby World Cup in France?'

I have no real interest in his reply, but some of his words slide into my consciousness. He mentions England winning in 2003, and South Africa having a strong team this time. I nod at what I think is the appropriate point and sneak a look at Grace when he gets into a debate with George.

I smile at her. She looks at Dick to make sure he is not looking, and quickly smiles back.

I have a plan.

*

It's the Wednesday following the "Pirate" after-show party and I am sitting with the girls; they have been asking me for days to continue with the story. I tell them that I am under strict orders to wait for their daddy because he wants to hear what happens next.

Poppy is sitting with us. She is chattering away but I am not paying much attention because I am excited and nervous in equal measure about putting my plan into action tomorrow.

Amelia shakes me from my thoughts. 'I wish Daddy would hurry up.'

I shout, 'Come on Flash, we're waiting for you.'

Emily asks. 'Why do you call my daddy, Flash, Runcletez?'

'Oh, it's just a nickname.'

Emily continues. 'What's a nickname?'

'It's a special word for people, which is used to emphasise something special about them, or because their name reminds us of something. For example, I had a friend in the Marines called Teddy who was a giant nearly seven feet tall. Can you guess what his nickname was?'

'Bear!'

'That's very good Amelia but we called him Tiny.'

'Tiny? That's silly.'

'I know but…'

Emily interrupts. 'Do you have a nickname?'

'I did at school, after discovering something in a physics lesson; it's a bit complicated but they called me "Voltage."'

'Can we have a nickname?' Amelia asks.

'Well you're a bit young…'

Emily pipes up again. 'Please give us a nickname Runcletez.'

I look at Poppy for her agreement; but she just shrugs her shoulders, which I think means "it's OK." I look at Emily. 'Well I will call you "Pancake," because you were named after a very famous lady called Emily Pankhurst. I look at Amelia and say, 'And you shall be called "Earache," because you were named after another famous lady called, Amelia Earhart, who was a very brave pilot.'

I see they are pondering as I look at Emily again, pull her to me and pretend to nibble her neck. She giggles as I say, 'Yes, Pancake, because I love to eat them a lot.'

I hug Amelia and whisper. 'And you, Earache my love, because you're the very opposite. You're like my friend Tiny, you're very quiet. I love that about you.'

Suddenly, I hear heavy feet rushing down the stairs. Emily shouts. 'Hurrah here's Flash; we can start the story now.'

Poppy tilts her head to one side as she looks at me. Her eyes are wide conveying the unspoken words, "See what you've started." She shouts. 'Girls, you must call him Daddy. Only grownups can call him a nickname.'

They both say, 'OK Mummy,' as they snuggle in next to me,

I say, 'Now where was I up to?... Oh Yes, I remember.'

"That's odd," said Spencer. "The only item that hasn't fallen off the shelves is my pair of Spectacular Spectacles. I think that must be an omen." He picked them up and handed them to the Prince. "I'd like you to have these as a thank-you for helping me."

"But I don't need any spectacles thank you Spencer; my eyes are true and clear."

'"But these are very special. I believe they were spared in the accident for a reason. So I'd like you to have them."'

"What do they do?"

"They'll show you how to 'see'."

"I don't understand. My eyes are perfect."

'"Look around you. What do you see?"'

254

The Prince said. "I see the clouds in the sky and the tree where Stan is tied." He noticed that Spencer had climbed up to the front of the carriage and had Pony's reins in his hands; it looked as if he was ready to leave.

*The tiny man said. "Now close your eyes put them on and say 'Spectacular Spectacles help me to **really** see.'*

'The Prince felt very foolish but did as he was told.'

The tiny man said. "Now slowly open your eyes, what do you see now?"

I pause for a moment. The girls wriggle in anticipation. 'What did he see Runcletez?' Amelia asks.

'First he saw the sky. It was the most wonderful blue he had ever seen and he could see multitudes of shapes in the clouds, each one amazing and interesting.'

'He forced himself to drag his gaze from the heavens and looked in wonder at the tree. The bark was made of the most complex patterns; he could study it all day but then he saw the leaves shimmering in the breeze. Each one seemed a miracle of creation, as if it had taken a million years to perfect.'

'Then he gasped when he saw Stan, his stallion. He knew his horse was special but when he looked at him through the "Spectacular Spectacles" he could see he was truly magnificent. The Prince realised that the spectacles gave him the ability to see the objects' inner beauty and enabled him to notice and appreciate what he had always taken for granted.'

'He turned to look at Spencer, to thank him for his generous gift, but the image through the lenses began to blur. Disappointed he said. "Spencer, the spectacles aren't working anymore…'

'"I know, I'm afraid I've had to limit the time you're allowed to look through them, to just five minutes."'

'"Why?"' asked the Prince.

'"Because of what happened to the man who had them before you."

He pushed a heavy looking lever beside him to release the brake on the wheel. "I have to be going now. Thank you for your help.'"

'The Prince pleaded. "Tell me what happened?"

"He went mad because he never took them off. Come on Pony, let's get moving."

'The carriage shuddered as it suddenly moved forward. The Prince persisted. "But Spencer, tell me, how can anyone go mad looking at such wonderful and beautiful things?"

'The tiny man looked over his shoulder as his carriage seemed to float silently down the road. He said. "I told you. The 'Spectacular Spectacles' show you how to **really** see. You will realise that some beautiful objects are actually hideous and wicked."

Emily breaks the tension. 'Runcletez, I don't understand what the little man is saying.'

'What he's saying Pancake, is the glasses helped him to notice all the things he had taken for granted; he could see their inner beauty. But they can also show him that there are other things that look good on the outside but deep down they're bad, even evil.'

'Oh.'

'The Prince put the spectacles into the inside pocket of his robe, untied Stan and was about to mount him as Spencer shouted to him. "By the way, I forgot to tell you something very important…"'

The carriage appeared to be miles away now. The Prince thought, 'How could it have got so far in such a short space of time?' Spencer shouted something else but the Prince couldn't hear.

"What did you say?" he yelled as loud as he could.'

"I said you must never look at people through the glasses." And with that Spencer Spackman and his carriage and Pony of course, disappeared from view.'

'The Prince was thirsty and filthy when he arrived in Grimingtown. He tied Stan to a post and sat exhausted, in the sunshine, on a wooden walk way at the side of the road. He was desperate for a drink. He was pondering where to stable his horse and where to get some refreshments and a bath when a shadow fell upon him. He looked up to see a young maid standing before him. Her face was dirty, she had a piece of her front tooth missing, hair stuck up at odd angles, and her clothes were very plain.

'She offered a jug to the Prince. "Here, I can see you are thirsty, please take a drink Sir.'"

'The Prince took the jug and drank every last drop. He looked at the plain but kind girl and said "thank you."

She said, "You can water your wonderful horse at the stables near the palace. I have to go now to fetch more water to wash the feet of my Princess.'

'Your Princess?' said the Prince.'

'Yes, I am her maid. She is dancing tonight for the King and Queen at the annual jousting tournament, so I have to help her get ready. With that, the young woman ran off towards the palace entrance, across the road.'

'The Prince left Stan with a stable boy and went to a tavern to wash and change. He then followed the crowds into the gardens of the palace to watch the entertainment. He managed to get a spot near the front of a stage just as the music began. A group of girls skipped into view followed by a tall majestic looking woman in a crimson regal costume. Her robes were held at four corners by maidens dressed in white silks.'

'The people around him whispered. "Here's the Princess, isn't she the most beautiful in the land. "He couldn't believe his eyes; her loveliness was stunning; she was the most beautiful woman he had ever seen. She walked haughtily to the front of the stage, held up her arms and drank in the adoration from her father's subjects. She then threw her *heavy robe to one of the maidens and started to sing and dance."*

'He noticed that the maiden who had caught the Princess's robe was the woman that gave him a drink when he arrived in the town. She was standing nearby, in the wings of the stage.'

'The Princess sang and danced. He felt she was performing especially for him. She seemed to glide across the floor as if on a cloud. He was dizzy with pleasure; he looked around and saw that everyone else was under her spell. He thought, "I wonder if she is really as beautiful as she appears. One little look wouldn't hurt and besides, Spencer Spackman wouldn't find out."*

'So he took out the Spectacular Spectacles, closed his eyes, put them on and said, "Spectacular Spectacles help me to **really** see." And then he very slowly opened his eyes."

'He saw that the Princess no longer looked beautiful, she was hideous, like a crooked witch. The sight of her offended him, so he quickly looked away and saw that he could see the inner blemishes of those around him. It was like a nightmare, he thought he would go mad; he didn't want to see all the wickedness. "I wish I had listened to Spencer," he screamed. He was just about to rip them from his face when he felt a strange sensation, as if he was being watched.'

'He turned and saw the maiden with the chipped tooth smiling at him. Her hair had been washed and combed, but it still stuck up, defiantly in places. She still looked humble and plain but he realised she really was the most radiant and exquisite woman he had ever seen. He knew he had found who he was looking for.'

'So he decided he would wait until the end of the entertainment, seek out the maiden, and humbly ask if she would consider marrying him. He moved to the side of the stage and was about to take off the "Spectacular Spectacles" when he accidently caught his reflection in a mirror. He screamed, pulled savagely at his hair, then ripped the*

"Spectacular Spectacles" from his face and threw them on the ground.'

The girls are sat stock still, they are not making a sound. I have only just noticed that Poppy has appeared and is sitting on the floor next to the coffee table. I can see Jacob out of the corner of my eye, standing in the doorway. They are all looking at me expectantly. 'Do you know what he saw that caused him such distress?'

They all shake their heads. Amelia breathes, 'No.'

'Well I think it's best to finish it next week.'

The noise erupts instantly. They are all babbling in protest. Poppy slaps me hard on my knee. 'Stop teasing Tez and finish the story.'

I am laughing out loud, which triggers a coughing fit. I eventually manage to compose myself. 'OK.'

'The Prince had seen all his lies and hatefulness in the looking glass. He saw he was loathsome and realised he could never expect to be loved by the maiden, so he turned to leave the castle. He felt worthless and full of despair and as he crossed the moat; he had just got to the stable when he heard a soft voice behind him. He turned; the kind maiden was standing there.'

'"Excuse me Sir, are you all right?"'

'He turned his eyes from her in shame. "I've searched for years to find someone to care for me but I understand now that I don't deserve to be loved. I'm truly bad inside."'

'"But you're not bad, Sir, you're just human, everyone has imperfections."'

*'"But the spectacles made me **really** see what I'm like inside."'*

'"No, they just highlighted the scars and pain from your life. I can see into your soul, I see your hurt and suffering can be removed with love.'

'"But who will love me? I have done so many wicked things?"'

'The maiden held the Prince's hand and said. 'I will.'

'The end,' I say and give each girl a kiss on the forehead.

'That's a lovely story,' Poppy says as she beckons my nieces into the kitchen. 'What was the maiden called?'

'Mary,' I say as I close my eyes and visualise Grace's smiling face.

Chapter 22

I have never been nervous when formulating a plan to win a woman, but I am this time, because the outcome really matters. Failure didn't concern me before because I could always move onto the next likely conquest but I don't want to spoil it with Grace.

I was careful to make my offer of lending the book within earshot of Dick. He has given his approval, and it's important I have his blessing. I was telling the truth when I said I had a copy of my favourite Daphne Du Maurier novel, but it was in my apartment, over 300 miles away. So on Monday morning, I divert from my early morning walk to have a coffee in the town centre, while I wait for the second hand book shop to open.

I find a suitable copy that I could pass off as my own, and go back to Poppy's to sit at my laptop, trying to write. I discover it is difficult to concentrate, as the time creeps slowly towards midday on Thursday.

*

I am standing part way up the public footpath. I can see the quiet avenue before me and the gates of Grace's drive if I stretch up and look over the hedge. I have been here for ages waiting for her mother-in-law to go to play golf. Each time I see someone approaching; I put my mobile phone to my ear and pretend to have a conversation, conscious that I must look furtive. I am not sure I look convincing. I think "I wish I could act as well as Grace" as I hear a "CHUNK" as the automatic motor engages to open the gates. I pocket my phone when I hear the crunching of gravel as a car approaches. I watch as Isabella's car emerges across the pavement, pauses for second then drives slowly down the avenue. I wait for it to disappear from view and walk casually towards the entrance. There is a faint metallic groan, increasing in volume, as the gates gradually shut. I quickly slip through, and am heading up the drive as they slam together.

I arrive at the front door, take the book from my pocket and look around to see if anyone has spotted me. "Look at me; I'm only delivering a book," is my message should anyone be interested. I see no one, so I ring the bell. I can't stop myself from tapping my foot impatiently and rolling a piece of hair on my forehead around my finger. A searing pain flares at my temple, as I hear my heartbeat hammer between my ears. I find it difficult to breathe as the pounding in my chest escalates until it feels as if it's crushing my lungs.

The door snaps open and she stands before me. Her hair is tied in bunches but some of the strands have worked loose and are stuck to her cheek and forehead. Her sky blue shirt, dark in areas from perspiration, seems to be undecided as it hangs part in, part out, of the belt of an old pair of jeans. She is holding her hands in front of her as if she is carrying an imaginary box; they have a white substance sticking to them. Brushing away a lock of hair that is stuck in the corner of her mouth, she accidently smears the gunk across her cheek.

She looks beautiful.

But it's her eyes that un-nerve me. Emotions flit across her face; if it was a performance, it would be world-class. She looks surprised, then pleased to see me but this turns to anguish, as her eyes and mouth open wide in fear. 'What're you doing here?' she says, her voice shaking. She looks like a cartoon character as she performs two double takes to see if anyone has seen me.

'Gosh, that's a nice welcome.'

'Why've you come here, you have no idea what he'll do if he finds out.'

'I just popped round to give you the book I promised to let you have. Don't forget Dick was there when we had the conversation. He won't mind will he?'

There is no reply, she now looks terrified.

'Grace. What on earth's the matter, you look as if you're in the middle of a catastrophe?'

'I've done something stupid in the kitchen and he'll…'

'Let me come in and help you.'

'No, it's too dangerous.'

'Look. If anyone asks, I just came here to drop the book off and you let me use the toilet before I left. OK?'

I move slowly towards her and she turns to her left, opening the door slightly; this is my invitation. I brush past her as I enter the hallway. Being so close makes me want to hold her, but I resist. She takes one last look down towards the drive and the avenue beyond to make sure no-one has witnessed my entrance, then closes the door and walks past me towards the rear of the house. I say 'Grace,' as I put my hand on her forearm.

'Don't.' But she doesn't pull away completely.

'No one can see us. What's happened?'

'I poured some cooling candle wax down the sink. It's blocked the pipes.' Her voice is trembling. 'I can't get the water to go down the…oh I'm so stupid. He'll be so angry if I have to call a plumber out, and I've got to do the shopping and…'

I interrupt her. 'Let me have a look to see if I can sort it for you. I did the same once when I poured fat down a sink, it should only take ten minutes. You go and get ready and I'll have this fixed by the time you come back.' She didn't move; she seemed rooted to the spot. 'Listen, do you take a list with you when you go shopping?'

This question must have come out of left field because it seemed to shake her. 'Yes of course I do, why?'

'You go and get ready and I promise that you won't be delayed. I've had an idea.'

'What idea?'

'Please, just get me a bucket and go and get ready.' I roll up my sleeves, kneel down and open the doors beneath the sink. I turn to see her still standing there. 'Go, go, go…' She finally moves and brings a bucket from a cupboard near the back door, then leaves the room

I unscrew the waste pipe and junction fittings. I can immediately see where it's blocked when I dismantle the connections. I find a skewer and a long thin knife in one of the drawers; fortunately the wax hasn't hardened yet, so it takes no time to breach the blockage, releasing the water trapped above. I have managed to clear all the debris, reconnect the fittings and have boiling water running through the system when I feel Grace's presence behind me. I shut off the water. 'There, it's fixed,' I say as I turn to her.

She is smiling at last. 'Thanks.' Her hair looks damp, I assume from a shower. She is wearing a white blouse and khaki calf length cotton pants; a rope belt finishes off her casual look. There is an aura around her. The panicking woman from earlier seems to have been replaced by someone oozing confidence. I detect that Mary Russell is partly present with me. 'Why did you ask me about the shopping lists?'

'Simple. Give me the list for the supermarket, I'll do that for you whilst you go to the department store. That'll mean I can get the bulk of it done for you, which will buy us, sorry, you – an hour at least.' She is about to interrupt again, so I continue. 'I can be discreet and meet you in the far aisle near the checkout? Grace, let me do this for you. I can't see a flaw…'

'I don't know Tez…' She pauses as she considers my idea.

I move towards her. 'Please let me?' I put my hand on her arm and change the subject. 'You look lovely Grace.'

'Lovely? I look like a tramp; I've had to rush to get ready.'

'Grace, I've told an awful lot of lies to a hell of a lot of women in my time but I'm telling the truth when I tell you that you look stunning...' She blushes as I pull her gently towards me. '...you always have,' I say as I kiss her. She moves into me, our bodies pressing. I put my arms around her. 'Grace, I've wanted you for years, I think Poppy always suspected but I could never admit it to her.'

'Me too.' She turns away from me, and leans on the kitchen unit, her arms supporting her. I wrap my arms around her again as she says, 'I wish you hadn't left to go into the Marines.' I start to turn her back to me as her hands make a swift movement at her waist. I pull her towards me, kiss her again and she responds passionately. It feels like tiny firecrackers are exploding in my head. God I want this woman so badly. I am disappointed when she releases me and stands with her arms by her side.

I notice her khaki pants are hanging off her hips. The rope belt has been undone. She is giving herself to me.

I am speechless as she grips my belt buckle and pulls me to her.

Our kisses are inaccurate and mistimed as I fumble with the buttons on her blouse and she rips the belt from my jeans; it drops with a clang onto the tiled floor.

Chapter **23**

I am parked at the supermarket again. It is exactly four weeks since we made love for the first time. Grace has gone missing. I feel sick in the pit of my stomach. I'm worried; I need to see her. When I say she has gone missing, I don't mean that people don't know where she is and there is a police search for her, I just mean she has disappeared from my life. I have walked past her house every day, hoping to catch a glimpse of her, without success. I have sat for hours in the car park at the supermarket for the past three Thursdays hoping to see her but she hasn't shown. I have seen her leave the house a couple of times with Isabella but that is all.

There have been two meetings of the GADS that I didn't need to attend but I went anyway just to see if she would be there, but there was no sign of her. I overheard Toby ask Dick if Grace was OK because she hadn't turned up. He just shrugged his shoulders and said, 'The silly cow's been under the weather for a while.'

This is the fourth time I have parked Jacob's van in front of the hedge. I believe I know each leaf individually after the hours I have spent gazing at it whilst hoping she would come to meet me again.

I have run that wonderful Thursday through my mind hundreds of times.

I had carried her into a room adjoining the kitchen and laid her gently on what looked like a futon. Losing my belt made the act of walking with my prize difficult, as I struggled to prevent my jeans from cascading around my ankles; I smile as I consider how tripping up and dropping her could have destroyed the moment.

Her blouse was completely undone; I pulled up her bra to release her breasts. It rested under her chin like a clown's bowtie. I kissed and bit her nipples as I started to remove all her clothes but she stopped me. 'No, what if someone comes to the gate?'

I didn't want to disagree with her, so clothing hung from limbs as we improvised our urgent intimacy. She quickly straddled me and slid me tentatively inside her. 'God, that feels wonderful,' she said, as she writhed on me. My breathing became laboured and guttural as her tempo increased. I closed my eyes as it seemed the firecrackers were igniting in my groin. It was as I was about to ejaculate, that she moved off and knelt next to me. I was about to protest but she said. 'Finish me with your fingers,' as she leaned forward and took me in her mouth. I tried to work out why she wouldn't let me climax inside her but the wondrous feeling of her darting tongue drove the conundrum from my mind.

She knelt up abruptly, causing my hand to be clamped between her thighs. Her movement juddered to a halt as she gripped my wrist. Then her body started to vibrate as she moaned. I tried to continue to please her but she held my hand tighter and giggled as she pleaded 'Stop, it tickles!' She had a mischievous smile on her face as she held my gaze and returned her attention to my groin.

She kissed me softly when I was spent, quickly pulled up her khaki pants, buttoned her blouse and ran off into the kitchen. She returned seconds later with paper towels to clean me. Then hurried off again as I pulled on clothes and re-looped my belt into my jeans.

I was savouring the encounter as she walked past me, in her coat. I went to hold and kiss her again but her uncertainty had returned. Her face looked strained as she pulled away and said, 'Come on, we've got to go.'

I persuaded her to give me the shopping list as she opened the front door and looked to see if the coast was clear. I said, 'Do you know what Daphne Du Maurier has in common with us?'

She seemed to be preoccupied as she steered me out of the house. 'No.'

'She was born on the same date that I kissed you for the first time.'

My remarkable revelation appeared to have little impact as she pressed the button to open the front gates and said. 'Really? Make sure no one sees you when you leave.' She set the alarm, locked the front door and went to her car.

I said, 'I'll see you soon in the far aisle.'

I had no idea if she had heard me. There is no acknowledgement as she starts the car and it creeps slowly down the drive. I slipped out onto the pavement and ghosted round the corner as she drove away.

I rushed home to get Jacob's van then set off to complete my task. I was granted a rare insight into the private preferences of the "Perritano's" as I went from shelf to shelf selecting so many alien products. I wondered what our shopping list would be like if Grace and I were ever together one day.

It was exactly fifty minutes after I had finished my assignment that she came into view, past a promotional display of biscuits. Her face was still etched with worry as she took the trolley from me and said, 'Thanks,' then walked away without another word. I followed her at a distance and watched as she queued to pay. I left and waited in the van for her to join me. She didn't.

*

So I am waiting for her yet again. I reflect that I have fucked numerous women, and made love to only a handful, but that lunchtime on a folding bed in "Perritano Towers" felt like nothing I had ever experienced before. It felt like...well I can't describe what it felt like to be honest, but it was special.

I am just about to leave when I see a familiar figure walking towards me. It's Mary Russell.

*

Grace told me she had imploded with the realisation of what she had done. She was so convinced her adultery would be found out that she drove herself into a pit of despair and anxiety. She had tried to perform her duties as normal, but some days she had been physically sick with worry. She couldn't even go to GADS, fearing a glance at me would give her away. It was only after a month had nearly passed, and doom hadn't befallen her, that she decided to meet me again. She told me "she missed me and couldn't stop thinking about my sweet, sweet kisses."

She decided to keep the disguise so she could use it when she came to see me. The props won't be missed by GADS. She keeps them hidden under the springs of the back seat of her car as it's the only place that she is confident that Dick won't look.

We formulate a plan and rules that should give us quality time together without attracting attention. My walks near her house cease, it's far too risky to be seen anywhere near there. We are always polite to each other whenever we are in company but we put on a display of irritation between us to throw people off the "scent."

For the first few months I do the basic shop for her, which means we have at least an hour together. We sit and talk, but she is always on edge, nervous each time a car passes. I suggest one day that we go for a drive to a nearby park. I am delighted when she reluctantly agrees.

I drive out of the car park and along the access road with Grace cowering in the foot well of the van. I have pulled out into the bustling commuter traffic when she slides back onto the seat and crouches beside me, to avoid detection by people in passing cars. I don't know who will recognise her in the disguise, but I am happy if it helps her have the confidence to be with me. I am uncomfortable that she doesn't fasten her seat belt.

Our drive to Brookesward Park becomes a regular Thursday feature. We sit and talk and laugh and learn about each other. We kiss and hug of course. Sometimes our kisses lead further and we do things that could get us arrested if we were caught. When the weather is fine, we take the risk of walking through the woods at the perimeter of the car park. The sensation of simply holding hands, as if we naturally belong to each other, is wonderful. We often end up at the farthest, most deserted point, a place rumoured to be only visited at night by drug addicts and doggers. We sit on a tiny decaying wooden bridge, dangling our feet over the sluggish dark water, as it struggles to make its way through the litter, used condoms and discarded syringes in its path. It might not be the most romantic setting but to us it's our special place.

I love to hold her close, imagining we are sat on the jetty next to "Sunbuoy."

I dream about sailing away with her and of being together, forever, one day.

*

My relationship with Jenny is still a challenge. Her moods swings and behaviour are even more erratic than usual, but I don't care, because I have the one time each week when I can be with the woman that excites me. I know Grace is still fearful each time we meet, but our Thursday becomes set in stone, except when she is away on holiday or if something unexpected happens.

I hate those rare occurrences when she doesn't show up. I try not to panic and start to imagine all kinds of scenarios.

270

Has Dick found out? Has she been involved in an accident? Has she got bored with me?

As I picture my life without her I realise my feelings for her are special.

*

It's the middle of October when Grace tells me that the next Thursday will be our last together for a while. After that, she won't be alone when she comes to shop. She cries as she tells me that Isabella will now be with her most days, because the golf season is about to end. It starts to sink in that it could be over five months before we can be alone again.

We are both quiet when we meet the following Thursday. She sits beside me; our hellos are subdued. The weather seems to mirror our mood as I drive through the teeming rain towards the park.

I have thought about this, our last meeting, it has made me realise the depth of my longing for her. I can't handle the thought of zero contact.

I stop the car in a secluded area; we are surrounded by sullen gray puddles. There are no other cars or dog walkers to be seen, we are alone.

I lean over, kiss her, and hold her close. 'I'm going to miss you so much Baby.' She is silent apart from her sobs. 'I can't handle not being able to contact you, so I've bought you something.'

She moves away from me and wipes her tears as I hand her a mobile phone, but she shakes her head, refusing to accept it. 'I can't have this Tez. Dick will find it. He is always checking up on me. He goes through my handbag and my belongings. It's too dangerous.'

'Grace, you can keep it under the back seat of your car, along with the disguise. He won't find it there.' I can see that she is unsure, so I continue. 'You can leave it there switched off until you want to use it; the battery will last for weeks. I've also got you a charger that you can put in your cigarette lighter, so you can top it up if you are out alone in your car.'

I hand it to her again. This time she accepts it. 'But I'll hardly be able to contact you, Tez.'

'I know, but just one message or call from you over the coming months is better than nothing. Here, let me show you how to use it, it's different from your other one.' I show her how to send a text; there is only one number programmed, it's under speed dial "T".

Her tongue protrudes slightly as she concentrates on the tiny keyboard. She smiles at me as she presses "send." It feels as if I am opening a Christmas present when I click on her first-ever message to me. It reads, "*Going 2 miss u. 143.*" She has never told me she loves me, but the numbers come close.

It's my turn. Her phone shakes with a, "FRHZZ FRHZZ" as she gets my reply. She asks, 'What does "Ditto 831 mean?'

I take it from her and switch off the vibrate facility. Better to be safe than sorry. 'It means I will miss you.'

'Yes, but what's 831?'

'Eight letters, three words, one meaning,' I kiss her again. 'I promise I won't abuse this Grace. I'll want to send you messages to let you know that I am thinking of you but I won't. I'll only contact you if you let me know it's OK.'

'But what if Jenny finds my number in your phone?'

'Don't worry; I will put a password on it and I've put you in as an alias, "Russell," in honour of your part in "the Pirate" and it makes you sound like you're a bloke.' She lowers her head slightly; I can see she is blushing. 'She won't know it's you – even if she does find the name.'

She is silent as she tinkers with the keyboard. I feel a momentary buzz before the opening bars of "Thursdays Child" by David Bowie brings a welcome interruption to the percussion of the rain on the van's roof. She asks, 'Is that my ring tone?'

I smile. 'Yes, of course. You're my Thursday girl, plus the words have a very special meaning for me.'

'Which words?'

'The whole song has lines that have relevance to my life, but to you in particular.'

'Me?'

'Yes, there's one line that reminds me of the time I saw you properly at the first rehearsal at GADS. It goes something like this…' I take hold of her hand; fix my eyes on hers as I clear my throat to ready myself to serenade her. I hum a couple of bars then I am thinking about how romantic this will be as I start to sing.

'Nothing prepared me for your smile, lighting the darkness of my soul.'

I don't get any further. Grace puts a finger to my lips; I guess the emotion must be too much for her. That thought is dashed when she smiles and says, 'Please don't sing Tez, your voice is awful.'

I must look hurt because she leans over to me, wraps her arms round my neck and kisses me deeply. The rain is hammering down, and the world outside is invisible through the steamed up windows. I start to undo the buttons on her blouse, but she stops me. 'We are not going to start that now. We'd better be going.' I reluctantly start the engine and drive back to the familiar parking space behind the hedge at the store.

We kiss and delay, kiss and delay and then kiss until we can't delay our parting any longer. We hug each other one final time and she weeps for what seems like an eternity before she pulls away from me and climbs out of the van.

I watch her hurry to her car and give one final look back before driving away. Emptiness and desolation overwhelms me as I linger for those final moments, as her car disappears from view.

Chapter 24

A sickening emptiness spreads through me during the winter months when I am apart from Grace. I try to keep busy and occupy my time, so I don't think about her too often – without success.

I love my time with the girls. I take them for walks and to the leisure complex for a swim and I read them loads of stories. I also sit for hours, bent over and suffering with cold and cramp as I entertain them in what used to be the "Bethlehem Hotel." The stable, their magnificent Christmas present from 6 years ago, is now situated between two apple trees at the far end of the garden. I am amazed at how quickly the girls have grown. They use to look so small when we originally played in here but now I see their heads are not far from brushing the ceiling when they stand. The stable transforms into a Castle when it's Emily's turn to direct the day's play and I am a dragon trying to capture them; their squealing when I chase them nearly makes my ears bleed but I adore it. If it's Amelia's turn, then the stable turns into a mystical Palace and I become a Prince trying to win a damsel's hand. Sometimes my mind wanders, and I picture myself scaling the gates at "Perritano Towers" to carry my beloved prize away.

I throw myself into writing and revisiting my music collection on the days that I am alone. I lock myself in my room; chain smoking, as I fill my head with words and familiar melodies. I manage to complete "Amazon" and hand it to Poppy to proof read, a couple of weeks before the clocks go forward. It's remarkable that I've actually finished it, considering how many times I find myself gazing out of the window, fingers poised over my keyboard, wondering where Grace is and what she is doing.

There are rare occasions when I do hear from her over the long dark months. The joy of receiving a text message, is tempered by whether I can reply. I am delighted if I read, "Tez, I am alone for a while. Call me." I am honoured that she has risked contacting me. But if the message reads, "Tez I'm missing you SO much. DTB," I know it's too risky to text back but I'm happy she has let me know she is thinking about me.

I attend every GADS meeting of course, praying that she will be there. I see her there twice which turns out to be more painful than I'd expected. To see her so close to me, yet not be able to hold her is torture.

Jenny's tireless swirl of activity, organising holidays and visits to the theatre and cinema, fails to fill the hole left by my "Thursdays Child. "But two parties that she arranges give me the priceless gift of seeing Grace again.

The first is an informal get-together at the home of George and Victoria Stanton, the couple that we sat with at the "Pirate" after-show party. It is extraordinarily good luck that Grace and I are left alone in the dining room when the others go to freshen up their drinks. We are both clumsy as we whisper hurriedly, at the same time, with the same comment. "I'm missing you." We daren't risk touching let alone a kiss. The strain is unbearable.

The second is a black tie affair at Toby's cricket club. It is one of the few times Jenny and I are out with Poppy and Jacob. It's patently obvious that the girls don't get on but it's nice to see them making an effort when we are confronted with the seating plan.

Poppy knows she looks hilarious in her ball gown but she doesn't care. She loves a good party but hates dressing up, so it's her way of sending up the occasion. I swear that the red fabric of her dress is made of the same stuff as the safety curtain at Gramplington Theatre. She smiles radiantly as she passes amongst the guests, creating a buzz of chatter.

Jenny on the other hand looks flawless, she reminds me of a cross between a "Stepford wife" and a "Barbie doll." She flinches each time someone approaches to give her a welcome hug; she fears they will tarnish her perfection. I find myself wondering if her makeup will crack and cascade to the polished wooden floor if she smiles.

The maître d announces that the banquet is about to be served so we take our seats at the table. 'That was hard work,' Poppy says as she plonks down beside me.

'What was?'

'Reading your manuscript for the "Amazon."' She shakes her head. 'The grammar was ok but your tenses were all over the place.'

'Oh God, is it that bad?'

'Yes. I didn't really notice how your tenses switched from past to present in your script for "Pirate" but they did in your novel. Why don't you use a grammar checker?' Poppy's directness cuts deep, I am surprised at how much my book must mean to me. 'That's the bad news; the good news is I think the story is wonderful. I found it romantic, exciting and sad; there are parts that made me cry, which is a good thing.' I am puffing my chest out in pride now. 'I had a word with Terry at my publishers; he looked at the first few chapters last time I was down in London. Hope you don't mind?' I shake my head. 'He was very impressed. I knew that he couldn't do anything for you because he only specialises in travel and cookery books but he has recommended someone to send it to…'

I see Grace at the entrance.

Poppy passes me a piece of paper. I am not concentrating. She continues '…name is Kurt Devlin at Black Elk Books… first three chapters…takes about three months…'

My whole spirit soars as Grace walks into the room. She pauses at the door, her eyes sweeping, seemingly looking for Dick. I know it is me she is seeking when our eyes meet for the briefest moment. There is more warmth in that glance, (which lasts no longer than a second,) than there has been from Jenny, in all the time I have known her.

'…and I can help you with the synopsis if you want?' I am grateful that Poppy's question rekindles my attention because I am staring as Grace descends the stairs and approaches her husband's table. I'm going to give myself away if I'm not careful.

'Thanks Sis, I really appreciate your help. I'll sort it all out next week when I'm back at your house.' I give her a kiss on the cheek, just as she half-stands and waves across the room saying, 'There's Grace.'

I join in and wave across. Our eyes meet again; I smile as I remember what had happened between us when I delivered the second hand copy of "Rebecca."

Dick acknowledges us then points the little finger and thumb of his right hand to the side of his face and mouths the words, "I'll call you."

*

Later the following week, I hear the sound of the telephone downstairs. The ringing ceases then Poppy bellows from the hallway. 'Tez! It's for you.' She is still talking to the caller, as I make my way down. I begin to pick up what she is saying. '…yes, and he's just sent off his first novel to the publishers…so fingers crossed. Oh, he's here now, I'll put him on.' She puts her fingers down her throat and pretends to vomit as she whispers, "Dick." There is a hint of sarcasm in her voice as she laughs and says, 'Cheery bye.' into the mouthpiece before handing it to me.

'Hi, it's Tez.' We exchange pleasantries. I say 'Fine,' when he asks how the family and Jenny are. I feel uncomfortable and a little guilty when I enquire about Grace.

'Oh she's fine,' he says abruptly. 'Listen, I was wondering if you and Jenny would like to come with us to the Takkenappi? It's a new Japanese restaurant that's opened in Upper Gramplington; I understand you can speak the lingo, so I thought it would be fun.'

'Yes, that'll be great.' I know Jenny would be up for it because she gets on well with Dick and I will get to see Grace again. Result! 'Give me some dates and I'll check Jenny's availability.' I make a note as he reels off a couple of Friday and Saturday nights over the following month. 'OK, I'll get back to you before the weekend.'

'Excellent, you can tell us all about getting published. I'm not into books but I like an excuse to celebrate. Bye.' The line goes silent as he hangs up.

'But I haven't been published yet,' I say to the dead handset.

Poppy comes from the hallway. 'What did Mr Makemyfleshcrawl want?'

'He's invited me and Jenny out to a new restaurant.' My tone is curt.

'What's up with you Grumpydrawers?'

'Piggin Doggin Poppy, why'd you have to mention my book to him? He thinks it's been accepted. I've only submitted the bloody thing.'

278

Chapter 25

Grace has sent me a message saying that Isabella is playing her first competitive golf match of the season that Thursday, which is my cue to meet her at the supermarket. There has been no opportunity for me to help her with her purchases, so I know our time together will be severely limited. I am astonished as she jumps into the van and crouches in the foot well and commands me to. 'Go, go, go!'

I drive a little too quickly, pitching her from side to side in my keenness to be alone with her. One speed bump too many causes her black wig to get caught on the bottom of the glove compartment. I want this moment to be so romantic between us, after so long apart, but I fear it's ruined when I see her hair hovering at an acute angle over her head; she looks like she's been scalped.

Our kisses at Brookesward Park are urgent and brief. We have so much to talk about, so much to catch up on and so many pent up feelings to quench but there just isn't time. No sooner have we parked, than we are on our way back to drop her off at her car. I really don't want her to leave me. Being this disciplined, is one of the hardest things I have ever done especially when you consider that I was trained by the SBS.

This is our first proper embrace in almost six months, but it will be over a year before we can spend regular Thursday afternoons together in a nearby hotel. The fact we accomplish this, given Grace's overwhelming nervousness and fear, is nothing short of a miracle.

It is the following week, when we are back into our routine, that I tell her how I think we can spend more time together. My plan currently hinges on one key question. 'Do you have access to a computer at home?'

'Yes, of course. Why?'

'So you won't draw undue attention when you use it?'

'I know Dick checks my e-mails and my internet usage and he certainly won't let me use social networks but apart from that I can use it when I want.' I am happy with her reply; I know my plan will work if I can convince her to try it. 'Why?'

I tell her about how I had experimented with "click and collect" over the Christmas period. The idea had come to me whilst sitting in the van at the supermarket, waiting for Grace. I had watched as a trickle of cars made their way to an obscure location at the side of the store and I decided to trial my idea by going with Poppy to do the next weekly family shop. She uses the same store chain as Grace but it's a different branch located to the north of the town, not far from the Gramplington Care Centre. She likes to pop in to see Jacob's elderly mother before going to the store. I am amazed to find it takes nearly an hour and a half, to complete the task, from selecting a trolley to loading up the car.

Poppy unsurprisingly seems suspicious when I offer to do it for her the following week. 'Why on earth would you want to do my weekly shop? You were bored out of your skull last week.'

'Oh, it's research for a new novel I'm writing.'

'What's it called?'

'Haven't got a title yet but it's about a character called Aaron Jacks.'

'Ok.' She still doesn't look convinced but gives me her shopping list anyway. It takes two visits to perfect my system; I reduce the ninety minutes to less than ten.

I am nervous when I meet Grace the following Thursday, as I know it won't be easy to convince her that the process will work. I give her a note with my user name and password. I explain that I have used my name and Poppy's address to register the account, so any junk post and e-mails will come to me, not her. All she will need to remember is the login details, so she can place the order from her own computer. I can see she isn't comfortable but I continue and try and console her by adding that there's no risk of Dick discovering the plan. I tell her. 'It's best to log on, on Wednesday evening to make sure that there is a slot available for the pick up the following afternoon.'

'It won't work! What if Dick or Isabella add something to the list just before I leave at Thursday lunchtime?' There's real concern in her voice as she adds, 'I'll be scuppered, it's too dangerous Tez!'

I hold her hand and soften my voice. 'I've thought of that; just hear me out, please. If you aren't happy then we can forget it. OK?' She nods. 'If that happens, then just ring or text me, I'll pick the items up for you.'

She takes a few seconds to let this sink in. 'OK.' She seems to relax a little as I gently finish explaining the procedure.

'Always choose a time slot as late as possible, preferably on your way home, after we have met, so that any refrigerated stuff isn't affected.' I can see anxiety start to well up in her now, as she obviously hadn't considered this. I plough on regardless. 'And don't forget to delete the record of visiting the site from your computer history.' I feel I'm spiralling out of control. I lose my composure when she speaks.

'But what if they find out I've done the shopping online?'

'Just say you're giving it a try so you can spend more time at home.' This comes out louder than I intend. 'Say you want to spend more time in the garden or preparing their evening meal.' There's real nastiness in my tone as I mistake her nervousness as a reason to find a hole in my plan. She looks hurt.

I am silent for a moment. Then I take her hand, lean over and kiss her. 'I'm sorry; I didn't mean to raise my voice. I'm such an arsehole. I just want to have more time with you. I promise I'll back off if you aren't happy.'

It's her turn to be quiet now. I'm in turmoil as I consider that my eagerness may have destroyed any chance of my plan working. She squeezes my hand as she looks at me. There's a distinct Cornish lilt to her voice when she says, 'OK. I will give it a try.'

*

There are a few false starts as expected, but I keep patient as Grace builds the confidence to give the scheme a try. It's three weeks later that she texts me a message to tell me she has completed the order online. The wonderful luxury of having nearly two hours together is tempered by her worrying whether her order will be ready.

Later, even I am nervous when I see her drive to the collection point. She sees me as I cruise past her down the one-way system and park near the exit. She looks scared to death as I watch an assistant help to load her car. I am pleased to see she has remembered to move her order from the store's distinctive "click and connect" packaging into the ones she normally uses, failure to do this will be a disaster if Isabella discovers any evidence. It takes less than ten minutes to complete the task.

The assistant waves as Grace gets back into her car but she doesn't drive off immediately. My heart starts pounding as I think something has gone wrong but then I sigh with relief as she moves off. She waves as she passes me and I see her beautiful smile just as I feel a "FRHZZ FRHZZ" in my pocket. I fish my phone from my pocket and see I have a message from "Russell."

"It worked! See you next week, I can't wait. 143."

*

'Hello, is that Tesla Coyne?'

'Yes.'

'Hi, it's Kurt from Black Elk Books.' It has been over three months since I sent my sample chapters to the publishers. I have to admit I had started to give up hope. 'My apologies for the delay in getting back to you but my department's been devastated with a bout of flu. Are you OK to talk?'

'Yes, of course.' I wonder if my voice gives away the excitement I'm feeling.

'Well, we've evaluated the first three chapters of "Amazon" and I'm pleased to tell you that we like it.' I want to jump in the air and shout "yippee" but he keeps my feet on the ground as he continues. 'Please don't get your hopes up yet Tesla, there's still a long way to go. I have to tell you that only a small percentage get through to actual publication but if the rest of the story is as good as what you have already sent, then there might be good news in the future.'

I am confused; he's telling me not to get excited but then building my expectations. 'So you want me to send the complete manuscript to you?'

'Yes.'

'Ok, will do. There's just one thing…'

'What?'

'Oh, nothing, I'll wait to see if you like the rest of it first.' I realise there is no point in complicating the matter. He'll soon realise there's a problem when he sees the page numbering.

Chapter 26

Our plan works like clockwork. Grace completes the online order on Wednesday afternoon, whilst Isabella is having a nap, and meets me the following day. She has also placed an on-line order for her requirements from the department store next door, which gives us even more time together.

I am relishing the opportunity to get to know her better and find out what makes her tick. We talk about music, books, art, theatre, films, politics and even sport. It's remarkable to find how much we have in common but it's also our differences that make our hallowed time together seem like a real partnership. The occasional disagreement between us seems to strengthen our bond, like grit in an oyster.

There are three subjects however, that I learn to avoid, for fear of her being upset or clamming up – her marriage, Faith and children.

I have tried asking her about her relationship with Dick. Why she is rarely trusted to be alone? Is it true that Dick broke her ankle when he pushed her down the stairs? Why does Isabella speak to her so harshly? I see real sadness in her eyes when she tells me she won't discuss her marriage. She rounds on me furiously when I make the mistake of commenting that I can see she isn't happy, and why on earth does she put up with it? It's the first time she has really raised her voice to me. 'I don't want to talk about it Tez!' I concede she has a point when she follows this up with. 'You've got room to talk, why do you stay with Jenny?'

Her reaction is different when I ask about Faith. She seems to crumble in front of me when I mention her sister's prison sentence; and her expression turns to despair when I ask gently whether it's true that she was raped by Dick? 'Tez, I can't discuss it, it's too painful.'

I am surprised and distressed by her response, when I tell her another day about my love for Amelia and Emmeline and how much I'd love to have my own family; she starts to cry. Her sobs shake her body; it's painful for me to watch. She tells me she would also love to have children but it's a dream that will never come true. They've been trying for years without success and she feels so sorry for Dick who wants an heir to follow him into "the business." I think it odd that she should mention feeling sorry for Dick, I want to ask more questions but resist as I don't want to cause her any more pain.

There is an occasion when I get a rare insight into her relationship with Dick and his mother. It is late in the summer and we are sad that our time together is coming to an end for another six months. We are sitting on our little wooden bridge; overlooking the stream as it chokes its way through the debris below. Grace is leaning into me; my arms are wrapped around her. I kiss the top of her head and say. 'Can I ask you something?' She nods. 'I've always wondered why you shop so far away from home, when there are stores much closer.'

'It's partly habit but it's mainly connected to what I need to get from the department store next to the supermarket. Dick and Isabella always have something that they want me to buy there, so I kill two birds with one stone and do it all together whilst Isabella is golfing.'

I have a feeling of trepidation as I ask the next question; I am expecting her to lower the shutters again. 'It sounds like a military operation, as if each second of your time has to be accounted for. It can't be that bad, surely you've got some freedom?'

'You don't know what it's like. I am watched virtually all the time, and when I'm not, I am afraid of slipping up even if I haven't done anything wrong.'

'What do you mean?'

She lowers her head. 'It doesn't matter Tez, I don't want to discuss it. Let's just enjoy our time together.'

'Please tell me Grace, I want to understand your life. I don't mean to pry.'

She is quiet for a spell; I think she is weighing up whether to finally open up to me. 'OK, I will give you an example,' she says as she takes a deep breath. I can tell this is going to be difficult for her. 'He couldn't get hold of me one day when I came here to do the shopping. I only noticed I had a missed call when my phone beeped on my way home. I stopped and called him as soon as I could but it was too late; he was apoplectic. He screamed at me, said he didn't believe that I didn't get his call and he accused me of being up to no good, he…' She pauses; she's wringing her hands, the pressure is turning her finger tips darker.

I reach over, unlock her vicelike grip and hold her hands as I say, 'What did he do?'

'He slapped me when he got home. Isabella just watched as he dragged me into the kitchen by my hair, screaming that I was no good.' I feel sick at the thought of him hurting her. 'I showed him that all the shopping was done and my chores had been completed but he didn't believe me. He didn't believe me until…'

'Until what, Grace?'

'…until he came to the supermarket with me one afternoon to get some wine for a party we were having. It was only when we were on our way home that he realised he'd a missed call and an urgent message on his phone. He finally believed me, having realised that you can't get a signal in the store.'

'Why, what had happened?'

'Isabella had fallen in the kitchen and badly twisted her ankle. She had crawled to the phone and called Dick for help and left a couple of messages when he didn't answer. She was in a right state when we got home, and he wasn't happy to find Marcus there, playing the virtuous Son. Dick was furious when his brother suggested that "he was more concerned about buying booze for a party than he was about being there for Mother." 'Dick said he couldn't have got there any quicker, because he couldn't get a signal on his phone.'

'So, he realised you were telling the truth, did he apologise?'

'Dick say sorry?' She laughs sarcastically. 'Never, if anything it made things worse for me.'

'How?'

'He blamed me for taking him shopping, when he should have been looking after his mother.'

I am indignant. 'But that doesn't make sense.'

'Welcome to my world.'

'So why does he let you still shop there if he can't keep in contact with you?'

'Because he is very particular about me using the stores next to each other, he knows how long it will take me. Besides he can't be bothered to check the mileage to any other stores.'

I have to take a moment to let this sink in; I can't quite grasp what she's saying. 'Grace, I don't understand.'

She looks at me, silent for a moment. Her amber eyes have lost their lustre as her unsettling gaze displays unbearable sadness. She lowers her head; there is shame in her voice as she says, 'He knows the exact distance from home to here and back again. He sometimes checks my speedometer to make sure I haven't deviated.'

'You're joking!'

'No, I'm not joking Tez.' She sounds exasperated. 'I once went to a garden centre near Atabara Country Park to buy Isabella a nice bouquet for her birthday. It was a bit out of my

287

way but I knew that they grew the best in the area, which was why I went. Unfortunately, it was shut for refurbishment. I didn't think anything about it until later the same evening when he asked me where I had been. I didn't fathom what he was on about until he told me that he had noticed there was an extra nine miles on my speedometer. I felt a chill run through me when I realised I was being monitored, plus, he didn't believe me when I told him I had gone to buy Isabella a spray of flowers. He just said, "OK, so where the fuck are they then?" I tried to explain about the garden centre being shut but he wouldn't listen. He hit me so hard across the face that his ring chipped my tooth.'

She looks so tiny and vulnerable now. I cup her face in my hands; her cheeks wet from crying and move her slowly towards me. 'I could never hurt you Grace,' I say as she leans into me, her arms wrap around my neck. She closes her eyes as I kiss her.

*

There is excitement in the air at Poppy's, as the girls reel off what they would like for Christmas. I smile at the banter as Jacob says "too expensive" and Poppy declares, "don't be greedy" to each of their suggestions. I am so happy to be with them of course, but part of me is empty, as it's two months since I've seen Grace. I just want the festive season to be over and for spring to arrive, so I can be with her again.

I have tried to immerse myself in the Aaron Jacks trilogy. I have most of the plot mapped out but I am finding it hard to motivate myself, partly because I miss Grace so much but also because my confidence has been dented by the lack of response from the publishers about "Amazon." It's been months since I sent the rest of the manuscript in for them to read but as each day passes without a letter or phone call, I find myself getting more and more despondent. I know that ringing them for a progress report will be the kiss of death.

I have a weird niggling ache in my arm, so I decide to go up to my room for some painkillers and a sly afternoon snifter to wash them down. I am halfway up when my phone rings. I am a little out of breath, so sit on the stairs to answer it.

I don't go to my room after all when the call has finished, I return instead to the family debate in the kitchen. First Jacob, then Poppy, and finally the girls fall silent as they see me standing in the doorway. 'What on earth is the matter Tez? You look like you're in shock.'

I stammer the four words that Kurt has just uttered; words I thought I would never, ever hear.

Poppy screams as she grabs me and guides me in a crazy jig around the room. A tear escapes and I am embarrassed as it trickles down my cheek. Jacob slaps my back as he kicks off the chant. The girls don't know what's really going on but they join in anyway; it feels as if we're at a football match.

"They want to publish"

"Oh Yes! They want to publish"

"They want to puuuuuuuuuuuuuuuuuuuuuuuublish"

"Oh Yes, they want to publish!"

"Again"

"They want to publish!"

"Oh Yes! They want to publish"

"They want to puuuuuuuuuuuuuuuuuuuuuuuublish"

"Oh Yes, they want to publish!"

*

Grace is still apprehensive about meeting me but her anxiety is nowhere near as acute as it was when we first started seeing each other. I have bided my time before suggesting we move our Thursday afternoons from the park to a hotel round the corner from the department store. She shrieks, 'A hotel, have you gone mad?' I swear I see her eyes roll to the back of her head. I fear she's going to faint.

She doesn't meet me, the first time I book a room, so I tell her I will book it each week until she feels confident enough to do so. Each week she ignores my offer, until finally she texts me one Thursday lunchtime to ask "which room?"

Grace enters room twenty two. I have left the door off the latch so she can enter without delay. 'This is so naughty!' she says with a distinctive accent as she leans against the door. It clicks shut. She is wearing the black wig, Alice band and horn rimmed glasses. 'What if someone sees me come in here? Dick would kill us.'

'Gosh Grace or is it Mary? Who's going to recognise you? I hardly do.' I walk over to her and embrace her.

*

She is lying in my arms in our hotel bedroom; it's the tenth Thursday she has met me here. We have made love and argued, playfully, about whose turn it is to make the post-coital coffee. I count my blessings if she capitulates and slides from under the covers. She takes the miniature plastic kettle into the bathroom to fill with fresh aerated water. I watch as she walks naked, her pert, muffin shaped backside enticing me. I can feel myself getting aroused again as I notice a tiny skip in her step as she walks from the room; I know it's a good sign. I appreciate that this normally shy person is comfortable in my company; her nakedness in my presence seems so natural. It means the world to see Grace is happy.

I really value the tiny pleasure of sharing the single packet of dry, complementary biscuits with her. It's probably the closest we will ever come to having a "romantic" meal together but Grace has other ideas. I have discovered a cheeky side to her that I adore. She pretends to be ravenous as she tries to negotiate with her kisses and "sweet nothings" to get me to give her my half of the treat. I tell her I have to be firm

290

for the sake of fairness and equality, and laugh as I place my portion of confectionary out of her reach on my bedside table. 'Sorry, you can't be trusted.'

I reflect on our love-making as she potters around before me. I will never compare her to any of my previous relationships but I have to admit that she seems to be an amalgam of the elements that excite me.

Her kisses make a muddle of my head like a fine whisky but the feeling is infinitely more pleasurable. When I hold her close, she just seems to "fit" into the place I have made for her. Her shyness makes it all the more provocative when she demands that I make love to her. Her fake coyness as she crawls towards the head of the bed and kneels invitingly in front of me and beckons me with her finger to enter her, drives me wild with longing. Her tongue and the way it darts over my body is a sensation I have never experienced before.

As much as I adore our intimacy, my favourite time together is when she returns with our coffee and she snuggles up to me for our final hour together before she has to rush off to pick up the pre-ordered shopping. She often lies across my chest and witters on about what she has been doing during the week. It is so special that she can be so relaxed like this with me, it feels like she is giving me a priceless gift.

I stroke her hair, wishing that we could both drift off to sleep together, never to be parted. I let her words wash over me, making sure that I acknowledge the important ripples of information. I am content and relaxed to be with her but I don't want to be lazy and miss something important.

I'm enjoying feeling totally relaxed when her voice suddenly drops to a whisper. The change in her tone alarms me; I am wide awake in an instant and ask her to repeat what she said. I wish I hadn't bothered.

'Dick has decided that we're going to Portugal in August.' It's like a slap in the face. She already spends so much time away from me, which I have to accept, but today it just cuts a little too deeply. 'I'll be so sad and lost and lonely without you.' I hate the thought of her so far away, with him, so I pull her tighter to me. She props herself on my chest, sighs and says, 'I wish we could go on holiday together,' She absentmindedly starts curling a lock of hair on my forehead; her elbows are jabbing into my stomach.

I gaze up at her and say as naturally as possible, 'Well maybe we can.' The pressure of her leaning on my belly is having a profound effect on my bladder.

Grace suddenly sits up. 'How?' I really don't want to break the moment of lying naked with her but I welcome the relief as my internal organs relax. I love the way her breasts wobble as she sits upright at my side. I am about to reach and cup them in my hands but this action is overtaken by a more urgent necessity.

I move from the bed and walk quickly on tiptoe towards the bathroom holding my groin. My mouth is in the shape of an "o" as I display the universal body language of someone needing to relieve themselves. 'It's better you don't know, as you'll have to look surprised if it happens,' I say through the open door.

'Tez, tell me,' she shouts as I flush the toilet.

'No.' I return to the room but stop dead in my tracks. She has my prized biscuit in her hand; it is aimed at her mouth.

She says, 'Tell me or the…' She picks up the wrapper and inspects it closely '…Scottish Butter Shortbread is history.'

'You wouldn't dare,' I say as I make a move towards her; but it's too late. The golden brown ingot is already stuffed sideways into her mouth. I see her cheeks are now the proud owners of square protrusions on either side. She starts to giggle girlishly and backs away from me. She sits at the top of the bed, grasping a pillow as protection for her nakedness and leans back against the headboard. I think I am about to melt with happiness when I see the sugar stuck to her lips, evidence of her crime. It's as her cheeky grin disappears, to be replaced with the beginnings of a choke that realise I can't bear the thought of losing her.

I reach the bed as she pulls the soggy piece of biscuit from her mouth. I think she will throw it away because it has almost asphyxiated her but she takes a deep breath then throws it back into her mouth and chomps away. She is laughing at my startled expression as she ducks under the covers and makes loud munching noises. She squirms as I playfully try to extract her from her linen fortress. She turns this way and that as she wriggles frantically to try to avoid capture but I simply wrap a sheet around her until she is cocooned below me. Her head sticks out from the makeshift shroud; her hair is sticking up at erratic angles. Suddenly I realise she isn't happy being trapped. I see a flicker of fear in her eyes and wonder. "Has Dick pinned her down like this before when he's hit her?"

I quickly release her and start to carefully remove the giant bandage. Her delicious smile returns and we hold each other's stare as she is finally released. I stoop and kiss her. The tingling coursing through my body is like an electrostatic charge. I don't want it to stop. Grace gives a little shudder as she releases me and says, 'I love your kisses.' Her eyes are glistening and her voice seems to purr as she continues. 'I'll make you tell me your "holiday" plan.' She slides down my body and takes me in her mouth. I try to delay the inevitable by examining the solitary picture on the wall above the dressing table.

There is a single tree on a hill, overlooking a sweeping bay and the sea beyond; the tree is blue and the sea is green…I don't notice the colours of the sky or the land in the picture. My attention has been diverted, as I twitch with pleasure for the second time.

Grace slowly slides back up and wraps herself around me. She looks longingly into my eyes, kisses me again and says, 'Now are you going to tell me?'

'No.' She makes a move to pull away but I hold her hand firmly. 'Let me do this my way Baby and we might be able to be together. Ok?'

She moves a fraction towards me so I pull her gently closer. 'Ok,' she says. We linger for no longer than a couple of seconds before reaching for our clothes, as our time to leave has come.

Chapter 27

The call from Kurt had informed me that Black Elk Books were interested in publishing my novel but the euphoria of receiving the information had triggered an element of selective hearing. I had not appreciated, at the time, that there were a number of stages that had to be agreed before "Amazon" could be published the following year. The image of me and the "Floods" dancing around their house in a premature celebration makes me shudder with embarrassment.

I receive a letter a few days after the call, inviting me to meet him at their HQ. It confirms that the first stage is to meet; to see "if we get on and can work together," and if we do, then the next step will be to draw up a contract.

I travel to their offices in my Citroen; it is wonderful to feel the breeze in my hair. My mind switches from imagining my novel in a bookshop window, with me inside signing copies for enthusiastic buyers to the probable reality of driving back to Gramplington with my tail between my legs. I am more apprehensive about the meeting with Kurt than when I crawled alone into a guerrilla camp in East Timor to booby trap their arms cache. How does that work?

I needn't have worried. Kurt meets me in the reception only minutes after the secretary at the front desk calls him to tell him I have arrived. I had imagined I would be met by a tall lanky bloke with a pony tail, half-moon glasses and sandals. But the man in a pin-stripe suit who offers his hand to me is wearing a dazzling white shirt and patterned red and green tie, and wouldn't look out of place in the consulting rooms of a private hospital.

'Why don't we chat at my local round the corner?' He guides me out onto the busy pavement. My willingness to keep pace with him is my answer when he adds. 'Come on, let me buy you lunch?'

He is obviously well known as he acknowledges the greetings as we make our way to a table towards the back of the pub. We order drinks and food, and then he sits back and asks me to tell him about myself. I try to keep it interesting. I touch on my childhood in Germany, my love of languages, sailing and music. I tell him a little about the Marines, the explosion and end by saying that I like to make up stories for my nieces and have even dabbled at writing a play.

He leans forward when we finish our meal and says, 'Well Tez, I'm delighted to tell you that I'd like to publish "Amazon."' He extends his hand again. 'Congratulations.' I pause for a second, partly from shock, but mainly because I'm not sure of the legal ramifications. What if I get ripped off? He must have encountered this before. 'Don't worry about the contract, it's standard terms, and I'm sure you can get it checked by your sister as you don't have an agent. I understand she has friends in the business?'

He's right; I'd forgotten that my sister has contacts. I grab his hand before he changes his mind. 'Thanks Kurt. I am dead chuffed.'

'You should. It's a great story and I love the twist; it's a refreshing angle on an old enigma.'

I can't resist having a couple of celebratory whiskies as he tells me about Black Elk and the publication process. I am startled when he says it could take eighteen months before it hits the shelves. 'You might think a book is ready to be printed when you submit it, but that is when the real work starts. When you ask the public to hand over their hard-earned cash, you will appreciate that the book has to be at its best, and that comes with editing and proof-reading, typesetting, jacket design, promotion and marketing.'

I frown as I say, 'But I have already had it proof-read and edited.'

'I know, don't worry, I'm not talking about wholesale changes that will affect your story. Every writer, even Dickens, has benefited from a bit of trimming, here and there.' I nod my understanding. 'Now, I have one question for you. Why do you want to change the page numbering?'

*

Jenny and I have been spending more and more time in the Perritanos' company. It is clear that Jenny and Dick are friendly when working together at the Dramatics Society, but they appear to be even closer when we are out as two couples.

I encourage this increase in our contact of course, as it means I can be close to Grace and it seems to lure Dick into a false sense of friendship. Having been told that my book will be published, he now seems much keener to include me in his inner circle. He parades me like a mascot, which doesn't bother me, as the benefits of being out socially with Grace far outweigh the negativity of having to associate with her bullying spouse. This however, does make Grace pathologically uncomfortable, as a slip up by either one of us could lead to the discovery of our affair. We have sworn to avoid the risk of suspicion by keeping up the pretence by being polite but distant to each other. We even go so far as to argue when Dick actually allows her the rare opportunity to have an opinion in one of our many discussions. Dick actually comes to my defence on one occasion when she is particularly cutting towards me on the subject of convertible cars and how pretentious it is to have one in our climate. I know she adores my Citroen and would love me to take her away in it; her performance shows what a great actress she is.

Concentrating on entertaining Dick seems to divert all attention from us. I find he is interested in my boat, and would like to have a try at learning to sail. I have also stockpiled enough information, gleaned from Grace, about his other likes and dislikes; I think I am ready to put my plan into operation.

I have previously broached the subject of going on holiday in late summer with Jenny, but it was met with little enthusiasm. She has auditioned for a couple of roles in provincial theatre productions and is keen to be around "if she gets the call." I can see she warms to the idea when I mention we will only be away for a week and that as she has a mobile phone, she should still be able to get any good news immediately.

I suggest a number of destinations in order to plant a seed, but don't emphasise anything specific in order to avoid suspicion. I do suggest going away with "The Floods," knowing her response will be swift and uncompromising. She doesn't let me down. 'With them? Not a chance.' Part of me is angry at her attitude towards my "family," especially the girls, but her reply implies that she is prepared to consider going away with someone else.

*

'Come with us?' I have been scheming for months to hear Dick utter those words to me.

We are sitting with Grace and Dick in a restaurant. It was Jenny who suggested going out with the Perritanos' and it was Dick who chose "The Conservatory Grill" as the venue. It is a warm spring evening but the weather has a touch of Armageddon about it. Foreboding darkness is joined by lightning, then ear-bursting thunder, and torrential rain and hail. I decide it's time to steer my plan into action, even though speaking below the glass canopy will be difficult, as the cloudburst sounds like the clacking of a demented typewriter above us.

I raise my voice, for dramatic effect; look up to the curtain of ice pellets sliding uniformly down the panes above and tut. 'The weather in this country...' I pause to shake my head a little, '...can really get you down if you let it.' I look at Jenny and say. 'I don't think we'll need any sun block this year darling.'

I catch a knowing glance from Grace as I pick up my glass, and take a gulp of Chateau Lafite Rothschild. Dick is such a show-off ordering a six hundred pound bottle of Bordeaux but I let the red wine's warmth course through me, as I silently pray that he takes the bait.

He says, 'I know it's crap isn't it...?' then pauses for what is only a nanosecond but seems like an age. I cross my legs and dig my nails into my thighs. '... Are you two going away this year?'

Bingo! 'We haven't planned anything yet. We've talked briefly about maybe going to Turkey, Greece or possibly Portugal, but nothing definite.'

'Have you been to Portugal before?'

'Oh yes, quite a few times. I love the Algarve; I've been sailing around there a few times when I've been on my way back from the Med.' I take another taste of the wine and raise my glass to Dick. 'This is a fine wine by the way.' He nods and raises his glass in reply. 'I don't really have any preference about where we go but it would be nice to get away for some sun.'

I look at Jenny as I continue. 'Have you thought about where you'd like to go?' She leans back to consider the question but doesn't get a chance to reply.

'Where in the Algarve do you like?' There is a hint of excitement in Dick's voice.

'Oh, let's see.' I pause as I pretend to sift locations through my memory. My voice is quieter, now that the onslaught from above has abated and I have his full attention. 'I remember that I enjoyed Portimao and Lagos when I stayed there. I particularly like the coast around Alvor as well. The sailing there is quite challenging as you can get some pretty dramatic tidal changes.' Most of what I say is true, but I have only stayed in the area fleetingly, that doesn't matter in the overall objective, as I have done my homework. Grace can't look me in the eye as the conversation takes place. Excitement runs through me as her foot runs gently over my shoe, under my trouser leg and touches my skin. I know her risky action isn't meant to be sexual; it's her way of saying. "I know what you're up too! Good luck!"

Dick says with obvious pride, 'Our villa is on that coast you know.'

'Really?' I say as if I don't know. I try to show an interest without making what I'm angling for look too obvious.

'Yes, it's in Praia da Luz, about half a mile from the beach.' I already know where the villa is, as Grace has told me almost every detail and I have had plenty of time to do my research, although I already knew that two of Dick's other passions are food and good wine.

I casually present the bait and hope he swallows it. 'Praia da Luz? That's amazing; one of my favourite restaurants is there. I think it's called the Condor or something like…'

'…The Albatross!' Dick's voice is loud enough to attract attention from some of the diners at other tables. 'I'll bet that's the one you mean?'

'I'm not sure, it's overlooking the bay. The entrance is really inconspicuous but it has a fantastic wooden veranda on the first floor.' Dick is bouncing ever so slightly on his seat. He is visibly excited as I describe what I know to be his favourite haunt. 'I've not been for ages but they did have a massive lobster tank at the back of the bar and…'

'…That's the Albatross! That's the Albatross! We eat there all the time.'

'Yes, that must be it. Fantastic food and one of the best wine lists in…'

'...Portugal.' Dick's voice squeals as he interrupts me again. Grace glances at me fleetingly. I can see hope in her eyes. 'When were you thinking of going away?'

Jenny and I look at each other. I bite my tongue as it's important that the next sentence is hers. I think all is lost and I am about to reluctantly reply when she utters the words I have been hoping for. 'Well we have nothing definite but we were thinking about sometime in August.'

'That's when we're going.' I brush away some imaginary crumbs as I pray that an invitation is winging my way. I can't look at Grace as he leans back in his chair and booms the words I'd been steering him towards. 'Come with us?'

It's worked. He sounds eager, but I can't be over zealous in my reply. I shake my head as I say, 'That's so kind mate,' (I can't believe I'm calling him mate), 'but it wouldn't be fair to gatecrash your holiday.' (Yes it would if it stops you ill-treating Grace for a week). 'Besides you haven't had a chance to discuss it with Grace, yet.'

He doesn't even look at her as he says, 'Oh, she won't mind, it's up to me who I invite to my villa.' Part of me is delighted that my plan seems to be nearing completion but my core is angered by the way he talks as if Grace isn't even present. It pains me further that her expression doesn't change when he speaks about her like this. Has she become so anesthetised by his nasty behaviour that she no longer notices? Dick's hands are twitching excitedly as he continues. 'I'll hire a yacht. The girls can sunbathe while you teach me the rudiments of sailing. What do you think?'

I pause for a moment before answering. I try to keep calm as elation sets in. Giddiness swells inside me as I think about being with Grace. I am just imagining her in a bikini when I realise there could be a fly in the ointment; Jenny hasn't said a word throughout the exchange. It is highly probable she will say "no" out of spite because she hasn't been included in the conversation. I have to move quickly and choose my words carefully. I top up Dick's glass with wine and say. 'Sounds like a great idea. I would be delighted to be your "skipper" but it depends on…' I turn to Jenny; it's her chance to give her view. She leans forward slightly and is about to speak just as a blinding flash illuminates the room. A woman at the next table screams and jolts out of her chair as the room is filled with the lightning's searing brilliance. Jenny's eyes are wide open, alarmed by the sudden atmospheric surprise. I don't want to lose the impetus, so say, '… so what do you think?'

Her lips move but her reply is drowned by a clap of thunder, so loud and near, it shakes the light fittings. This time it's me that jumps. I have been trained to expect the unexpected but the explosion in the cave has changed me. The vision of Grace in a bikini is instantly erased from my mind. I hear nervous giggles and expletives around me then the steady drum roll of hail becomes audible again, as I look at Jenny and say. 'Pardon?'

Jenny leans forward, looks at each of us in turn and says, 'Fuck this weather! Yes, Let's do it, it'll be nice to get some sun.'

Dick is smiling broadly. 'There, it's settled. We can sort the logistics later.' We raise our glasses and toast the decision.

Fortunately no-one is looking at Grace as her eyes transmit sheer happiness in my direction, although her smile appears demure and devoid of emotion. It feels like all my good days rolled into one as I realise that I will get to spend a week in her company. I relish the thought of seeing her virtually all day of every day. Then it dawns on me that it's going to kill me even more to be so close to her, for so long, but not be able to hold and kiss her. I push the negative thought from my mind and replace it with the image of her in a bikini again, but this time covered in oil. Suddenly, I realise just how we could be alone. The plan came to me in an instant; all it will require is timing, cigarettes and sun tan lotion.

*

302

Kurt was right about their editing, proof reading and typesetting of "Amazon," the old adage of less is more, definitely works in defining the plot. Their changes are subtle, but make reading the book more pleasurable. I show Poppy the revisions just to be on the safe side and she agrees, laughing. 'It's much better now.'

It is months later, when we start the discussion about the jacket design that I believe that publication is actually going to happen. My preference is a simple picture of the Mary Celeste, perhaps with a small boat sailing away, and the two lovers and a baby shown in silhouette. But their design, (which I have reluctantly signed off), has a banana yellow cover, with what appears to be a crimson sun, dripping blood which is pooling into the shape of the boat. The designer, Christian, says it will be perfect because modern day readers want something a bit more obscure to lure them to pick it up and browse. I think it looks a fucking mess and I'm sure that Pancake or Earache could do much better blindfolded.

The promotion and marketing is geared to start in the second quarter of the New Year. Kurt says, 'It's best for this type of book to avoid publication near Christmas. There are so many shitty celebrity autobiographies, cookbooks, travel books...' I feel a bit annoyed for Poppy's profession, '...and boy band annuals on the bookshelves, that we advise waiting until spring. We're going to send it to all the usual chat shows, to see if we can get it on their list of recommended reads and to our contacts at the relevant TV and radio stations. Finally, Noah in marketing suggested sending it to Xander Root at our sister company in California, there seems to be a lot of interest over there as it will soon be the anniversary of the Mary Celeste's launch, two hundred and fifty years ago.'

I am excited when I leave but I "ground" myself as I realise it probably won't sell a single copy.

Chapter 28

I hear crying. I can see it's just past 3am on Jenny's bedside clock but she isn't beside me. I find her in the kitchen with a newspaper open, nursing a mug of cocoa when I go down to find her. Her body jerks as she sees me; I don't think she has heard me approaching.

'What on earth's the matter?'

'Nothing.' Her tone isn't as brutal as usual, there's a hint of real melancholy. She seemed to be upset when I arrived earlier in the evening, but I just thought she was in one of her moods. Now I'm sure there's a problem, I have never seen her like this before.

'Bloody hell Jenny, of course there's something wrong.' I can see part of the headline of the article she is reading.

"DISGRACED ENTERTAINER, SELWYN TRENT, 67, DIES IN BLINDOWER PRISON."

Her arm moves to cover it when she sees me looking. 'Isn't that the paedophile off the TV who got banged up for interfering with young girls?' I stoop down to hug her.

She shrugs me off and stands up, her voice is barely audible. 'He worked at the same studio as me…' She finishes her drink, folds the paper and puts it in the waste bin. She quickly adds, '…I never met him though,' as she turns her back. I've known her long enough to realise she is lying.

'OK, let's get you back to bed; we have to leave in a few hours.'

Wednesday

Jenny looks tired and heavy-hearted as we wait for the taxi to take us to the airport. But she brightens up, just before we leave, when she gets a call from her agent saying she has been shortlisted for an audition the following month.

*

Dick is really pissed off by the delay at the check-in desk. I am ecstatic; I am standing so close to Grace, I can't believe we are going to be together for a week. Dick turns his exasperation on me when it takes me longer than a couple of seconds to find my passport. It has dropped into the lining of my jacket. Jenny tuts and says, 'I wish you'd throw that old thing away.' I ignore her and ask the check-in girl if I can use her stapler to make a temporary repair.

I deliberately avoid buying any duty free booze and cigarettes. It's part of my plan to be alone with Grace.

*

I had no idea that the villa was so grand. Grace's description was very modest compared to the reality. I can't see much of it as Dick drives the rental jeep up the steep gradient and stops in front of ornate gates, to enter the security code. But as we continue up the private road and approach what appears to be a single-storey building, I realise I am looking at three levels of opulence.

The view from the marble floored living room is magnificent. It overlooks the private pool, the sloping manicured gardens and a hill dropping dramatically towards the bay and the sea. Directly below the window is the shared balcony of the two bedrooms.

I bump into Grace in the basement when we have unpacked; I have no more than a couple of seconds to tell her about my plan. I think she is going to die with shock when I steal a kiss.

Thursday

It's mid-morning and the temperature is soaring when I get the opportunity to see if my ruse will work. I wait until Dick and Jenny have smothered themselves in lotion then tell them I have to pop into town to get some cigarettes because I forgot to get some at the airport. I also suggest that I pick up some food and booze for a BBQ. Dick says it's a good idea as he looks at Grace and says, 'Why don't you go and help him?' I ask Jenny if she would like to come as well but she predictably snaps, 'No, can't you see I'm covered in sun cream?' I find it hard to suppress a smile as Grace follows me into the villa to get my wallet.

I stop the jeep on a deserted dirt track, just off an access road to a golf course. Grace is initially nervous as I kiss her but this switches to eagerness when I slide my hand down the front of her shorts. I am boiling with desire as she releases the zip and guides my fingers. She gasps and nips my bottom lip as she pulls down her shorts then fumbles with my pants and exposes me. I am dizzy with expectation when I see her shorts and knickers hanging off her right ankle. I am scared when I slam into her as I fear I have hurt her. But I see a wicked smile and her eyes glaze over as she tries to pull me deeper. 'God, that feels so good,' she says as she pulls up her halter neck top and pulls my mouth to her nipples.

Later we are grateful for the air conditioning in the supermarket as it dries the dark patches on our clothing; the sweaty evidence of our exertion. We are relieved when we return as there is no mention of why it took us so long.

*

I have a feeling of dread when we head out to the "Albatross" that evening. I had described the layout to Dick and told him I had been there many times but it was all a lie. I had only relayed what Grace had told me. I was concerned in case he asked me specific questions about it or expected me to know the staff but he was so busy showing off that it all passed off without incident. Jenny loved it when one of the customers recognised her and insisted on buying her a drink.

Friday

I have mixed emotions when I see Grace preparing to go sun bathing. The sight of her putting oil on herself and glistening in the light drives me crazy with desire but this turns to a jealous fire when I see Dick applying it to her back. I hate him touching her.

It's almost noon when Grace goes into the villa, alone, to fix some food for us. I follow five minutes later on the pretext of giving Kurt a call.

I can see Dick and Jenny on the loungers below when I stand at the living room window. They are having what appears to be an animated conversation. I quietly whistle to Grace who comes to me from the kitchen. I tell her to watch as I move behind her and start kissing her neck. The lace curtain shields us from their eyes. She sighs as I release her breasts but says 'No,' as I gently begin to pull down her bikini bottoms.

'Just keep watching them,' I say as I slide them further down her legs and lower my shorts with the other hand. Grace dutifully obeys and doesn't take her eyes from the scene below as she bends over and pushes herself against me.

It's over in a matter of seconds. Her tanned and oiled body, along with the potential risk of discovery, and her beautiful white bottom, fuel one of the most erotic experiences ever. Dick and Jenny don't notice as Grace blushes when a smile passes between us later at dinner.

Saturday

The day starts out well. I get up early to walk the mile or so to the beach, and go for a swim. Jenny decides to come with me. We actually have a lovely time together; she seems to have cheered up a lot since we arrived. We dive over the huge rollers as they smash into the shore and we hold hands as we walk in the rising heat back up the hill.

The temperature is in the high nineties when we get back to the villa. Dick is complaining that he has a massive headache. He snaps at Grace when she timidly mentions that it could be sunstroke but he decides to go to bed when Jenny suggests that a nap might do him good.

The heat is oppressive so Jenny and I decide to go for a cool shower and a siesta. We can hear Dick snoring as she takes the initiative and pushes me down onto the bed. 'I enjoyed today with you,' she says as she takes off her damp swimsuit. She pulls down my trunks and squats on me in a reverse "cowgirl" position. The brightness in the room suddenly changes as a shadow passes across the window. I think for a moment that there is an intruder on the balcony but the sight of Jenny grinding down and against me focuses my attention.

*

Dick is feeling better when we meet up later. Jenny is perky and unexpectedly gives me a kiss on the head when she gets up to fill our glasses. Grace hardly looks at me, let alone speaks. She is cold and distant all evening. I lie awake for most of the night trying to work out what I have done wrong.

Sunday

This is the day that I have an opportunity to let Dick die but more importantly, I find out what is vexing Grace.

Dick and I are about to leave to pick up our hired yacht when I bump into her in the garden. I ask her what the hell is wrong and why is she being so horrible to me. She tries to avoid me but I hold onto her and plead with her to tell me.

She relents and explains that she had decided to go onto the balcony to get away from Dick's snoring. She had seen me and Jenny when she walked past our window. She tells me it made her sick to see me with her and so obviously enjoying myself. She breaks from my grip and runs back up to the villa when she hears Dick calling me.

*

Dick is a complete arsehole. He is impatient as I run through the safety checks and complains when I have to check the weather reports. 'Why do you need to know? Anybody can see it's bloody beautiful out there.' I try to hide my exasperation as I explain that we need to know as it affects the wind, tides and currents.

Getting him to wear the automated life jacket is a chore. He keeps taking it off and fiddling with it. I am sick of telling him it's dangerous. In addition, I have to ask him repeatedly to fasten himself to the life rail. He often forgets when moving backwards and forwards when following my instructions to trim the sail. 'It's like a mill pond out here, stop worrying.'

I compromise my authoritarian standards by letting him get away with it, once too often, which is when disaster strikes. We are hit by a freak wave which causes the boom to swing violently, cracking him square across the back of the head.

It all seems to happen in slow motion as he sinks to his knees and serenely topples overboard. I spring from my position at the tiller and manage to grab him as the boat shoots past him. I see to my horror that the sea is already cloudy red from the split on his head. I see he hasn't fastened his life jacket correctly so it hasn't inflated. He is lying face down. He is unconscious. He is drowning.

The boat is out of control as I fight to pull his dead weight up onto the deck. My lungs are on fire as I try to haul his sodden hulk out. I shout and shake him vigorously, radio for help as soon as I realise he is safely breathing, and then bandage the wound. The rescue team arrive twenty minutes later and air-lift him into a helicopter. I sail back to the marina and call Jenny to tell Grace what's happened. I am detained briefly for questioning by the police as I provide a statement; they commend my quick thinking as I leave them to drive to the hospital.

I don't like the way Grace fusses over him. The doctors say the wound looks worse than it really is and he is lucky that I acted so quickly, as my actions have definitely saved him. They say he should be fit to be discharged next morning, and even fly home, provided he has no after-effects.

Monday

It is early morning when they release him from hospital. I have a message from Kurt on my phone when we get back to the villa. He says that they are about to print a sample copy of "Amazon" to see what it will look like with the proposed cover design. He is laughing when he asks if I would like to see it.

I ring him back and ask if I can have two sample copies. He says yes.

Tuesday

There are lights on in their house when the taxi drops them outside their front door. Grace has called from the airport to see if Isabella is back from her sister's. She is and has told Grace she will open the gates and wait up for them to get back. The mood is pretty flat when we say our goodbyes. Grace gives me a small kiss before linking Dick's arm and escorting him into the house.

Dick never thanked me for saving his life.

Chapter 29

Grace has finally agreed to meet me but flatly refuses to come to the hotel. Its three weeks since we got back from Portugal. I have spent each Thursday, sitting in room twenty two working on the "Aaron Jacks" trilogy and praying in vain that she will appear. I have plenty of time to appreciate how it must have hurt her to see me and Jenny fucking. I can't imagine how I would have reacted if I had seen her and Dick at it.

She is still cool when I pick her up at the usual place in the van. I give her a little kiss and say. 'I've missed you.' I start the engine and move off. I have no idea that my next words would open a can of worms. 'Can you put your seatbelt on?' She looks at me nervously, and turns away, ignoring me. I am only trying to protect her. 'Please put it on Baby, I can't understand why you always refuse to wear it; I'd hate you to get hurt if we have a bump.'

There is harshness in her voice which is new to me. 'Well just drive carefully and make sure we don't have a "bump." Dick would smother me with a pillow in my hospital bed, if I was unlucky enough to survive an accident.'

I can't understand why she's so obstinate. The change in her tone and making such an odd comment irritates me. My voice is rising. 'Put your belt on, please, it'll make me feel better.'

There is a look of defiance and absolute dread as she says, 'I can't Tez.'

I don't like where this is going. This has all the makings of one of Jenny's mood swings. I want to avoid a confrontation, so I speak softly. 'What do you mean Grace when you say "you can't?" I don't understand.'

She is irritated now. 'Just leave it.'

'Please tell me. I witnessed one of my mates hitting a windscreen in a collision when I was in the Marines; he was a right mess. He also refused to wear his seatbelt.'

'Look, I've been trapped in my car when the belt has jammed before. I don't know if there is a fancy name for it like "seatbelt phobia" but I just can't do it. I start to panic because of what has happened to me in the past. I know it sounds daft but I actually feel safer.'

'Ok but I know that the belt in this van is ok…'

She cuts me off, shouting. 'Tez, I don't care if this belt is perfect, I'm not fastening it. Just leave it. OK?' I can tell I have hit a nerve and I realise that she won't budge, so I don't mention it again.

It takes some of our special hugs and kisses to lighten our mood. We are both calmer as we walk slowly, arm in arm, to the bridge in the park. We talk about the holiday and giggle when we remember our stolen sex in the jeep and the villa. Life is good now we are together again.

She leans into me and says she is sorry for being horrible earlier, she was angry to see me and Jenny together; it made her jealous that it wasn't her lying there with me. I say I'm sorry she saw us, and emphasise I would be devastated, if I saw her like that with Dick.

I am surprised when she says, 'Well, that will never happen – willingly.'

It's "off limits" to ask her to elaborate but I can't resist. 'I don't understand.'

'He hasn't touched me in years, apart from when he hits me.' I am about to react to this distressing revelation but she stops me. 'We've tried for kids but have had no luck. I

313

suggested going to a clinic years ago but Dick just said, "What's the point, you're barren just like your fucking crazy sister, it must run in the family.'" The anguish on her face when she relates this is hard for me to witness.

'I know he's unhappy he hasn't got an heir, and Isabella doesn't help. She has never liked me; I think she has always regarded me as a "trophy wife." She stokes the fire of his discontent by saying his brothers have all got boys that can enter the business, so why hasn't he? I made the mistake of getting angry one day and suggested it might be Dick's fault that I couldn't get pregnant. That earned me a cuff round the ear for doubting his manhood but do you know what she said?' I shake my head. '"How can it be his fault? You haven't had a regular period for years."'

I have to admit it had crossed my mind, when we had so many consecutive Thursday's together, that there hadn't been an awkward conversation, ("I'm not feeling very well or it's ladies time"), every four weeks when I wanted to make love to her.

Grace says, 'Reading the book you gave me was ironic. I know you were comparing me to the "new Mrs Danvers" I love you for that...' Did she just say she loved me? '...but I know now I'm more like Rebecca. She had a malformation of her womb so she could never have got pregnant. My problem's slightly different, but the end result is the same. Nothing.'

I want to say something comforting but nothing constructive comes to me. I want her to tell me she loves me again. I hold her hand tighter, hoping it helps. 'I don't care that Dick and I don't do it anymore, I'm happy as long as I have you.' She smiles at me, I am enveloped by a warmth I've been searching for all my life. 'Besides, I know he's seeing someone else but he's usually very careful to cover his tracks.'

'How do you know?'

'I overheard him on the phone in his study. He thought I was out at the top of the garden but I'd come in to get a drink. His door was slightly ajar so I heard him talking. I don't know who she is but I guess it's someone from GADS. I think it's Mandy Bentley; she always seems giddy in his company.'

I am thinking it's more likely to be Jenny; they are very alike, as I say, 'Why don't you confront him?'

'What's the point? He won't admit anything and he wouldn't risk divorcing me because he'd rather die than give me half his money.'

'Why don't you run away?' There is anger in my voice as I can't understand why she stays with him. I want to state, "I will look after you."

'I can't, I have no money to call my own and the only place I would go is Sebastian's in Greece. But I can't escape there because I can't get my passport.'

'Why, where is it?'

'He keeps it in a safe in his desk.'

'There must be a way for you to get away.'

'There isn't. I've told you he won't divorce me, and he would hunt me down if I left him. He would be happier if I was dead.'

'Dead?' I feel like I am being carried away in a flood. I am helpless, as I listen to Grace opening her heart to me about her marriage. I doubt she has ever told her best friend, my sister, any of this.

'Yes, dead. I'm convinced he tried once when he pushed me down stairs after I told him Faith was coming to stay. Isabella backed him up when he told the hospital staff I'd been clumsy and tripped. He made it clear that Faith would suffer if I said anything, but…' She is crying now, part of me wants her to stop but I need to know the rest. '…he raped her anyway.'

I hold her in my arms. 'You don't have to continue.'

315

'No, it's time, I want to tell you everything. Remember how I reacted when you asked me to fasten my seatbelt?' I nod; how could I forget? 'Mine stuck in the buckle each time I used it, because the retractor seized; I couldn't even wriggle my way from under it. I was humiliated when I had to drive to a garage to get released, the mechanics made fun of me, they even laughed when I told them I didn't have enough money to get it repaired. To make matters worse, Dick kicked up a fuss when I got home, questioning where I had been for so long. He eventually accepted there was a problem with it and said he would get it repaired, but so far he hasn't bothered. That was over a year ago and I know for a fact that he will beat me if I get it fixed behind his back. It's made me panicky about fastening it in any car.'

'Oh Grace, I had no idea things were that bad.' I am now beginning to appreciate how much she is risking being with me.

'He hates me Tez. He really would like me to die which would be the perfect solution. It wouldn't cost him half his estate, he would probably collect an insurance payout, but more importantly, he would be able to try and get someone else to have his children.'

'You do a good job of covering this up when you are together in company. I know he can be offhand with you and I often see the pain in your face but I see that in lots of couples.'

'I know, I have to keep up appearances, otherwise I suffer the consequences when we get home.' This is getting into scary territory now. She is talking casually, as if she is describing a recipe. 'You already know he checks my mileage and phone records. Well he also monitors every transaction in my account so every penny is accounted for. I get a slap if anything is untoward.'

My temper is festering. It is hard to believe he wants Grace dead, but the mention of physical violence is too real to accept. My face must show some incredulity.

'Oh, he's hit me for important indiscretions,' a heavy tone of sarcasm in her voice, 'like when I haven't filled the kettle with water, or if I haven't cut the hedge straight enough. There are things like toasting his bread the wrong colour, or if his eggs are not runny enough.' She seems deranged now; I couldn't stop her if I wanted too. 'Oh, he's beaten me loads of times Tez, particularly if I've smiled or spoken to a man in his company. He certainly doesn't want me, but he gets jealous if anyone shows an interest in his property.'

'There was the time Dick came home drunk and found Isabella angry with me because I'd not ironed her favourite golf shirt. He hit me that hard in the belly that I was laid up in bed for nearly a week. That's his favourite target for his punches you know, my tummy. Very little bruising. It's a good job I'm infertile, no baby would survive in my body.'

I wince when she paints this description.

'To be honest, it's partly my fault Tez. Dick and Isabella have told me what they want, but I'm just a bit dozy at times and have to face the consequences. It's probably because I am thinking about you most of the time.'

I shake my head in disbelief; now she is making allowances for his abusive behaviour. I am distraught at how he could possibly have convinced her that any of it could be her fault.

*

OK, I admit it; I am consumed with excitement when the package arrives at Poppy's. The code on the shipping label has a clue to its contents, *"PB-87-4BLKBKS."* I rip open the wrapping to find the sample copies from Black Elk Books. There is a letter inside but I ignore this momentarily whilst I look at the gaudy yellow cover. I have to admit it looks brilliant. The mock-up seemed cheap and boring all those months ago, but now I see the design is eye-catching and

317

mysterious. I ask myself, "Would I pick it up in a bookstore?" Well yes, I would, so well done Christian, you were right.

I waste no time in turning to page 143 and am happy to see that Kurt has been true to his word, it isn't there, and it has been replaced by 322. I then read his letter; it says he has high hopes for my book, as there's been some great feedback from the proof-readers.

I hide one of the samples in the hallway bookcase; I will present it to Poppy later. I place the other in a bag, along with the other items I have for Grace. I am truly happy and relieved that our Thursdays at the hotel have resumed. I feared that the horrific revelations about her abusive marriage might scare her from coming to see me again.

She still enters our room nervously; wearing the disguise, but immediately relaxes as she walks to me and holds me tightly. We talk, laugh, argue over who makes the coffee and make love of course. I tingle when I hold her; it's so right to lie with her in my arms.

She has previously told me that her brother Sebastian moved years ago, to the island of Hydra in Greece, where he makes money as an artist. He has a share in a bar and spends his spare time on the beach. I met him a few times when he came to our house to drop Grace and Faith off to play with Poppy. I liked him.

Grace is unconsciously curling a piece of hair on my forehead when she says, 'If I could have one wish, it would be to be with you in Hydra. I would love us to live there together. I know a beautiful cottage, just three blocks from my brother's studio, opposite a bar called the "Aphrodite." It's been up for sale for years. It would be perfect. It has a powder blue door, is surrounded by bougainvillea and it overlooks the sea. It even has its own jetty, so you could moor Sunbuoy there. You'd adore it Tez.'

'That's a wonderful dream Miss Russell; I would go anywhere to be with you, if only our circumstances were different.'

'Tez, I'm not Miss Mary Russell today. I am Grace, your "Thursday's Child" and I so want to be here. You have brought me happiness. I've never told you this before; I've always loved you but I thought I was too young. I didn't think I had a chance because I saw how other women desired you.'

'What did you say?' I have waited all my life to hear those words spoken in a sincere way. I can't believe it.

'I said "I love you, Tesla Coyne." Or to put it more clearly, I am in love with you. It destroyed me when you left to join the Marines. I never thought I would see you again.'

I am shaking as I hold her in my arms. It's a mixture of shock and revelling in the overwhelming emotion. I repeat the words in my head over and over again. "She loves me, she loves me." I have to check. 'You really love me?'

'Yes, I love you. I always will, forever and ever, even when you're old and feeble.'

I laugh as I say, 'What, you'll still love me when I need a bed bath or if I'm incontinent?'

She laughs too. 'Well, I hadn't quite envisioned that romantic scenario, but yes, I will love you, whatever life throws at us.'

I plant this moment firmly in the centre of my memory. I have waited so many years for someone to love me for who I am. I can't find a word to describe how I feel, now it's finally arrived.

I reach under the bed and say, 'I have something for you.' I put the bag in my lap, and extract the first item, an envelope. 'Here is a bank statement and debit card, I have opened an account in my name and deposited some money for you in case of an emergency but only you have access. The passwords and security questions are in there along with some cash of different denominations.'

She begins to protest. 'But I can't take your money…' She tries to hand it back to me. '…besides, Dick will find it.'

I refuse to take it. 'No he won't if you hide it with your disguise.' I take a set of keys out of the envelope and hand them to her.

She scowls. 'What are these?'

'They're the keys to his desk and the safe.' She looks at me in disbelief; I guess she is trying to work out how I got them. 'I got them from Jacobs's workshop when he was on holiday, he always keeps spares.' I can tell by her expression that she still doesn't understand. 'He renovated the desk you bought as a Christmas present remember? When I first moved up here all those years ago.'

'I forgot about that. God, that was ages ago. I didn't realise he kept spares – won't he miss them?'

'No, they're copies. I have to admit it was a bit difficult to get the safe key cut, though. All the local hardware stores refused, saying they couldn't do it, without the relevant security documentation. They moaned, "More than my job's worth mate." So, I just sent them by courier to Jordi who got them back to me the next day.' She looks worried. 'The originals are back in Jacob's filing cabinet.'

She holds them in her hand as if they are some kind of alien object. She seems to be processing data, confused about why I have given them to her, or what to do with them. 'What's the matter?'

She looks perplexed. 'I don't understand why you've given them to me.'

'If you ever have to get away and need your passport, then you have the means now. Just hide them somewhere in the house where Dick or Isabella will never dream of looking.' She looks like someone who has just had the cage door unlocked and left ajar. Freedom is a step away but her face signals what a massive leap it would be.

There is a tear in her eye as I pull out the book and pass it to her. She holds it delicately in both hands as if it will crumble into dust. 'Oh Tez, I'm so happy. It's such a great achievement to get your story published, I'm so proud of you.'

'I wanted to leave you a message in the book, so I explained to Kurt the publisher what I wanted him to do. He said my request was highly irregular and it was something he'd never heard of before. But he agreed when I said, "what harm can it do?"

'I don't understand.'

'Remember how you would always put 143 in your messages to remind me you loved me?' She nods. 'Well, I have left a message for you on that page in the book.' She opens the book near the middle then flicks one way, then the other until she finds…

'Page 143 isn't here Tez.'

'Are you sure?'

'Yes, the sequence goes 140, 141, 142, 322, 144, 145…'

I smile. 'OK, turn to page 322 and read from the sixth paragraph down, the last line will explain what you mean to me. Only you will understand its true significance.' She turns the pages again until she finds the missing number. She starts to read.

'Sarah clasped Sophia to her breast. "But they will kill us all Edward, they've done it before, they won't let anything get in their way."

He took the small, multi-faceted, black bottle from inside his tunic and turned to the heavy pot, bubbling over the flames. 'I will protect you both; I'll never let them hurt you. I love you with all my being'. Heavy, running footsteps exploded down the stairs.

Edward hid the Captain's wife and her daughter behind a secret panel in the galley. He replaced the wood gently, making sure that no one would know they were there. He put his lips to a small gap in the boards of the hiding place and whispered. 'Love…

Grace stopped reading. She started to cry when she read the final line in the chapter. 'Oh Tez, that's beautiful, I never dreamt you felt that way about me.'

'Well now you do. I couldn't imagine life without you.'

'I will hide this with the other things in my car; I will always treasure it.' She underlined Edwards's words in eyebrow pencil. 'This will remind me of our special time together today.'

'Love is not who you can see yourself with, it is who you can't see yourself without'

Chapter 30

I am at Poppy's getting ready to go out. She has arranged a party, at the Green Man, to celebrate the book launch of "Amazon." Most of the GAD's have been invited; Jenny won't be there because she is away for a couple of days, auditioning for a part in Madame Butterfly. I honestly don't want the fuss but I am really looking forward to it, because Grace will be there.

The phone rings just before we are due to leave, the babysitter Suzanne hands it to me. She whispers. 'For you – someone called Kurt.'

'Hi Kurt, great to hear from you, we're just about to leave for the party.'

'That's one of the reasons I'm ringing, I'm sorry I can't make it. I would've liked to meet your sister and see if I could work out who the mystery woman is.' I go cold as I realise my request to have a secret message in the book, is something I had to share with him. I ignore his comment.

'It would've been great if you could have got here but it's good of you to call.'

'I also have some news for you that I thought you'd like to know before you left. The sales of "Amazon" are what we call in the trade, "moderate," but it's actually tremendous for your first novel when you consider that the main publicity programme starts next week.'

'Brilliant.'

'There's something else.'

'What?'

'I just got off a call from Xander in Hollywood; he has had an approach from a producer about the possibility of buying the rights. It doesn't mean it'll be filmed but it could be serious money if they go ahead and make an offer.'

I am delighted to hear this news of course, but I want to get off the phone because a pain suddenly sears in my head. 'Kurt, can you hang on a sec?' He says "yes," I holler towards the kitchen. 'Pops. Can you get me some painkillers please? I've got a blinding headache.' I wonder if it is a migraine, I'm getting spots in my vision.

I hear her laugh as she shouts, 'Bloody hell, he writes one poxy book and he starts commanding everyone around.'

I resume my conversation with Kurt. He tells me a bit more detail of Xander's feedback and confirms he will arrange to get a written draft of what they are proposing. Poppy walks into the hall, with a glass of water and some pills in her palm. She kisses me. 'Here you go Mr Steinbeck,' she says sarcastically, 'sorry about the delay.'

*

I drink in the congratulations and the attention when I arrive at the Green Man, but this only occupies ten percent of my consciousness, the rest of me is thinking about Grace; the woman I love, the one who has turned my world upside down.

She is sitting in front of me. Her light brown hair is longer than usual and it's streaked by the sun. I love how a wayward strand still sticks out at the back. I see joy in her piercing amber eyes as she looks at me. She is wearing a crisp white silk blouse with the top button undone, she isn't wearing a bra. I can't help watching the way her incredibly pert nipples move beneath the fabric; it's as if they are writing me a message.

324

Dick can't help witnessing that every male in the room is looking at her. I guess part of him will be proud to see them coveting his wife but I know this attention from them and his jealousy, will spell trouble for her later. I am honoured she loves ME.

I am sitting with Poppy and Jacob, Dave and Mandy Bentley, and Dick and Grace of course. I know I'm drinking too much but I am so happy. Can you imagine how wonderful it is to have someone come up to you and say, "Please can you sign this for me Mr Coyne?"

I am having a great time. The champagne, beer, whisky and painkillers, have evicted the searing spike of discomfort from my temple. I get the feeling during the evening, that Dick resents the attention I am getting. He has tried on a number of occasions to initiate a conversation but these quickly peter out as the focus around the table returns to me and the "approach" from Hollywood. I have to thank Poppy of course, for blabbing the detail of the call from Xander, I know she's proud of me, but nothing is set in stone yet. I wish she had kept it quiet.

The happy party mood changes however, near midnight, when Dick turns nasty. Everyone notices his visits to the bar have become more and more frequent. His eyes are glazed over when two of the younger male members of the society come over to say hello and casually comment that Grace looks wonderful. Dick laughs sarcastically and slurs his words. 'She *was* a head turner a long time ago, but she just turns my stomach now.'

The red mist envelopes me instantly. How can he say something so cutting about his wife? I wonder if it is a barbed comment about her infertility. I want to hit him; it's "my" Grace he's talking about after all. I see the pain in her beautiful amber eyes. I am about to say something but its Jacob who leaps to defend her. 'Hey, come on Dick, that's a bit nasty. She looks bloomin' gorgeous.'

I notice Grace flinch as she sees Dick's head turn slowly towards my brother-in-law. 'Oh, fuck off chippy, what do you know? You're just a loser who can't make serious cash. You just piss around all day with woodworm riddled furniture.'

Jacob looks shocked, I can see he is stung by the comment; Poppy squeezes his hand and whispers something to him. The sight of them, upset like this, causes my restraint to snap. My mouth engages before I can introduce my brain. Even I think my voice sounds sinister when I quietly sneer, 'Well at least he's talented and his rewards are from his own efforts, unlike you.'

Dick looks surprised, as he registers it's me that has spoken. Grace looks at me as he responds, she looks horrified. 'What did you say?' I can tell by her eyes that she's pleading for me to shut up but the verbal lava is about to gush. I can't stop myself.

'I said that Jacob's rewards are from his own efforts. The truth is, you wouldn't have a job if it wasn't for your dad starting the company in the first place and your brothers who keep you employed.'

He jumps up, eyes bulging, hands coiled into fists. 'What the fuck are you on about?'

I smile serenely as I speak each cutting word slowly. 'Let me spell it out for you Dick. That's a perfect name for you by the way. You wouldn't have got a job if it hadn't been for your dad. You failed at rugby because you're a talentless, overweight bully. You strut around as if you're something special, but everyone knows you're very ordinary and it's your educated brothers, who're gentlemen by the way, who run the business.'

His fury is cataclysmic as it explodes. Every eye in the room is on him as he screams. 'You cunt.' I look on in horror as Grace touches his arm to try and placate him. He knocks her away with such force that she topples off her seat.

I am up in an instant; Jacob manages to restrain me as I seethe. 'I should've let you drown in Portugal you bullying bastard.'

Dick heads for the exit as Grace follows obediently. My heart is torn as she leaves, without a backward glance. Poppy says, 'Oh Tez, what've you done, you know Gracie is going to cop for it when he gets her home.'

All eyes are on me as Jacob releases me from his hold. I want to crawl under a stone, for my lack of discipline but I don't want to lose face. I raise my arms to indicate I want to make an announcement. The alcohol causes my words to falter slightly. 'Ladies and gentlemen…thank you for your attention…That was a sneak preview…of a scene from my forthcoming play…about a bloke who has his soul removed…to give his stomach more room to be filled with bile…I'm going to call it… "The Bullying Gobshite."'

Laughter breaks out, I can tell by the reaction that the majority are delighted that someone has finally stood up to him. I realise there are times when the truth has to be told but it's not a good idea to involve alcohol, I can see by Poppy's face that this is one of those occasions.

*

It is over a month till I see Grace again. I understand her reluctance to meet me after my behaviour. I get a message one Thursday morning, to say she will meet me later at the usual place.

I ask her what had happened when she got home from the party but she won't tell me.

She won't let me make love to her. She just lies, very quietly in my arms. It's up to me to do the talking today.

I notice she isn't wearing any jewellery, her hands have a rash. I ask about it, she says, 'I've had it a few days now; I'm going to see the doctor about it tomorrow morning.'

I mention that Jenny is going to London again in a couple of weeks; it looks like she might get the role in Madame Butterfly.

I tell her I have been recognised around the village. My picture appeared in the paper, with an article about the launch of my book. I didn't tell her the receptionist recognised me when I checked into the hotel earlier today. That unnerved me a little. I'm thinking I might use up some of my savings to buy a small apartment nearby, where we can meet.

I make her a cup of coffee. She manages a smile when I give her my shortbread biscuit.

I tell her about Amelia and Emily's tenth birthday party last week. I wrote them a short story and had it made into a picture book with their faces superimposed as the princesses. They were delighted with the present. It was good of Kurt to do that for me.

I reveal that I am travelling to London next Monday to record an interview for a late night Arts program. They want to discuss "Amazon", especially as there has been publicity recently relating to the anniversary of the discovery of the abandoned Mary Celeste.

I kiss her when it is time to leave. She gives out a small cry when I hold her. I am sure I didn't squeeze her too hard. I am convinced he has hurt her again but I don't say anything. She stops at the door on her way out, she is wearing her disguise. She looks so tired and sad but she manages a small smile as she says, 'I love you.'

*

I had received a worrying message from her saying she was going to see the doctor, so I watch from a distance as she arrives with Isabella. She enters the surgery, as her mother-in-law parks her car in the spaces at the rear of the building. I see them leave half an hour later so I cross the road to intercept them. There is a look of alarm on Grace's face when she sees me approaching. I have a broad smile as we meet. I ask how they are. They say 'fine.' Isabella is pressing to leave, I wonder if she realises I am the one who had the spat with her son. I ask Grace if she will be at the GADs meeting next week. She says 'yes.' Isabella starts to move away and says, 'Come on Grace.' She says 'goodbye' and moves away.

They have moved no more than ten paces from me as Grace suddenly shouts, 'Tez, I forgot,' and runs back to me. Isabella is watching as Grace reaches me. Her voice is barely audible as she whispers, 'See you on Thursday darling; it's going to be special.'

I am stunned at her boldness. I see a strange look in her eyes. I quietly say, 'Can't wait.'

She turns to go and says over her shoulder. 'I have something important to tell you and I've made a decision.'

Isabella is beside her now. 'What're you doing Grace?' she says as she grabs hold of her elbow and starts to lead her away.

'Sorry Bella, I was just telling Tez how much I enjoyed his book, especially what happened on page 322 or was it 143?

*

The recording is scheduled for ten am. I have been up since six, reading through the pack they sent me. I have had a really bad night, I try to blame it on the hotel bed but in truth I have felt like this for a couple of days. Searing headaches and the numbness in my arm keep returning.

The team at the studios are brilliant; they congratulate me on my book appearing at number ten in the best seller list. I start to feel better when they give me some painkillers. The interview goes well but the spots before my eyes return as I am being chauffeured back to the station.

I ring Toby's surgery for an appointment when I get to the platform. The receptionist informs me there is nothing available with him until next week but I can see a locum if it's urgent. I say no it's not an emergency, and accept a time the following week.

My health has improved on the morning of the appointment but I don't want to be rude and not turn up to see Toby. I tell him why I'm there but emphasise that I am feeling fine now. He asks me many questions whilst he is examining me.

'OK, you can put your shirt back on now Tez,' he says as he finishes checking my blood pressure and listening to my chest. 'I suppose you are still smoking and drinking like a fish?'

'I have cut back a bit.' I think I see him shake his head. He looks disappointed.

'You really need to be careful Tez; I can see from your records that you have not been requesting repeat prescriptions, so I know you're not taking the medication.'

'But I'm fit and strong most of the time and I'm still pretty young to have a real problem.'

'Have you heard of a writer called Patricia Neal?'

'No, why?'

'She was Roald Dahl's wife, she was only 39 when she had her first stroke, so don't make the mistake and think that age is a deterrent.'

'But she was hardly as fit as me Toby?' I regret the words as soon as I utter them. I sound so arrogant.

'How do you know?'

'I'm sorry Toby, I didn't mean it to sound like that.'

'I really wonder why you don't look after yourself. What's the point in coming to see me, if you ignore my advice?' I want to say something but he continues. 'Have you finished the Aaron Jacks trilogy?'

'No, I'm dropping off the first draft to Poppy before she goes away to the Cotswolds. Why?'

'Oh, I just wondered.'

A chill runs through me, as those four words seem to indicate he doesn't expect me to be around to finish it.

PART THREE

Chapter 31

I awake with a start, on this, the last morning of my life. It takes me a moment to realise that I am back in my own bed. I guess I have only slept in this room half a dozen times in the past decade. The noise that wakes me sounds like a giant centipede, attempting a rendition of River dance on the skylight above. The faint light coming from the street lamps outside helps me see that the real source of the cacophony awakening me at four twenty two in the morning, is hailstones the size of ball bearings. I am convinced the glass will be raining down on me at any moment and I won't be able to move quickly enough to avoid the shards. It has taken me a couple of moments just to move my body and head far enough to see the time on the clock radio on the table beside me.

My yearlong rehabilitation has improved my mobility considerably, but all the care, attention and hard work afforded me by the staff at the hospital, especially Tammy, will be considered a waste of time when I am found dead later today.

I had worked hard, for so long, just to be strong enough to say goodbye to Grace, which I did yesterday when I paid my respects to her at the Crematorium. I grieve at the thought of her, because it triggers the memory of Jenny standing over me on the day I awoke from the coma, informing me joyfully, that Grace had been cremated. Twice.

*

I decide to leave two days before my official discharge. Poppy expects me to go back home with her, which isn't going to happen of course. I have a date with a bullet. Getting away early will avoid any confrontation.

She has been so lovely; she is so excited about me leaving the hospital. She has bought me a complete set of new clothes, because I have lost so much weight. She said, 'It will be a fresh start Tez,' when she handed them to me. I try not to think about how my actions will tear her apart.

I have abandoned the new clothes in my hospital room along with most of my papers and medication, I won't need them. I left the hospital with my rucksack and in the clothes I was wearing when I was admitted. I have told the nurses I am going to the garden to write but I left by the side entrance, it was hours before they noticed I'd gone.

Nurse Tamara Flint was the other reason I left early. She was a brilliant proof reader for my story but one day she said, "I wish my Terry was as loving as you," after she had read one chapter about my love for Grace. There was a look of rejection on her face when I turned my head away as she tried to kiss me. On another day, she held my hand and said, "I am glad you had a stroke, I wouldn't have met you otherwise." I thought that was a very odd thing to say, there was something scary about her.

I panicked when she told me she thought she was in love with me; I said I was flattered and explained that in different circumstances we could have been good together. I think she eventually accepted that I could never love her, I lied when I said she was more like a sister.

She got suspended briefly, when she had fallen asleep in my room one evening, after working with me on my journal. She was re-instated when I convinced her bosses that we were just friends – well that's all I was but her boyfriend thought otherwise, when he discovered she had bought me the briar cane and spent most of her overtime with me; which was when she fell asleep in the chair beside me. He even suspected that I was the father, when Tammy announced she was pregnant.

I had to get away to avoid any complications with her.

*

I decided to walk to the Crematorium from the hospital.

The combination of the rucksack over my shoulder, my damaged lungs and the weakness on my left side resulted in the journey taking nearly two hours, even with the aid of my cane. It was raining, just as it was on the day I was due to meet Grace all those years ago. The day that began with me believing I was invincible yet it led to death, paralysis and ruined lives.

As I slowly made my way, I fully appreciated my disability wasn't being partially paralysed; it was living without Grace. I had plenty of time to think through what had happened in the past year.

*

Kurt came to see me in hospital to inform me that Xander had called from Hollywood to say there is a producer who is definitely interested in making a firm bid for the rights to Amazon but he wants me to go to Los Angeles. I thought I would die laughing.

There is a steady trickle of news about Dick during the year I am in hospital. There is an article in the newspaper about him being arrested when Isabella died in suspicious circumstances. He was later released when it was revealed it had been a terrible accident, she had inadvertently been taking the wrong tablets. I am told that Jenny moved in with him, which doesn't surprise me, they will be perfectly suited. Dick was arrested again, when a massive hole was discovered in the

335

companies' books; millions had gone missing. He eventually got released but his brother Marcus was charged and is currently out on bail.

Finally, Poppy tells me on one of her many visits that a plaque for Grace has appeared at the crematorium. She says she thinks it must be from her brother. She added that the message might have got lost in translation when it was sent from Greece because "it's a bit odd."

*

I found her plaque in the Rowan Chapel, where Poppy had said it would be.

GRACE PERRITANO
ALWAYS HAVE FAITH TO REMEMBER
1977 – 2012

The tributes to the deceased nearby declared: In Loving Memory or Eternally Loved. In comparison hers seemed brief, impersonal and almost cryptic. Perhaps her brother in Greece had decided on these words. Maybe they had a special meaning known only to him.

I reached up and touched the small rectangle of white porcelain. There was no rush of joy or spirituality, just an incredible sadness and loss. I was thankful the chapel was deserted, as my eyes began to sting as the tears welled up. I had had a year to think of what to say at this precise moment but my mind had gone blank. A lyric from her ring tone came to my rescue.

"Nothing prepared me for your smile; you lit the darkness of my soul."

'I miss you Grace, so very much.' I kissed her name and left the chapel.

As I made my way back to the main road I remembered my previous visit to the same chapel about ten years ago. I had been to see my sister just after she had had the twins. She had been kept in for a few days after the birth because of complications with her blood pressure and there was a possibility that she may have suffered a fit. Even as I sat at the side of Poppy's bed and held the new born babies snugly in my arms, I realised I could already detect a difference between them.

Emily had a slightly narrower bridge on her nose and was restless; her eyes darting around the room, as if she was afraid she would miss something. Amelia on the other hand, lay quietly in the crook of my arm; she had slightly sharper features with tiny freckles dusted across her cheeks. Emily gripped my index finger as if she would never let me go; Amelia's eyes were steady, never leaving my gaze. I was overwhelmed.

I remember when I passed the girls gently back to Poppy I remarked how they reminded me of the "Skyler Girls." I said it was funny that her best friends when she was growing up were identical twins as well and how it was virtually impossible to tell them apart by appearance. But their demeanours were strikingly different, Gracie was calm and reserved, whilst Faith was like a firework that could go off without warning.

Poppy had said that Faith had been in trouble with the police and been arrested a few times and that Grace had married a local businessman. She had rolled her eyes when she said the word "businessman," I was about to ask why, but the conversation was interrupted when Amelia started to cry. I remember thinking at the time that I had liked Gracie Skyler.

As I was leaving, Poppy suggested, "Seeing as you're in the area, why don't you go and see "Mother"? After all," she said, "the Crematorium is just down the road." It always amused me that this final resting place had been built so close to a large hospital. I had nothing better to do that day so I walked there; it only took about thirty minutes that time.

I hadn't attended my mother's funeral as I was "on a job" in East Timor at the time, monitoring the process of its political separation from Indonesia, which resulted in it becoming a sovereign state. My CO, Lieutenant Ray Kelsey had told me I was free to go but I had decided that my job was more important than being a hypocrite and paying my respects to a woman who had despised me. Apparently, she had died alone in her studio, having choked on her own vomit, brought about by acute alcohol intoxication. Well, anyway, that was what the Coroner had said. She was only forty five.

I realised I hadn't bothered to ask Poppy where her ashes were scattered or whether there was a memorial plaque. I went into one of the chapels, looked at the large "Book of Remembrance" in the glass case which was a waste of time and turned my attention to the small plaques around the walls. I had just left the wonder of my nieces' new life at the hospital but here there were so many sad stories of loss and pain.

One of the plaques had a photograph of a lovely looking lady, with what appeared to be a picture of a cook book and some words. Her name was Joyce. She had died when she was forty nine and was sadly missed by her husband, children and grandchildren. I particularly liked the verse, "God couldn't be everywhere, that's why he made mothers."

I pretended this pleasant looking woman was my mum. I said out loud, the words I had thought, every night before going to sleep since I was eight years old. Just as a tune can stick in your head and drive you crazy, this was the sentence that would never leave me.

'It wasn't my fault Mum.'

*

338

I shake the words from my head and decide to lie in bed a while longer. I had travelled here by taxi from the Crematorium. I no longer owned a mobile phone so my call from a public payphone to the cab company had been met with disbelief when I requested a price to take me on a one way trip to Dorset. To give them credit, they found me a driver willing to take me on the six hour journey. I thought the price was pretty reasonable; after all it would be my last big capital outlay.

It had been over nine years since I had actually lived here for any length of time. My visits here had dwindled since leaving the SBS and moving in with Poppy, so I was grateful that Jordi, had kept an eye on the place on a regular basis; checking the post, occasionally letting in some air and making sure there were no leaks during the winter.

Jordi had got an unwelcome surprise when he had tried to call me to discuss the authorising of a repair that was needed to the fire exit door to the roof. An irate Jenny, who had taken the phone from my jacket when I was in the Acute Stroke Ward, had answered the call; strains of Peter, Paul and Mary singing If I Had a Hammer alerting her to the fact that someone was trying to contact me. He told me afterwards that she enjoyed telling him about my stroke and coma and suggested it would be a waste of time securing the door. She had said, "With any luck, the bastard will be on his way to a fire door in Hell, not Dorset."

Almost as suddenly as the storm had begun, its energy seems to be depleted as it starts to move away, resulting in a dramatic reduction in the noise level. I really want to go back to sleep but realise the pressure on my bladder means I will have to get up, unless I want to spoil my recent sustained efforts at keeping a dry mattress. Urinating, an act once so simple and subconsciously performed, now requires absolute motivation to move and a precise plan of approach to complete the task. By getting my right arm under my body and pushing upwards together with my right leg I manage to sit up and swing myself onto the edge of the bed. The bedside table is at the perfect height for me to place my palm on before pushing up so I can stand unsteadily on the carpet. My briar cane is within reach but I decide to go solo which will leave both hands free should I topple.

In all the time I had lived here I had never appreciated it would only have taken about sixteen strides from the front door next to the toilet to the far wall where there was a sash window overlooking the bay. Yesterday, I discovered that it now takes forty one shuffles, not paces or strides, to cover the same short distance and this task is anything but a routine.

Shuffles one to five I liked to call freestyle, in truth the performance is more like a hopping tumble with a slight falling sideways motion towards my dressing table and wardrobe, where I can gratefully hold on for a moment to rest. The next fourteen are relatively easy, moving from the bedroom door across the lounge to the support of the chair at my writing desk. I count nineteen more into the open kitchen area where the small table and sink provide excellent support for my final journey to urinary salvation. The kitchen clock next to the window informs me, the time is sixteen forty one. Below the timepiece that has required new batteries for at least eight years is the 2004 calendar, depicting a picture of farm workers bringing in the harvest. There is one bold cross, indicating Thursday, 23rd December, the day I left to stay at Poppy's for Christmas, after my medical discharge from the SBS.

Two final lunges towards the bathroom door complete the task. By supporting myself on the door handle I can press the switch, but no light is forthcoming. I limp in wondering why Jordi hasn't replaced the bulb and quickly support myself on the rim of the bath before lifting the seat and sitting down. It doesn't matter which "discharging" operation is required in the bathroom; they are both performed in this manner as its uncomfortable and sometimes dangerous to risk trying to stand up with an unreliable left leg

Having completed my ablutions I make my way to the door, close it behind me and press the switch to the "off" position. Why am I turning off a light that wasn't working in the first place?

I turn my attention to the task of retrieving the box. I cross the passage and open the storage cupboard in front of me, tried the switch and thank God the lamp is still working in here; otherwise it would be very difficult to find what I was looking for.

I can't remember where I had stored it all those years ago, I hope the box will be at ground level, to save me time and effort, but it isn't. It doesn't surprise me to find it's on the top shelf, which means I will have to clear the cupboard floor before I can get the step ladders in place to reach it.

It takes nearly an hour to make enough room on the floor. I am hot and sweaty, wishing I had changed out of my pyjamas before starting the task. By standing on my good leg, on the very last rung, I manage to rock the box slightly from side to side whilst edging it towards me. As it begins to see-saw forward, years of dust and dead spiders cascade over me, causing me to turn my head away. This is fortuitous as the human ledge made by my neck and cheek acts as a brake when the box topples off the shelf. It is heavy but I manage to get it down without falling. I squeal like a little girl when I realise that one of the spiders that has fallen down my shirt, is alive. I slam my back into the wall until the movement ceases. I try and comprehend how a trained killer can still get un-nerved by such a tiny creature. I shake the remaining debris from my hair, face and shoulders and place the box on the table.

The faded writing on the top says, "KEEP."

Chapter 32

I am sitting precariously on a wall, with the drop to oblivion behind me. I am looking to my right, towards the skylight of my apartment. The area is still wet from the earlier downpour, the dampness is drawn into the seat of my jeans but that is really the least of my worries considering what I am about to do. The seagulls, that so often awoke me when they perched on my glazed roof, are now circling overhead. Maybe they are preparing to greet one of the early morning trawlers returning to the port or later, an unfortunate child with an ice-cream.

Gaining access to the roof had not been as easy as it was all those years ago when I had come up here on warm days to jot down ideas for my novels and play. This was where the notion of "The Amazon," was born when I saw what I thought was an unmanned yacht sailing out to sea. This time, it takes me a little longer to climb up the stairs. Progress is slow, one step at a time, with a compulsory pause to adjust the balance of the pack on my back. Emerging onto the roof, I hear the door close behind me with an unfamiliar click. I limp over to the gap in the barrier and sit down. Looking behind me I see the length of the drop down onto the rocks and the beach.

I pull my favourite jacket around me as I am chilled by the fresh sea breeze buffeting me. I can hear the engine of a car, making its way along Minecliff Road as I look beyond the satellite dishes and safety barriers towards the New Forest. On my right, with the early morning sun glistening off the waters of Poole Bay, I see the Isle of Wight in the distance. I am especially grateful for this beautiful crisp dawn and the magnificence of the sky as it is my favourite time of day. I also know it will be the last time I see this or any other view for that matter.

I turn my attention to the small rucksack on the floor next to me. Looking inside I can see the pistol, the hip flask, lighter and cigar case. Alcohol and nicotine have played such a big part in my life, that I had thought it would be pleasant to have one last drink and a smoke. Instead I find I really have an issue with this. It must be nearly a year since I'd had my last smoke and drink; this is the cleanest I have been since I was seventeen. I think, "Why spoil everything on my last day?"

Ignoring these items, I grasp the only other object in the bag. It makes a distinctive sound like rice sliding on a baking tray when I pull it out. The handle is made of mother-of-pearl, tiny but perfect for a baby's grip. The body is oxidised silver, in the shape of a rabbit with an ivory "teething" ring attached by a solid silver band.

Rocky's rattle.

*

I was eight when Rocky was born in the hospital next to the barracks. He was named after one of my dad's favourite films, which was released a couple of years earlier.

My parents had always been undemonstrative in their love for me but they seemed to warm to Poppy when she was born which I understood, because I adored her too. It was only when Rocky was born that I really appreciated the chasm between their "feelings" for me and those for my brother. My parents were unrecognisable; such was their love for him. Looking back, I realise their devotion verged on a form of worship.

I had often seen my mother drinking alcohol during the day and this would increase when my father returned from his lengthy absences. The accusations from both sides would start, followed by arguments resulting in even more drinking and verbal abuse for me. Their relationship had improved dramatically with my brother's arrival. It seemed to bring them closer together for a while. Then just after Rocky's second birthday they had another major row. Dad had informed her he had to leave for a training exercise in the Brecon Beacons and Mum was furious because she wanted us all to go back with him to Dorset.

Dad had been away for over a month when Poppy was taken ill and confined to bed. She must have been in some pain because she cried constantly. Mum's patience was wearing thin, so I stayed off school to try and cheer Poppy up.

I was upstairs in her bedroom with Rocky when Mum shouted upstairs to tell us she was going out for some milk from the NAAFI shop. I thought it strange because it seemed like we had loads in the fridge when we had our breakfast cereal.

I was chasing Rocky, pretending to be a "monster" when Poppy started a violent coughing attack. As I went into the bathroom to get her a drink, I caught sight of Rocky running out of the bedroom.

He stopped on the landing, looking directly at me. He bent his little legs, held out his arms and made claws with his hands. His "growl" was interrupted by his giggles as he turned away and started to run towards the top of the stairs. I can visualise his thick blond curls now, they were bouncing as he ran. I dropped the glass in the sink, and sprang forward to stop him. I heard the front door slam as I shouted. 'Rocky! NO!' (I remember thinking, "good, Mum's home".) The noise of the door shutting made him falter, he caught his foot in a small piece of torn carpet at the top of the stairs and fell forward just as I was about to grab him. I saw the laughter in his eyes as he spun in the air and disappeared from view.

My mother was at the bottom of the stairs; I must have come into her view as he crashed at her feet; a sickening crack reverberated in the stairwell. She screamed and dropped the bag she was carrying. There was a loud smash as the contents hit the floor and the unmistakable stench of brandy met me as I ran down the stairs.

When I reached the bottom step, she was tottering, shaking her head and whimpering, 'Rocky, Rocky.' She slowly lifted her head to look at me, eyes glazed over; the words slurred as she hissed. 'You pushed him, didn't you, you little bastard?' I couldn't compute the words or their implication as she bent down unsteadily, and stroked his cheek, whispering. 'Why did you push my little angel?' Then she got up and staggered away.

I swear I saw his arm spasm as she left him. I yelled, 'Mummy, Mummy look.' She just continued to shuffle away. 'Where're you going? Look I think he's…' But she had gone. Some glass stuck in my knee as I knelt down and tried to lift him. The sparkle in his eyes seemed to dim as he looked at me. He died in my arms. He was just two years old. I was eight.

I spent hours answering questions about what had happened. I was thankful that Poppy, although only four years old, could add weight to my version of events. It was accepted that it was a terrible accident and resulted in all of the family accommodations having new carpets fitted.

It didn't take long however, for the silent gaze of contempt to fall upon my mother for leaving us alone. The military personnel, civilians and my father all demonstrated an outward display of support underlined with an unspoken accusation of neglect. My mother in turn piled all the guilt and blame upon me, she seemed to truly believe I had pushed him to his death.

I hoped, that in time Rocky's death would bring me and Mum closer together and that as her grief subsided she would realise I was innocent and begin to love me. I wanted her distance and bitterness to melt away and for her to share her love with me. God knows I needed the reassurance that it wasn't my fault. I wanted her to tell me she loved me, not as an obligation or as a response to my declarations of love but because she meant it. I tried many times to discuss what

345

happened, to explain the true sequence of events so we could be reconciled before it was too late but she would always fly into a rage.

Mum and Dad didn't love each other anymore because there was nothing but sadness now for them; they were missing their little boy. The memory of holding his body in my arms, with his blond head twisted at an acute angle across my knee, forever fuelled the deep pain and emptiness inside me. I spent the next four years, (prior to moving back to England) reliving the loss all over again every time I tiptoed past his room, as if he was still asleep inside. Poppy didn't realise that she was the glue that held the family together now.

I wish I could go back to the small children's chapel in Monchengladbach, where he is buried, just to say goodbye. But the memory of Dad, carrying that tiny box into the Lutheran church, the heart broken wailing of the congregation and the look my mother gave me as his coffin was lowered into the grave, would be too much to for me to bear. His miniature granite headstone read.

"Don't stop the children from coming to me! Children like these are part of the kingdom of God."

I could never begrudge their grief for little Rocky but where was the compassion for the eight year old boy, left to look after his much younger siblings; who ended up at the bottom of some stairs, holding his brother's broken body, in a pool of alcohol?

I don't think anybody noticed his silver rattle had disappeared. I put it in my box along with my comics and stamp album. I wrote "KEEP" on the lid with a red crayon.

'It wasn't my fault Mum.'

*

I put the rattle back into the bag and realise that it is time. I take out the pistol, put it on my lap and take a deep breath.

346

This is it. I take another look at the drop behind me which is integral to the plan. I hear a car pull up below as I run through the exit procedure, one last time.

I will put the muzzle in my mouth, pull the trigger and my corpse will fall and be dashed on the rocks below. High tide is in ten minutes so with any luck my body will be washed away. Simple.

I take the pistol from my lap, turn it so it's facing me and put my thumb on the trigger guard. I am just about to push the decocker lever and fire when I hear a distinctive sound. It's Jordi opening up the shop.

Thinking about Jordi reminds me I haven't said goodbye to him. I put the pistol down carefully on the wall beside me, as I don't want it to go off by accident and injure me. You have to laugh.

I have already written a letter to Poppy and Jacob, trying to explain why I am doing this. It mentions Rocky's death and Mum's hatred of me. It covers the explosion in Iraq, Eddie, my lungs and losing the job I loved. Finally my stroke, the coma, my disability and waking up to learn that Grace had died in horrific circumstances and that I don't want to live anymore without her. I re-iterate my love for them and tell them I am sorry for what I am about to do. I finish the letter by detailing what I would like to happen in the absence of my "Will." I realise this will not be legally binding but I can only hope that my wishes are considered.

The deeds to my apartment are to be passed to the Stroke Association; the sale of which will help the charity provide counselling for fellow victims. All my savings, my car and the remaining contents of the box downstairs are to go to Poppy and Jacob. The royalties from my writing and the film, if it happens, are to be passed, in trust, to Pancake and Earache. I realise I have completely forgotten to mention Jordi and my yacht and to thank him for looking after things all those years I was away. I decide to leave "Sunbuoy" to him and to write a short note for him on the back of the envelope and leave it with my rucksack.

I feel for the envelope in the side pockets of my jacket but it isn't there. I remember that I put it in the inside pocket, when it was hung on the back of the chair in my apartment. I can move my left arm now but not sufficiently to reach that far. I cautiously remove my jacket and lay it carefully across my lap. I lean forward slightly for balance as I remove my right hand from the barrier and insert it into the pocket. It is empty, I say, 'Piggin Doggin,' I know I had put it in there. I realise it must have slipped into the lining. I had forgotten about the torn pocket. I push my hand further inside and find the envelope and something else.

The crisp white envelope, written a matter of hours ago, is accompanied by a sheet of printed paper that looks as if it's been in there for a long time. I remember I was absolutely sure that I had emptied the contents of my jacket lining just before I had left the car to meet Grace on that fatal Thursday.

I stare in disbelief when I realise it is a page ripped from a book. I am faint for a moment, when I recognise what I hold in my hand. I accidently drop the page, onto the wet floor. I grab hold of the barrier to stop myself overbalancing and falling backwards to my death on the rocks below. Once the light-headedness has passed, I bend forward and pick up the damp page knowing that it is 143 from my book, "The Amazon." One of the sentences has been underlined in what I know is eyebrow pencil.

'Love is not who you can see yourself with,

it is who you can't see yourself without'

Chapter **33**

My mind is in turmoil. The page I have found is definitely from the copy of "The Amazon," that I had given to Grace when she told me she was in love with me. She had underlined the sentence, my secret message to her, and hidden the book later, with the other things, under the back seat of her car.

All thoughts of ending my life are displaced by an avalanche of enigmas. I can't concentrate because the sound of traffic on the street below has increased, so I decide to postpone my demise and get back to my apartment where I can at least attempt to think. I put everything back into the rucksack and go back to the fire door. It's locked.

I notice that a new security catch has been fitted, which accounts for the unusual click when it closed earlier. I am trapped. I try banging it a few times but know there is no way anyone in the apartments below mine can hear me. I figure that I have three options available to get someone to come up and open the door. I can throw something off the roof or fire my pistol to attract the attention of the early shoppers below or I can just wave and shout. I opt for the last.

*

Jordi opens the door after being alerted by a traffic warden and helps me down the ladders and back to my apartment. I'm pretty certain he doesn't believe me, when I tell him that I had gone up onto the roof at dawn, just after a hailstorm, to do some writing. That doesn't matter now as I have some serious thinking to do. Something isn't stacking up.

I've found a unique link to Grace, who is dead. Yet something is troubling me, something that I have to try and work out. I sit on the bed, with page one four three in my hand and pray for inspiration as I run through the questions flashing into my mind.

Who put the page in my pocket?

A. It must have been Grace.

Q. Couldn't someone else have put it there?

A. Yes but it's very unlikely. We were the only ones who knew the meaning of the page.

Q. OK. When did she put it there?

A. Sometime between me arriving at the hospital and her death because it wasn't there when I left the car to meet her.

Q. Couldn't the page have been put there after the accident?

A. I shout. 'How the fuck could she put it there if she was dead?' I am talking to myself now. Stop it!

Q. OK. Why did she leave that page?

A. She wanted to leave a clue that she had been to see me.

Q. Why not just leave a note or a letter?

A. Perhaps she didn't have time, plus a letter might have been found by Jenny.

Q. Jenny would be suspicious anyway, if she had found the page.

A. True, but unlikely, it's just a page torn from a book.

Q. OK, but why did she put it in the lining of my jacket?

A. She didn't. She put it in the pocket without knowing it was torn.

Q. So you're saying she wanted you to know she had come to see you.

351

A. Yes. I guess she expected me to find it if I woke up.

Q. So Grace definitely came to see you?

A. Yes. The nurse said I had had a mystery visitor.

Q. Doesn't mean it was Grace though?

A. True, but according to the nurse, she had black 'glossy' hair, a red Alice band and horn-rimmed spectacles.

Q. How can you be sure it was Grace?

A. Because she often dressed that way when she came to meet me.

I am depressed. I feel like I'm in a pitch black room and my intuition tells me that there's a hidden door for me to walk through, if only I can solve the puzzle. But I keep slamming into a brick wall. I know what I'm doing. I'm desperate; I want Grace to be alive and finding that special page has given me hope that she is.

I am such an idiot, what have I actually worked out? I now know that Grace did come to see me shortly after I was admitted to the Acute Stroke ward. She wore a disguise because she probably thought Jenny might be there. She only had seconds to be with me so she left a special message for me and went home.

I experience an overwhelming wave of love for her, knowing she had been there for me when her world was about to fall apart. She would have rushed home, knowing it was only a matter of time before Jenny worked out who it was on the phone at the hospital and called Dick to tell him about our affair. I know now that she was probably trying to get away when the crash happened.

I look across at the bag containing the pistol. I realise it is time to resume my task. I can die now in the knowledge that Grace was with me shortly before she was killed, something I would never have known had I not found the page.

The image of her in the car comes back to me as I pick up the rucksack and retrace my steps to the roof. I shudder as I imagine her pain as she frantically tries to get out of the burning car. It is at this moment I remember Jordi had to open the fire escape door for me. I have used that access hundreds of times and it has never locked behind me before. Something about the word "locked" triggers my mind. The interrogation starts again.

Q. So what's troubling you now?

A. Everyone said there was evidence that Grace couldn't get out of the car.

Q. Why is that important?

A. It means she was alive.

Q. How do you work that out?

A. Because of something I'd forgotten. She'd managed to get the door open.

Q. So why are your eyes sparkling as you walk back to the apartment?

A. Because it wasn't Grace who died in the car.

Q. How do you know?

A. Because Jenny also said. "Grace couldn't undo the buckle; she was trapped."

Q. So why is that good news?

A. Because Grace would never fasten the seat belt because it was faulty.

*

I am thinking about who could have been in the car if it wasn't Grace, as I empty the contents of the rucksack onto the table. I give up on the conundrum as I realise my passport and the envelope full of Euros are still there. I put these into my jacket pocket and laugh out loud and say, 'Piggin Doggin,' as they fall through the torn pocket into the lining. I am still smiling as I put everything else back into the box, replace the lid and put it under some old carpet in the storage cupboard. I am too excited to waste time putting it back onto the high shelf. I go into the bedroom put on some fresh clothes and bung a few items into the rucksack. I am happy; I punch the air, grab my cane, gave it a little twirl and leave the apartment. (I wonder how long I will be away this time.) I exit into the brilliant sunshine, pause, close my eyes and drink in the fresh air.

Prayers hadn't seemed to help Eddie after the explosion in Iraq but I have to try. I really want some help. 'Please Lord, let me be right. Please let Grace be alive. Please bless me with some good luck this time.'

I turn towards the wheelbarrows, coloured buckets and stacks of firewood on the pavement to my left. The door announces my entrance as I go into Jordi's shop. His smile is broad as he says, 'Hi buddy. Have you locked yourself out of your apartment?'

'No ya cheeky bastard. Could you call a taxi for me please? I still haven't got a phone.'

'Sure. Where are you going?'

'Airport.'

'The airport, blimey, that's a bit sudden. Where are you going?'

'Greece.'

'Why are you going to Greece?'

I have the broadest smile for years when I say, 'To find a "Blue Door" Jordi. To find a wonderful "Powder Blue Door."'

Chapter 34

The taxi driver is really helpful. He radios his control room to find out which is the best airport to go to. I haven't thought that far ahead, I'd just assumed there will be a flight available. They confirm there is a flight from Heathrow later that afternoon with plenty of spare seats.

The plane takes off on time and four hours later, I am in a taxi, in stifling heat, leaving Athens airport heading towards the millionaire playground of Glyfada. I stop for a meal in an upmarket restaurant on the marina, where the owner, Hector, arranges accommodation for the night in a holiday flat around the corner. He also arranges the next step of my journey.

At six the next morning, I sail out of the marina on a chartered yacht. Hector had offered to arrange for a fishing boat to drop me off, which would have been cheaper, but I want to sail. Ideally I would have liked to have travelled on my own of course, but my disability prevents it. So I sit back and enjoy the journey as my hired crew takes me across the gulf to the island of Hydra; home of the artist, Sebastian Skyler, Grace's brother.

*

Grace told me she often dreamt of running away with me and of spending the rest of our lives together. She told me about a run-down villa that had been for sale for years. She said we would buy it together, renovate it and live there happily ever after. It had a powder blue door, was surrounded by bougainvillea and the garden faced south, overlooking the sea. It was three streets down from her brother's house, at the end of an alley, opposite a bar. I couldn't remember if she'd said the bar was called the "Acropolis" or the "Aphrodite." My task was to find the bar and the blue door and then maybe, just maybe ask around to see if a successful English artist lived nearby. Doubts crossed my mind; what if the bar had changed its name, or maybe the villa had been sold and now had a red door? Maybe Sebastian had moved from Hydra. I thought about page one four three and the seat belt buckle and hoped against hope that if she were alive that she had fled to her brother's.

I pay off the crew when we dock in Hydra Port and watch them go to a local bar before I go into a shop to buy a map of the island. I reckon I should be able to get a list of the island's bars and restaurants to check out and cross off systematically but I quickly find out that the majority of small family run establishments are not included in the tourist information. I have run the plan through my mind numerous times on the way over; it will be like a military operation but I seem to be thwarted before I have even started.

I find a street café and sit at an outside table studying the map and considering my next move when the man on the next table leans over. 'Good afternoon sir, are you looking for anywhere in particular?'

'Afternoon, I'm trying to find an old friend but I've lost his address. He's called Sebastian and I know he lives near a bar called the "Acropolis" or the "Aphrodite." It might sound silly but there is a villa opposite the bar that I'm looking for which has been for sale for years. It has a powder blue door and is surrounded by bougainvillea. 'He slaps the table with the flat of his right hand, causing his espresso cup to rattle in its saucer.

'Well sir, I don't know Mr Sebastian, but I do know the villa you speak of.' He turns and points to the top of the town.

'You've described the old Ptolemy place. It's less than one kilometre away.'

My heart leaps at the news. 'Thank you,' I say as I stand, grab my cane and stoop down to pick up my rucksack.

'It's too far and too hilly for you to walk sir.'

'Ok. Where can I get a taxi?'

He grins broadly. I notice the gaps in his mouth where his teeth should be as he says, 'No cars here sir.' He moves to my side and offers to take my bag. He points to a sorry looking donkey tethered to a railing. It's in the shade but still seems to be suffering in the heat. 'That's my taxi over there...' he says, as it deposits three steaming orbs of dung onto the road. 'I can take you...'

*

And so my English speaking "driver", Icky, drops me and my bag outside the Aphrodite bar. I choose a table giving me a view of a distinctive blue door, (with beautiful bright flowers cascading around it), at the end of an alleyway. I order a cold drink and put my briar cane and jacket on the chair beside me. I am curling the hair on my fringe and considering asking the waiter if he knew an artist called Sebastian when the core of my body tightens. There is a woman across the street, walking in the shadows. I can't see her too clearly but my whole body begins to shake as if it knows that my search has ended.

Chapter 35

She goes into a small bakery at the corner of the square across from me. I ask the waiter if I can leave my bag for a moment, clutch my cane and cross to the fountain where I can get a better view of her. I am walking better, it seems that the possibility of seeing Grace has improved my gait. I think. "Please don't let me trip up now." I hear laughter as she pays, which is my cue to walk to the window of the fashion shop next door.

I am shaking with nerves when she comes out and turns away from me towards the bar. I step behind her and sing.

'*Something about you stood apart, a whisper of hope that couldn't fail.*'

She stops. I don't think I have ever been as anxious in my life. Will she be pleased to see me? I know she always hated me trying to sing to her. I feel stupid and childish as she turns and smiles. I take this as a good sign but notice the tears. I say, 'Did the sound of my voice make you cry?'

She moves towards me and says, 'Oh Tez. You took your time to find me.' I realise the tears are tears of joy.

I pause for a moment to look at my supposedly dead soul mate but this is no cadaver. There is a golden glow around her, as if she has eaten radioactive porridge. Her hair is streaked and virtually white in places, probably bleached by the sun and sea air. She looks as if she has gained a few pounds which actually make her look even more beautiful and content than the last time I saw her. Was it really over a year ago? She appears to be serene, calm and happy.

My insecurity comes flooding back, as I notice her fleeting glance at my cane. Will she find my disability hideous, or even worse, feel sorry for me? Did she notice my impaired speech when I sang to her? What about the sag in my cheek? Has she found someone else? These thoughts run wildly through my mind, as she looks furtively around her, then moves towards me and kisses me discreetly on the cheek and says, 'I've missed you so much.'

These are the words I want to hear. I can tell by the way she is acting that she doesn't want an open exhibition of emotion so I say in a hushed voice, 'It broke my heart when I thought I had lost you for good.' With no consideration for timing I rush on to ask. 'If it wasn't you, who was it in the car Grace?'

The expression on her face, when I ask the question, looks as if she has been electrocuted. She appears to regain her composure instantly, however, as she takes hold of my hand and whispers. 'Don't call me Grace, I'll explain why. Let's sit somewhere peaceful and I'll tell you everything.'

She guides me back towards the Aphrodite. My bag and jacket are still at the table at the front but she guides me towards a smaller table in the alley, next to the side window. I see one of the waiters wave and call something indistinguishable to her as she takes her seat. A small pang of jealousy surfaces in me as she smiles broadly, waves back, and shouts, 'Hello Belisario.' I ask her if she wants something to drink, walk back to the entrance and say. 'Two white coffees please.' The waiter seems to look at me suspiciously as I re-join Grace.

Grace reaches across the table and holds my hand. A rush of energy floods through me. That single gesture makes me feel wanted and loved again, I don't consider myself to be ugly or deformed anymore. Is it possible to send a message and convey your love for someone through a touching of hands? I think she must surely be able to sense me saying, "I love you."

She suddenly releases me and sits bolt upright as a young woman turns the corner and says, 'Kaliméra,' and then in broken English, 'how are they?'

Grace waves to her and shouts, 'OK,' then turns to me and says, 'That's my doctor,' as the woman continues past the bar.

I am conscious that we are in a public place and that Grace is acting in an odd way but I don't care. I will go along with whatever she wants. The fleeting gentle kiss and holding of hands is just like old times, it is truly wonderful knowing she is alive. The alleyway is deserted, but Grace looks around anyway to make sure there is no one listening. She leans forward and whispers. 'How did you know I was alive?'

'I didn't know for certain until about four minutes ago. I've believed for a year that you were dead until I found the page from my book that I gave you. It was only after I found it that I started to consider the implications of it being in my jacket.'

'Why did it take you so long to find it?'

'That doesn't matter now; please tell me who was in the car.'

'I promise I will tell you everything Tez. I've not had to talk about what happened since I had to tell Seb. It's so painful. 'She squeezed my hand imploringly and said. 'How did you find my "clue" after so long?' Tell me everything, please.'

'It was in the lining of my jacket. The inside pocket was torn and it had slipped through.' I reached across for my jacket and showed her the tear in the fateful pocket and my passport now residing in the lining. 'I found it when I tried to retrieve my suicide note, about five minutes before I'd planned to blow my brains out.'

She gasps and I hear my knuckle crack as she squeezes my hand tightly. 'Oh God, Tez, you can't be serious?'

'I was going to kill myself.' She increases the pressure on my hand even more as tears begin to well up in her eyes. She starts to speak but I carry on. 'I just didn't want to live in a world without you. Remember my message to you in my novel? *"Love is not who you can see yourself with, it is who you can't see yourself without."* Well it's so true; I couldn't face a future without you.'

Tears start to roll down her cheeks. I can see the waiter who had served us, looking our way, protectively, probably wondering why this stranger is upsetting his friend.

'You need to understand that I have only considered myself to be invincible twice in my life. The first time was when I joined the Marines. I fitted in and I was happy. I had found a purpose in life after all the shit I put up with at home. Then my job, my best friend and part of my health were taken from me in tragic circumstances. I was lost and found it hard to carry on, but then I met you and rebuilt my life. I was indestructible again. I had you, I was loved and wanted, happy and complete for the very first time in my life. I had also had my book published and there were even overtures from Hollywood. I know that isn't all that important in the scheme of things but it would have been nice to walk down the "red carpet" with you. I didn't have a hole in my soul anymore, I had a purpose. Life was *so* good.'

'But then I awoke from my stroke and found I had lost you. Every waking moment became filled with the horror of me not being there for you on that Thursday. I knew Jenny would tell Dick about us, so you would be in for a beating but nothing could prepare me for the anguish when I found out that you had died in such horrible circumstances.' She makes a choking sound and I can see grief etched into her face. I want to stop but she nods and waves her hand, indicating she wants me to continue. 'Then I found out the extent of the damage to my body caused by the stroke. I felt worthless, disabled, weak, pathetic, ugly and alone.'

She said, 'You're not ugly darling, you are still handsome to me.'

I smiled inwardly as her kind comment could imply that she agrees I am worthless, disabled, pathetic and weak but I know she doesn't mean it. I say, 'I just didn't want to carry on. I know it sounds insane but I just wanted to get strong, so I could go and say goodbye to you at the Crematorium and then end it all.' She gently strokes my left cheek and I know she has noticed the change of pitch in my voice. She probably detects sadness in my words, perhaps there is, but frustration begins to surface. 'What I can't understand is why you didn't get a message to me letting me know you were alive? At least then I would have had something to live for.'

Grace moves her hands back onto mine. 'Oh Tez, I couldn't.' I am angry at this point. What possible reason could she have had for not telling me she was alive? How could she have been so cruel? I am about to interrupt her but she puts her finger on my lips to stop me. 'Let me explain, I hope you'll understand. Initially, I thought you had got tired of me when you didn't turn up at the hotel. It wasn't like you not to answer my calls or texts, so then I thought there must be something wrong. I'd told you that I'd made a decision, and had something very important to tell you. I thought I'd scared you off or perhaps you'd got cold feet.'

How could she have thought I would ever desert her? My tone has sharpness. 'How can you say that? You know how much I loved you.'

'Tez, I was in turmoil. I promise you'll understand when I tell you everything. What did you do when you found the page from the book?'

This is beginning to sound like a game of dysfunctional tennis with me serving important pieces of information but getting no returns.

I still feel irritated but continue. 'I knew it could only have come from you because it had the quote underlined in your eyebrow pencil.' I smile as I add, 'Do you remember the day I gave you the book and explained there was the special message for you on page one four three?'

'Yes, I remember we were in bed together.' She blushes. 'I was amazed you had convinced the publisher to put the special quote on that particular page.

One of the waiters is making his way towards our table but Grace raises her hand and politely says something in Greek. It's a language I have little knowledge of but I think it means, "ten minutes please" but I can't be certain. She looks at me again and nods for me to carry on. 'Ok. I knew from the page in my pocket that you had come to see me when I was in hospital, because it was definitely not there when I went to meet you at the hotel on that "fatal" Thursday. Though what I didn't know was when you had put it in my pocket. If it was put there before the accident then you would still be dead.'

'What made you realise I was alive?'

'One of the nurses had mentioned ages ago that there was a woman in the room shortly after I was admitted. They knew it wasn't Jenny, they will never forget her! They thought it was Poppy at first but she was still on holiday. They told me that when they challenged her she said she was in the wrong room and left, so that got me thinking about who the mystery woman could be. One day I asked Tammy, that's the name of the nurse who cared for me, if she or her colleagues remembered what the woman looked like.'

Grace smiled broadly, not a hint of jealousy in her voice. 'I'd like to give her a big hug for taking care of you.' A lump the size of Ayres Rock jammed in my throat at the scale of her love for me.

'She said she couldn't remember except she had long "glossy" black hair. She emphasised about how shiny it was and remembered a red Alice band with black horn-rimmed spectacles.'

'Yes that was me. I obviously wore my Mary Russell disguise when I came to see you, just in case Jenny was there. It was a good job that I did, because she didn't notice me when I came into your ward and saw her at the nurses' station. I heard her demanding to be the first to be told when you awoke. She appeared to be distraught and said she wanted to be there to welcome you back. I could hear the insincerity in her voice. I waited in the stairwell until she had gone and then came into your room.'

'I cried when I saw you hooked up to all those wires and you didn't respond to my voice or my special kisses.' She gives my hands another squeeze as she changes the subject. 'I'm sorry; we went off at a tangent. Tell me how you worked out that I might be alive.'

'I had the unique page from the book, and guessed it was you who visited me. I was ninety nine percent certain it couldn't have been you in the car.'

'How did you work that out?'

'Simple, it was the seatbelt. I knew you would never have fastened it, as it was faulty. I remembered what you'd told me when you'd been trapped before, the difficulty you had getting out and that Dick couldn't be bothered to fix it. I realised someone else must have been driving, fastened the belt and perished in the flames' A look of pain flashed across her face again when I mention the fire. 'No wonder they thought it was you who had perished. '

All the happiness has drained from her face. I ask. 'Are you ok darling? 'She nods and asks me to carry on. 'You always told me that your dream would be to come to Hydra to be with your brother and buy our dream villa with the powder blue door. So this was the only place I could think of, to come and see if you really were alive. I'm so happy I was right.' I pull her hand to my lips and kiss it.

Grace has regained her composure and her smile is back. She says, 'Now tell me what happened on that Thursday.'

'Ok. I had dropped the manuscript off at Poppy's and had taken Jenny to the airport. She was being her usual nasty self so I decided I was going to leave her.' Grace's eyes widened. 'Yes. I decided I had had enough of her venomous attitude. I couldn't wait to be with you and find out what you had to tell me. I was excited and nervous in equal measure trying to work out what you were going to say. I had parked up at the hotel and was on my way to check in when I started to collapse. I really thought I was going to die at the very moment I knew you were calling me, I heard your ring tone just as I was blacking out.'

'My ring tone is still Thursday's child?'

'Yes of course it is. My last terrible thought, was, I would die, and never hold you again. I also realised that my phone would give us away, Dick would find out about us and I would not be there to protect you. I'm so sorry; I was so stupid not to have had a password on it. Then I awoke after ten days to be told by Jenny that you had died.'

The spark of pain flashes across her face again.

'Oh Grace, she said you had been cremated, twice. She actually relished telling me, God, it hurt me so much.' Grace is crying again, her shoulders heaving. I can't understand why she is so distraught. I say, 'I'm sorry to upset you, I'll stop now.'

'No Tez, please carry on. I need to hear the rest.' She holds my hand tighter as she smiles weakly and nods for me to continue.

'There isn't much more to tell. The doctors told me I'd had a stroke and been in a coma for over a week, any longer and I would have been in a real mess. They implied I was lucky, which of course was ludicrous considering how I felt.'

I am ready for a coffee. I point to the cup and say. 'Another?' Grace nods, so I wave to Belisario and continue. 'The thing is I was a mess anyway, paralysed down my left side and it had affected my speech. I had also lost part of my vision on the left.' (I didn't tell her about soiling the bed.) 'Basically, I felt deformed, worthless, and ugly.'

Grace says, 'What did I tell you ages ago when we talked about my dream of us living together? I told you I would love you forever, even if you were old and incontinent.' It was funny and romantic when she told me that day in the hotel but it is a bit too close to home this time.

'I started the rehabilitation in the hospital, where I learned to walk and talk again. I moved to a rehab bungalow to continue the therapy as I couldn't bear to move back to Poppy's and have the girls see me in that state. Everything was going well but I suffered another setback.'

'What was that?'

'It's not important now darling. I've told you most of what has happened to me.' I decide to tell her what I had been thinking earlier. 'I have to say our conversation feels like a one-sided tennis game, with only me taking part. I am desperate to know your side.' So I ask her the question again, 'Please tell me, who was in the car?'

She looks at me for a moment before lowering her head and releasing a muffled cry. I can hear her weeping. She must have been really holding herself together before, because these are not small tears now, but deep shoulder shaking sobs. It is unbearably distressing to witness her pain. 'I will never get over what happened and it was wrong what I did.' I thought what an odd thing to say but she continues. 'It hurts so much to say this.'

She sits upright, takes a deep breath, she is ready to speak but the facade crumbles. She lowers her head then starts to wail. The only time I have heard a sound like it, was at the funeral of a teenage soldier; the mother's grief displayed a world of anguish that I had never witnessed before.

I hold her hand for an age. Her sobs gradually subside as she turns to me. She is silent for a moment as she composes herself. It seems an eternity since I asked who was in the car. Grace slowly raises her head and gets involved in the match. Her first serve is an ace, she utters one word.

'Faith.'

*

That simple five letter word slams into my chest with the force of a concrete slab falling from a great height. My mind is in turmoil, did I hear her correctly? I have a raft of questions I need answering, but they can wait. My poor Grace has lost her twin sister. I cannot imagine the grief she must be experiencing. How would I feel if I lost Poppy?

Grace has turned away from me but I can see she is using her paper napkin to dab at her tears. I can't get my head around this. It couldn't be Faith because she was in prison; we had both talked about her being diagnosed with hepatitis C only days before I was due to meet Grace at the hotel. Also, if it was Faith in the car, why did everyone think it was Grace that burnt to death? How did Grace get here? A headache blossoms as my head fails to cope.

I really want to ask the questions that are eating away at me but she is too distraught for me even to consider trying. I can see Belasario is looking at her through the window, as she continues to weep and I realise that the tray of drinks he is hurriedly preparing to deliver, is ours. The last thing we need is an interruption, so I leave Grace for a moment to collect the coffees before he can approach us.

Belisario begins to make a mild protest, telling me in excellent English that he will bring them to us but I just say, 'It's ok, I'll take them out.' and give him some money to pay for them. When he goes to the end of the bar for change I can't help noticing that the walls are almost completely covered with photographs of famous musicians and writers and numerous paintings. One of the canvasses above a black and white photograph of a young Leonard Cohen looks familiar. I am trying to work out where I have seen it before as Belasario returns with my change.

He nods towards Grace and says, 'My friend, she is ok?' Does he mean that I am his friend or Grace? I realise he means her and is obviously concerned about her; maybe he wants to protect her. I say, 'Yes she's fine thanks,' and she forces a smile as she waves to us. I take the tray and some extra napkins and unsteadily return to our table. Carrying a tray of drinks hadn't been part of my rehabilitation.

I take my seat and see her eyes and the tip of her nose are an angry red. I pass her some fresh tissues. 'Thanks. I'll be ok in a minute.' She takes a deep breath, has a sip of her coffee and says, 'Right, now it's my turn to tell you what happened.'

Little did I know, that very soon, Grace would win the Grand Slam for storytelling.

*

'I honestly don't know where to start. I've had the opportunity, over the past year or so, to think about how I would approach this moment if it ever happened, but now that it has...' Her voice trails off. I am just about to utter the cliché that she should start at the beginning, when she resumes. 'I know I need to tell you about what happened on that Thursday and how Faith became involved. I also have two important things to tell you but I will leave those until the end. I'll begin by telling you about the decision that I had made.'

'I was thinking about that when I was collapsing in the car park. I remembered you saying our meeting was going to be special because you had something important to tell me.'

Grace takes a sip of her coffee and follows that with a deep breath saying, 'I'd made the decision to leave Dick.' I can't believe what I am hearing, I had asked her numerous times why she had stayed with him but she would just change the subject. 'I was going to tell you this when we met, as I hoped you would help me.'

'Good God, of course I would have helped you but what finally made you make the decision?'

'There were a couple of good reasons that triggered it, but I don't think I would have even contemplated it if you hadn't helped me build the confidence in myself. I had decided to get away on the day I had been to the doctors about the eczema on my hands. That's when I saw you briefly, remember?' I nod. I feel a wave of sadness as I realise it was the last time I had seen her. 'I was ready to start making the plans, with your help, to get as far away from him as possible. I had set myself a couple of months to plan my freedom which would also give me the time to work out what to do about Faith.'

'What do you mean?'

'Sebastian managed to get a message to me informing me that she was due to be released from prison. The decision was made because she had completed half her sentence but also on compassionate grounds; her hepatitis C was more serious than we thought, possibly terminal, so my plan was to bring her here. No one knew if she had days or months to live, so I thought she could have what time she had left in a beautiful, warm place. It would also get her away from the dealers who were waiting for her to be released, to get the money they were owed.'

I remembered the life Faith had made for herself. The failed marriages, the drug abuse, the attempted rape and the prison terms. Grace continues, 'It was Jenny's phone call that messed with the timescales.'

'I think it's time for you to tell me what happened on that Thursday.'

'OK. I was looking forward to seeing you so much. Can you imagine the change in me that day?' The tears have gone now. Her eyes are bright and animated as she leans forward in her seat. 'I had finally decided to get away. I knew you loved me, I couldn't doubt that but I couldn't presume you would leave Jenny for me,' she smiles as she says mischievously, 'but hoped you would. I was confident, strong and happy; I had so much to tell you. I was apprehensive but mainly very excited. Life felt so good.'

'Dick had left as usual in the early morning, so all I had to contend with was his mother as she was following me around, keeping an eye on me as usual. I had just finished listening to the eight o'clock news when she went up to her room to shower. I knew I had about twenty minutes before she would be back downstairs to check on what I was doing.'

'I went into his study and logged in to the PC. I had already ordered a "full shop" from the Supermarket, the day before with clear instructions that I would pick it up later that afternoon. I logged onto the website of the department store next door and purchased some underwear for Dick and some new kitchen knives for Isabella. Finally, I treated myself to some silk underwear from the Designer Pod. You know that if I had gone to the stores in person, including being measured, the whole thing would have taken over four hours.'

I am enraptured as she tells me this story. Despite all the tears and sadness since our reunion and the knowledge that the fate of Faith would be raised soon, I couldn't help but be impressed by her animation. My love for her swells if that is possible. She stops to smile at me.

'What?' I ask.

'It's just funny watching how you still twist your hair around your finger when you are concentrating on what I'm saying. I've missed seeing you do it, it's lovely.'

'Glad you find it appealing, Jenny hated it.'

'Appealing? Tez, I love you. I can't believe you are here again with me. I have dreamt so often that this moment could be possible.'

It is my turn to look around to see if anyone is looking. The two waiters are talking to a chef next to a screen at the corner of the bar; the rest of the Aphrodite is empty. There is only one table occupied outside, at the front, where a young couple are trying to pacify an infant in a pram. Happy that no one is watching us, I rise out of my seat and turn to Grace, only to find her leaning forward and puckering her lips. Her eyes are sparkling as our lips meet briefly. 'I love you too Grace,' I say as I sit back down.

She continues telling me the events of that day. 'I got the transaction reference numbers written down, deleted the history and checked I hadn't left anything in the re-cycle bin before switching the PC off. I had just left the study and entered the kitchen when I heard Isabella coming downstairs. I sat and read a book for an hour or so while she did a jigsaw puzzle. She told me what clothes she wanted ironing before she went to get ready to go to the golf club. She left at midday having said hardly more than five sentences to me the whole morning.'

'I left the house just after twelve but it had started to rain quite heavily. It took a few minutes to clear the screen because it was all misted up. That's when I noticed the very strong smell of petrol fumes again, whilst the engine was idling. I set off to meet you when the screen had cleared.'

'You said you smelt the fumes again. When had you noticed them before?'

'I think it was a couple of weekends before, when I had to rush out to get Dick a bottle of scotch from the shop. I mentioned it to him when I returned home but he just shouted. "Stop bleating about the fuckin' car will ya; you can get it fixed, along with the seatbelt when it's due for a service." Obviously I don't know much about cars so I thought that was reasonable because I don't really do many miles.'

It was only minutes ago she described how she had come to understand she was an abused wife and had decided to act upon it, so why revert back to making excuses for him? I am just about to make the mistake of mentioning this when the opportunity is taken from me.

'I had a great journey to the hotel. I arrived a bit early and found my favourite parking spot. I was happier parking there because it was behind the high bush near to the service entrance, so it was unlikely that anybody would see my car. I got the disguise and "our" phone from under the back seat to wait for your call. I also got your book out from under the seat and decided to read it until you called me.' My mind drifts away remembering all the times she walked into our room in her disguise.

'I called you a couple of times to tell you I had arrived but there was no answer. I also sent you a text message from "your little detective," asking if we were in the usual room. I even considered going into the hotel to see if you were already there, but thought I would leave it for a little while. By the time it got to half past one I was getting a bit worried so I called you again. Your phone had just started to ring when an ambulance tore into the car park, its siren was deafening so I aborted the call because I wouldn't have been able to hear you even if you did answer.'

Grace pauses, leans forward again and takes both my hands in hers. 'Tez, you know it was at this point that our lives changed. I say "our" because I know now that it must have been you in the ambulance and because what happened next to me is very difficult to tell you.'

'You know how you mentioned before that you felt invincible and then everything fell apart?' I nod. 'Well the same thing happened to me at roughly the same time. Remember I felt confident, strong and happy and I had told you that life was good?'

Our hands are interlocked, as I squeeze tightly and say, 'Yes.'

'Well I was just about to call you again when I heard my other phone ringing. I didn't recognise the number but I answered it anyway as I thought it might be Dick checking up on me. It was Faith. It was hard to make out what she was saying.'

The sparkle and animation has departed from her now as it's obvious the story is entering a dark place. 'She said she had been released early on the recommendation of the Governor. Apparently the Home Office had agreed on health grounds, stating that the decision would also ease overcrowding. Then she told me she was on her way by bus to my house to confront Dick about him attempting to rape her. I knew I couldn't let this happen because she would only get arrested again, so I tried to talk some sense into her and calm her down. It was no use though, she sounded as high as a kite, which spelt trouble. I couldn't understand how she could be in such a state until she told me where she had been. "I need your help Sis, I had to see my "candy man," and he's after me because I owe him money."

Grace shakes her head in frustration. 'I couldn't believe it. She's just got out of serving a sentence on medical grounds, but goes straight to her dealer to get a fix. Then she decides to confront Dick and asks me to give her money to clear her debt. I had to think quickly so I asked her what time she would get to my house. She said "just before four o'clock." I knew how I could sort this out without Dick knowing.'

I am intrigued. 'How?'

'I had her passport.'

'You never told me. I knew she'd come to stay with you on her way back from holiday and that Dick had attempted to rape her whilst you were at the hospital, but I didn't know you had her passport.'

'I know. I got it when I returned from the hospital after he'd pushed me downstairs.' I flinch at this. 'I'd just got back after having my broken leg put in a cast, just as Dick was being checked in for second degree burns. I'd found Faith's passport in her bag on the evening she was arrested for scalding him.

'Didn't she have her passport confiscated when she was arrested?'

'No, you wouldn't believe it but even criminals are covered by the Human Rights Act, so taking their passport is a big thing as it restricts their freedom. I hid it just in case the police asked for it, but they didn't. In fact I'd forgotten about it until she called thought that if I could get home before Dick and his mother turned up, that I could give her the passport and book a flight for her to Athens, using the debit card you gave me, where she could catch a ferry to Hydra. That way she would avoid both Dick and her dealers of course, who were bound to come looking for her. That would still leave me time to plan my escape and join her later.'

'You would have been proud of me Tez. I didn't panic. I thought you must have had a good reason for not turning up, so I decided to concentrate on Faith. I still had to go to pick up all the shopping, so that Dick wouldn't suspect anything and I knew I had time to do everything before he got back from work and she got back from golf.'

'I left the hotel car park just before two o'clock and picked up the order from the store round the corner and then went to the supermarket to the "click and collect" desk. It was exactly two thirty when "our" phone rang, I was so happy that you'd finally called me. I answered and said something like, "Oh Tez darling I'm so glad you are ok." My world started to cave in when I realised it was Jenny who had called me and it changed forever when she told me what had happened to you. Although something died inside me, I realised she didn't know my identity, yet, so I knew I had to act quickly. My plans would now have to be changed as she was bound to eventually work out who I was from my voice but I didn't know how much time I had.'

She is about to continue but I see her smile as she looks through the window into the bar. A waiter is approaching us to see if we want another drink. I am sure he includes a little skip as he turns the corner. I hadn't seen him when we arrived earlier. He is very tall and slim and I am positive he is wearing eye shadow. His black trousers are moulded to his backside, when he bends over theatrically to pick up a crushed cigarette packet. Grace stands up with arms outstretched and says, 'Aggie, how are you?' They hug as he says, 'I am very well Miss Faith.' I am about to correct him but Grace flashes a glare at me and shakes her head vigorously.

She turns him to face me. 'Agamemnon, this is my fiancé, Tez.' This comment completely throws me. 'He's been away on his travels but he has finally come back to be with me. Tez, this is my favourite Greek and Sebastian's best friend, Aggie.'

I was expecting a handshake but receive a strong hug and a kiss on each cheek. He says in an outrageously camp accent, 'I'm so glad to meet Faith's future husband, you are so lucky.

She has many admirers but she always say she wait for you.' He may not look like a Greek warrior but I instantly like this man who could be mistaken for the world's most beautiful hairdresser. 'I'll go and get you some fresh coffees; it's nice to meet you Tessie.' He gives me a cheeky wink as he skips off back to the bar.

Grace is smiling at me when I say, 'Fiancé, bloody hell, when did we get engaged?' She puts her index finger to her mouth; she wants me to keep my voice down. She encourages me to sit down and says, 'I was asked a lot of questions when I got here. People are naturally inquisitive, especially on a small island where nearly everyone knows my brother, and a number of men tried to court me. The thing is Tez; there will never be anyone else for me. I love you and when I knew you were out of the coma, I told everyone I was engaged and that you would join me soon. I didn't know for certain but that's what I told everyone.'

I am confused again. 'But why couldn't you get a message to me in the hospital when you knew I was conscious?'

'I promise that you'll understand everything when I explain what happened.' She stands and takes a mobile phone from her bag. 'Tez, I was on my way to meet Seb when you surprised me. He's out walking with some friends of mine. Do you mind if I call him to tell him we will meet him later? That will mean we can talk some more.'

'Of course, it will be good to see Sebastian again.'

Grace walks across the road and into the small square and sits on the raised wall of the fountain. The sun is streaming down; its light is bouncing viciously off the whitewashed walls of the villas and the marble of the fountain. It is very quiet now, as I assume that people are sheltering from the heat. I marvel again at Grace's beauty as she waves to me during her animated conversation. I want her to return to me but realise my unexpected appearance will need some explaining to Sebastian. Having ended the call she returns to me and sits down.

'Seb sends his regards to you and says he'll meet you later. He can't believe you're here.'

'I'm so glad to be here, believe me. I like it. Everyone seems to know you.'

'Yes, people are very friendly. Most know me through Sebastian who moved here permanently over twenty years ago. He is one of the few foreigners to be involved in local politics, he has settled down and he even has a share in this bar. Many of those paintings on the wall are his.' That explains why I recognised one of them when I went to pick up the coffees; it was a picture that was used on the cover of a music compilation CD some years ago. 'Anyway, where was I up to?'

'Jenny had answered your call and told you what had happened to me.'

'Oh Tez, that's when I knew I had to run. I knew she would work out that it was me on the phone and then she would tell Dick. I couldn't allow him to beat me again.'

I interrupt. 'I understand.'

She looks at me sternly and slowly says, 'No Tez, you don't understand yet.'

I want to challenge her but she continues. 'Consider my position. My soul mate was in hospital with a stroke and I didn't know if he would survive. My heart was breaking Tez. My sister who was dying from hepatitis C was drugged up and on her way to confront Dick, which would probably result in her ending her days back in prison. Finally, I might only have had a matter of hours before Jenny worked out who I was, which would mean...' She lowers her head now '...an amazing thing happened though, I didn't panic. I think part of me became Mary Russell. It was as if I could see each of the issues as a puzzle that I could solve. I didn't hesitate as I started the car and drove from the supermarket to the hospital. I knew I had to see you before I went away.'

'How did you know which hospital I was in?'

'I guessed. It seemed logical that it would be the big one near the airport and the hotel. It wouldn't make sense to take you anywhere else.'

'Was this when you came to see me and saw Jenny in the corridor?'

'Yes. I parked at the hospital and put on the disguise. It was still raining heavily so I had the added chance of "invisibility" because I could pull the hood of my coat over my head. I found your room easily by asking at the front desk and saying I was a relative. I wanted to leave you something to let you know I had been there but I was afraid of Jenny finding it, so it had to be something which only we knew about. That's when I thought about the book. I had put it in my handbag when I went to pick up the groceries from the supermarket. I ripped out page one four three and put it in your pocket knowing you would know it was from me when you found it. I knew it would be meaningless to Jenny if she discovered it. I had no idea the pocket was torn and that you wouldn't find it for nearly a year. I gave you one of my special kisses and was just about to leave when a nurse came in.'

There was a call from the corner of the cafe. 'Faith,' Aggie is waving, 'see you later.'

She waves back and continues. 'I just said I was sorry and this was the wrong room and left. It was about three thirty when I got back to the car. I was now in a rush to get home so I just threw the book and my disguise into one of the supermarket bags and set off to meet Faith. I would put everything back under the car seat when I got back and had sorted her out.'

'I arrived home just as the four o'clock news was starting on my car radio. Faith was already waiting for me at the end of our front wall, behind the trees, near the public footpath; she was in a manic state. She was ranting about paying Dick back for trying to rape her and then pleading for money to pay off her dealers. She was shivering, very pale and dreadfully thin. She had a holdall with her so I just picked it up and I told her to follow me inside, I could make her something to eat as I had a couple of hours before they got home.'

'I wanted to keep her busy because she was so agitated. She helped me bring the shopping from the hall into the kitchen. That's when I sat with her and explained my plan. I told her I had her passport and that I would sort everything so she could go to Hydra and I would follow within a couple of days.'

It's getting busier around the bar with customers taking seats at the front and a well-dressed, elderly couple taking the table next to us. The 'traffic' is also increasing along the road next to the square, as donkeys and bicycles jostle for space and pedestrian flow builds past us in the narrow alley. Grace begins to fidget, I can tell she is uncomfortable, and she says, 'Tez, do you mind if we go somewhere a bit quieter? I've so much more to tell you and this is not the right place.'

I say, 'Of course,' as Grace stands. I follow suit but not as quickly, my left leg has seized from sitting for so long. I manage to get moving again with the aid of my cane and say, 'I've already settled up for the drinks.' She links my left arm, as she guides me towards the street running parallel to the alley. We hear shouts from the bar; we turn and wave to Belisario and the chef as we cross towards the entrance to a small park.

It feels cooler amongst the trees as we walk silently up a slight incline, adjacent to a small playground. A number of olive skinned children are squealing excitedly as they run across the sandy ground and jostle for the swings and a brightly coloured seesaw. I suddenly miss Earache and Pancake so much. I wonder if I will ever see them again. I remind myself, "You wouldn't see them again if you had shot yourself, would you?" I shake the thought from my head as I realise that I now have a lot to live for.

Grace interlocks my hand and pauses. She is smiling as she watches the little ones having fun. I marvel at the beauty of her profile as the joy of seeing her again wells up inside me. The carefree happiness of the children along with the rich scent of the pine trees being carried on the warm breeze settles into my memory. I will never forget this moment.

We begin to move away, nodding to the women sitting on the benches facing the play area. With the odd exception of a splash of red here or blue there, they are all dressed from head to foot in black. The sound of the children diminishes as we enter a deserted tree lined grove. Grace changes the subject. 'When did you get here?'

'Today. I flew to Athens yesterday, and then got a taxi to Glyfada. I chartered a yacht early this morning then came looking. I didn't have a lot to go on to find you. The only information I could remember, was a powder blue door on a villa overlooking a beach, opposite the Aphrodite or Acropolis bar.'

'How did you find me so quickly?'

'A man called Icky knew exactly what I was looking for and brought me here on his donkey.' We are totally alone in a grove of olive trees. I pull her towards me and kiss her, it's our first for over a year. I feel a sparkle, shivers and my heart is exploding like a firework with happiness. I don't want the moment to end.

Grace gently pulls away from me. Her eyes are sparkling as she tugs at the curl on my forehead and says, 'I've missed you so much. Come on, let's sit down here.' We emerge from the park onto a concrete platform overlooking the sea. We take a wooden seat facing the west coast of the island where a number of yachts are sailing around some buoys and markers. She is quiet for a moment as she looks out over the ocean.

I want to get back to what happened to Faith, so say. 'You said you had both brought the shopping in and you had told her you had her passport and could get her a flight to Sebastian's.'

She moves away from me slightly as she twists sideways, tucks one of her legs beneath her, holds my hand again and says, 'Faith was ranting. She said she didn't want her passport or to go to Seb's, she wanted to pay Dick back for what he had done to her and needed money to pay off her debts. She begged me to get her some money as the dealers were after her. I managed to calm her down a little bit when I suggested that I could book her into a hotel nearby and try to get her some money. I told her I would come with her as I wanted to get away as well.'

She was quiet whilst I made her a drink, so I went upstairs to get the keys you had got for me, to open Dick's desk and safe. I was taking out a wad of cash when I heard the front door slam and the sound of the car as Faith drove off erratically. I ran downstairs to find she had taken her holdall, "our" phone and my handbag, containing the keys for the car and house, my other phone and my watch and rings as well, as I'd taken them off because of the nasty rash on my hands. I have no idea why she shot off like that without the money, maybe she thought there was cash in my handbag.'

'I just sat on the stairs trying to work out what to do. You were in hospital with a coma. I was sure that Jenny would be calling Dick soon telling him about our affair, which was bound to result in the worst beating he'd ever given me. Faith was dying from hepatitis C, high as a kite and wanting revenge on Dick and had stolen my car. It was too much to handle Tez. I knew I had to run. There was no time to lose. I didn't think it could get worse but it did.'

'I took your book and disguise out of the shopping bags and quickly packed a holdall with as much as I could. I got Faith's passport from its hiding place and went back into the study and took the pile of cash and my passport. I planned to get somewhere where I could call Faith to arrange to come and meet me; it shouldn't be a problem contacting her, as she had taken both phones. I could actually see a light at the end of the tunnel. But then the house phone rang.'

She pauses at this point and holds my hand tightly. 'I just froze and then the answering machine clicked into life.' I look at her. I don't think I have ever seen a sadder sight. Her face is streaming with tears as she continues. 'It was Dick leaving a message for his mother. His voice sent a chill through me when he said he'd just had a call at work from the police saying I'd been involved in a serious road accident. His voice was so matter of fact. And then he said, "Anyway Mum, it looks like I'm going to be late. I have to drive over to the compound to see the police and try to identify the body. It looks like she lost control of the car, which left the road, crashed and burst into flames. It seems the barren bitch forgot about the faulty seatbelt. She must have fastened it, been trapped, and burnt to death in the fireball."'

She stops for a moment, her amber eyes flooding with tears. 'Do you know what he said then Tez?' I shake my head, I am genuinely afraid to find out. 'He said, "The cops tried to break it to me gently, but apparently everything was vaporised when the petrol tank exploded." Finally, he said. "Anyway, there's no need to wait up for me."'

There are tears in my eyes now. I thought I had been exposed to every variety of hatred and bad luck but this was off the scale. I have no idea what to say, but that doesn't matter because she continues. 'Something snapped inside me Tez but I didn't fall apart, I was amazingly calm. Maybe I became Mary Russell...I don't really know, but it seemed so clear what to do. Dick had used the word vaporised, so I assumed everything would have been destroyed, including my sister. I know it sounds cold, but I saw this as my chance to get away. I went back to the desk and took all the remaining money, the bank savings books, the deeds to the house, and the ledgers and papers connected to his business. I cleared everything, knowing this would cause him the maximum stress.'

'I realised that I probably only had minutes before Isabella came home, so I ran around the house finalising my disappearance; I had just got through the front gates and onto the public footpath when I saw her return. The house looked abandoned, all the lights were on, the front door was unlocked because I had no keys and the alarm wasn't on. It looked as if someone had left in a hurry, which was exactly what had happened.'

I am just about to ask what she means by "finalising her disappearance," when she suddenly brightens up and points to the promenade on my right. The sun is low in the sky now and blinding me, so I find it difficult to make out what she has seen. I can make out two men walking towards us; it looks as if they are hand in hand. One is definitely the waiter who I had seen earlier in the cafe, the other looks familiar. They are pushing something.

Grace is excited when she says, 'Sebastian and Aggie are here.'

EPILOGUE

I see they are pushing a pram or buggy of some sort. The look on Grace's face is one of sheer serenity and pure happiness. The two men are smiling as they approach; it's as if they are all sharing the most wonderful secret.

They stop in front of us; the breeze off the sea is scorching now. Sebastian is talking to me; I think he is saying hello but I can't be sure. All my senses, well, those still working correctly, are telling me something is afoot.

Then Grace is standing; she is pulling me to my feet. She pulls back a white cover from in front of the buggy; I shield my eyes to reduce the glare and look in. There are two babies, wrapped snugly in cotton sheets. One is wearing a pink bonnet, the other, blue. I realise now what is happening. The men are obviously taking someone's children for a walk. I wonder whose kids they are...

My thoughts are interrupted, Grace is talking. 'Tez, I'd like to introduce you to my children.' I literally do a double-take. "Your children?" My brain can't handle the computations of what's going on here. My legs buckle slightly. I have seen this happen in the movies, when people receive devastating news, but never actually thought it was for real, until now.

There must be an obvious explanation. Grace must have adopted the children. Phew, of course. But hang on, she has only been here for a year, how can she have arranged that so quickly, in a foreign country?

Oh God, they must be hers, which means she must have met someone and got pregnant and…

… Fuck, fuck, fuck, fuck, she must have given birth in the last…

… Slow down, that can't be right; she has told me so many times that Dick had beaten her because she was barren. She can't have children. What the fuck is going on? My brain is going into meltdown, as she speaks again.

'Tez, I know this is going to come as shock to you,' I hadn't noticed that we had all walked to take shelter beneath an olive tree. Its leaves are chattering in the wind. 'Take another look darling.'

I am shaking as I slowly draw the sheet from under their faces. I can see them more clearly now. They are beautiful. They look identical. Strangely, I think about Emily and Melia and how I had abandoned them without saying goodbye.

I am smiling dutifully, but my mind is a bucket of mush, as I see the "Blue bonnet's" eyes are amber and he looks like… I lean forward for a closer look. Grace puts her arm around my shoulder; why is she is holding me so tightly? I am about to say something but she removes the knitted hat. He has a full head of hair and… a tiny kiss curl.

I see "Pink bonnet" has tiny freckles across her nose and upper cheeks, her eyes are cornflower blue. She has miniscule pink lips, tiny dimples in her rosy cheeks and dark hair like her brother. Pure unadulterated love cascades through me, even though I don't know them.

'Tez, this is your son, Tesla junior.' I am dizzy as I try to understand, my left leg gives way; Sebastian leaps forward to help Grace support me…

'And this is Faith, your little Princess.' The cornflower blue eyes sparkle as she smiles up at me. Her image is obliterated as tears explode…

'Yes. They're your babies, darling.'

Grace looks into the buggy and addresses the babies.

'Tesla Junior.'

'Faith Rebecca.'

'This is your daddy…'

*

I am lying on my side on the dusty concrete of the viewing platform; I have no idea how I got here. Arms are lifting me onto a bench, I am hot and confused. I appreciate the shade, looking up I see I am beneath the olive tree, a tree that I will remember for the rest of my life. It reminds me of the solitary picture in our hotel room.

'I don't understand darling, how can they be ours?'

'It turns out that I wasn't infertile after all. Remember when I had a rash?' I nod. 'It was so bad that I had to remove my watch and rings etcetera? Well, I went to the doctor's and he gave me some cream and I also mentioned that I had been sick a few times and my breasts were sore.'

I interrupt her. 'Grace?'

'Yes darling?'

'Please can I hold them?'

'What, my breasts?'

'No, not now, but I would very much like to later.'

Aggie groans as he makes a face and turns away. Sebastian says, 'Yuk.'

'I was actually wondering if I could I hold the babies?'

She's laughing. 'Oh Tez, of course you can.' I slide into the centre of the bench and hold my right arm out to accept Tesla Junior, I lay Faith Rebecca on my lap, I will not trust my dodgy left arm with something so precious. I marvel at the two most beautiful things God has ever created and I take a moment to silently thank him for bringing my soul mate, Grace, back into my life. I don't take my eyes off them for a single moment, as Grace's words wash over me.

She says her doctor recommended she did a test when she went in with the rash as he thought she could be pregnant. It was then she decided she would have to get away if it was positive; she couldn't afford another beating when Dick found out she was pregnant by another man. *("He hasn't touched me in years Tez.")* He might kill the baby and probably her as well. That was the decision, and the news, that she wanted to tell me.

She was worrying about how she could keep the tests secret from Dick and Isabella but that issue was taken away, thanks to Jenny getting the phone call and Faith turning up. It was only when she finally had stomach pains, shortly after arriving in Hydra, and was flown to the hospital in Athens that she discovered she had polycystic ovaries and expecting twins.

The doctor said it was unusual, but not impossible, for a woman with PCOS and no periods, to ovulate and become pregnant. Grace says that could explain why she and Dick never had a baby, but she likes to think it was a blessing in more ways than one. I like to think that as well.

She laughed later, when I told her that I thought the babies were Sebastian's. 'No, Tez. Seb moved here to escape being persecuted for being gay. He has been "married" to Aggie for over fifteen years.'

*

Grace and I are lying on the bed after making love. The breeze coming off the bay is warm and rattles the dry leaves of the Bougainvillea around the open window of our villa with the "powder blue door." I can faintly hear the twins being entertained by Seb and Aggie in the paddling pool on the balcony below our room.

It was difficult when I telephoned to make the peace with Poppy, having disappeared from the hospital. I am not sure if she will ever forgive me for hurting her so, but I hope she may realise one day that I didn't have a choice. She has reluctantly, accepted my promise that I will return soon to explain, face to face, what happened. I can never tell her of course, that I was going to kill myself and as for informing her that Grace is alive and I have twins, well, that is a shock that I am going to have to time very carefully.

Grace is sleeping; I watch as she breathes softly beside me. Words can't express my contentment. I let my mind flood with the thoughts of her and how my life is so complete now. I smile as I recall her refusing to let me penetrate her earlier. She said, 'No Tez,' but that's ok, I understand she is cautious, seeing as our third is due in a little over six months. Just one heartbeat this time though, the Doctor assures us.

I am pleased that this story has a happy ending. Nothing can go wrong and spoil this now after all we have been through.

I imagine that if our story was made into a film, the closing shot would be of Grace and me walking along the beach. I still have a slight limp as I carry our baby Rocky (or it could be little Poppy), in the crook of my right arm; the twins are screaming with joy, as they run through the edge of the surf. The camera closes in on my face.

It's a vision of a truly contented man. He is laughing loudly, his smile is broad. Only then do you notice his eyes as he passes the baby to his love. What have you seen? Something isn't quite right… Then the screen goes blank and the credits roll…

THE END